Murder
in
Carcassonne

ROBERT HARDAWAY

WESTERN REFLECTIONS PUBLISHING COMPANY®

ISBN: 978-1-937851-59-0

Printed in the United States

Text and cover design by Steve Smith
FluiDesigns

Cover photo credits:
Carcassonne: Alexandre Fagundes De Fagundes
Girl:Milla Fedotova

Western Reflections Publishing Company
P.O. Box 1149
951 N. Highway 149
Lake City, CO 81235
www.westernreflectionspublishing.com
(970) 944-0110

Critical Praise
For Novels
By Robert Hardaway

MURDER AT MONT. ST. MICHEL

"A Colorado John Grisham!…Truly an engaging book from first to last. I loved it!

~ Richard Lamm, former governor of ColoradO

ALIENATION OF AFFECTION

"…an extraordinary novel…a superbly crafted novel of obsession, sex, scandal, betrayal and prejudice which raged through the high society of Chicago, Paris, Denver, and even the doomed voyage of the Titanic. Attention Hollywood! Alienation of Affection is the very stuff of which block-buster movies are made…"

—Midwest Book Review

"University of Denver School of Law Professor Robert Hardaway has seamlessly incorporated reports from Denver's daily newspapers and transcripts of the trial proceedings into his own creative work to produce a spell-binding book…More than just a riveting tale…(Awarded an "A" rating)"

—*Rocky Mountain News*

"…a fascinating look at a bygone era…"

—Bob Ewegen, *Denver Post*

LILY QUEEN

"…A compelling story set in the context of a great American tragedy, which educates, entertains, and enlightens…"

—Richard Lamm, former governor of Colorado

SIX QUEENS NAKED

"…a wild heartstopping ride…"

—Richard Lamm, former governor of Colorado

MURDER ON THE CONCORDE

"The saga continues…with verve and style!"

—Richard Lamm, former governor of Colorado

BOOKS BY ROBERT HARDAWAY

Novels (Western Reflections Publishing)
Alienation of Affection
Lily Queen
The Papyrus
Six Queens Naked
Dreamlet
Murder on the Concorde
Murder at Mont. St. Michel

Academic Books on Law and Public Policy
Colorado Evidence (Lexis-Nexis, co-authored, 14 editions)
The Great American Housing Bubble (Praeger)
Marijuana Law and Politics (Praeger)
Saving the Electoral College (ABC-CLIO)
Airport Law and Regulation (Greenwood Press)
Crisis at the Polls (Greenwood Press)
America Goes to School (Praeger)
Population, Law, and the Environment (Praeger)
The Electoral College and the Constitution (Praeger)
No Price Too High: Victimless Crimes (Praeger)
Preventive Law Casebook (Anderson)
Aviation Law and Regulation Treatise (co-authored) (Butterworths)
Preventive Law in corporate Practice Treatise (Mathew Bender)
Colorado civil Rules Annotated (West Publishing, co-authored)
Aviation Law and Regulation—student Edition
　　　　(Butterworths, co-authored)

DEDICATED TO

JUDY TREJOS

AUTHOR'S NOTE

Readers sometimes ask me where I get ideas for my novels. Because law is my profession as a law professor, and my primary interest outside the law is history, I generally get my ideas from either of those two areas of endeavor.

In the fifth of the Judy Alexander mystery series that follows, I draw from both the law and history to frame the plot. In the case of the former, my interest derives from the jurisdictional issues I teach in my Civil Procedure class. Such issues become particularly acute and problematic in the international arena. In Europe, both the UK and countries within the European Economic Community continue to grapple with such matters as extradition, reciprocity, and enforcement of European Arrest warrants. One case in particular caught my attention. It involved a 1996 murder that occurred in West Cork, Ireland, a victim who was a French citizen and socialite celebrity, and a primary suspect who was a citizen of the UK. Over the last twenty-five years, both Irish and French courts have battled over jurisdictional, reciprocity, and extradition issues. When the Irish Prosecution Service declined to prosecute the suspect for lack of evidence, a French Court took the bull by the horns, tried the UK suspect in absentia in 2019, found the suspect guilty, and sentenced him to twenty-five years. Even this failed to resolve the jurisdictional issue when the High Court of Ireland rejected the subsequent French request for extradition of the suspect in 2019. To date that saga continues unresolved, while the suspect remains in jurisdictional limbo in West Cork, Ireland.

The plot that follows also gave me the opportunity to delve into the fascinating chronicle of the ancient besieged city of Carcassonne in southern France, which in medieval times was saved from destruction by the casting of a fatted pig over the ramparts. The more recent history of London's notorious "death trains" also captured my imagination, which for over a century carried thousands of bodies and their accompanying mourners from London to the now infamously haunted Brookwood Cemetery in Surrey.

I therefore prevail upon the indulgence of my readers as our intrepid heroine, purported to be the first American female barrister, weaves her way through both legal entanglements and historical pathways to defend a woman charged in Crown Court with the murder of a man whose billion dollar inheritance had depended upon whether he was born fifty seven seconds before, or after his fraternal twin.

RMH 2021

"Very few of us are what we seem, (so) whenever great sums of money are at stake, it is advisable to trust no one."
~Agatha Christie

CHAPTER ONE
Present Day

*M*ichael Hodges, Q.C., stretched back in his leather chair and clasped his hands behind his head. He thought for a few moments, and then impulsively lurched forward over his massive and uncluttered mahogany desk, grabbed the phone and rang chambers Clerk Archie Harold. He could have simply gotten up, walked fifty-five feet down the corridor to the chambers' central receiving room and caught Harold's attention in person, but he was not in the mood for facing the daily bedlam. In any case, Hodges was the Quadrangle's senior barrister and Queen's Counsel, and he expected Clerk Harold to come to him when summoned, no matter how trivial the matter at hand.

Archie was pacing back and forth at one end of the chambers' giant central table yelling into his phone above the din of eight junior barristers, six assistant clerks, and five aspiring barristers in pupilage, all fielding calls from and to various solicitors, clients, and investigators.

"No chance, Max," Archie shouted into his phone at his least favorite solicitor. "We aren't taking two bit burglary cases right now. Now be a good chap and bring us a good felony coming down from CPS, or better yet a juicy libel case against the *Mirror* and we'll talk!"

Archie slammed down the phone and was about to take a call from another solicitor when he noticed the intercom call from Hodges. With exasperation, he picked up. "Yes, Mr. Hodges. Can it wait?" he asked with little attempt to disguise his impatience.

"No it can't wait, Archie. I'm trying to find Braxton. Where is he? I haven't been able to reach him on his mobile."

That was why Hodges was interrupting his management duties? No solicitor had requested Hodges' representation in months. Solicitors knew that while Hodges demanded fees commensurate with his Q.C. status, his courtroom skills had diminished considerably since his younger glory days when he had achieved fame for his brilliant courtroom performances in some of England's most high profile cases, both criminal and civil. However, womanizing, partying, navigating the celebrity circuit, and heavy drinking had taken their toll.

Most barristers had retired long before they reached Hodges' age; those aging barristers who could not land a judicial sinecure contented themselves with lucrative and less demanding "consulting" work. Hodges' narrow escapes from numerous scandals had foreclosed any chance he might have had for a judicial appointment, and he disdained consulting work as the final road to oblivion.

For Hodges, the courtroom was still the preferred venue, the measure of his self-worth, even if he rarely if ever now set foot in it. Of course he would never agree to sit second chair to a mere junior barrister. Nevertheless, his name as Queen's Counsel on the chambers door—one of only three at the Quadrangle— gave chambers a competitive advantage, at least on paper. He also paid more than his fair share in chamber expenses, and the other barristers in chambers were reluctant to push him out as long as he did so.

"I think he's still in final arguments in the Hamilton case, sir," said Archie, making little effort to hide his impatience at the interruption. "If he comes in before leaving for the day I will tell him you want to see him."

"Be sure that you do. And you would do well to remember who pays your salary, Archie."

"Yes, sir. Is there anything else, sir?"

"No, that will do."

"Yes sir. Goodbye, sir." Archie shook his head, thinking how silly it was to say "Goodbye" to a man who was sitting just fifty feet down the hall.

Braxton Thomas rapped on his old mentor's office door.

"Entre!" came the booming voice of the Queen's Counsel.

Braxton opened the door just wide enough to poke his head in. "You wanted to see me, Michael?"

"Yes, come in my boy!"

Since his days of pupilage with Hodges a decade before, Braxton had gotten used to indulging his old mentor even when he still treated him as a pupil; but this was not a particularly good time for a chat. "Well, actually, I…"

"Nonsense! Come in and shut the door."

As Michael Hodges sat back behind his enormous desk, Braxton took a seat and waited patiently for Hodges to say whatever he was going to say.

"So, my boy, how is that case you're working on…the…"

"Hamilton case. We just concluded final arguments, and recessed for the day. Instructions first thing in the morning, which is why I need to prepare."

"Well, perhaps you can spare a few moments for your old mentor. I am having a little soirée at my home in Newbury this coming weekend, and was hoping that you and Judy might join us."

Braxton sat back and smiled indulgently. It had been almost four years since he and Judy had visited Hodges at his magnificent country home outside Newbury. At that time, Judy Alexander had just come into his life after arriving in London from America to investigate a case in which she had become involved as a co-counsel with her friend Amber Hartman, a defense lawyer in Houston, Texas. As a recent graduate of the Oliver Wendell Holmes School of Law in New York City, Judy had spent her first year after graduation as an associate in her partner's small criminal defense law firm where, under her new partner's guidance she had honed her skills in all matters relating to criminal defense. Her partner's untimely death in a commuter air crash in Maine had ultimately led her to leave her New York firm and associate with her friend Amber's firm in Houston.

"Well, "said Braxton cautiously, "I appreciate the invitation and I can certainly ask her, but she's so busy these days I'm lucky to catch her for a short lunch."

Michael Hodges now returned the indulgent smile and shook his head. "I really would have thought that after these past several years that you would have married the girl by now."

"Not for lack of trying, Michael, so I can't help that. As you know, she divorced her first husband when she was in her twenties, and her partner, with whom she was deeply in love, died in a plane crash less than three years into their relationship. She just isn't ready for a third try, and I'm not inclined to push her."

"Nonsense, my boy!"

Braxton sighed. He had long since given up trying to convince his old mentor to stop calling him "boy," but Hodges, like an old uncle, was now too set in his ways to be persuaded to change his old habits of address to a former pupil. Once a pupil, always a pupil.

"You are aware," Hodges continued, "that these days it's not necessary to get a piece of paper to live together, are you not?"

Braxton started to get up. He was not interested in listening to his old mentor's advice on matters of the heart.

"Sit down, my boy! I've been meaning to talk to you about Judy, so now's as good a time as any."

"Michael, I'm really too busy to talk about…"

"You will listen to me, Braxton, because I have concerns about her continued role here in chambers."

Reluctantly, Braxton sat. Although he knew the rant that was coming, he realized that he'd have to hear it again before being allowed to escape.

"Look, my boy, you know as well as I that things have not been the same since she was admitted to chambers here. It is extremely difficult for an American lawyer to become a

British barrister. Only a handful have ever managed it, and even those who do usually do so only to practice what is essentially American law in large UK financial firms. You spent three years helping to usher Judy through the process of becoming a barrister, first with navigating her application and admissions process at the Inns of Court School of Law, then tutoring her in preparation for the Bar Course Aptitude Test."

"Which she passed with flying colors. She also paid all her applications, fees, and tuition, which were most considerable."

"Nevertheless, I doubt if she could have done it without your help. And then there was your most monumental feat of engineering, a pupilage offer from Mortenson here at the Quadrangle."

"Mortenson was only too pleased to offer it. He considered her an outstanding prospect, as did you. I seem to recall you telling me that you thought she would make a most decorative addition to our chambers."

"Well, I suppose that is true," Hodges admitted sheepishly, "but that was not my reason for supporting her tenancy. I also thought she would make an outstanding advocate based on her performance at the Inns of Court Law School."

"As did we all. She also performed well during her pupilage and has since made something of a name for herself. So what is the issue here? Since the Quadrangle granted her tenancy here, she has become one of our top advocates. You saw the article in the *Mirror* last month with the headline 'American Beauty a Rising Star at the Inns of Court.'"

"Yes, with a cheesecake photo of her underneath the headline."

"Hardly a cheesecake photo, Michael. An aggressive paparazzo happened to catch a photo of her during her early morning jog through Hyde Park—fully clothed I might add in her jogging outfit."

What a sly dog you are, Michael. I know you've been lusting over her ever since she and I visited your house of iniquity several years ago. Admit it. If you can't have her, you're just insanely jealous of her.

"Yes, yes, "Hodges sputtered, "but she still cuts a fine figure, and the tabloids love that sort of thing."

Imagine!

"As far as making a name for herself," Hodges continued, "you know how she has done that. She takes cases, almost all from indigent criminal defendants, the kind of cases that often make for sensational stories in the tabloids and are more apt to make the headlines. That hardly serves our longtime goal here at the Quadrangle to become a prosecution-oriented chambers that can command the best referrals from the Crown Prosecution Service and insure a steady and reliable source of fees. Unless, of course, you're comfortable with attracting the kind of solicitors who offer us only indigent clients who pay only the pitiful fees offered by our woefully underfunded Legal Aid Agency."

"Actually she turns down many of the Legal Aid cases, but not because of the low fees. She insists on only taking cases in which she feels the client is at risk of an injustice, and she often charges no fees at all. In fact, many of her indigent clients have been those who bypass Legal Aid and come to her directly without a referral from a solicitor. They know that if she takes their case, they will get the kind of dedicated and zealous representation usually available only to the very rich. She's that good, and you know it."

Hodges grunted. "Perhaps. That's all very fine for her, as you tell me she's independently wealthy—though you've never told me how she came to be so. Some day we should look into that. I suppose this is all just a hobby for her. In any case, I don't see how that helps the rest of us. How can we command decent fees if solicitors see us as some kind of down and out legal aid society?"

*You mean, **you** don't command top fees anymore, Michael. You've lost most of your courtroom skills even as you try to coast along on your QC laurels. You've bedded so many beautiful women in your time, you can't accept being overshadowed by a* *beauty who could run circles around you in court if it ever came to that.*

"You know the firm is doing quite well, Michael, and truth be told, it's in large part because of Judy. I don't suppose you heard that the BBC has asked her to give an interview on *UK Law Today.* That's the kind of publicity that helps the firm. We've already gotten referrals from solicitors for very wealthy women who identify with Judy after reading the story about her in the *Mirror* and inquire whether she will take their divorce case against their wayward husbands."

"Well, that's more like it! I didn't know that. No one ever tells me anything around here, least of all Archie, who is worthless as far as I am concerned. So has she taken any of those cases?"

You should be happy that Archie even puts up with you, Michael.

"Of course not. As I said, Judy could care less about the generous fees those cases can command, and she knows that divorce is not her area of expertise, though I think she could be brilliant if she ever chose to enter that field."

The fantasy of seeing Venus nail faithless husbands to the wall gave Braxton a momentary shiver of excitement, as he was sure it did to the society women who had sought forlornly to retain Judy's services.

"I suppose she pays her fair share of chamber expenses."

Just as you do, Michael, as the price of maintaining the master office keeps going up...And everyone knows you can afford it.

"Of course, double in fact. She is also happy with that small office at the end of the hall."

Unlike you, Michael, who still insists on the most palatial office in chambers, despite your dearth of paying clients.

Hodges finally broke into one of his endearing smiles. "You've convinced me, Braxton. Don't take me wrong. I know we are lucky to have her, and I was just testing you to see the extent of your commitment to her."

"It is the same."

"Of course. Now, about this weekend."

"I'll talk to her and let you know."

"By tomorrow if possible?"

"Sure, I'll try."

CHAPTER TWO

*I*t was late in the evening when Braxton finished his proposed jury instructions in the Hamilton libel case. He yawned, turned off his computer, put on his hat and quietly entered the hallway and locked his office door. Looking down the corridor, he was surprised to see the light on in Judy's office. He went to her door and tapped.

"Who's there?" came the response.

"Just me, Meow. I saw your light on." Meow was Braxton's pet name for Judy whose cat was named Chloe.

"It's all right. Come on in."

"Sorry, I was surprised to see you still working this late."

"I have a pre-trial hearing in Magistrate's Court tomorrow morning, and need to finish this motion to suppress."

"Big case?"

"Big for my client, Janet Tomlinson, yes. This one may go to Crown Court."

"You've been there before. You didn't mention this case before."

"I didn't think it would get this far. Ms. Tomlinson's been abused by her husband for years, but is being charged with assault for refusing to accept another beating...and rape."

"Which solicitor referred the case to you?"

"Peter Mayfield."

"Ah yes, Peter Mayfield."

"I know you don't think much of him, but he knew his client would never get a proper defense with any barrister who agreed to take the case for the pitiful fee Legal Aid would pay.

I may not be the most experienced barrister here, but I have resources at my disposal. Archie would have declined it without consulting me, but I just happened to hear about it and I insisted he let me call Peter back and take the case."

"I'll talk to Archie. He really should let you know when any solicitor asks for you, regardless of what the case is."

"Thanks. I just found out Archie turned down a burglary case today without asking me."

Braxton sighed. "Judy dearest, we're not Legal Aid. You know that in ninety-nine out of a hundred of these cases, the client is guilty as sin."

"That still leaves one in a hundred who is not, and probably many more who are at risk of injustice, and who can be exonerated if they get a proper defense. You know that's why I'm here. That's why I became a lawyer in the first place."

"I understand, and admire you for wanting to take on these hopeless cases without a fee. But..."

"But?"

Braxton paused. "Hodges called me in today."

"Don't tell me. He doesn't like me taking criminal cases. He wants the Quadrangle to handle only CPS prosecutions, and high profile civil cases."

"Well, yes. But he has a point. Being on the CPS radar would finally get us a regular and reliable source of income, and the fees Legal Aid deigns to pay our young barristers are ridiculous. Some of them could make more money working a double shift at McDonalds.© You know you're the only one here who even considers taking that kind of case."

"Braxton, you know I almost always waive my fees—unless they can afford it, in which case I supplement our office fund—and I pay more than my fair share to keep us in these rather extravagant digs, even though I only get a broom closet for an office, though as I've said I don't mind that. I know I'm still the junior here. It's fine. In fact, I prefer it. So why should Hodges care anyway?"

"Look, Meow, I'm on your side, but it's a matter of perception and reputation. Some of our best paying clients are put off by some of the dubious characters they see wandering around here looking for you."

Judy sat back and crossed her arms. "Braxton, honey, haven't we had this conversation before?"

She considered whether to play her trump card—which was to tell him that if Hodges wanted her out, she'd find another chambers—but she resisted playing it. She cared for Braxton too much to hurt him, and despite her misgivings about practicing in the same chambers for fear it would harm their relationship, she had agreed to the "arrangement." This included, at her insistence, that they would not live together until she was ready to take their relationship to the next level. To Braxton's chagrin, she had also made it clear that despite her feelings for him, she was not yet ready, and was not even sure that she would ever be ready to marry again after one divorce and the death of her partner. Although the two had not tried to hide their relationship, they had also agreed to keep it low key for the sake of propriety and to fend off whispers that were acting in concert. They were both independent barristers and had so far avoided any conflict of interest.

Braxton had long been aware that Judy was independently wealthy, though she had never told him any details regarding the source of her wealth. She had confided only that she had inherited a great deal of money from her godfather in America. Her first priority, which she never tired of telling him, was to honor the legacy of her late partner, Professor Robin Hammond, who had been her supervisor in the Exoneration Clinic at the Oliver Wendell Holmes School of Law in New York City.

Braxton held up the palms of his hands in submission. "I understand. I just wanted you to know what Hodges was about. I won't bring it up again."

"Thanks, please don't."

"You know I support you, and always will."

"I know. I wouldn't be here without you."

"I did try to explain to Hodges that you've probably given the Quadrangle as much good visibility as anyone here—if not more. He saw the picture and article about you in the *Mirror.*"

Judy recoiled at the mention of the article. "Oh my God! I was so embarrassed! I don't know how that creep with a camera tracked me down, or even why."

"Really? How many female American lawyers who look like a goddess have come to the UK to become a British barrister—which isn't easy to do as you well know—and get an acquittal in a high profile case that nobody else would take?"

"Stop it."

"If you'd called me that morning I would have joined you, you know, protected you from that sort of thing."

"You're sweet but I woke early that morning and couldn't get back to sleep. It was spur of the moment. I can't imagine how he even knew I would be out running that morning. I didn't know myself."

"He'd probably been trailing you ever since the trial, sensed a story if he could get a picture of you jogging, followed you home, and waited. I mean you look like a jogger. You know our London tabloids by now—cheesecake photos on the front page, followed by some real news inside. You were lucky you didn't make the front page."

"Thank God!"

"I did think the article was unfair, though—implying that you got that acquittal by wrapping the male jurors around your little finger during the trial."

"Oh come on, I read it. It didn't say that. Please."

"Implied."

"Oh right. I looked so glamorous in my loose black barrister's robe and white-haired wig that the jurors just had to acquit my client."

"As I said, implied—your picture jogging in shorts and tee juxtaposed above the article recounting your miraculous feat in getting an acquittal in that case before a jury of middle-aged males."

"I was running at five in the morning when there's hardly anyone about in the park to ogle!" she protested. "Moreover, that trial was only my third trial on my own—nobody else in chambers would assist me of course—and I lost my first two solo trials before that. Yes, I got an acquittal, but the article was dead wrong about the male jury because there were three women on the jury, and if I had any emotional edge, it was because the women jurors identified with my female client as a battered woman."

Braxton smiled. "Well, whatever, Meow, but I still love it. If nothing else, you drove Hodges into a state of insane jealousy. He still lives in his glory years in which it was he who got all the attention."

"Okay. Can we drop this as well?"

"Sure, babe," Braxton said with a wide grin, "but I still love it. Fancy a pint?"

She thought for a moment but then shook her head. "I'm afraid I'm fading, so a pint's the last thing I need right now. I guess I could finish this back at my flat. Walk me home and we can stop on the way for a Cappuccino."

"Of course. I'll take what I can get. Oh, I just remembered why I came by and bothered you. Hodges wants to know if…"

"You said you'd drop it, darling."

Braxton chuckled, and blurted, "He's invited us to spend the weekend with him at his Newbury house."

Judy opened her mouth in amazement. "You've got to be joking! Was this before or after he told you he wanted to get rid of me."

"I didn't mean to say that he said that. He just wanted to suggest that you let up on the criminal cases and consider taking some civil or prosecution cases."

"Let up? I've only tried three criminal defense cases on my own since my pupilage, so I'm hardly experienced enough to be in any kind of a rut. I wouldn't mind taking a prosecution case if I thought it was fair, and if someone in chambers would take first chair to give me the experience. I'm surely not on the CPS radar right now—despite, or maybe because of— the *Mirror* article. I did work with my friend Amber in Houston on a big civil case, though, so I'm perfectly willing to take a civil case if a solicitor offers one. That's how I happened to come to England in the first place—and meet you, if you recall."

"Yes, I do most certainly recall."

"It's been, what, four years since the old lech last invited us? You may also recall it was something of an ordeal. He must have something up his sleeve."

"You mean other than getting in your pants? I know you only agreed to go last time because I went with you and he implied he had some critical information regarding the case you were working on in America."

"He did, as it turned out."

"So there you are. It wasn't that bad, was it? I'd be with you this time as well. And you enjoyed his little fox hunt, didn't you?"

"I don't know, Braxton. He's such a…"

"I know, but it wouldn't hurt our cause to have him on our side, and he is a…"

"QC. Yeah, this whole QC thing. I still don't quite get it."

"It's just an honorific. That's all. So you'll go?"

"Can I think about it?"

"He wants me to let him know by tomorrow."

Judy sighed. "Okay, if you think it's important. I hope your Spitfire is up for it."

"Just got it tuned, and it's ready to go."

"Famous last words," she said, remembering the Spitfire's breakdown on the A-4 during their last visit to Newbury four years before.

Judy packed her briefcase with her files, rose from her desk and took Braxton's hand. "All right, I hope the Cappuccino does its job. I'm going to be up all night working on this motion."

CHAPTER THREE

As the chapel bells signaled the end of the class day at Brianhurst School for Girls, Miss Muriel Wright picked up the briefcase containing her French lesson books and dismissed her Sixth Form French class.

"See you all on Monday, girls," she said cheerily in French to her fourteen young, eager, and fresh-faced students, whose ages ranged from eight to eleven.

"Remember that your essay on Mont St. Michel is due on Monday, so don't let this weekend go to waste. And don't forget to practice your conjugations!"

As most of the girls picked up their workbooks and headed noisily to the classroom exit, a short red-haired student with pigtails and freckles, the youngest in the class, stayed and approached Muriel at her desk.

"Miss Wright" she asked, "Will you be staying here…"

"Remember, Cynthia," Muriel reminded her, "we only speak French in this class."

"Yes, Miss Wright," said the girl, embarrassed that she had neglected the class protocol. She thought for a moment trying to remember the correct words, and then haltingly repeated her question in French. "Will you be staying here this weekend at the school? I wanted to know because…" There was another long pause as she grasped for the right words.

"Yes? Take your time, Cynthia. It's all right."

"I think I will need…help. An essay…"

"I understand, Cynthia. Yes, I will be here for the weekend, but I have to leave the school now, and won't be back until later this afternoon. Why don't you come by my room at nine tomorrow morning?"

In a rush, and late as she was for a low-tea visit with an old friend at the Lock, Stock, and Barrel in Newbury, Muriel realized she had spoken too fast for her youngest student.

Unlike preparatory schools in America, students were not automatically promoted to the next form at the end of each year. Rather they were promoted only when they had reached a certain level of proficiency in a particular subject. For this reason it was not uncommon for students in a particular class to have a range of several years in age.

Cynthia understood, and nodded. "Tomorrow at nine?"

"Yes. You know where my room is?"

"Your room?"

"On the fourth floor, south side, at the end of the hall, overlooking the chapel. Yes?"

Cynthia nodded, but did not seem sure.

"Okay, then. See you then."

Ordinarily Muriel would have taken more time to make sure an inquiring student knew how to get to her room, but she was satisfied her young student could find it. If not, Cynthia could ask Matron.

"Bye, Cynthia!" Muriel picked up the last of the papers and exercises on her desk, jammed them into her briefcase, and headed up to her room.

Muriel's room at Brianhurst was a small one, encompassing a space just large enough for a bed, chest of drawers, sitting chair, and a small desk and chair. It was certainly a step down from the comfortable two-bedroom house she had lived in with her former husband for three nightmarish years. Nevertheless, the little room has proved a welcome sanctuary after her grueling divorce. Moreover, it provided her with absolute privacy and safety away from her ex-husband. Because the divorce had left her in a precarious financial condition, she had soon thereafter accepted Brianhurst Headmistress Charlotte

Weathersby's offer of a small salary plus room and board to teach French at Brianhurst as a resident teacher.

The room also had a wonderful view of the quaint and charming thirteenth century chapel just beyond the trees amid the lush greenery which surrounded Brianhurst. In the early mornings before rising and dressing for chapel, Muriel treasured the moments she spent gazing out at the meticulously manicured grounds and listening to the morning chirps of the many birds who nested on the grounds.

Brianhurst School for Girls had been established in the early 1920s. Prior to that time, it was the family home of Ebenezer Farnsworth, the Biscuit King, who had made his fortune building a network of bakery factories making what Americans called "cookies." His brand of biscuits was still popular and found in specialty food stores across the United Kingdom. When Ebenezer passed away in 1919 at age eighty-nine, his many offspring and heirs found that after paying heavy death duties, it was both impractical and too expensive to maintain. By the time the heirs sold off the manor in 1922 to wealthy widow Eleanor Davis, an activist in educational reform movements, it had fallen into disrepair. Davis subsequently transferred title to a non-profit group that refurbished the manor and its environs and established it as a girls' school. They named it after Davis' deceased husband, Brian, and added the name "hurst," which in Old English meant hill or wooded hillock.

After checking her face, applying light make-up, and brushing her luxuriant dark hair, Muriel changed from her schoolteacher's prim skirt and blouse to more comfortable black leggings and sweatshirt. After locking her door tightly, she bounded down the back stairway to the second floor grand staircase, entered the Great Hall, and then speed-walked out the front doors to the stables where she kept her bike in an anteroom. Mounting her bike with aplomb, she began pedaling furiously down Pemberton Lane to the nearby town of Newbury, Berkshire, some five miles away.

After coasting down Badgers Way to Balfour Crescent and completing the circuit, she turned up Coachman's Court Road to the Lock, Stock, and Barrel. Standing outside was her former college roommate and friend, Samantha Sterling, smoking a cigarette and glancing at her watch.

"So sorry I'm late, Sam!" Muriel said breathlessly as she linked her bike to a post. "You should have gone in and ordered."

"It's fine," said Samantha. "I need my nicotine fix anyway, but I did get us a table." The two hugged.

After claiming their table and ordering two Cappuccino's and pastries, Samantha sat back and crossed her arms. "I've really been missing you, Muriel. Ever since you left my house I hardly ever see you."

"I know. I've missed you too. I couldn't presume on your hospitality for any longer than I did. I'm not sure Eddie approved of me staying so long. I'm sure I intruded on your privacy."

"Nonsense. And the heck with Eddie. We can always use the company, and of course, you were a great help with the cooking. Now with the kids off to boarding school, it's just Eddie and I, and truth be told, he can be spectacularly boring. Half the time he isn't here anyway, doing God knows what, and I'm just here alone. And when he is here, he just sits in his office in front of his computer. When we do talk, all he wants to talk about is the wankers in parliament, the high taxes, and the high price of petrol."

"You were so kind to let me stay as long as I did, Sam, I really mean that. Once I finally got the teaching job at Brianhurst, which came with room and board, I couldn't justify imposing on you any longer. But I do miss our time together. You have such a beautiful home, and I dearly loved my early morning walks in the forest nearby."

"Did you have to take that teaching job in residence?"

"That was the offer, and I wasn't in a position to bargain. Norman insisted I stay at home when we were married, so after the divorce from Norman. I had no job, no money at all really. In residence, I have other duties every other weekend at the school.

You know, taking the boarders out on pony treks, organizing archery practice, supervising study halls, bed checks, that sort of thing."

Samantha shook her head in disgust at the mention of Norman Yates. "What a bleeding bastard! I suppose you still aren't getting any support from him. The Court did order…"

"To be honest, Sam, I don't want anything from him! All I want is for him to leave me alone and get out of my life."

Samantha nodded sympathetically.

Muriel shuddered as she remembered the constant abuse, the frantic calls to the police after the beatings. "And even now," she continued, "and even now…that's another reason I really had to leave, Sam. The restraining order I finally got—after draining what little money I had of my own to hire a solicitor—turned out to be worthless. You remember the night Eddie caught him on the grounds of your house, creeping around. I was so sorry you had to deal with that."

"Eddie gave him the what for, Muriel, got him arrested for trespassing. The Constable told him the next time it was the clink. Constable Myers would have put him in the clink anyway for violating the restraining order, but said that because Norman was beyond the 100 feet specified in the order, he couldn't do that. Our house is on four acres. I really think you'd be safe if you came back and stayed with us. Really I do. But I understand. Well, at least you don't have to worry about him stalking you at Brianhurst, a little girls' school. He'd never dare…"

Muriel hung her head and let out a low sigh.

"Muriel, what is it?"

"He did…he did…"

"Did what, Muriel? He did what?"

"Oh Sam, he did come to the school. Two weeks ago. Alexa—she's the Assistant Headmistress—found him over by the stables talking to a couple of the girls, asking them if they knew where 'Miss Muriel' was. Alexa confronted him and asked him what he was doing on the school premises. He told her he was my husband and urgently needed to talk to me."

"Your husband?"

"A lie, of course. We've been divorced for over a year. Alexa just told him I wasn't available, that visitors had to register at the office before entering the premises, and that otherwise he must leave. Apparently, he did leave, so she didn't call the police. I wish she had. Or maybe it was better she didn't, because the last thing I wanted was for Headmistress Weathersby to get wind of it. Of course, Alexa had to report it, though, so she knows. Now I'm worried, Sam. If he were to come around again bothering any of the girls…I mean I could lose my job. I can't lose this job, Sam. I love this job. It's probably the only thing I'm qualified to do now—other than maybe waitressing here at the Lock, Stock, and Barrel. You remember I majored in French when we roomed together at Cheltenham, and I got my A levels."

"I know you did, and I've been jealous ever since. I never got my A levels in history. I was always out socializing while you were back in the dorm hunkering down with your French."

Samantha could have added, but diplomatically did not, that life wasn't fair. Samantha had socialized and slept her way through Cheltenham, finally landing her future wealthy and successful husband who, while not much to look at, now provided her with a most comfortable and lavish lifestyle. Muriel on the other hand had worked hard at her studies, earning the highest grades and A levels, but had had the bad luck to marry a man who, despite first impressions, had given her nothing but heartbreak, grief, and abuse. The irony was that Muriel was the true beauty, far more attractive than Samantha, and could have landed any husband she wanted.

"I'm so sorry," Samantha continued, "you don't deserve this. I probably shouldn't say this now, but I never liked Norman Yates from the moment you introduced me. Even his name gave me the creeps—reminded me of that demented Norman Bates character in that Alfred Hitchcock film—what was it?"

Muriel finally managed to crack a reluctant smile. "*Psycho*. And yes, Sam, you did tell me once that it was a creepy name, but I suppose you were nice enough not to say anything else bad about him given that his name was not your only reservation. Was I supposed to dismiss him because he had a name that reminded you of some odious film character?"

"Hey, girl, he was good looking, certainly up to your level in that department anyway, and he seemed nice enough at the time. All the girls liked him. How was I to know how he'd...?"

"I didn't see it, and in retrospect I should have. There were warning signs, but like they say..."

"Sure, sweetie. Love is blind, I know, but half of the married and divorced couples in the world only figure that out after the fact."

"I have no one but myself to blame. I did jettison the name at least —after the divorce."

"Thank God! Wright is a good old-fashioned British name. I always liked it."

Muriel took a long sip from her Cappuccino and this time managed a real smile. "If we can stop talking about you-know-who, I do have some positive news to share with you."

Samantha opened her mouth with excitement.

"Don't tell me! You've found someone! Someone who really deserves you! Tell me!"

"I can't tell you all of it. Not now. But I have found someone, and he's amazing. He's already making me deliriously happy."

"I can't believe it, but I'm so pleased, sweetie. May I say it is about time? So what are your plans? When can I meet him?"

"I'd rather not tell you his name—not yet. He's a Latin instructor. We met at a language symposium at St. Johns last fall. We're going on a trip together. In three weeks, it will be the spring intersession and I have four days off to go with him."

"Wow. Where are you going?"

"You have to promise me you won't tell a soul."

Samantha crossed her heart.

"We're going to France. In my last review session I had with the Headmistress, I told her that I'd like to take some of the girls in my class on a field trip next summer—you know, so they can practice their French. She seemed receptive to the idea if enough parents agreed and were willing to put up the travel and accommodation costs."

"So you and your Latin teacher friend are taking the kids to France?"

"No, no. Just he and I are going there together over the spring break."

"Paris, I assume."

"Actually, no. He and I have both seen Paris. I convinced him I'd like to go to a town in southern France that I've read a lot about, but never seen. I want to scout it ahead of time. You know, make plans about what to show the kids—when and if I finally get to take my students there next summer."

"Hmmm," said Samantha. "Just the two of you. Sounds very romantic. Tell me about this Latin teacher of yours. He must be caring, sensitive, considerate, intelligent, good sense of humor, not to mention an Adonis."

"Yes," said Muriel. "All of that."

"Natch. Now you must tell me what place it is in southern France. "Marseille, Nice, Avignon…?"

Muriel shook her head. "I have to keep it all a secret for now. I don't want to jinx it, you know."

"Oh come on. You can at least tell me where you are going. Let me guess. St. Tropez, Toulouse?"

Muriel kept shaking her head. "I've got to keep it a secret, at least for now."

Samantha now gave her old friend a look of skepticism. "So you can't tell me his name, even though you've already told me enough to look him up. Can you at least tell me where you're going? I'm just excited for you. Come on, Sweetie. You know your little secret would be safe with me."

"I know it would. I just can't. Believe me. Not right now."

There was a long pause before Samantha ventured, "It's Norman, isn't it? You don't want him to find out."

Muriel leaned over the table and took Samantha's hand. "That is part of it, not all of it. But yes, it would send him over the edge if he found out. Please understand."

"Jesus, Muriel. What is it about divorce that creep doesn't understand? Okay, sweetie, I won't press you. You'll tell me when you're ready."

"Thanks, and I will."

Muriel could see that Samantha was hurt that she wouldn't confide in her, but she knew from her days as Samantha's roommate in college that Samantha was a terrible secret-keeper. Muriel could foresee telling Samantha where she was going with her mystery man, Samantha then confiding to Eddie, and Eddie casually mentioning it to someone at his downtown offices. Somehow, someway, Norman would find out. He was proving to be a master stalker. She didn't know how he tracked her down on previous occasions, or how he managed to find out about her activities and whereabouts. Just as well that she tell no one—not even her blabbermouth best friend until after she returned.

"Well, I'd better get back to the school," Muriel said as she rose. "I'm supposed to supervise vespers tonight. Here, let me take care of the coffee."

"Don't be silly. You're as poor as a church mouse, and can't even afford a little car. Let me drive you. It'll be dark soon, and we can put your bike in the boot."

"I'll be fine, but thanks for the coffee."

"Call me. Don't forget."

"I won't."

The two embraced and said goodbye.

CHAPTER FOUR

At 9 AM sharp on March 4, the preliminary hearing in the case of Regina v. Janet Tomlinson was called to order in the Highbury Corner Magistrate Court, London. The purpose of the hearing was to determine, among other legal matters, whether the indictment charging the defendant with assault with a deadly weapon would remain in Magistrate Court or be referred to the Crown Court, which dealt only with the most serious offenses. If so referred, the defendant faced a more severe punishment if convicted at trial of the offense, up to and including life in prison.

Judy Alexander in full gown and barrister's wig sat on the first tier bench, looked back at her client in the upper dock, and nodded to her as a gesture of confidence. Don't worry, Janet, we'll keep this in Magistrate's Court and go on from here to final acquittal.

Behind Judy in the lower gallery sat a scattering of interested onlookers, among whom sat Braxton who had come to see Judy in action. Braxton noticed two men and a woman who looked suspiciously like tabloid journalists.

Although the matter in Magistrate's Court on this day was only a pretrial hearing, and not an actual trial, it had nevertheless attracted tabloid attention. At a suppression hearing several weeks before, Judy had lost a motion to exclude, on grounds of hearsay and relevancy, certain statements Janet had made to police after a domestic violence call several years before. While this loss might have caused tabloid interest in her motion to subside, a story in the prior day's *Morning Star* had run on the bottom of page nine—using the same picture of Judy jogging in

Hyde Park—under the headline "American Barrister Beauty to Defend Another Battered Wife in Magistrate's Court."

Neither Judy nor Braxton would have had any reason to notice another young woman in the gallery who, after seeing the story in the *Morning Star* and anxious to get out of the house, had taken the early train from Reading to come see the beautiful young barrister that everyone was talking about.

Judy did not disappoint. The prosecution had called the defendant's husband, Rupert Tomlinson, to testify to his wife's dastardly and unprovoked attack upon his person with a kitchen knife. With great emotion, he described how he had come within minutes of bleeding to death before the timely intervention of the medics on the scene, and doctors in the emergency room, had narrowly saved his life.

Judy's cross-examination was masterful. Braxton marveled as her crisply crafted questions revealed the victim's ugly history of domestic abuse going back many years—not just against Janet but a previous wife as well. When he denied ever having lied in court before, Judy confronted him with the transcript of an eleven-year-old fraud case in which he had been caught lying about the circumstances of the fraud in which he had been involved.

How did you ever find that particular transcript in such an old case? Braxton wondered. Judy's direct examination of Janet was also thoroughly prepared. Avoiding all manner of leading or objectionable questions, Judy had Janet describe what actually happened. With emotion, she described how Rupert had come home in the middle of the night and awakened her in the bedroom. He then fell on top of her, demanding sex. When she resisted, he became belligerent and tried to force himself upon her, viciously striking her several times. When she was finally able to break free, she ran out of the bedroom down to the kitchen. He followed her down the stairs into the kitchen where he shoved her violently against the kitchen counter and ripped open her bodice. As she fell back upon the counter, she desperately grasped for a kitchen knife from the knife stand behind her, and frantically plunged the knife into his stomach. As he fell and released her, she ran upstairs to the phone and called 999. The medics arrived in less than fifteen minutes and took him immediately to the hospital where they managed to stop the internal bleeding, gave him a transfusion, and saved his life.

The prosecutor's cross of Janet was perfunctory, making the mistake of simply asking her to tell the same story again, apparently hoping to find a discrepancy in her testimony.

By then the magistrate had heard Janet's story twice, thus magnifying its effect.

Although an actual dismissal of the case against Janet was never in the cards—the injury inflicted upon Rupert had come too close to actually causing his death for the Magistrate to dismiss summarily all the charges against Janet at this early stage of the proceedings—his decision not to refer the case to the Crown Court was a victory nevertheless. After listening to the testimony of both the husband and the wife, few in the courtroom had any doubt that the prosecutors would ultimately move to dismiss; or if it actually went to trial in Magistrate's Court, an acquittal on grounds of self-defense now seemed very likely.

As the hearing was adjourned and Judy gathered her books and files, Braxton came up to congratulate her.

"Great job, Judy. I was impressed."

As Judy was about to thank him, an earnest young woman with note pad in hand approached the two of them. She eyed Braxton for a moment, but then held her hand out to Judy.

"Hi, Ms. Alexander. I'm Nora Phillips from the *Express*. Do you have a minute?"

Judy took her hand, but said, "Actually I was just going..."

"It will just take a minute," the journalist persisted.

Braxton turned to Judy. "It's okay. Go ahead. I'll meet you out front if you want to grab some lunch."

Judy nodded and turned to Nora. "Well, I suppose we can talk, just for a minute. But not here in the courtroom."

"Outside in the hall is fine. I just wanted to ask a few questions."

"I can't really talk about this case. I'm sure you understand that."

"Of course. Shall I follow you?"

Judy latched her briefcase. "This way."

Nora followed Judy outside the courtroom to a vacant bench down the hall.

As they sat, Nora said, "I think a lot of our readers would be interested in your story."

"My story?"

"Yes, you were an American lawyer. What made you come to England and become a barrister? It's not supposed to be easy to do that."

"No it wasn't. Not at all. It took three years as a matter in fact. There were times when I was ready to give up, to be honest."

"I'll bet. According to my research, you are among only a handful of American lawyers who have managed it. I think, if I'm not mistaken, you may be the only female American lawyer who has done it. There's a number of female American lawyers who have become solicitors here, but not barristers—at least not that I have found."

"I didn't know that, but I'd be surprised if that's really the case."

"So what gave you the idea to do it?"

"Several years ago I came here to investigate matters relating to a civil case pending back in Houston."

"Houston, Texas? And after you finished that, what made you decide to come back here."

"There were a couple of considerations. For one thing, I liked what I saw in your court system. I particularly liked the way you separate the office lawyers, the ones who prepare the paperwork, and the barristers who specialize in trying cases. During my law school days back in New York…"

"Which law school may I ask?"

"The Oliver Wendell Holmes School of Law. I was a student in the Exoneration Clinic there in which we investigated cases in which we believed there was an unjust conviction. We were successful in several cases in overturning convictions. The supervising professor in the clinic inspired my interest in the area, and I guess that's what got me started."

"Your professor must have been a great role model for you."

"He was. After he returned to his criminal defense practice in New York, he hired me as an associate and…"

Judy paused.

"And…?" Nora asked.

"We ended up living together."

"Oh my!" Nora made busy notes in her pad.

"He was killed in a commuter plane crash less than three years after we were together."

"I'm so sorry."

"Thank you. Perhaps we could talk about something else."

"Did I sense that the young man who was just here might have had something to do with you coming here to begin a new life as a barrister?"

"He helped me immensely with the American case that I was working on here and introduced me to the life of a barrister here. He was and is a barrister at the Quadrangle…and yes, he did have something to do with me coming back here. He is a very good friend. I owe him a lot."

"Perhaps more than just a friend?"

Judy nodded and smiled.

"And plans to…?

"Ms…. Phillips, is it?" asked Judy, changing the subject.

"Yes, but please call me Nora."

"Nora, I'm very flattered that you have taken such an interest in me, but I probably should go now."

"Your friend is waiting?"

"Yes, so…"

"Just one more question?"

"Sure."

"You've garnered a lot of attention as a result of winning an acquittal several months ago in that assault case against a battered wife…and now you seem to have reprised that performance here today."

"Not really. This was just a preliminary hearing on whether to refer the case to the Crown Court. What's your question, Nora?"

"I guess it's just that…well, a zealous defense in these types of assault cases involving a battered woman's defense…I mean it requires resources…investigative resources…how do you manage?"

"I only take cases that I believe are just. I almost always waive my fee."

"Then how do you make a living?"

Judy was in no mood to go into the circumstances of her legacy and inheritance, which enabled her to take on meritorious cases without regard to cost or fees.

Rising from the bench, but not wanting to be rude—even to a tabloid journalist—she held out her hand. "I really must go now, but before I do could I ask you for a favor?"

Nora took her hand. "Of course."

"Can you promise not to use that jogging photo of me in any story you run about me?"

Nora resisted reminding Judy that the photo had already gone viral on the internet. "Absolutely, I promise."

"Thanks," said Judy, and turned to go out and meet Braxton.

He was sitting on a railing nursing a Starbucks. "Everything okay?" he asked. "What did she want?"

"Just the usual. You know, why I came to England, why I wanted to be a barrister…"

"Did you tell her?"

"Sort of. Come on, let's go. Where are we going?"

"The Brass Monkey? We can take a cab to the Embankment and walk from there."

"Fine. Lead on. I'm not really hungry but I think I could use a pint."

"You deserve it." Braxton flagged down a cab and gave the cabbie instructions. "You know," he said, taking Judy's hand as they climbed in the back seat, "you really were brilliant this morning."

"Thanks. But why do I feel there's a 'but' coming?"

"There is, but it's a good 'but'. It struck me that you really are developing a natural British accent. Not completely, of course, because it's been so gradual I didn't notice it until today in court."

"Really? That's nice, I guess, but not surprising given that except for a few visits to see Amber in Houston and check on things at my New York firm, I've been immersed in my studies and cases at the Quadrangle for the past three years."

"You've got a way to go, but you've definitely lost your American accent."

"So what is my accent now?"

"Something in-between. That's all I can say."

"You're silly."

They took in the bustling sights of London for several minutes before Braxton took a big breath. "Any chance I could come over tonight? It's been a while, you know. Celebrate your victory with a little…"

Judy patted his hand before saying, "Tempting, and I know I've been so busy lately with this Tomlinson case, but I'd better take a raincheck. Tomorrow, maybe? I really want to just unwind tonight and get to bed early. I've also been meaning to give Amber a call."

"Sure, Meow," he said, trying not to show his disappointment. "Tomorrow would be great."

After a hot bath that evening, Judy called Amber at her private office number at their Houston law firm.

Amber answered after one ring. "Sister! Where have you been? I haven't heard from you all week!"

"I know. I am sorry. I had a pretrial hearing this morning in the Tomlinson case I told you about, and I've been preparing for it all week."

"How'd it go?"

"Not bad, even if I say so. Not an outright win, no dismissal. But it wasn't referred to the Crown Court."

"That's good, right? I still don't understand all those different courts they have over there."

"It's good. I think the case will ultimately be dismissed. How about you? How are you and Harvey doing these days?"

"Okay, I guess. He is a little distracted these days. He's in another one of those re-election campaigns for DA, so I haven't seen a lot of him."

"Keep me posted. Any good new cases?"

"Actually I do have a couple that might interest you. Of course I've given up ever enticing you back to the firm here."

"I've worked too hard to make it here, and I do like it here, but hey, any chance you could come out and visit again?"

"Maybe I could. I've given up trying to get Harvey to come there with me, especially now—what with this re-election and all. What about you and Braxton? Are you ever going to let him give you a ring? I know he really wants to."

"I know, but like you and Harvey, Uncle Timothy's legacy makes things complicated, you know…at least right now. We're fine. I told him that once I've firmly established my career here, we can think about playing house, and I haven't ruled out marriage. I do think I need more time for that."

"I don't know, Judy. I hope it works out. Much as he loves you, he may not wait forever. Listen, sister, I must run.

Meeting with a new client coming in any minute. Call me soon when we have more time."

"Will do. Braxton's coming over tomorrow night, but let's plan a long call to catch up the night after."

"Talk to you then. Bye."

CHAPTER FIVE

*I*t was the last class before the Easter Break and the girls in Muriel Wright's French class were in a state of anticipation.

"Now, girls," Muriel scolded the class as she clapped her hands, "let's calm down and listen. I'm not giving you any written assignments for the break."

There was a cheer from all the girls.

"But you still have an assignment."

The cheers subsided as the class waited for the bad news.

"When you go home, I want you to try to speak only French when you're with your family and friends."

Cynthia raised her hand vigorously in apparent protest. "But Miss Wright, my parents don't speak French, and neither do a lot of my friends. They won't be able to understand me."

Muriel realized she would have to modify her assignment. "If your parents ask you to stop speaking French, you must obey them. However, from my conferences with many of your parents, I think they will appreciate your efforts, and many of your parents speak at least some French and I think would be most pleased to engage with you."

Catherine Pierce, the oldest girl in the class, raised her hand to lend support to her teacher, and perhaps earn some brownie points. "All my friends are taking French. I can talk in French to them. It will give us a lot of practice."

"Well, there you go. All I'm asking you to do is try. Remember, it's one thing to speak French in class, but to really learn a new language you must practice speaking it in your everyday lives as well. I think you'll find it much more fun too.

When you come back after the Easter break, those of you who tried to do so can tell us how it worked out."

Without raising her hand, Georgina blurted out "Will we get a grade for this?" Georgina was Muriel's most diligent, but also her most grade-obsessed student.

"Georgina, you must raise your hand. No, there will be no grade. Now before you all leave, be sure to come up and pick up your essay. I thought they were very good. Many of you seem to be doing better on your vocabulary than on your grammar and conjugations, so we'll have to work on that after the break. I could tell that many of you had also done research on the history of Mont. St. Michel."

Susan Bradley raised her hand.

"Yes, Susan."

"I visited Mont St. Michel last summer with my parents."

"I'm sure that was a help in writing your essay," Muriel replied. "Did you practice speaking French while you were there?"

"Yes, Miss Wright. My parents let me order our food in the restaurants."

"There you go! All right," Muriel said with a final clap of her hand, "I think the bells are about to chime, so please line up in an orderly fashion to pick up your essays. Have a wonderful break, and I look forward to seeing you when you return and hear how your practice sessions worked out."

Muriel handed out the last of the essays just as the chapel bells chimed. The students left amid noisy farewells and goodbyes. After they had all left, Muriel began tidying up the classroom when she noticed Matron Ratchet, Brianhurst's resident dormitory mistress and mother hen figure, standing at the door.

Hello Matie," Muriel said cheerfully. "Are you looking for one of your girls?"

"Hello, Miss Wright. No Ma'am. Headmistress Weathersby asked me to come by and tell you that she would like to see you before you leave for the break."

"I see. Thank you. I'll be right up. Is she in her office or her apartment?"

"Her office, Ma'am. She said right away."

"I'll be right there."

Muriel hurriedly packed her briefcase. It was now 3 PM, and she hoped that whatever the reason was for the Headmistress's summons, it would not keep her past 4 PM when Arthur Edgeware was to pick her up at the front gate. She had planned this trip for weeks and had tickets for the 4:57 train to Reading. From there they would connect to the 6:22 to St. Pancras in London, and from there the 8:16 to their final destination in France.

"Enter!" came the sharp response to Muriel's knock.

Muriel entered and stood before the Headmistress's massive desk.

"One moment," said Mrs. Weathersby as she continued signing some papers while Muriel remained standing. "Take a seat," she finally said without looking up from her desk.

Muriel sat and waited. She looked at her watch nervously.

Mrs. Weathersby finally laid down her pen and looked up. "I understand you have plans for this Easter break."

"Yes, Ma'am."

Mrs. Weathersby took off her glasses. "I won't keep you long, Miss Wright, but I must talk to you about a situation that has come to my attention, and which has caused me grave concern."

"Grave concern, Ma'am?" Muriel began to flush.

Weathersby sighed deeply, and sat back in her chair. She was obviously struggling with how best to broach the matter that concerned her.

"Alexa has told me that she was obliged to confront a strange man who entered the premises without signing in, and who began talking to several of our girls out behind the stables. I understand this man may be connected to you in some way."

Muriel shifted uneasily. "Yes, Ma'am. I'm afraid he is, and I'm so sorry…"

"What is his connection to you? He told Alexa that he was looking for you."

"He is my ex-husband, Ma'am. We were divorced over a year ago."

"Then what business have you with him that would bring him to Brianhurst?"

"Absolutely none, Ma'am."

"The divorce is final, then?"

"Absolutely, Ma'am. I have no business with him whatsoever. But he…he…"

"You did not invite him?"

"No Ma'am. I would never invite him here. Never. Not for any reason. I want nothing to do with him whatsoever, but he…"

"You have made it clear to him that he must never come here for any reason without signing in at the entrance?"

"I have made it as clear as I can to him that I do not wish to see or hear from him for any reason."

"So he is stalking you, then?"

"Yes Ma'am."

"How long has this been going on? Have you called the police?"

"Yes, Ma'am. Many times. I have a restraining order against him."

"Then why has he not been put away?"

"He knows how to work the system, Ma'am. He knows exactly what he needs to do to avoid arrest…how many feet he has to stay away…what to say to the police when they confront him…and so far, at least, he has not actually harmed or directly threatened me."

"What is it that he wants, then?"

"He says he just wants to talk to me…to show me that he has changed…that we can work it out. I only agreed to talk to him once, but just to tell him in no uncertain terms that I do not wish to talk to him, or see him, or have anything to do with him, but he is delusional. He says he does not acknowledge the divorce because he never appeared in court or responded to a summons. He says..."

Weathersby held up both hands. "Enough...I don't need to hear all this, Miss Wright. You must understand something very important about this school—and all the best public schools in the country. Nothing is more important to this school than its reputation. Our girls come from the finest families. We have four girls here whose fathers are MPs. One is a subcabinet member of the government. One whiff of scandal or perceived risk to the safety of any of our girls and we could no longer continue in our educational mission."

"I'm so sorry, Headmistress. I..."

"I don't mean to suggest in any way that any of this is your fault. I have no doubt that it is not, but you must see the situation from my vantage point. Having a strange man wandering these premises and interfacing with the girls cannot be tolerated...ever."

"Of course, I understand, Headmistress. I will do everything I can to make sure it never happens again."

There was a silence before Muriel ventured, "Ma'am, would it be possible for me to leave my residence here, and just commute to school during the day? I can find a room in Newbury and..."

"I'm afraid not, Muriel. We retained you with the understanding that you would be in residence and be available to our students and, in particular to our boarding students at certain designated times in the evenings and on weekends. All our female instructors are unmarried and in residence. We only allow our two male instructors—Mr. Hailey and Mr. Smith-Hancock—to live off the premises. Of course, we require our male instructors to live off the premises. You cannot expect us to change our policies just for you, Miss Wright."

"Yes Ma'am..."

"In any case, I do not see how that would resolve our concerns here. Your ex-husband entered our premises during the day. If it happens again…"

"It will never happen again, I promise you."

"Very well. Let us say no more about it. Now, since you are here, let us turn to a more pleasant topic. How are the students in your French class coming along?"

"Oh, very well, Ma'am. They just turned in an essay I assigned them."

"An essay? Quite an assignment to give second year French students. At that age, I did well to master simple translations and conjugations. How is our little Cynthia coming along? She is the youngest in the class as I recall."

"Yes, Miss Webster recommended her for promotion to Sixth Form French because she mastered the material in Seventh Form French after just three months. There was no point in keeping her in Seventh Form French when she so quickly mastered the material…but, yes, she is the youngest."

"She may have had some outside tutoring as well. Her father is an MP from Sussex I believe. Have the age differences in the class—she's what, eight—caused any problems? I believe the oldest in your class is eleven?"

"Yes. They all get along well."

"I'm glad to hear that. Now tell me about this field trip you want to take the kids on in the summer."

"To Carcassonne, Ma'am. It's an old medieval walled city just north of the Pyrenees near the Spanish border."

"I know it well, Miss Wright. I spent my entire summer break at Oxford in Carcassonne working on my A levels. Have you been there before?"

"No, Ma'am. That is why I want to scout it out ahead of time…check out the museums, the castle, hotels, and see if I can line up a group or educational rate for the kids. In fact, that's where I'm going now for the Easter break. I have the whole week off this break. I made the request several weeks ago."

"Yes, I believe Miss Winters will assume the residential duties. Several of the boarders will be staying with us over the break."

"Enjoy yourself. You understand that before I can give final approval to this field trip for this summer, you will need to line up the parents of at least seven girls to make the trip count as a field trip. That means you must return with an exact summary of all the costs the trip will entail—hotels, rails fares, museum fees, meals—everything."

"Yes Ma'am. I will do that."

"I also suggest that you try to line up at least one or two of the parents to help you chaperone. Watching seven or more children that age can be a challenge, as I am sure you are aware. If you can do that, I'll post your proposed field trip on our website. Would you be willing to take kids from Miss Webster's French class too?"

"Oh, yes. Of course."

"Perhaps Miss Webster could come along as a chaperone as well."

"I would like that."

"Now, for your trip this week. Are you going alone?"

Muriel hesitated, but knew she had to answer. "Well, no Ma'am. I'm going with a friend."

Muriel held her breath, praying that the Headmistress would not ask who she was going with—male or female. Not really her business, but Muriel knew she would have to answer truthfully if asked, and that might in turn open up a can of worms.

To Muriel's relief, Headmistress said only "Quite so. Not advisable for a young woman to travel alone these days on such a trip. When are you leaving?"

Muriel looked at her watch. "Actually, Headmistress, my ride is coming to pick me up in fifteen minutes."

"Then I must let you go. Remember what we talked about earlier. You are a fine teacher, Muriel and I would hate to lose you."

"Yes, Ma'am. Thank you. I will give you a full report when I return."

"Stay safe and have a wonderful time."

Muriel rushed up to her room, fetched her purse and roller bag that she had pre-packed, and rushed down the back stairs to the second floor grand staircase and out the front door.

Arthur was already waiting in his old model Morris Minor on the far side of the courtyard.

CHAPTER SIX

Madeleine Edgeware and her new husband Chester sat enjoying breakfast on the patio of their manor house outside St. John's Village in Surrey. It was the first morning since winter when the weather was suitable for eating outside. As the housemaid served coffee, Chester sat buried in the financial pages of the *Times*.

"Chester," said Madeleine hoping to get her husband's attention, "I thought our dinner party last night went well. What do you think?"

"Yes, quite well, dear," came the perfunctory reply.

"But I didn't quite understand your story about Winston Churchill which everyone found so amusing. I don't suppose you could explain it to me?"

When there was no immediate reply Madeleine repeated, "Chester?"

"Yes, dear. I'm sorry, what did you say?"

"That story you told about what Winston Churchill said about…about…"

Chester put down his paper and reached for his coffee. "Primogeniture, dear. It was a remark Winston once made explaining the reason for the primogeniture laws in England."

"Primogeniture? I thought those laws were, you know, repealed a long time ago."

Chester dropped two cubes of sugar in his coffee. "Not entirely. Titles can still be handed down to the eldest son."

"Then why aren't you a Lord then? Your father is a Lord, isn't he?"

Madeleine's lawyer had explained the answer to that question when she had posed it to him eleven months before when she was contemplating accepting Chester's offer of marriage. A fashion model at age seventeen and but twenty-two to Chester's forty-one when they married, Madeleine was proud of the fact that she came from royal blood and was 138th in line to the British throne. That Chester's father was a Lord had played a large part in agreeing to marry him—that and the fact that Chester was heir to one of the largest fortunes in England.

Chester smiled. His young wife's beauty was more than ample compensation for her relative lack of intellectual acuity. Had she only now realized that his friends and business associates did not address him as Lord Edgeware?

"Honey, as I told you, I will be a Lord, and perhaps quite soon, but as a rule the son does not inherit the title until his father's death."

"Oh yes, I remember you told me that. Anyway, what did Winston Churchill say about primo…primo…"

Chester put down his paper to give his lovely wife the attention she deserved. "Primogeniture, dear. The laws made sense back in the day. The reason the Holy Roman Empire broke apart back in the 840s was that Lothar—or maybe it was Louis the Pious—split his empire among his three sons. Each of those parts later developed into separate European countries—France, Germany, and so on—leading to untold wars for the next Millennium."

Basking in her husband's attention, she gave him one of her wondrous smiles. "You are so knowledgeable, Chester. Now I know why I married you!"

"Guilty as charged, my dear. It all comes with an Oxford education and a major in medieval history—all worth it if it enabled me to win you as my wife."

Madeleine glowed.

"In England," Chester continued, "Parliament adopted the primogeniture laws to insure that the great estates were not broken up into smaller and smaller plots to the point where food production became inefficient and unproductive. The only way to keep the estates in tact was to provide by law that the eldest son must inherit everything—the house, the land, all the means of production on the estate. Second and third sons got nothing and were usually sent off, penniless, to sea or the church. If there were only daughters and no sons, then the estate was entailed and passed to the nearest male in line before it would pass to a daughter."

"Like in those Jane Austen stories."

"Absolutely. What would poor Jane do for a plot without entailment?"

"I know all about that, sweetie, but you still haven't explained the Winston Churchill story you told at dinner. I hate it when everyone else gets the joke, and I don't. I think I missed the punchline."

"It wasn't really a joke, just an amusing anecdote. Apparently Winston Churchill and Franklin Roosevelt met at Placentia Bay…"

"Where is that?"

"Not sure. Canada?"

"Go on."

"The two were enjoying after-dinner liqueurs, Roosevelt smoking a cigarette and Winston his cigar and somehow the subject of primogeniture came up. Roosevelt told Winston that he did not understand the British aristocracy's idea of primogeniture, and that he intended to divide his estate equally between his five children. Churchill responded that 'British aristocrats view equal distribution of property as the *Spanish Curse*. We give everything to the eldest and the others strive to duplicate it and found empires. While the oldest, having it all, is free to marry for beauty…which accounts, Mr. President, for my good looks.'"

Madeleine chuckled. "Okay. I did miss the punchline. Is it true, though, what Winston said?"

"It's documented in the president's notes, yes." Chester's demeanor now became more serious. "I felt I had to lighten the mood, because Mr. Holliston—who sat next to you at dinner, dear, and I might mention seemed, not surprisingly, very much taken with you—is the Guardian and Conservator of Dad's estate, and the cloud of primogeniture very much affects our present situation."

"Our situation? I thought primogeniture had be abolished"

"As I said, not entirely. Titles are still handed down to the eldest son—not that that means very much today if an estate doesn't come with it. As your lawyers no doubt explained to you, I am Father's oldest son."

"I know. And your father's will provides that he leaves everything to his eldest son."

"Yes, that is true." *Of course you know that, darling Madeleine, and I have no illusions that you would not have married me had your lawyers not assured you of that well before you said your "I do's." Nor would they have failed to apprise you that the appraised value of father's 95% ownership interest in Edgeware Industries exceeds 2.4 billion pounds.*

A look of apprehension suddenly flashed across Madeleine's face. "Chester, I hadn't thought of this before, but there's no chance your father could change the will, is there—I mean split the inheritance between you and your brother, Arthur?

"My fraternal twin? Not at all, my dear. I am sure your lawyers assured you of that. Father was adjudged mentally incompetent fifteen years ago—Alzheimer's—and control of his shares in Edgeware Industries was put in the hands of a Conservator."

"Mr. Holliston."

Chester nodded. "Father wrote his will long before he was adjudged incompetent and now, of course now he would never be deemed sufficiently competent to write a new will. Even if he were so capable, I doubt if he would change a word of it. He was old school and like his fellow Lords, he believed most fervently that estates should not be broken up into pieces. After my mother passed away many years ago, long before my father was ruled incompetent, he always said his greatest fear was that

Edgeware Industries, which he had spent a lifetime building, might be dissipated and torn apart by warring sons. Even when my brother and I were young boys, he would tell us the history of Henry II, whose sons fought over the inheritance—Henry's son Richard even rebelled against his father with force of arms. Father wanted none of that. I think he was preparing us for the day when only one of us would inherit—everything."

"Did he ever tell you which one of you was the oldest?"

"No, he never told us prior to him being judged incompetent—the only thing he ever told us was that we were born fifty-seven seconds apart. I didn't find out that I was the eldest until Hollister was appointed conservator and he showed me the medical documents of our births."

"Oh my God, Chester. The lawyers never told me any of this. Fifty-seven seconds between the births of you and your brother and you're just telling me this now—that what separates you and your brother from inheriting your father's company is just fifty-seven seconds? Why didn't you tell me this, and why are you telling me now?"

I wish now I hadn't, Madeleine. Maybe neither my lawyers nor I told you before because I didn't want them to tell you anything that might spook you into breaking our engagement. I was momentarily obsessed…God help me…but in for a penny…

"Actually," Chester continued, "fifty-seven seconds is not even close to the record for closely timed twin births. On April 6, 2017, a Canadian woman, Amanda Dorris, delivered twins born twenty-two seconds apart. Perhaps it was a Caesarian."

"How would you even come to know that?"

Chester shrugged. "When Hollister told me about the fifty-seven seconds I thought it might be a record, so I looked it up. If it was a record, Amanda beat it."

Madeleine resumed the shaking of her head, letting her luxuriant blond locks tumble down on her forehead. "This really is too much to take in. Why did your father not tell you who was the first born?"

"I guess that was father's way of making sure that both Arthur and I would never take anything for granted—make sure that we both prepared for making our own way in life until the time came for one of us to take control of his company."

"So Mr. Hollister definitely knows that you are the eldest and sole heir?"

"Yes! There's no question of that, darling. I told you. Father kept all the medical records of our birth in a safety deposit box for years. When the probate Court appointed Mr. Holliston as Conservator of Father's estate, the contents of the deposit box, including the medical records of birth, were retrieved by court order and given to Mr. Holliston."

"Have you seen them?"

"I told you. Yes, I have seen them. There is no question about it. I was born first. The doctor and the medical records are quite clear on that. Why do you think Holliston has advanced me the funds sufficient to maintain our lifestyle?"

"What advances are you talking about?"

"Except for what I earn at the hedge fund, those advances are pretty much what we live on."

"You mean we're in debt?"

Chester laughed. "Not at all. As Conservator, Hollister has the documentary evidence that I am the oldest and sole heir under my father's will. He has sole discretion to disburse funds from the estate, and now forwards me the dividends from the company shares. He distributes those funds on a monthly basis. At such time as my father passes away, the Conservator will transfer to me 95% of all the shares in Edgeware Industries in accordance with the will."

"And this house? Is it not in your name?"

"Technically, title will remain in the name of the Conservatorship until Father passes—at which time the house title will be transferred to me free and clear."

"One final question, dear husband of mine, does your brother Arthur know that he is the second son and will receive nothing under the will?"

"Of course he does. Both Hollister and I showed him the medical records."

"Is he at all resentful of you inheriting everything?"

"I don't think so, no. We both knew from the time we were kids that only one of us would inherit, and he has known since the Conservatorship was created that I was first born. In any case, he seems perfectly happy with the quiet academic life he has chosen. He teaches Latin and Greek at a boys' school in Berkshire—Coldbridge School for Boys, I think it is. I do insist on advancing him funds sometimes, though he never asks for it. He is in residence at the school, which includes room and board, so his needs seem to be few. I did offer to buy him a new car, but he said he's attached to his ancient Morris Minor, and didn't need a replacement."

"I knew you had a brother, but you've never told me much about him. Shame on you, Chester. You invited him to our wedding, didn't you?"

"Of course I did, but he was off at some conference giving a lecture and said he couldn't come. I'm sorry, I've been remiss. I promise to introduce you soon, invite him to come visit us. He always seems to be quite busy with his classes and academic work. He's written several Latin grammar books, and often participates in language symposia—mostly in Eastern Europe it seems. I believe he said he planned to go to one in Budapest sometime next month."

"Does he look like you?"

"People say they can see the resemblance, but he's only a fraternal twin, not identical—so not that much. I have a picture somewhere. I'll find it and show you."

"Is he married?"

"No. He's dated on and off. Mostly bookish types he meets at the various conferences. I did go to see one of the lectures he gave explaining how the Phoenicians adapted certain hieroglyphic symbols in the alphabet, which in turn were incorporated into the Hebrew alphabet and later the Greek alphabet—something like that. Didn't understand most of it."

Chester finished his coffee and stood. "I think I'd better go and see Dad at the home. Do you want to come?"

"Hmmm. I'd better not. I feel a little uncomfortable there." *They all think I'm you're daughter, you know, Chester.* "And of course your dad doesn't know me at all."

"I'm afraid he doesn't know me either, but I still need to go and sit with him. They're talking weeks now, even days. He's ninety-six, you know..."

The ring of the house's private telephone line interrupted Chester in mid-sentence. It was Holliston.

"Yes, James, what is it...no...just sitting here having breakfast with Madeleine...yes, I'm sitting down...you mean... oh...oh no...when...?"

Chester looked up at his wife.

"What is it, Chester?" she asked with concern.

Chester held up a finger. "Was the doctor there when...I see, that's good...see...thank you Holliston...I know...we knew this was coming...it's just that I thought he had a little more time...just last week they were saying he might have a few more weeks...I know, I was just about to go out to Parkington to see him...yes...we'll talk later about the arrangements...yes, I know...Brookwood...the whole family is buried there, though I still think cremation would be better...I understand...you have to go by the will...call me tomorrow and you can fill me in on your plans for the probate...thanks for letting me know...talk tomorrow..."

Chester hung up and looked at Madeleine. She said nothing, but he couldn't help but detect a glow in her face as she said, "I'm so sorry, Chester, but it really is for the best, isn't it? I mean..."

"Yes...he wasn't really living..."

The two sat silently for several minutes as they finished their final sips of coffee. Madeleine finally said, "So, does this mean you're a Lord now?"

Chester nodded. "And you're a Lady, dear."

Madeleine beamed. How long for the probate...I mean before..."

"It will take a while, dear, but there shouldn't be any problems."

CHAPTER SEVEN

*M*uriel Wright stepped out on to the Reading Station tarmac and looked out for Samantha's baby blue Lexus that would be coming up from Forbury Street. Not seeing it in the heavy traffic, she called Samantha on her mobile.

"Hi, Samantha. I'm here. Are you near?"

"Hi babe, glad you got in okay. Just coming up on Chatham. Sorry, I was out front a few minutes ago, but there was no parking and I had to go around. Be there in two minutes!"

"No rush, Samantha. I know it's a mob scene out here. I'm at the front entrance and will wave when I see you. I'm wearing my red jacket."

"See you in two."

Moments later the Lexus stopped at a space that momentarily opened up in front of the station entrance. Muriel took a quick look through the car window to make sure it was Samantha, opened the back door, threw in her roller bag, and then plumped into the front passenger seat.

The two hugged.

"Whew!" said Muriel. "Thanks so much for picking me up! It's not easy getting a cab this time of day, and Ubers have a hard time connecting at this location—not to mention saving me twenty quid and saving me from waiting another hour for a connection to Newbury."

"You know I'm always happy to come for you, babe," said Samantha as she adroitly wheeled the Lexus between lanes to get to the A329 to Newbury. "Since you left for Brianhurst I hardly ever get to see you. Can we stop somewhere for a pint and catch up before I drop you off at school?"

"I'd love to, but I better not. I have residence duties starting tomorrow, which is why I had to get back early before the weekend."

"I had thought you were getting the whole Easter break off."

"I wish. I was lucky to have five days off, and I have to sign in by four today." Muriel looked at her watch. "It's after two now, and I'd like time to get settled in. Do you mind just dropping me off?"

"Not at all."

"Maybe we can get together at the Lock, Stock, and Barrel next Saturday."

"It's a date. Saturday it is. We have forty minutes before I drop you off, and I'll tell you what the fare will be: you simply must tell me all about your secret little trip to the South of France with your mystery man…and I insist on all the details!"

Muriel chuckled. "I couldn't believe you weren't able to guess where we went."

Samantha looked back sharply to her right at the traffic behind her, and made a sharp turn on to the A329 on-ramp. "Come on, no time for guessing. Now tell me, or the fare goes up."

"Okay, if you must know it was Carcassonne."

"Carcassonne! I should have guessed. Of course! Silly me. I love that little medieval town. So historical! Like stepping into the medieval past. Eddie took me there for our anniversary two years ago. I'd never been there before, and I loved it! Now tell me all about how you pulled off this little trip."

"Well, where should I start?"

"At the beginning, dearest, and don't leave anything out, or I might just forget which turnoffs to make on the way to Brianhurst to get you back in time."

Suddenly, Muriel emitted a squeal of pleasure. "Oh Samantha, it was wonderful! It was like a dream! He picked me up at school last Friday afternoon, and we caught the train to St. Pancras. It was too late to catch the Chunnel that evening, so we stayed at the Savoy for the night."

"The Savoy! Oh, honey. Your mystery man must be loaded."

"Hardly. He's just a poor boarding school teacher—like me. As I told you, he teaches Latin, Greek, and the classics. We both scrimped and saved for months to make this trip together, but he paid for most of it. He makes twice my salary, which isn't much either."

"All right...and now dare I ask if my little Catholic girl shared a room with this nameless, and I assume, most charming travelling companion?"

Muriel didn't answer, but sheepishly smiled before finally saying, "We couldn't really afford two separate rooms."

Samantha raised her eyebrows. "Uh-huh. 'Nuff said. And what did you do the next day?"

"We slept in and got permission for an extra hour before checking out. Then we took the underground to St. Pancras, had lunch at McDonald's©, and caught the afternoon Chunnel to Paris."

"You stayed in Paris before taking the train to Carcassonne?"

"Yep, at the Avalon just a few blocks from the Gare Du Nord. Not that expensive. That night...he..."

"He...he...you almost let it slip Muriel."

"Okay, okay. I'll tell you his name...his first name...if you promise on a..."

"Stack of Bibles...yes...now, his name for your fare... though I can't imagine why it's such big secret."

"It's Arthur. His father named him after...you know, the king."

"You still can't tell me his surname?"

"Later, I promise. Not right now. Please understand."

"I won't push..."

But you are pushing, my sweet friend.

Muriel quickly moved on from the surname issue. "That first night in Paris we walked along the Moulin Rouge, had a nice dinner in a little café, and returned to the Avalon. The next morning we took the train from *Gare Du Nord* to Carcassonne. It's about a seven and a half hour trip, so we arrived in Carcassonne about 9 PM. The walled city is about a mile up the hill from the modern city of Carcassonne, so we just walked up with our roller bags. The desk clerk at the *Hotel Ville Fortifiee* met us at the city gate to authorize security to let us in. Security lets in hotel guests arriving late if a member of the hotel staff greets them."

"I take it you were tired and checked in to the hotel right away."

"Yes, but they dine late in France, so after signing in at the hotel we walked around and checked out several charming little restaurants that were still open within the walled city. We had a wonderful dinner and then walked in the moonlight back to the hotel and went right to bed. It was a lovely and quaint little hotel with a beautiful view of a garden behind the hotel."

"This was Sunday night, then?"

"I guess it was, yes. We had reservations to stay that night, Monday, and Tuesday. I was to leave on Wednesday morning, catch the very early 4:57 AM train to Paris, stay at the Avalon by myself that night in Paris and take the early morning Chunnel this morning back to St. Pancras in London. From there I took the train to Reading, and here I am early on Thursday afternoon."

"Whew. You really planned your trip tightly."

"It was the only way we could work it out. I had to be back at Brianhurst by four today, and Arthur had to arrive in Budapest Wednesday night for a language conference the following morning. He was not due back to his school in St. Johns until the following Sunday night because he got the whole week off for Easter break. I had to be back by today."

"No wonder you're tired. Arthur didn't go with you back to Paris?"

"No, he had to take a different train late Wednesday afternoon to get to his language conference. As I said, he didn't have to be back at his school until the following Sunday evening."

"He didn't wake up with you at 4 AM to take you to the Carcassonne station?"

"No, he offered to, of course, but I absolutely insisted that there was no reason for him to wake up at 4 AM just to take me to the station. His train didn't leave until 2 PM that day, so I told him to sleep in, and prepare for his lecture. I had ordered a cab the night before to pick me up the following morning at 4 AM at the front gate."

"So he was asleep when you left?"

"Oh, yes. I think I may have awakened him, though—didn't mean to—and he said something, so I went over to his bed and kissed him goodbye. He was still groggy, but he pulled me close to hug and kiss me. Then he said 'goodbye, see you back in Newbury,' or something like that. He was so sweet. Then he turned over and went back to sleep. I left him sleeping at the hotel when I went out to meet my cab. Fortunately, the cab was waiting for me outside the gate."

"Sounds like you worked the whole trip out to the minute."

"It was the only way for us to have this trip together—get me back to Brianhurst by Thursday afternoon, and still enable him to get to his language conference in Budapest and back to his school in St. Johns by the following Sunday."

"It all sounds very romantic."

"Oh, it was, Samantha. I had a wonderful time. I can't tell you."

"You certainly have a glow in your face. I'll say that for you. I take it you also had time to do some 'scouting' for your planned field trip with your French students this coming summer."

"There are only four hotels inside the old city walls, but I visited all of them to see what deals they could

⚜ 54 ⚜

offer us for as many as six rooms. I also needed to line up two rooms with two beds each for the adult chaperones."

"Were you successful?"

"I was! It turned out that the Hotel Ville where we were staying offered the best deal, but only for the week of July 13-18."

"That works for you?"

"I would have preferred the week after, but hopefully that week will work for most of the kids and their parents as well. The hotel proprietor, Martin Aubert, kindly agreed to hold the reservation for two weeks with a deposit of only a hundred Euro. I maxed out my credit card to hold it."

"What about the train fares?"

"I've got time for making those arrangements. Arthur and I got a good deal by getting the tickets in advance, and a group rate is even cheaper."

"Looks like you're a go, then?"

"Not yet. The Headmistress says I need to line up at least seven girls—though maybe I can get by with six if necessary since we could then get by with just three rooms for the kids—in addition to two rooms for four chaperones."

"Good luck on that. The kids would be lucky to go on such a trip. I know I would. I'm sure the parents would too. What about museums and other sights?"

"Arthur and I saw as many as we could. Of course, we visited the Chateau Comtal, the inner city medieval castle, and the Basilique St. Mazaraine. Most fun was just walking through La Cite de Carcassonne—it's just like a Disneyland attraction except it's the real thing, untouched since medieval times. Outside the walls, but within walking distance, is the Musee Des Beaux-Artis—a great art museum. I think the kids would also enjoy the Musee De L'ecole, which has preserved actual primary school classrooms from the 1880s. If we have time I can take them on the barge trip on the Canal du Midi."

"Did you go to all those places?"

"We did, but in two days we could only see half of what we wanted to see."

Samantha made the final turnoff on to Willows Lane, which led up the hillock to Brianhurst. Minutes later, they arrived in the courtyard in front of the main doors.

Samantha turned off the ignition. "We're here, and..." she looked at her watch, "...with forty-five minutes to spare."

"Thank you so much, Samantha. I owe you."

"You owe me nothing. So Saturday at the Lock, Stock, and Barrel?"

They gave each other a final hug, and Samantha watched Muriel knock on the front door. When the residence Head Girl opened the door and greeted Muriel, Samantha waved and Muriel disappeared into the Great Hall.

Little did Samantha know that the next time she saw her friend it would be under terrifyingly different circumstances.

CHAPTER EIGHT

Muriel awoke with a start at the sound of her iPhone alarm. She rarely needed an alarm to wake up, but she had been so exhausted from the previous day's long trip from Paris that she had gone right to bed upon settling back in her room at Brianhurst. Before retiring, however, she had tried to call Arthur on her mobile, but had gotten only a recording. Doubtless he was already involved in the language conference in Budapest, so she thought nothing of it.

Muriel had slept soundly for ten hours straight, dreaming of a future life with Arthur. He was kind, unassuming, considerate, and most of all he cared for her in a loving way that she had never before experienced—certainly not with Norman Yates. Although he was not classically good looking, and even showing early signs of balding, she had enough bad experiences with the good-looking men in her life who had pursued her only because of her own rather spectacular good looks. So far in life her God-given beauty had earned her only heartbreak and disappointment, ending with the ultimate catastrophe of her disastrous marriage to Norman. She now had her future all worked out in her mind—that she and Arthur would apply together as man and wife for teaching positions at a co-ed preparatory school that could provide them with a little cottage. They would raise a family in a safe and protected environment where each of them could pursue their academic goals—perhaps write books together.

As she picked up her mobile, she went to her window to breathe the fresh spring air and look out over the foliage, much of it just starting to come into bloom. In the courtyard driveway below she noticed only two vehicles. The first was a food delivery truck, which she often saw at this time in the morning. The second was a black sedan from which emerged a heavyset middle-aged man with unkempt and barely combed white hair, and a younger well-dressed young woman who looked to be in her late twenties or early thirties. The pair did not appear to look like typical parents, and, in any case, visiting hours were only on Sundays from 2-4. Perhaps they were friends of the Headmistress, but it did strike her as out of the ordinary.

As she gazed out, she dialed Arthur's mobile number and waited seven rings before the recording came on. Thinking that Arthur might just be getting up, or showering and preparing for a conference meeting, she was about to try again when she decided to text instead:

Dearest Arthur, thank you so much for giving me such a wonderful time in Carcassonne. I enjoyed every minute of it, and my only regret is that our time was so short. We must do it again. It was amazing. I need to head down to the refectory now for breakfast to head one of the boarders' tables. We still have about thirty girls living here during the intersession— mostly girls whose parents live abroad or are too far away for the girls to go home—and we have to supervise their activities. We allow the older girls to do their own thing, but the younger ones have to participate. I have duties all weekend, which is why I had to leave so early on Wednesday morning to get back here in time. I'm leading a pony trek this afternoon and supervising vespers tonight—I'm trying to think of what hymns to sing—but except for those times, I'll have my phone with me so you can call when you have a chance. Hope everything is going well at the conference. I wish I could be there to hear your presentation on how certain Egyptian hieroglyphs were incorporated into Coptic and then more modern alphabets. ooxx Muriel

As Muriel entered the refectory, she was immediately greeted with a cacophony of cheers and entreaties from all the girls.

"Come sit with us!" Cynthia squealed.

"No, sit with us, Miss Wright!" Catherine Pierce shouted.

Being as popular with the girls in other classes as she was with her own students, Muriel could not help but beam and smile at all of them in spite of feeling sad for so many of them who could not be home with their families during the intersession. Mother Hen Matron Ratchet was too much of the grumpy and scolding disciplinarian to be endearing to the girls, but Muriel was adored as a much beloved second mother, especially by the homesick younger girls.

Muriel held up her hands. "How about if I sit down with all of you?" She pointed to Cynthia's table. "Cynthia, I shall sit at your table for juice and porridge. Then I shall sit at Catherine's table for Kippers and Fried bread."

Susan Bradley at the third table raised her hand frantically. "What about us, Miss Wright?"

"I shall then come to your table, Susan, and we shall enjoy our tea and talk about our pony trek this afternoon. How's that everyone?"

There were cheers as Muriel looked around the refectory for signs of Matron Ratchet who was usually hovering and assisting Cook Manson with the breakfast. Without supervision, the girls could be unruly this early in the morning.

To much laughter and cheers, Muriel took her seat at Cynthia's table next to the picture windows of the heath.

"Do we need to speak French now?" Cynthia asked. "I'm the only one who speaks it at this table."

"No, Cynthia. "That was only if you went home, and I thought you said you were going home for Easter."

Cynthia frowned and shook her head. "They told me they would come and pick me up, but my dad called the Headmistress and said he had to take Mummy to the hospital this week, so they couldn't come."

"Oh, I'm so sorry to hear that, Cynthia. I hope your mother is okay."

"Dad told Mrs. Weathersby that she was fine and not to worry."

"I'm glad to hear that, Cynthia." Muriel turned to the other girls at the table. "Now, are all of you signed up for the pony trek?"

All the girls raised their hands enthusiastically except one, a girl named Brenda, who said, "I signed up, Miss Wright, but they said it was all filled up."

"Well, Brenda, why don't you come over to the stables after high tea and we'll see what we can do. I'm sure we can find a pony for you."

"Thanks, Miss Wright. Can I ride Cinnamon? She's my favorite…"

Before Brenda could finish her request, Matron Ratchet appeared and stood next to Muriel, who looked up. "Oh, good morning Matie, I didn't see you. Just a minute, Brenda. Did you need me for something Matie?"

Dour-faced, Matron Ratchet intoned dutifully, "You have visitors. You're to go to Mrs. Weathersby's office."

"Visitors? For me? My, I can't imagine who would be visiting me this morning. I'm not expecting anyone. I'll be right up."

"You're to come right now, Miss."

"I see. Very well. Girls, I'm afraid you'll have to excuse me. Don't worry. I'll be right back. I imagine there's some mistake."

"We'll wait!" cried Cynthia.

"No girls. You go ahead and eat. I'm not sure how long I'll be, but I'll be back as soon as I can."

"*Okaaaay*" the girls moaned with disappointment.

"But I'll see you after tea for the pony trek." Muriel waved goodbye.

Muriel had hidden her concern from the girls, but as she made her way up the Grand Staircase to Mrs. Weathersby office, she began to imagine a parade of potential horribles. What if these two visitors were the man and woman she saw exiting the black sedan—police officers in plain clothes responding to a call of an intruder on the premises? Had Norman again trespassed on the property looking for her? If so, the Headmistress had made it clear that she would be terminated. What would that do for her dreams and plans of a quiet and contented life with Arthur? How could she ever get another teaching position if she were unceremoniously dismissed at the very first school where she had taught? She thought of what Samantha would say to her, for she had said it to her many times, "Life is what happens while you're busy making other plans."

Muriel stopped at the top of the staircase to gather her thoughts before she stepped into Mrs. Weathersby's office. If the police were really here to respond to a report of an intruder on the school premises, surely the Thames Valley police would send a uniformed constable, not plain clothed inspectors. She was letting her imagination run away with her.

Just as she dismissed this possibility as unlikely, an even more horrible thought came to mind. Could Mrs. Weathersby possibly have gotten wind of her long weekend tryst with a *man*? The Headmistress had made it clear that reputation was everything when it came to a girls' school being able to perform its educational mission. Every teacher, but especially the resident women teachers, had to be the model of propriety and set the moral example for the girls in their charge.

Muriel took a deep breath. Surely not! This was the twenty-first century after all. What right did Mrs. Weathersby have to look into her private life outside the confines of the school? Even if she did have that right, what possible justification would she have to call in the police—and plain-clothed inspectors at that—to charge her with adultery, fornication, or some other moral offense long abandoned as a crime in England. Wouldn't she more likely avoid a police presence at the school, and just quietly terminate her with no publicity?

Muriel took a deep breath. She was being paranoid. Her visitors could not be the man and woman she saw emerge from the black sedan. Perhaps her visitor was Samantha—perhaps with Eddie in tow, though that did seem unlikely—who dropped by the school to ask permission to take her to lunch, and was referred to the Headmistress for permission.

Muriel now straightened and held her head up. Stoically, she tapped on the door of the Headmistress.

"Come in!"

With trepidation, Muriel entered the threshold. Her heart sank.

At first sight, her first fears were quickly realized. Mrs. Weathersby was seated behind her desk looking at her with a very unpleasant expression. Standing beside her were indeed the same man and woman she saw exiting the black sedan.

"You sent for me, Ma'am?"

"Yes, Miss Wright. These two visitors are from the Thames Valley Police Department and they wish to speak with you."

"What…what is this all about?"

The man held out his credentials. "I am DI Stone, and this is DS Graham."

"Yes, sir. How can I help you? If it's about my ex-husband, he's…"

"Ma'am. Are you Muriel Wright?"

"Yes sir, but…"

"Your address is 187 Willow Lane, Shire of Berkshire?"

"Yes, that is the address of this school, and I am in residence here."

DI Stone turned to Mrs. Weathersby. "Ma'am, would it be possible to speak to Miss Wright alone?"

"Yes, officer," said Mrs. Weathersby with a distressed expression. "I can leave and let you speak to Miss Wright here in my office, or if you prefer, there is an empty classroom down the hall."

"Perhaps that would be better, Ma'am."

"Of course. Please come with me."

Weathersby led Muriel, who was by now in a state of nervous panic, and the two inspectors down the hall to an empty classroom. Much to Muriel's chagrin, it turned out to be the classroom in which she taught her class.

"Please be seated," said Inspector Stone. All three took seats on the small classroom chairs.

"Now," said Stone, "we would like to ask you some questions, but first I must advise you that you need not say anything, but it may harm your defense if you do not mention when questioned something which you later rely on in court. Anything you say may be given in evidence."

Muriel sat in mortified silence. What could all this possibly mean?

"Do you wish to answer some questions?" Detective Sergeant Graham asked.

"Yes, of course," Muriel managed to say, "anything, but can you tell me what this is all…"

"Miss Wright," Graham continued, "did you leave England this past week?"

"Yes, I did. I took a trip with a friend to Paris, and then to Carcassonne."

"When did you leave here?"

Muriel breathed heavily, trying to think. "Umh, last Friday evening. My friend picked me up here at the school around five or so, and we drove to Newbury station where we took the train to London."

"What was the name of your friend?"

"…Arthur."

"Arthur what, Ma'am?"

Muriel tried not to hesitate in answering, but she did.

"…Arthur Edgeware, Ma'am."

Inspector Stone and Graham looked at each other as if her answer was the one they were looking for. They also seemed to be familiar with the last name.

"You transferred in Reading?" Graham continued.

"Yes Ma'am."

"Did you stay in London for the night?"

"Yes, Ma'am."

"Where?"

"The Savoy."

Stone and Graham again looked at each other.

"What did you do the next morning?"

"We took the Chunnel to Paris, and stayed the night at the Avalon, just a few blocks from the *Gare du Nord.*"

"You stayed in the same room?"

Muriel answered quickly. "Yes, Ma'am."

The detectives exchanged another knowing look.

"Please, please, can you tell me what this is all about?" Muriel begged.

"Just a few more questions, Miss Wright. When did you travel to Carcassonne from Paris?"

"Well, let me think. We stayed in Paris last Saturday night. Then the next morning, on Sunday we took the train to Carcassonne."

"You arrived in Carcassonne last Sunday evening then?"

"Yes Ma'am."

"How many nights did you stay in Carcassonne and where did you stay?"

"The *Hotel Ville Fortifiée.*"

"And you again shared a room with Mr. Edgeware?"

"Yes Ma'am. We stayed three nights—Sunday, Monday and Tuesday. I left on Wednesday morning very early."

"With Mr. Edgeware?"

"No Ma'am. I had to catch a very early train back to Paris at 4:57. I took a cab to the Carcassonne station."

"So you left Mr. Edgeware alone?"

"Yes, Arthur offered to take me to the station, but I didn't see the reason why he needed to do that—just to drop me off and then come back to the walled city, go back to the hotel and go back to sleep. He planned to take a 2:30 train later that day to Budapest where he was scheduled to give a presentation to a language conference."

"So when you left your room, Mr. Edgeware was still asleep?"

"Actually, he did wake up for a few moments. We kissed each other goodbye, and then I left."

"And how was he at that time?"

"He was fine, a little groggy, I suppose, since I had unintentionally awakened him while dressing, packing, and also showering."

A final exchange of glances between the two detectives now caused Muriel to stand up in distress.

"Is Arthur all right? Please tell me! Has something happened? Please tell me!"

Detective Stone said, "Please sit down. I am sorry to tell you that we have some very bad news."

"Oh my God, what is it? What has happened to Arthur? You must tell me!"

Detective Graham looked over at her superior, as if to ask: *should we ask her to come down to the station now?*

DI Stone hesitated and then shook his head. There would be time enough for that. Then he nodded, and DS Graham understood. It was time to tell Miss Wright what information they had received early this morning from the *French Gendarmerie Nationale*.

CHAPTER NINE

*J*udy was about to pick up her mobile when it rang. She smiled when she saw Amber's name appear on the screen.

"Hey, girl. I was just about to call you!"

"I'm sure, sister. I was sorry I couldn't talk last time you called. Is this a good time?"

"Absolutely. There's been a lull in my caseload recently, so I was thinking of playing hooky anyway, and lounging and resting at home all day. How's Harvey's campaign going?"

"He's still gearing up for it, but the election isn't actually until November. He may have a real challenger this time who has some money behind him, so Harvey's getting a little worked up over it."

"This will be his third term for DA, so I would think he'd be pretty established by now."

"He is, but there's a lot of oil money sloshing around down here in Houston, and a lot of attorneys who would love his job and see it as an entry job for higher political office."

"Everything's okay, though—between you and him, I mean?"

"Oh yes. I'm pretty busy too, you know, so we don't get to see each other that much."

"I don't suppose you've invited him to move into that beautiful new house you bought?"

"I'd really like to, but it's kind of a dilemma for him. Running for office, he can't give his opponent the opportunity to make political hay out of him playing house with a woman he's not married to. This is Texas, after all."

"Simple solution to that one, you know."

"I know, but I'm not pushing it. I hate to admit this, but with this incredible legacy Uncle Timothy left us, I mean, I've got to be sure…is that what's hanging you up with tying the knot with Braxton too?"

"I don't think so. If I were sure…"

"See what I mean? Who wants to begin a marriage by asking the prospective husband to sign a pre-nup—it's usually the other way around and all men have their pride."

"I know, but it's not just that. At least I don't think that has anything to do with me keeping Braxton at arm's length for now. Timothy has given me the chance to do what I've always wanted to do, and I want to give myself a chance to see if I can be a success at it—on my own."

"No need to convince me, Judy. I get it. Speaking of your new career in helping the powerless and disadvantaged fight the privileged and powerful, what's happening with that case you were working on so hard?"

"The Tomlinson case? Nothing new since we last talked. The case is still in Magistrate's court, and I think the CPS is still brooding over whether they really want to bring it to trial. After Janet's heart-breaking testimony at the preliminary hearing— she clearly acted in self-defense for her own life—no barrister worth his salt would want to touch that case with a ten-foot pole, but we'll see. I'll let you know."

"What about the New York firm you left behind?"

"I didn't really leave them behind. I consult with all the partners on a weekly basis. They hired an excellent male litigator as an associate—Carol convinced me that an all-female law firm would be a bit intimidating, especially to male clients."

"I suppose you still subsidize the firm."

"Yes. The firm still loses about three million a year, and I make sure all the partners receive a monthly salary commensurate with their skills and experience. All I ask in return is that they take only meritorious cases in which there is a risk of injustice if they do not, and keep me posted."

"Are they?"

"I think so. They all appreciate a set monthly salary so they don't have to be forever chasing clients and fees or spending endless hours filling out time sheets."

"Lucky them. I can't really do that with my firm yet. I'm just one of three senior partners, and they all are interested in the high contingency commissions they earn in their high profile civil cases."

"We can't save the whole world, Amber—even with Timothy's legacy."

"I know, and I respect what you're doing over there across the pond. I still don't understand how it works over there. The 'chambers' you're now in…"

"The Quadrangle. It's not like an American law firm at all. As barristers, we're all independent contractors, and available for hire by either the Crown Prosecution Service to act as prosecutors on behalf of the Crown, or as defense counsel if retained by a client's solicitor."

"Clients can't come to you directly—they have to first go to a solicitor, and then the solicitor retains you to try the case if it goes to trial?"

"Customarily and traditionally, yes. I heard Braxton try to explain this to one of his American clients who was arrested for vehicular homicide. He said it's like the way a general practitioner sees a patient in his office and then refers the case to a surgeon if surgery is required. Personally, I think Braxton was oversimplifying."

"How so?"

"I think Braxton's explanation gives the impression that barristers are necessarily more skilled or experienced than solicitors, but that is hardly the case. Over ninety-five percent of British lawyers are solicitors, many of them highly skilled and experienced in their areas of specialty. The difference is that barristers specialize almost exclusively on trying cases in the courtroom. Solicitors give the barrister the entire case file wrapped in a blue ribbon—literally."

"Do you like being a barrister in that system?"

"I do, very much. You know I've never been one for sitting at my desk all day writing documents and filling out time sheets. I have come to love the excitement, challenge, and drama of the courtroom. Time goes by quickly in the courtroom, and I never watch the clock. We barristers become highly proficient and experienced in our specialty of trial work because that's all we do—day in and day out. Nothing else."

"Is that so different from the skills of American trial lawyers?"

"Very different, I'm sad to say. Any American law school graduate can enter a courtroom and attempt to try a case. It is painful to watch many of them. Without real courtroom skills, many of them rely on back room wheeling and dealing for people's lives and liberties. It's now very rare that defendants in American courtrooms ever actually get their day in Court."

"Wow. What does that make me, Judy?"

"Of course you're the exception, Amber. You've developed your courtroom skills. I've seen you in the courtroom."

"Well, thanks for that."

"I think I told you that Robin and I took a sabbatical year from the firm to come to London and observe the Inns of Court to see what experienced and skilled barristers could do in the courtroom—not just for their clients but for the cause of justice. It was seeing the barristers in action that inspired me to someday become a barrister. It remained a dream and fantasy until you and I received our amazing legacy from Timothy."

"And help from Braxton too, so you tell me."

"Yes, much help from Braxton as well."

"So now you've set yourself up as a one person legal aid society."

"I suppose you could say that, but I hope I'm not anything like Legal Aid here in the UK. They offer only a pittance to those representing indigent defendants. I cannot yet claim the experience that I need to properly represent them, but I have something Legal Aid cannot offer them."

"Which is…"

"Resources, Amber. You'll remember how I finally tracked down the murderer of Timothy's daughter at Mont St. Michel, and the murder of your client's mother on the Concorde?"

"I remember well."

"It wasn't my courtroom skills that brought them to justice, but my access to the scientific and investigative resources of NXR Investigation Services in Chicago."

"Oh, yes, Jake Everett. I know his firm's investigative services cost you…"

"Millions, yes. How do you think I ever tracked down Rupert Tomlinson's former wives, one of whom now lives in Canada, to interview them about Rupert's treatment of them— not to mention an obscure perjury charge, which Rupert pleaded down to a misdemeanor for Obstruction of the Course of Justice over a decade ago? I like to think of myself now as a judicial equalizer. Without those resources, now unavailable to indigent defendants, Janet's case would now be at the Crown Court on charges of Assault with a Deadly Weapon and Attempted Murder."

"You are amazing, Judy. If you are now to take the most hopeless cases—without remuneration I might add—and be the Batman of Justice, who will be your Robin? If you fancy yourself a female Sherlock Holmes, who will be your Doctor Watson?"

Judy paused before answering with serious intonation, "I was kind of hoping you would, Amber."

Amber laughed. "Whoa, sister! I understand your wanting to continue the path that Robin first opened up to you at the Exoneration Clinic at Holmes School of Law, but be honest…haven't you ever thought of just enjoying the legacy Timothy left us? Have you ever even visited our estates in Paris and the South of France? Do you even have a nice car—or any car for that matter?"

"None of the above. The traffic in London is a nightmare, so I don't need a car. When Braxton and I travel out of town, he drives his old Spitfire, or we take the train."

"That reminds me. Last week you told me that you and Braxton travelled out to a little town…"

"Newbury…"

"…to spend the weekend with…"

"…the Quadrangle's QC, Michael Hodges. Yes, it was fine. Braxton protected me from him the whole time."

"This is the Hodges who's trying to get you booted from the Quadrangle?"

"That's the impression Braxton gave me. I have no idea why Hodges invited us, but it was important to Braxton that we humor him and not decline his invitation."

"You're a good mate…and Braxton has no idea about your…"

"My legacy. Like I said, I only told him that I had received a generous inheritance. He knows I make ample use of expensive investigative services and receive little or no remuneration, so I didn't want him to think I had robbed a bank or something…"

"…but you never told him how much."

"No, and if he really loves me, he shouldn't care…and he'll support me with what I'm trying to do until I'm ready to marry or play house."

"Babe, I've got to start getting ready to get to the office. One more question."

"Sure. Like I said, I'm playing hooky today, curling up with Chloe—she's purring up a storm right now—and enjoying my view of the Thames."

"Your condo sounds fantastic. Your one indulgence I take it."

"Yes, guilty…and you're right that it cost me a bundle. I wanted the view up here more than anything else…it really helps me unwind at the end of the day…floor to ceiling windows on the eighteenth floor, and the night skyline is amazing. I think Timothy would approve."

"I'm sure he would…and you deserve it. I can hardly wait to see it."

"Plenty of room, two bedrooms, but a monster kitchen, and huge patio. When are you coming?"

"I'm working on it. Maybe in June I can get out there."

"That would be great if you could. You had a question before we sign off?"

"Okay. You said earlier that a client has to contact a solicitor first, and then the solicitor calls chambers and asks for a particular barrister on behalf of the client."

"Customarily and traditionally."

"Then how are all these indigent clients of yours going to access you if they have to go through a solicitor first?"

"I was hoping you wouldn't ask that question. First of all, indigent defendants don't get to choose their own solicitors. Judges or court personnel simply assign them one from a list of solicitors who are desperate enough to take the low fees."

"Which must make it almost impossible for them to approach a barrister directly."

In most cases, yes. However, a client, whether indigent or not, is entitled to directly approach a barrister who is listed on the Direct Public Access Portal as authorized by the Bar Standards Board."

"Are you on that?"

"It was my first priority after I completed my pupilage and joined the Quadrangle."

"So you're on it."

"Yes, Janet Tomlinson was the first client who approached me directly for legal advice using that portal, and bypassing the solicitor."

"How did she get your name and know how to contact you?"

"She was a little vague on that. It was before I gained some unwanted notoriety with that jogging picture of me in the *Mirror.*"

"Since that picture and story about you was published, have you received any more potential clients trying to contact you directly?"

"I'm embarrassed to say that I have—several. Though at least one of them said they heard about me after a short interview I gave to *UK Law Today* on BBC-2."

"Have you agreed to take any of them?"

"I did agree to speak with them, but ultimately declined to take any of them. All but one of them were women who wanted me to sue their husbands for divorce, and none of them was indigent. There was one man who contacted me, a habitual criminal charged with domestic violence. He was indigent, but I chose not to take the case after reviewing the charges against him."

"Do you still plan to stay on the Direct Public Access list?"

"I think so, for a while anyway. I still think it is my best chance to find indigent clients who have a meritorious defense and are at risk of an injustice. An hour before you called, I got a call from Archie…"

"Archie…?"

"…our chambers clerk…he said a woman called in to the Quadrangle earlier this morning who wanted to talk to me. I'm looking at my notes…a woman named Samantha Sterling. Anyway, Archie tried to give her the name of a solicitor, but she insisted on talking to me directly. Archie tried to talk her out of it, but Archie knows I'm on the Direct Access Portal, so he finally relented and told the woman he would contact me and ask if I would meet with her. Archie doesn't approve of me taking Direct Access clients, but said he wouldn't stand in my way if I wanted to meet her—but only if I met with her outside chambers. He suggested The Brass Monkey, and I said yes."

"The Brass Monkey?"

"The Quadrangle's favorite watering hole. It's probably just another woman who saw my picture, or heard me on *UK Law Today,* and thinks I can pin her husband to the wall in a divorce proceeding. They think that if they can land the only female American barrister, the publicity and subsequent embarrassment to the husband will help their cause. I'm not expecting anything else coming my way right now, but if it's what I think it is, I'll be declining that case as well."

"Maybe you'll be surprised."

"Maybe. By the way, before you go, if you're really interested in how the courts and chambers work out here…do you get Amazon Prime Video?"

"I think so, why."

"Pull up a series called *Silk*. It will give you the flavor of how chambers works and how barristers, solicitors, and clients interact. The fictional female barrister on the show, Martha Costello, has become something of my role model. Of course, like all telly dramas, it's a bit over-wrought. It turns out that Martha and her on-and-off love interest Clive Reader become pitted against each other as they both compete for the honor of being awarded the coveted honor of 'Queen's Counsel' and thus entitled to wear the 'silk' in court."

"Sounds like a variation of the theme in that Spencer Tracy and Katherine Hepburn film *Adam's Rib* in which the two are both lawyers married to each other and face off against each other in court."

"Maybe, a little."

"Sounds like fun. I'll take a look."

"Bye, babe. Call soon."

CHAPTER TEN

"**W**hat did the Chief Inspector say about an arrest?"

DI Stone and DS Graham were sitting in the canteen of the Thames Valley Police Department enjoying an early morning cup of coffee.

Stone shook his head. "He says we can't make an arrest now, even if we wanted to."

"Why not?"

"Brexit, if you can believe it."

"What does Brexit have to do with it?"

"It seems that when the UK withdrew from the EU, it also withdrew from the EAW."

"From the what?"

"The European Arrest Warrant protocol, Sergeant. You'd better brush up on all this before you take your Inspector's examination. Under that protocol, adopted by the UK back in 2002, any country in the European Union can issue a warrant that is valid in all EU countries. Once issued it requires another member state to arrest and transfer a criminal suspect to the issuing state."

"The UK had to withdraw from that protocol when it left the EU? Why was that?"

"The UK offered to continue with the protocol even after withdrawing from the EU, but the EU declined the offer unless the UK was willing to accept freedom of movement and the jurisdiction of the European Court of Justice—which of course it was unwilling to do."

"So how does extradition work now?"

"The old-fashioned way—by having an extradition hearing. The process can take months, or even years."

"So if Muriel Wright did kill Arthur Edgeware at that hotel in Carcassonne, she gets away with it?"

"Not necessarily. Look at this report." He handed it to Graham, who began reading it.

"These pictures! Jesus, sir!"

"We knew when the Gendarmes first called us last week that Arthur was found dead in his hotel room with his throat slit and multiple knife wounds to his chest—one of which punctured his heart. According to the pathologist's report, there is no question that these wounds were the cause of death."

"I know sir, but these pictures…"

"You'll see much worse if you stay with the force and ever make Inspector, Sergeant. Now turn to page six."

Graham nodded and turned the page.

"Read it."

"It says that a toxicology test showed that Arthur had several times the normal dose of the drug Ambien. However, it doesn't say that Ambien was the cause of death, or even a contributing cause of death. If that is so, why is the Ambien in his system so important?"

"You tell me, Sergeant, and then turn to page twelve and we'll see if Inspector Marceau of the French Gendarmes agrees with you. Look at the pictures."

"Well, the pictures are terrible, but I suppose it is unusual that there is not more blood all over the sheets and covers. The blood seems confined to the body itself, and where it just dripped off the body onto the bed without the splatter you would expect from such a violent attack."

"And what does that tell you?"

"I suppose that there was not a struggle?"

"Excellent, Sergeant. If you turn to page twelve, you'll see that that is precisely what the French Inspector also concluded."

"In other words, you're saying that the victim must have been so sedated that even after the first stabs of the knife he was unable to resist the attack or even to thrash about. But isn't it possible that the first stab to his heart killed him instantly before he was even able to mount a struggle?"

"That is a possibility, but I agree with Inspector Marceau that it is more likely that except for the victim's extreme state of sedation he would have thrashed about much more during the attack and splattered his blood over a much wider area."

"So the Ambien did contribute to his death."

"Not in a direct way. Being attacked while he was asleep, his chances of survival or defense were probably nil. However, the presence of the Ambien does suggest that murder was premeditated. The murderer must have spiked the victim's drink some hours before the attack with the expectation that he would be less likely to struggle or cry out. Had any of the guests in the rooms nearby heard anything, they might have aroused the alarm and jeopardized any chance of the killer getting away.

"I see, I guess."

"We shall have to gather more evidence, but from what I can tell from the report I received, Muriel and Arthur were together almost all the time they were in Carcassonne. If we can find evidence that Muriel, say, bought the Ambien in England and perhaps even began spiking his drinks before they left London, it might be possible to bring charges against her in a British Court. The law is clear that it is possible to prosecute a person for the same crime in multiple states if elements of the crime occur in more than one state."

"If it can't be proved that Muriel bought the Ambien and sedated him, can she still be extradited to France to face trial?"

"Theoretically, yes. The French government would have to request extradition, in which case a UK court would hold an extradition hearing to determine if there is reasonable cause to believe Muriel committed the crime in France. It might take more time than under the EAW protocol, but she wouldn't necessarily 'get away with it' as you suggested."

"What can we do now, then?"

"For the time being all we can do is gather evidence. The French Gendarmes have requested that we monitor her movements and confiscate her passport to prevent her from fleeing the jurisdiction."

Graham frowned.

"What is it Sergeant?"

"I don't know. I have a hard time believing that she could have done it. I mean she just seemed to be a sweet young French teacher. I know she was nervous when we interviewed her, but who wouldn't be, especially after we told her that her companion was found brutally murdered in her room shortly after she left him in Carcassonne? I thought she was very forthright with the answers to our questions."

"Sergeant, if you stay the course in the Thames Valley Police Department, you'll see much worse than what you see in those pictures. I can also tell you that you can't judge a killer by appearance. I have come to believe that under the right circumstances, motivation, and opportunity, everyone is capable of murder."

"I still can't see it in this case. I mean, if she did kill Arthur Edgeware in that hotel room, wouldn't she know that she would be the prime suspect after she simply took off as she did? She must have known that the police could easily track her down and learn her identity."

"If murderers never made mistakes, very few would ever get convicted."

"Isn't it possible that after she left Arthur Edgeware in that hotel room, someone else came into the room and killed him?"

"Take that report home tonight and read it thoroughly. The evidence is overwhelming that Muriel Wright committed this crime. She admitted that she left the room about 4 AM. The night clerk confirms that while he locked the doors to the hotel at 11 PM the night before, he unlocked the doors for Muriel to leave at 4 AM to catch her cab to the Carcassonne train station. He locked the hotel's front door after she left, and no other guests entered or left the hotel until after Muriel left the hotel. The maid found the body when she entered the room to clean at 8 AM. Hysterical at seeing the body, she immediately ran to get the manager. When the manager saw the body he immediately called the Gendarmes, who told the manager not to let anyone enter or leave the hotel until Inspector Hugo Marceau arrived. When the Inspector and his team arrived at about 8:30 he immediately cordoned off the room. No one was allowed to leave the hotel until statements were taken from all the guests. All stated that they had heard nothing during the night. Neither the night clerk nor the manager had any indications that anyone had broken in or out during the night."

"I take it that the pathologist was able to give an estimate of the time of death."

"At the scene he gave a preliminary estimate that the victim died between two and six in the morning. After he conducted the autopsy, he narrowed the probable time of death as occurring between 3:00 and 5:00 AM."

"So if Muriel left the hotel at 4:00 AM, it's possible that someone could have entered the room after she left and attacked Edgeware."

"Possible, yes. However, you would have to believe that a stranger managed to spike Arthur's drink with Ambien either the night or day before…that he somehow just happened to see Muriel leave at 4 AM…that he then entered Arthur's room at just the right time and attacked Edgeware with a knife, returning to his own room without anyone seeing anything."

"I still don't see why Muriel had any greater opportunity to commit this crime than any other guest in the hotel."

"Sergeant, Muriel was with him the entire night until she left the next morning. Except for the maid who only entered the room the next morning to clean after she knocked and got no answer, no one other than Muriel had a key to the room. She relinquished that key when she asked the night clerk to open the front door of the hotel."

"Did they find the murder weapon?"

"Yes, it was lying on the floor next to the bed. The manager later identified its markings as those of the hotel. Of course, no fingerprints were found on the knife as might be expected."

"How was the victim identified?"

"His wallet, passport and driver's license were in his wallet on the nightstand. The Gendarmes quickly began calling and finally located his brother in England, a Chester Edgeware. He flew in immediately and identified his brother's body. Apparently, he's staying there in Carcassonne until the coroner and Gendarmes release his body. He told the police that he wants to bring his brother back for burial as soon as possible and won't be leaving France until he can do so."

"Edgeware. That wouldn't be the Edgeware family that owns Edgeware Industries, would it?"

DI Stone raised his eyebrows knowingly. "Oh yes, it certainly would be."

"Oh my. That does make it uhm…" Graham couldn't find the right adjective. "How did they track down Muriel so quickly?"

"She and Arthur both signed their names and addresses in the hotel register. When the Gendarmes found that Muriel's address was a Girls' School in Surrey, they immediately found the telephone number for the school and found that she had returned to England on the Thursday afternoon after the murder."

"I'm surprised the French authorities weren't able to intercept her before she left the country."

"Apparently they tried, but for whatever reason it didn't happen. As it is, it looks like she fled the country to avoid prosecution."

Graham resumed shaking her head. "I still don't buy it. I saw the way she reacted when we told her the terrible news, and I can't believe she faked that reaction. She answered every question we asked. If she's innocent, and my every instinct tells me that she is, she must be going through hell right now."

"Sergeant, we have to go where the evidence leads us. You know that. Instinct is not evidence."

"Ah yes, sir. As you always tell me, a wise man proportions his belief to the evidence. So far I can accept that Muriel had the means…the knife came from within the hotel itself…and opportunity…she was with him in the room just hours before and perhaps after he was attacked…but sir, don't we need a motive?"

"Yes, that is a problem, I agree, though it's not necessary to prove motive to get a conviction. Our victim is the son of one of the richest men in England. There may be something there."

"I don't see how, sir. As far as we know, Muriel was just Edgeware's playmate, not his wife. I don't see how she could benefit from his death."

"Maybe, maybe not. We'll have to check that out. Moreover, at this point we can't rule out the traditional motives— jealousy, anger, who knows."

"Well, sir, I'll read the whole file tonight, but I have to ask you why we need to do all this investigation for the French? Why not just wait until they seek extradition and let them come here to a UK court and make their own case. Is the Chief Inspector going to let us devote very much time to this?"

"You have a point, Sergeant, but I feel there's a lot more to this case than we can see at this stage. I already have the Chief's okay to pursue this matter. The Home Office has already contacted him and asked him to monitor Muriel Wright's movements and report back. I'm not sure we know all the ramifications of where this case could lead."

"Very well, sir. What do you want me to do?"

"First, check every pharmacy in this county and see if you can find any prescriptions for Ambien issued to Muriel Wright. Also, see what you can find out about the nature of the relationship between Wright and Edgeware. How long have they been dating? Also, follow the money trail if you can find one. If Arthur is an heir to any of the Edgeware money, we need to look into that. From the last I heard, Lord Edgeware is still alive. Check all of that out and get back to me."

"Yes, sir."

CHAPTER ELEVEN

*T*he Brass Monkey teemed with patrons who came for the popular afternoon Saturday roast.

Judy entered and scanned the room for the woman who had described herself as being in her 30s, with dark brown hair, wearing dark glasses, and wearing a dark blue blazer.

Samantha Sterling had claimed a corner table and kept her eye on the entrance. Having previously seen Judy in court, albeit in a barrister's black robe and wig, Samantha recognized Judy instantly and waved.

Judy, dressed in black skirt, white blouse, black tie, and black patent leather flats, waved back and approached the corner table.

"Samantha Sterling?"

Samantha rose and extended her hand. "Good afternoon, Ma'am. I recognized you from court. Thank you for coming."

Judy took her hand and sat. "I'm Judy Alexander. I'm sorry we have to meet here rather than in my chambers office, but our clerk insisted. You understand that approaching me as a barrister directly is not customary. I take it you have not seen a solicitor?"

"No Ma'am. I think I can explain. You see, I'm not here for myself, but for a dear friend who finds herself in desperate need of legal assistance."

Judy was surprised. Archie had not told her that she would not be meeting with a potential client at all, but rather with a potential client's friend on her behalf.

"Please call me Samantha."

"Of course…Samantha. Listen, Samantha, under these circumstances, I think it best that I refer you to a solicitor. I can give you several names…"

"Please, Miss Alexander. If you would let me explain, I can tell you why I came to you directly, and why I would prefer not to involve a solicitor at this time."

"You came to me in particular? May I ask why?"

"Several weeks ago I wanted to get out of the house. You see…I live near Newbury. It's in Berkshire about fifty miles west of…"

"I know it well. Go on."

"My husband was gone for the day, my children were all away in school, and I had been thinking of coming into London for something to do and maybe do some shopping."

Judy waited patiently, hoping that this friend of someone who might need legal assistance would soon get to the point.

"Well," Samantha finally continued, "on the train coming in I read an article about a preliminary hearing being held in Magistrate's court—the case of a woman being charged with assault against her husband."

"*Queen v. Tomlinson.*"

"Yes, that's the one. The case interested me because domestic abuse is such a problem in this country. I belong to several organizations that seek to address this problem."

Judy nodded.

"I also read that the 'American barrister' would be defending, and I remembered seeing an article in the *Mirror* some weeks before, how you had gotten an acquittal in an earlier case in which domestic violence was involved—a case that no one else wanted to take and that would otherwise have gone to Legal Aid—that you took cases based on the merits of the case and not on ability of the client to pay."

Judy shook her head. Would she ever live down that picture of her jogging in Hyde Park? "Oh dear. I hope you didn't come to me based on that article."

"Not at all, but I was curious to see you in court trying another domestic violence case."

"My client was the defendant and charged with deadly assault. Her defense was self-defense."

"I understand, but you brought up the prosecution witness's history of domestic violence."

"Yes…but go on."

"So, rather than shopping I thought it would be interesting to see what was happening in the Tomlinson case. I very much admired how you cross-examined the husband, and thought to myself, if I ever get in trouble with the law, you're the one I would want to go to."

"You are very kind, Samantha, but I did not win in the Tomlinson case. It was not dismissed, though it was kept in Magistrate's course. In fact, I have very little experience. I have tried only three cases on my own, and lost two of them. If your friend is in legal trouble, I strongly urge you to let me recommend a good solicitor who can best advise your friend. Has your friend been charged with a crime?"

Samantha shook her head. "No, not yet, but she and I are very much afraid that she will be…of a most serious crime. She has already been questioned by the Thames Valley Police and cautioned."

"In connection with what crime?"

Samantha took a deep breath and struggled to say the words. "First Degree Murder, Miss Alexander."

Judy tried not to let her face show her surprise. "First Degree Murder? Is this a murder that was committed in the Thames Valley?"

"No Ma'am. The murder took place in France…in the walled town of Carcassonne."

"Carcassonne? I know the town, but must confess I'm very confused. If this crime was committed in France, why is she being questioned by the Thames Valley Police?"

"Apparently the French Gendarme has asked that she be detained by the police in this country and returned to France for prosecution."

"That will be difficult. Since Britain left the EU, the UK is not part of the European Arrest Warrant protocol and under no legal obligation to serve warrants issued by any EU country."

"I asked my husband Eddie about that, and he said she can still be extradited."

"That's true, but that is a complex process—a process still under review by the British government in the aftermath of Brexit. At a minimum, it would require a UK court to review the evidence against your friend and determine that there is probable cause that your friend committed the crime in question. It might also require the acquiescence of the British government itself."

"But in the end, she could be extradited?"

"It is possible, yes, depending on what the evidence is. It is also possible that if the police here discover that any element of the crime was committed in the UK, a UK court could also assert jurisdiction and try her for murder. Given these legal uncertainties, I must again most strongly advise you to have your friend seek a solicitor who is experienced in such matters, and in particular a solicitor who is experienced in both criminal and extradition procedures."

"Have you ever defended a client in an extradition case, Miss Alexander?"

Judy thought for a moment. "I sat in on a case as a pupil, but did not participate in any way, and after I was admitted to the bar, I sat second chair in such a case. In both cases the detainee was returned to the requesting country—hardly the experience that your friend should look for in someone he…she…is your friend a man or woman, Samantha? You didn't say."

"She is a woman, about my age."

"Where is she now?"

"She is staying with me for the time being…at my home in Newbury. Ma'am, I need to tell you some things."

"Go ahead."

"First of all, I will tell you her name. It is Muriel Wright, and she is…or was…a French teacher at a very well regarded girls' school outside Newbury, called Brianhurst. Do you know it?"

"No, I'm sorry."

"Before she was dismissed, she was a resident there."

"She was dismissed because of the matters you have related?"

"Yes Ma'am. Her students, little girls aged eight to eleven, were devastated. All of them much loved and adored her. They do not understand any of this, and of course, no one has told them anything. I'm telling you this because I know that she could never afford any of the experienced solicitors you say she needs. What little money she had, she saved for months to take a trip to Carcassonne with the man I know she loved."

"This is the man she is accused of killing?"

"Yes, tragically, yes."

"Has Muriel talked to Legal Aid?"

"No, but I will tell you I do not believe that they could do anything for her at this stage—if they would even give her the time of day. The police have not yet charged her, but this matter should never get to the point where she is put in the dock. I know she is completely innocent of this hideous crime."

"You weren't there, Samantha."

"Please understand, Miss Alexander. Muriel's only chance of ever returning to a normal life after the death of the only man she ever loved and hoped to marry…after being fired from the only decent job she has ever had…after enduring the disgrace…for you can be assured that the reasons for her abrupt dismissal are already the subject of gossip in the community and will doubtless soon come to the attention of the tabloids, if not the more respectable papers and media."

At this point Samantha broke down in tears. Judy held her hand and squeezed it.

It was several moments before Samantha recovered enough to complete her sentence. "The only chance Muriel has for returning to a normal life is if this crime is solved well before she is ever arrested, charged, or deported. You can see that, can't you, Miss Alexander?"

Judy was about to say that it sounds like what Muriel needs is a good private investigator. Before she gave such advice, however, she fell silent as she realized that such advice would be worthless given Muriel's destitute circumstances. Judy also realized that she was in a unique position to help this woman because of Timothy's legacy. Judy now had access to the best investigative services money could buy, and had used them to great advantage several years before when she helped Amber solve the murder of her client's mother.

In the face of Judy's silence, Samantha pulled herself together, picked up her purse and began to rise from the table. "I'm sorry, Miss Alexander. I shouldn't have bothered you. It was wrong to take up your time. Thanks for listening."

Judy took her by the hand. "Samantha, I can't promise you anything, but it might be possible for me to help your friend."

Samantha dried her eyes with a tissue. "Really, you think you could?"

Judy was beginning to see that this might be the kind of case she had been waiting for since becoming a barrister— that is, a case in which she might not only be able to make a difference, but also prevent a great injustice. She wondered if it was the kind of case that Robin would have encouraged her to undertake when he supervised her in the Holmes School of Law Exoneration Clinic. If it was, she owed it to his memory to take the case.

"Before I can commit to anything, Samantha, I need much more information than you have thus far given me."

"I'll tell you everything I know."

"You said that Samantha is staying with you at your home in Newbury?"

"Yes."

"What is her state of mind at this point?"

"She is deeply depressed about Arthur—that is the name of the person she is suspected of killing. She is paralyzed with anxiety and fear and refuses to come out of her room or even leave her bed. She has not eaten or slept for days."

"Fear, you said?"

"Yes."

"Fear of what? Do you know?"

"She won't say."

Judy extracted a notebook from her briefcase and began taking notes.

"I need to know all the evidence that police have against her."

"I only know what Muriel told me about her trip with Arthur and what questions the police asked her after she returned to Brianhurst."

"Tell me everything."

For the next half hour, Samantha related as much detail as she could remember what Muriel had told her in the car the previous Thursday when Samantha drove her from Reading Station to Brianhurst School.

Judy carefully jotted down the dates and times of Muriel's itinerary, including the first night Muriel and Arthur had spent together at the Savoy on Friday; their night in Paris on Saturday; the three subsequent nights they spent together at the Hotel Ville Fortifiee in Carcassonne; and Muriel's early morning 4 AM departure on Wednesday morning while Arthur remained in the room.

"And what did the police tell Muriel when they later interviewed her at Brianhurst?"

"They told her Arthur was found stabbed to death in their hotel room several hours after Muriel left. They also told her that no one else had entered or left the hotel during the night, except when the night clerk had let Muriel out the front doors to get her cab—after which he locked the doors."

"She must have been devastated."

"Of course she was, and still is."

"Did the police tell Muriel anything about the murder weapon?"

"No, not that Muriel could remember. Of course, about the only thing she really remembered them telling her was the terrible news that Arthur was dead—brutally stabbed, though they gave her no details."

"And what does Muriel remember telling the police?"

"Just the details of their trip from Newbury to Carcassonne."

"So she admitted that she left Arthur at 4 AM?"

"Well, yes, but of course the night clerk must have confirmed it."

"Did the police ask her anything relating to a possible motive on her part?"

"Like what?"

"Whether they had a fight, whether she had left on good terms?"

"She didn't say. Apparently, they did ask her if she had talked to him Wednesday morning before she left at 4 AM. I think she answered that he had awakened while she was doing her final packing, and that she had kissed him goodbye."

"All right, that's enough for now. Before I can make any commitment to help Muriel, I need to talk to her. Is there a chance she could come to London and meet with me?"

Samantha shook her head. "I don't think so. She's not in any state to do much of anything. Is there a chance you could come to my house and talk to her?"

"I could do that, but...I should have asked you this before. Does she even know that you are talking to me on her behalf?"

Samantha hesitated.

"Samantha, please don't tell me you came down to meet with me without Muriel's permission to speak to me on her behalf?"

"I...I..."

Judy just looked at Samantha.

"You have to understand, Ma'am. She's in no condition to talk to anyone. She won't even come out of her room right now."

Judy shook her head. "I'm not going up there to talk to her until you can assure me that she consents and is willing to talk to me. Do you understand?"

"Yes Ma'am."

"I'm not doing anything more until you call me and tell me that she agrees to see me." Judy was already beginning to regret agreeing to consider getting involved with this entire matter.

"I'll talk to her and call you."

Judy took out a card with her home telephone number and handed it to Samantha. "After I talk to her—that is if she agrees to talk to me—I will do everything I can to obtain a copy of the police report, which I assume is the French Police report. They must have sent it to the Thames Valley Police."

"I don't know."

"I hope there's nothing else you've forgotten to tell me."

"No Ma'am, not that I can think of."

"How did the school administration get wind that Muriel was under investigation for a serious crime? I assume that that was what led to her dismissal."

"Muriel told me that she was having breakfast with the girls in the refectory when the Matron came and told her that the Headmistress wanted to see her. When Muriel went up to her office, two policeman were already there requesting to see her."

"Was the Headmistress present when the police questioned Muriel?"

"No, Muriel said the Headmistress left before the police questioned her."

"Then how did…"

"After the detectives left, the Headmistress came in and demanded that Muriel tell her what the police wanted. She was in a state of shock, but told her, confessing that she was being questioned and cautioned about the murder of the man whom she had spent five days with in France. Muriel said she was just so sorry, and knew she had to resign to protect the reputation of the school. The Headmistress gave her an hour to collect her things. And that was that."

"The Headmistress never asked whether she was in any way involved with what the police were suspicious about?"

"I don't know. You will have to ask her. I doubt if it would have made any difference. Just being suspected would have been enough for the Headmistress to dismiss Muriel."

"I'm sure you're right."

"So what do you think?"

"I don't think anything yet, Samantha. From what you've told me it doesn't look good for Muriel. If the hotel was locked during the night, with no one entering or leaving during the night except Muriel herself…"

"It could have been anyone else already staying at the hotel."

"Sounds unlikely, but possible of course. In due course, we will have to get the names of everyone in the hotel on that night, and get our hands on both the police report and the autopsy report. Until then, I reserve judgment. If it becomes clear that Muriel is in fact involved in this dreadful murder, you understand that I will decline to either defend or act in her behalf. If I come to believe she is innocent, I will do everything in my power to make sure that she is not unjustly convicted."

"That's all either Muriel or I can ask."

"Why are you so sure she is innocent, Samantha?"

"I have known Muriel since we were in secondary. I know her, Miss Alexander. To my knowledge, she has never so much as gotten a traffic ticket. I would stake my life that she could not have committed this crime. She has suffered the cruelty of an abusive husband and is the kindest person I have ever known."

"One final question, Samantha, and I then I must let you go until you call to tell me that Muriel is willing to see me. You said the name of the victim was Arthur. Do you know his surname?"

"Edgeware, Ma'am."

"Hmmm, that name sounds familiar. Do you know anything else about him?"

"He's a primary teacher also teaches Latin and Greek at a boys' school outside St. Johns. In Surrey, I believe."

"All right. If I take this case I will have to learn everything about him."

"Thank you, Miss Alexander. I will call you tomorrow and let you know what Muriel says."

CHAPTER TWELVE

"*E*ddie, please go away!"

Muriel buried her head in her pillow.

Eddie Sterling continued to tap on her door, which was locked. "Just wanted to make sure you're okay, love."

"I'm fine, Eddie. You know Samantha will be back in a few minutes with groceries. Just please leave me alone!"

Eddie heard the front door open downstairs, and backed away from the guest room.

"Eddie!" came the shout from his wife. "Where are you? Please come and help me with the groceries!"

"Ah, you're home, dear," said Eddie as he bounded down the stairs. "I was just checking on Muriel."

Samantha placed a bag of groceries on the hall table. "I'll go up and talk to her. Now, please go out and bring in the food."

"Yes, dear," Eddie said obligingly.

Muriel went upstairs to the guest room and knocked. "Sweetie, everything all right? May I come in?"

Muriel immediately rose from bed to unlock and open the door. "Coming!"

"Muriel," said Samantha as she took Muriel's hand, "you know you don't need to lock your door. One of us will always be here while you stay with us."

Bleary-eyed Muriel nodded. "I know. I'm sorry. I'm just so…"

"I know, honey." Samantha took her hand. "I know all this has all been so terrible for you. I can't even imagine how you must be feeling. Come, let us sit down and talk. The lawyer

I called earlier, Judy Alexander, will be here at ten. Are you up for it?"

Muriel nodded. "I guess so. I'm just not sure I can..."

"It will be all right. I really think she can help you."

"You told her I have no money."

"Yes, I told her, and she is fine with that."

"I can't afford to go into debt now either. I have lost my..."

Samantha hugged her. "I know honey...the man you hoped to marry. Such a tragedy."

"It's not enough that I lost the man I loved...now they want to say I killed him! Stabbed him with a knife! How could anyone think that? I loved him, Samantha!" Muriel began to weep.

Samantha kept her arms around Muriel until her sobs subsided.

"I have nothing, Samantha. No money, no job, and the police think I...I just don't know if I can go on..."

"Sweetie, I know you couldn't have done such a thing, and the police have no proof. All they have is that you left your hotel room in Carcassonne a few hours before they found Arthur. I'm sure the lawyer will tell you that is not proof."

"Try telling that to the Headmistress. It was bad enough when Norman began sniffing around the school, but now being suspected of...I can hardly say it...murder! I'm sure everyone in Sussex and Berkshire now knows I'm a murder suspect."

"I doubt it. Your Headmistress knows, because you had to tell her why the police wanted to talk to you...but she's the last person who would go around telling anyone that one of her teachers was a murder suspect—certainly not the other teachers, parents, or students. You haven't told anyone, have you—other than Eddie and me?"

"No, but the Headmistress let me go the moment I told her why the police wanted to talk to me. I had to tell her the truth."

"I know, but I'm sure she came up with some other reason to explain why you left the school...probably something like 'Miss Wright had a family emergency and needed to take a leave of absence'...something like that."

"What must all my little girls think—that I deserted them?"

Samantha shook her head. "I'm sure they will think nothing of the sort. As for your concern about money, you know you can stay here until this whole terrible affair is cleared up, and you can get back with your life."

"What life can that ever be...and I can't continue to stay with you."

"Why on earth not? You have your own room here...you certainly don't eat much...you've always eaten like a bird. Is there something you're not telling me?"

Muriel started to say something but then thought better of it. After a pause, she said "No, no, it's just that I can't...you know...impose."

"Well, you know very well you're not imposing at all. Besides, where would you go? Even a one room flat in Newbury would cost you a pretty penny...and you really shouldn't be alone now...you must know that."

Muriel sighed as she realized Muriel was right. Somehow, she would have to figure out a way to deal with Eddie without telling Muriel about Eddie's unwanted attentions toward her. It would crush her, not to mention jeopardize Muriel's own friendship with Samantha.

"The lawyer who's coming...why would she come without asking for a fee...is she from Legal Aid?"

"No. I checked with Legal Aid. They can't help you until you're actually charged with something. You wouldn't want them anyway. No, I've thoroughly checked out the lawyer who is coming to meet with you. She was originally an American lawyer who came here to be a barrister."

"A barrister? Why would I need a barrister? I haven't yet been charged with anything, let alone headed for a trial where I'd need a barrister."

"I've thoroughly googled up her background for you. She's represented victims of domestic violence and gained acquittals for them when they were charged with defending themselves."

"I never needed to defend myself from Arthur! He was the kindest, gentlest soul…"

"Of course not, not from Arthur…but you have been the victim of Norman's abuse and violence. As I told you, I went down to the Magistrate's Court in London to see this lawyer in a real case after reading about her in the paper. She's good!"

"Then why would she be willing to talk to me without asking for a fee—even before I've been charged with anything?"

"Why she'd be willing to help without a fee I can't really tell you, except that she must be in a position to do so, and she is by all accounts very passionate about wanting to help young women who are being abused…if not by jealous husbands or boyfriends, then by the judicial system itself. In any case, as I told you, I went to see her and she is willing to help you if you will accept it. I don't think we should look a gift horse in the mouth."

Samantha looked at her watch. "Look, she'll be here in about fifteen minutes. Can you make yourself presentable, come down, and talk to her? I thought we'd meet in the sunroom."

"Yes, thank you so much, Samantha."

"One reason I think it's so important to talk to her now is that you can't wait for the police to take their sweet time in accumulating evidence against you. Right now, it appears that you are the only…God forbid…the only suspect on their radar. If you don't find out before the police arrest you who really killed Arthur…and why…then just being arrested for such a crime…even if you are later acquitted…will beggar you the rest of your…"

"I know! I know. I'll come down."

Samantha patted her hand. "It certainly can't hurt. I'll call you when she arrives."

Samantha directed to the sunroom both Muriel, who had managed to brush her hair and even apply some make-up, and Judy, dressed in her black skirt and blouse. She introduced them to each other and offered them seats on the shaded side of the atrium. The two shook hands and sat.

Samantha clasped her hands together and said, "Miss Alexander, thank you so much for coming. Muriel is so pleased to talk to someone willing to help her. Can I offer you some tea?" Samantha asked.

Judy smiled. "That would be nice. Thank you."

"Cream and sugar?"

"No, just the tea for me."

"Of course. Muriel?"

"A little cream and two cubes?"

"Coming right up."

Samantha encountered Eddie on the way to the kitchen. "Eddie, I want to give Muriel and the lawyer some privacy. Would you mind?"

"Of course not, dear. I'll take Bruno out for a walk."

"Thank you dear."

Samantha returned to serve the tea. "Ladies, please let me know if you need anything. I'll be just down the hall."

"Thank you," Muriel said. "I think we'll be fine."

Samantha latched the door to the sunroom and retreated to her living room to read the paper and wait.

Muriel took a sip of her tea and spoke first. "Samantha has told me such good things about you, Miss…"

"Alexander. Judy Alexander. Please call me Judy. Your friend has also told me many good things about you as well. May I call you Muriel?"

"Of course."

"I can only imagine what you have been through these past two weeks. I am so sorry."

"Thank you."

"Four years ago, I too, under very tragic circumstances, lost the man I loved. For you to now be under suspicion for the death of the one you loved can only compound your grief."

"It is very much the case…Judy. Thank you for understanding."

Judy pulled out a notebook from her briefcase and turned to a page of notes. "Samantha has already given me a detailed outline of your itinerary to Carcassonne with your fiancé Arthur. You were planning to be married, I understand?"

"Umh, yes…we were…Although we hadn't set a date yet because I was teaching at a girls' school and under the terms of my teaching contract I had to be in residence."

"You didn't want to get married until you could live together, I take it."

Muriel did not answer immediately. "Arthur is a teacher as well—at a nearby school for boys—and was trying to arrange for a cottage in which we could both live…if not at St. Johns, then at some other school where he could continue to teach."

"I see. Now I'd like to go over the itinerary I worked out with Samantha, and make it as precise as possible in terms of exact times and dates."

"Of course. I think I can be exact…except perhaps during the days of Monday and Tuesday when we really flitted about from museum to museum."

"To the best of your recollection is all I can ask."

"Upstairs I have a lot of hotel, restaurant and museum receipts, and all our rail ticket stubs. I kept them because I was planning to make a scrapbook of our trip when I returned home. Would you like me to get them?"

"Please, Muriel. Those would be helpful."

For the next hour, the two went over the itinerary, and Judy made minor corrections to the itinerary that Samantha had previously given to her.

"May I keep the originals of these receipts? I will make copies of the originals and either return them by post or give them to you in person should you decide you would like to meet again. Is that satisfactory?"

"Yes, certainly."

Judy now turned to study the itinerary. After ten minutes she said, "Now, before I go, may I ask you a few questions?"

"Yes, anything."

Judy thought for several more minutes before framing her next question. "Tell me exactly when you got up that Wednesday morning."

"A quarter past three in the morning."

"You can be exact about the time?"

"Yes, because my iPhone alarm awoke me."

"Did the alarm also wake Arthur?"

Muriel thought for a moment. "I don't think so. Of course, I was not sleeping very soundly because I didn't want to oversleep, so I turned off the alarm right away when it buzzed in hopes that I wouldn't wake up Arthur."

"Samantha said you told her that Arthur did wake up before you left, though."

"Yes, I was about to leave when he woke up. I went over to kiss him goodbye."

"Did he kiss you?"

"Yes, he did, and said goodbye. He may have also said something like 'be safe,' and 'I'll see you back in merry old England.'"

"Hmmm. How did he seem when he said that?"

"He was groggy, of course."

"How groggy was he?"

"Half asleep, I guess you could say. It was 3:45 in the morning after all, and he didn't need to get up. We had agreed on that the night before."

"…and then you left the hotel at…you said…4:00 AM?"

"Almost exactly. I had ordered a cab for that time. Also, the night clerk had to let me out at that time because the hotel locked the front door at 11 PM the night before."

Judy then asked Muriel to try to remember everything the police told her during their interview with her at Brianhurst.

Judy took notes.

"What do you think?" Muriel asked.

"Well, I can see why the police focused on you as a suspect. From what the Thames Valley Police told you...and I assume they must have gotten this information from the French Gendarme...the body was found about four hours after you left the hotel...but that still gives someone else...presumably someone who was already staying at the hotel, since the hotel doors were locked for the night...time to come into Arthur's room and kill him."

"With that much time between when I left the hotel and when the body was discovered, why are they only focusing on me?"

"What we don't know at this point is the time of death. To get that information, I will need to get a copy of the autopsy report. If it turns out that the time of death was very shortly after you left, that time window becomes very narrow, and that makes it less likely that someone else had time to commit this murder."

"Can you get that report?"

"Not through traditional channels. Neither police nor prosecutors are much inclined to divulge what evidence they have prior to making the decision to bring charges—least of all to their prime suspect."

"So how can you get it?"

"Leave that to me." *And don't ask. Suffice it to say, it will take a generous expenditure of investigative resources, and even I don't want to know how it's done. I only commission it.*

Judy quickly changed the subject. "Now tell me everything about Arthur."

"He's a wonderful man, Judy. I met him..."

"I mean tell me all you know about who he is, his family and background."

"Oh. Well, his father is Lord Chester Edgeware. I know that. He has a brother, named after his father."

"Is the elder Chester Edgeware still alive?"

"I don't know. Arthur didn't talk about him much. I think he was in a home for the elderly."

"So he would be about…how old would you say?"

Muriel shrugged. "I don't really know. I don't even know if he's alive."

"Muriel, I did some preliminary research about Lord Edgeware based on what Samantha knew about him. She thought he might be the founder of Edgeware Industries."

"I think Arthur did mention something like that."

"If Lord Edgeware is still alive, he would be one of the wealthiest men in England. Did you know that?"

Judy looked closely at Samantha's expression. If Judy were to pursue this matter, she had to be sure Muriel was innocent. Judy knew from her experience in the previous cases she had undertaken that money was at the root of many if not most murders."

Muriel did not answer immediately, and seemed uncomfortable with the question. "Arthur did mention that his father was very wealthy. I guess his father owned the lion's share of the stock in that company."

"Edgeware Industries…"

"Yes, but Arthur was not an heir to his father's estate."

"He was disinherited?"

"No, not exactly. Arthur did mention to me that his father's will left all the shares of Edgeware Industries to his eldest son. Chester was the eldest. He and Arthur were fraternal twins, but Chester was born first."

"How did Arthur feel about that?"

"I honestly don't think he cared. He always said he was happy as a Latin and Greek master. He had no head for business, and wasn't interested in it. Why? Do you think that's important?"

"I don't know yet."

"So you will help me find out who killed Arthur? You know I can't pay you."

"I will not ask for a fee. But Muriel, I am a barrister, not an investigator, though I have access to some very fine investigators. Before I commit to anything, I have to ask you a very critical question."

"Anything."

Judy looked Muriel right in the eye and held her gaze. "Muriel, did you kill Arthur Edgeware?"

Muriel answered instantly and firmly. "No Ma'am I did not."

"All right. I believe you, and will start investigating what really happened to Arthur…with one very important proviso."

"Yes Ma'am, anything."

"You must be absolutely truthful about everything you tell me. And I mean everything. If I discover in the course of my investigations that you have not been honest with me—about anything and for whatever reason—I will withdraw from any further efforts on your behalf. Is that understood?"

"Yes, Ma'am."

"I'll tell you what I'm going to do. First of all, I am going to have you contact a solicitor."

"But if you're…"

"I have a good solicitor in mind whom we can trust. Solicitors can prepare documents and paperwork that barristers cannot. They also have avenues of inquiry not available—at least not directly—by barristers. Will you agree to go to London and meet with the solicitor I have in mind?"

"Yes, Ma'am."

Judy did not ask Muriel to revert to calling her by her first name. By committing herself to at least initiating a preliminary investigation on Muriel's behalf, it was best that Muriel continue to call her Ma'am.

Judy stood, packed her notebook, along with Muriel's receipts and stubs into her briefcase, and held out her hand.

"I'll be in touch, Muriel. In the meantime try to rest and divert your mind from these terrible events, as I will need your complete help and cooperation."

CHAPTER THIRTEEN

*J*udy was awakened not by her iPhone alarm, but by an incoming call. It was 6 AM, and she could not imagine who would be calling so early.

"Hello," said Judy groggily.

"Hi, sister. It's me."

"Amber?"

"Oh, I'm sorry. I completely lost track of time. I hope I didn't wake you up."

"I was just about to get up. You know you can call me anytime."

"You're sweet. It must be about midnight here in Houston but I just had to tell you some happy news."

"Oh my. Tell me!"

"Well. Harvey took me out to dinner tonight at *Brennan's.*"

"Nice. I remember you taking me there once...and...?"

Amber took a deep breath. "You won't believe it. Harvey proposed and gave me a beautiful engagement ring!"

Judy did not reply immediately, but finally said, "Oh..."

"Somehow I sense you're not overjoyed."

"No, I am pleased, Amber...of course. I'm just...you know...surprised...but truly I am most happy for you if that's what you want."

"Harvey and I had talked of possibly getting married after the election. He has enough going on now...but I guess he just decided to go ahead now full steam ahead and get engaged."

"Amber, you know I'm delighted. It's just that we haven't talked about how we would…if either of us got married…how it would affect our joint ownership of all the assets Timothy left us."

"Oh sweetie, there won't be any change at all. We will continue to go fifty-fifty on any expenditure either of us makes. I bought my house here in Houston, and you bought your condo there in London. We've already made all the charitable contributions Timothy suggested, all the taxes are paid, and all his staff have been fully provided for."

"I know…but it's just that up until now it's been only you and me making the financial decisions."

"That won't change. Of course, I will be making a pre-nup to insure that all our assets remain in our joint names alone. Harvey will have no say with regard to any expenditures you and I make together from those assets."

"And Harvey is fine with that?"

"Yes, he says he understands."

"You've told him the…how much we jointly own…I mean two and a half billion is…"

"Well…"

"You have told him, right?"

"Not the full extent of it…not yet…but I did tell him that my inheritance was substantial…that I owned in joint ownership with you…that my lawyers insisted…"

"Amber, there's substantial and there's substantial. You know you've got to tell him."

"I know, I know…no pre-nup would hold up if he's not advised of the full extent of our assets before he signs it."

"More than that. The full amount of our joint assets and your fifty-fifty joint interest in it will have to be spelled out in any pre-nup."

"I know."

"The sooner you tell him, the better."

"I will. We still haven't set a date yet."

"So you might not get married until after the election in November?"

"We didn't actually discuss that."

"It would be a long engagement if you wait that long."

"I know. Of course, I could use that time to...you know..."

"Be sure? You'd better be sure now, babe!"

"I am...I am...and I have checked with my lawyer. Texas is a community property state, but...as I understand it...if the unthinkable happens, he would only be entitled to the increase in value that occurs after the marriage, not any of the principle as of the date of marriage."

"I hope that's the case. As you know, after we liquidated Timothy's shares in Hoxsey, we had our financial advisor put half of all our liquid assets into a ladder of U.S. Treasuries, paying very little interest, and the other half in the S and P 500. The stocks have appreciated nicely since Timothy passed away, and the dividends from the stocks and rents on our estates in Catalina, France, and Switzerland have increased our net assets by a fair margin."

"I know. As a percentage of our assets we've actually spent very little—just my house, your condo, and of course all those subsidies you pay to your New York Law firm, not to mention..."

"My expenses getting my barrister's certificate. I know, and don't forget we're still maintaining and flying the G-500."

"Remember that Timothy insisted that we keep and use the plane...there's no question of not honoring his wishes. I've flown on it several times, but you've only used it...what...once or twice?"

"I used it to visit you last year."

"How could I forget. That was nice."

"I expect you to use it soon to come visit me here in London."

"As soon as I can get away. Promise. So, you're really okay about me and Harvey…assuming my lawyers can come up with a rock solid pre-nup…"

"Absolutely…"

"You know, Judy, both of us have the big number forty staring us in the face…"

"It's not something I worry about…though one of the pupils in chambers was cheeky enough to ask me how old I was…after asking me on a date…which of course I politely declined."

"You have a pupil?"

"Oh, no. I'm just a junior barrister, with less than two years' experience…the lowest of the low. Thank God I don't have to worry about how much I make, but if I did I'd soon realize I could make more working a double shift at a grocery store. I won't be getting my own pupil until I have at least four or five years of experience. This was Mortenson's pupil…just signed up a couple of weeks ago."

"So what did you tell him?"

"I told him I was twenty-eight."

"Not that you couldn't pass for that, but what did he say when you told him?"

"The cheeky little lad then asked me how long I'd been twenty-eight."

"And you said…"

"Maybe a year or two…"

Amber laughed. "I'm sure you broke his heart. I guess he didn't know that you were already taken by Braxton…okay, Judy, with your looks you don't have to worry about any of that. You've been married, had a child…but my biological clock has been ticking a lot louder lately. I don't want to end up as a rich old woman living in my mansion, childless, wandering its lonely halls all by myself…"

"I understand…of course I do…and I apologize if I seemed ambivalent about your wonderful news. You know I'm happy for you."

Amber sighed. "Who knows, maybe it won't even work out. Harvey and I have had our problems in the past. By the way, how is your son now?"

"He's doing great. He's almost eighteen now. As you know…after my divorce, I agreed to let him stay in China with his dad. It would have been a nightmare to gain custody of him when he was in China after that attempted kidnapping…but we email each other every day and talk several times a week. He landed an internship at one of those big tech companies in Beijing. He'll be coming to visit me this summer. I told him I would send the G-500 for him, and he was excited about that. Of course I've been paying for his educational expenses all along, and I also bought him a Tesla for his birthday."

"Maybe I'll come visit you about the same time and we can take a holiday together."

"That would be great."

"Enough about me. Sorry. How are things in your… chambers…have to get used to saying that. Any interesting new cases?"

"Not in my capacity as a barrister…at least not yet. However, I may be taking on a matter which may ultimately require my services as a barrister."

"Tell me."

"Archie called me…"

"The chambers clerk?"

"Yes. He called me and said a woman had called and wanted to contact me directly without going through a solicitor. Archie doesn't like that, and tried to persuade her to contact a solicitor first, but she would have none of it and insisted on seeing me. When I ended up meeting her, it turned out that she was meeting me on behalf of a friend who was suspected of killing her boyfriend in the town of Carcassonne, France."

"Oh my! Has the friend been arrested?"

"No, but based on my conversation with her, I don't see how the police can arrest her for a crime that occurred in France…although she could be deported. The girls' school where she was employed fired her. The main evidence against her is that just a few hours…or less…after she left him in her hotel room, he showed up dead from a stabbing attack."

"That doesn't sound like enough evidence to arrest her."

"It isn't. The police will need more, but it was enough for her employer to fire her."

"What can you do?"

"Not much in my capacity as a barrister…at least not now…but it would be a career and personal disaster for her if it became public that she was a murder suspect, not to mention if she were actually arrested, deported, or convicted of such a crime. I think the only way I can help her now is with my access to investigative resources."

"You mean the NXR Agency. And Jake in particular."

"I've just made arrangements…which I was planning to do anyway…to have Jake leave NXR and set up an investigative agency here in London where he can be closer to the sources of information I will need. He's also bringing two of his best investigators with him. He'll hire the necessary computer analyists and technicians here once he arrives."

"Your own private investigative service."

"Completely independent of me, though I will be staking it. He can also take other cases unrelated to mine, but I will always have first priority."

"Jake's willing to do that?"

"I'm paying him enough to make it worth his while."

"What does NXR say? I would think they'd not be too pleased."

"Jake will still need access to NXR's resources, so I've reached an accommodation with NXR as well."

"I guess that's what your share of Timothy's legacy is for."

"It's what I want to use it for."

"Hmmmm…okay…that's fine. As always, I'm in fifty-fifty. I know Jake really helped you find the murder of my client's mother several years ago."

"He's good…really good. I don't know how he gets the information I always need, but he does…and I don't ask him how he does it."

"I won't comment on that, but if it's in the interests of justice…"

"It always is, and he's the best there is."

"Well, Judy, if this is really what you want to be doing, you know I'm always in."

"It is what I want to be doing. Robin introduced me to this world, and I want to continue in that world. I've started to make a difference as a barrister…but in cases like this one, I know that there is no substitute for gaining access to information and sources. Information is what lets me make a difference, both as a barrister, and as in this case, before a case ever gets that far."

"I know…this woman, are you sure she's innocent?"

"It's difficult for me to believe that a young woman French teacher, much beloved by the little girls in her French class at a prestigious girls' school would suddenly turn into a vicious murderer."

"I agree. It does sound very unlikely."

"In the right circumstances…with the right motive…the most unlikely people can commit murder."

"So, when will you decide whether to take the case?"

"I can't really say until I get the police and autopsy reports. After that, I should be able to make my own judgment. I didn't make her any promises. She knows that if I can't believe in her innocence, then I can't help her. I intend to use Timothy's money to pursue justice…nothing more…nothing less. The police appear to be focused solely on this woman right now. Once I'm convinced of her innocence, I intend to focus on who else might have had a motive to kill her boyfriend. I'll also be looking for who might have had a motive to fit up the woman herself."

"Fit up?"

"British slang for frame. From what I know so far, any case against the woman is just too convenient…too perfectly timed."

"Wow, that would be something. For what reason?"

"I have no idea…yet."

"When do you expect to get access to the police and autopsy reports?"

"Not any time soon…or in any case, too late to help the woman once word gets out that she is a suspect."

"So what will you do?"

"Jake is already on it. Hopefully he'll have everything I need before he even arrives."

"Judy…"

"Amber, I better get going. Archie just left me a text that Peter Mayfield has a case for me and is waiting for me to get to chambers. Anyway, congratulations on your engagement. Talk soon."

"Bye, sister. Keep me posted."

CHAPTER FOURTEEN

*M*adeleine Edgeware had been looking forward to a weekend, or even an entire week, to be free to do as she pleased while Chester was away in France awaiting the release of his brother's body by the French Gendarme in Carcassonne. Her visions of uninterrupted shopping expeditions to Harrods and Selfridge's were dashed when Chester called to say he would be coming home later that day.

Chester had been prepared to stay in Carcassonne until his brother's body was released, but soon realized that he couldn't wait that long. The French Police were talking about doing further tests on the body and couldn't or wouldn't provide him with an estimate as to when they would release it.

Chester called Madeleine from his mobile while riding in the limousine from London Heathrow. "Hi babe, I should be in St. John's within the hour. However, Holliston just called me and wants me to drop by Parkington to pick up Dad's effects, so I'll go there before I come home."

"So glad you're coming, sweetie! I've missed you. It's lonely here in this big house without you. What effects do you have to pick up?"

"Holliston seems to think Dad might have kept some papers…documents in his room, which we should retrieve. He always kept a locked file cabinet in his room, and refused to give us the key when we visited—if he even had the key. Even though he had Alzheimer's, he was secretive and even fanatical about not letting anyone gain access to this file cabinet. I'm sure there's nothing of importance in it, but Holliston thought I should go and check it out. The staff told Holliston that they put the file cabinet in their storage facility and can't find any key to it. I doubt if Dad ever had a key for it. All I know is that when Holliston had him placed in Parkington, the cabinet was the one thing Dad insisted on bringing with him. Anyway, the staff want someone to come over and pick up the cabinet. I don't want to mess with bringing home the whole cabinet, so I'll probably ask the staff to break it open. If there really are documents in it, I'll just put them in boxes and bring them home."

"Yes, dear," said Madeleine, who was sorry she had asked about the effects and was not interested in hearing details about some cabinet. "I know this has been such a terrible week for you. First your dad passes away, and then…what, just a couple of days later your brother is killed. Horrible. Horrible! I'm so sorry."

"Thank you, dearest. Yes, it has been a terrible week, losing my father and then my brother…a double whammy you could say…but the damn police over there wouldn't say when they'd release Arthur's body, and I couldn't wait indefinitely."

"I understand, baby. So sorry. When will you be home?"

"I don't know. Depends how long it takes to get into that file cabinet after I get to Parkington."

"So you could be late?"

"Possibly…so don't wait up. I'll call when I know."

"Do what you need to do. I'll be here."

"I won't be too long, I promise."

Chester now dialed James Holliston at his law office. It was now after five in the evening, so he was not surprised that he received a recording. He began to leave a message:

"James, I just left Carcassonne, and am on my way to Parkington to look at that cabinet you wanted me to check out. I'll let you know if there's anything in there worthwhile. Please call me as soon as you get this message, as I'd like to go over your final plans for the funeral. If I had been able to bring Arthur's body back, I suppose we could have had one funeral for the both of them. Since that is not going to happen now, I was thinking we could have Dad's funeral at the Parkington Chapel, and then have the hearse take him from there to Brookwood for the burial in the family plot. We can arrange Arthur's funeral later."

Chester's recording was cut short when Holliston called.

"Sorry I couldn't answer your call. Glad to hear you're back. So you're going to check out the file cabinet?"

"Yep, I'll let you know if there's anything in there."

"Probably nothing, but you never know. You know, we need to talk about the probate of your dad's will."

"You don't foresee any problem, do you?"

"No, not really, but the chronology of your dad and brother's death is unfortunate."

"How so? What do you mean?"

"Well, if your brother had died first, the probate of your dad's estate would go much more smoothly. Since Arthur would have predeceased you, there would be no question that you would inherit the estate."

"Why should that make any difference? There should be no question now either, since I'm the first born, and Dad's will leaves everything to the first born."

"No problem, I didn't mean that. I have Dr. McAllister's medical report of the two births and his letter in which he clearly states that you were born fifty-seven seconds before Arthur. It's just that we will now have to present and authenticate both the medical record and McAllister's letter at the probate hearing and that will take extra time and cause delays."

"I still don't see why, now that Arthur has passed away."

"Arthur was still alive when your dad passed away. Before the Probate Court can designate you as the sole heir, it would have to be satisfied that the estate did not pass to Arthur."

"But Arthur is dead now!"

"But if it turned out that Arthur was the first born, on your dad's death his estate would have passed to Arthur before Arthur died. That would mean that your dad's estate would now be in Arthur's estate."

"You've got to be fucking kidding me!"

"Chester, calm down! We have the documentary evidence in the form of the medical records and McAllister's letter that you were the first-born. Once we present those documents to the Probate Court, there's no question that your dad's estate will go entirely to you...but even under a worst possible scenario, if these documents didn't hold up for any reason, and the court found that Arthur was first born...for which there is no evidence whatsoever...it's probable that by intestate succession you would inherit anyway from your brother's estate since you are next of kin to your brother. Do you know if your brother ever wrote a will?"

"Jesus. Of course not! Why would he? He's not the first born and his only asset is some silly old Morris Minor car."

"So relax, Chester. You were first-born and we have the documents to prove it."

Parkington Abbey was hardly a typical nursing home. It was in fact a Palladian mansion on a forty-acre estate, with Corinthian columns and a grand marble staircase. It was founded by the widow of the shipping magnate Cornelius Hightower who made it her life's work to create a comfortable home for the elderly. She spared no expense in making it not only the most comfortable but also the most luxurious nursing home in Sussex, if not the entire country. Within four years of its founding, it was full, with wait lists of up to seven years.

Like the best country clubs, an up-front payment of half a million pounds was required to procure a reservation, and only half of the initiation fee was refunded if the pensioner died before an opening occurred. Annual fees exceeded two hundred thousand pounds, and access to certain amenities could cost another fifty thousand or more per annum.

As the manager of the Abbey, Sir Henry Lichfield-Fletcher was fond of pontificating to recalcitrant heirs who might balk at the cost of providing such splendor for an aging mother or father, "You can't take it with you. Much better to go out with a bang than a buck, wouldn't you agree? They gave you the best in life, and it is only right that you should return the favor." Thus shamed, many did exactly that even if their parents were suffering from Alzheimer's and had no idea where they were or how to partake meaningfully of the amenities.

Residents enjoyed spacious rooms or suites, all with high ceilings, ornate plasterwork and magnificent views of the rolling hills and a lake filled with ducks that also had free rein of the surrounding grounds. All rooms and apartments came with ensuite bathrooms lined with marble.

Special care was provided for those afflicted with Alzheimer's, and an on-site hospital with round the clock medical staff was attached to the main mansion. A private theater showed the latest films, and troupes gave live performances of popular plays and musicals. Residents had their choice of taking their meals in their suites or in the grand teakwood-lined refectory where socialization was encouraged.

On Sunday, residents enjoyed fishing rights in a nearby stretch of the river Avon. A lavish game room filled every night with residents playing bridge, whist, and even poker, though bets were limited to no more than fifty pence. Poker losses, even among the unskilled, rarely exceeded five pounds on any given night. Nevertheless, some residents seemed to enjoy racking up losses of as much as fifty pounds a month—all of which were made good by the Parkington Abbey slush fund, which came from the annual fees and were never actually billed to the losers. Winners enjoyed having their winnings reflected in their private account books.

Residents were encouraged to bring their pets, which were housed in a separate pet residence, and ample time was set aside for daily interaction with their owners, though not in the mansion proper.

Had it been his decision, Chester would not have been inclined to provide his father with such splendiferous luxury. Lord Edgeware had Alzheimer's after all, and to Chester's way of thinking was not capable of getting his money's worth. It was the court-appointed conservator, James Holliston, who made the decision to place Lord Edgeware in Parkington Abbey, and Chester was not willing to appear churlish by suggesting that his father be placed in more modest accommodations. Had he done so, Holliston would doubtless have pointed out that as sole heir to his father's two and a quarter billion dollar fortune, he could hardly deny his father the best care and comfortable surroundings.

The receptionist, Marianne McAllister, was sitting at her large glass desk when Chester entered the Great Hall. She knew him well, and stood to greet him with a sympathetic hug.

"We are all devastated, Mr. Edgeware. He was such a fine man...never gave us any trouble at all despite his condition... never a harsh word to any of us." She continued in a low hushed voice, "not like many of our other Alzheimer's residents who can drive us quite batty, if you know what I mean."

"Yes, Marianne. My wife and I are much distraught as you can imagine. Actually, I'm here to retrieve the file cabinet which my dad kept in his room. I understand you took it to your storage facility here?"

"Yes, Mr. Edgeware. It was the only item of furniture which your father owned. Everything else in his room was the property of Parkington. Please follow me and I will take you to our storage facility."

CHAPTER FIFTEEN

"**J**ake? You there?"

"Yes, I'm here, Judy. Just arrived in London on Tuesday…staying at the Westchester. I received your wire with the money and entered into a five-year lease on the entire fifth floor of the Enterprise building here in Knightsbridge. Most of our equipment and computers should be arriving by the end of the week. Until then, I still have access to all of NXR's infrastructure, computers, and data bases…for which you will need to pay them directly."

"I'll let you take care of all that for me. Bill me for whatever you need, but I'll leave all those details to you. In the meantime, I really need to see the French Police and autopsy reports on the death of Arthur Edgeware."

"I've got them."

"Really? How on earth did you…?"

"Once I knew there was a transmission from the Carcassonne Constabulary to the Thames Valley Police, it was…"

"Stop. I didn't mean to ask."

"Understood…but it would be best if I didn't risk sending them, either by email or otherwise."

"Keep them in your secure files, but right now just give me any high points."

"Hmmmm. The cause of death was the knife wounds inflicted on Arthur Edgeware, one of which pierced his heart and would have killed him instantly."

"We already knew that. Time of death? Location?"

"*Hotel Ville Fortifiée*, room 213, Carcassonne."

"Time of death?"

"Wednesday, March 29 between three and five in the morning."

"Oh, dear…"

"Is that bad?"

"It's not good. Muriel left the hotel at 4 AM, so that only leaves a one hour window in which someone else could have killed him."

"Ouch…I see what you mean…but it is what it is."

"Anything else?"

"Looking…here on page twelve…the victim was found with four to five times the standard dose of the sleeping medication in his body—Ambien."

"Ambien…huh…do you happen to know if that requires a doctor's prescription in the UK?"

"I assume so. I've used it myself back in the states, and I needed a prescription, so I assume it requires one here."

"Check that."

"Anything else that stands out on the autopsy report."

"It says a cough bottle of Robitussin was found on the victim's bedside table. Chemical analysis revealed that Ambien was found dissolved in the cough syrup."

"Does it say how much?"

"Nope, but I'll watch for a follow up."

"No, you've done enough along those lines, and I don't want you to push your luck and maybe get both of us in trouble… no, I'm going to approach the police up front and see if I can convince them to give me any additional information."

"Good luck with that…oh; it says here that they sent the bottle out for testing for both fingerprints and DNA."

"I would like to get the results of those tests as soon as possible, but I'll wait and see what I can get on my own through the Thames Valley Police. Whatever you did to get a copy of the police and autopsy report…don't do it again. I don't want to know."

"Do you really think it's wise to approach the police? I mean...what would be your basis for asking the police for that kind of information?"

"I'll just tell the truth—that I've been retained by their suspect, Muriel Wright, and acting in her behalf, that Muriel is willing to cooperate in any way she can to help them find Arthur's real killer, and that she's retained me to help them find the real killer."

"Do you think they'll buy it?"

"I have no idea, Jake, but it happens to be the truth. If I can convince them that Muriel is just as eager to find Arthur's killer as they are, who knows, either they'll help me or they won't. Hopefully I can convince them I can be of use to them. Perhaps they might let me work with them in the hope that I might let something slip...any evidence that I find...that might be of use to them."

"Based on the evidence you were able to elicit in the Mont St. Michel and Concorde cases, and you weren't even a licensed lawyer in that first one, perhaps you can persuade them to keep you informed but aren't you concerned that just by retaining you Muriel is signaling to them that she might be guilty? Otherwise why would she want a lawyer before she's even been charged?"

"Potential suspects do that all the time, and not just because they're guilty. It could be because they know they're innocent and just want to be sure they won't be railroaded or bullied. Anyway, we'll see, Jake. Muriel is already the prime suspect and if the police are smart, they'll welcome Muriel's cooperation even if it's through her attorney. It's worth a try."

"I remember what Amber told me how your godfather Timothy explained why he retained you to find his daughter's killer on Mont St. Michel rather than relying on experienced investigators. Didn't he cite Aristotle for the proposition that 'beauty is a better recommendation than any letter of introduction?'"

"I was still in my thirties then Jake, and you know that I could never have solved that case without your expertise and NXR's investigative services."

"You got the entrées and gave me what I needed to work with."

"Jake, stay focused, please. Now one more thing before I let you go. I want to find out more about Arthur's father. Samantha told me that Arthur's father was, or is, some kind of tycoon, but Samantha didn't know if he was still alive. Could you check?"

"Way ahead of you, Judy. I knew you'd be asking me to find out everything about the victim's family ties."

"And?"

"Besides owning a controlling interest in Edgeware Industries, he is also a Lord, but he has been suffering from Alzheimer's for some time and been living in a nursing home—a very sumptuous one, in Sussex, and just passed away…let's see I have it here…he passed away on March 27, at 10:43 in the morning at the Parkington Abbey."

"…and Arthur was murdered on…"

"As I said, March 29."

"Interesting. So Arthur's father died before Arthur died."

"Is that significant?"

"I don't know. Probably not, but I need to know everything if I'm going to be any good to Muriel in finding the real killer."

"Arthur also has a brother."

"Yes, Muriel told me Arthur had a brother, but she didn't know much about him."

"He's a partner in a London-based hedge fund, but doesn't appear to do much work there, though he seems to live quite handsomely on advancements from his father's conservator. Let's see, he lives in a manor outside St. Johns, he's in his forties, just last year married some socialite in her early twenties, that's all I've got so far."

"You're amazing, Jake."

"That's what you pay me the big bucks for, Judy."

"Money well spent. Okay, keep looking for anything that might help me."

"Will do…and can I ask you something?"

"Not only can you, but you *may* ask me."

"Now you're reminding me of my mother."

"Okay, Jake…what's your question?"

"Are you pretty convinced that this Muriel person is innocent?"

"To be honest I'm not yet absolutely sure. From what I know about her from her friend Samantha, and from talking to Muriel directly, I must confess that it's hard for me to wrap my head around Muriel going from being a sweet schoolteacher to a murderer that viciously stabs him—by all accounts a very loving and modest boyfriend—multiple times with a knife. As far as I can see, the only real evidence against her is totally circumstantial—that Muriel just happened to leave a hotel room…"

"Just minutes before the time he was killed."

"Don't exaggerate, Jake. You said the autopsy gave a time of death as late at 5 AM—so an hour."

"Pretty strong circumstantial…"

"I know, it looks bad, but the police still have no idea of a motive, and without more evidence they can't even make an arrest, much less get a conviction…and there's countervailing circumstantial evidence as well."

"Like?"

"Like the fact that she made no effort to hide the fact that she left at 4 AM. Surely, the killer, if it was Muriel, would know that if she left the hotel immediately after killing him she would be the prime suspect. She left her name and address in the hotel register, so there could be no question in her mind that the police would soon find her and focus on her as the prime suspect. If she was actually going to kill him in the hotel room, it would have made more since to stick around and claim that an intruder…"

"I'm not sure that the police would find that story any more credible than the one she later told the Thames Valley Police."

"I suppose…none of it makes any sense…which is why I'm wondering if Muriel isn't the prime victim in this case."

"What do you mean? Arthur was killed, not her."

"There's more than one way to victimize someone. Killing a person outright is one way, but even with what must have been Arthur's moments of horror and agony, it was still over quite quickly for him. Muriel on the other hand, if she's arrested, convicted, and imprisoned for murder, becomes a victim for life…and perhaps along the lines of the killer's actual motive, still very much out of the way no less than if she herself had been murdered."

"Seems like a bit of a stretch…and for what possible motive? Are you saying that poor Arthur might just have been collateral damage? What obstacle could Muriel's very existence pose to the killer? Who could possibly gain from Muriel being put away for life in a prison somewhere?"

"I don't know, Jake. I just know there's got to be a motive somewhere…and I'm determined to find out what it is. Once we find that motive…we find the killer. That's why I need your help."

"Look, Judy…please don't expect any miracles from me."

"Jake, you've already performed many miracles for me."
"You've paid me well."

"You've earned it. Now, I have a critical task I need you to perform for me."

"Name it."

Judy laid out her assignment in detail.

When Jake was momentarily silent, Judy visualized his mouth opening wide and a light bulb going off inside his head.

"Wow," he finally said. "I see where you're going. Talk about a motive!"

"Let me know the moment you find something."
"Will do!"

CHAPTER SIXTEEN

DS Leslie Graham, holding two files in her hand, tapped on DI Raymond Stone's office door at the Thames Valley Police Station.

"Come in, Sergeant."

"Busy, sir?" the Sergeant asked.

"Not too busy if you've got something," said Stone without looking up from the file he was reading.

"I think I have, sir, but first, can I ask if we've gotten any new updates from the French Police?"

Stone looked up. "As a matter of fact, I have. Sit down, Sergeant."

"Thank you, sir."

Stone handed Graham the file he had been reading. "Just got this a few hours ago. Take a look."

Graham started reading. "It says the Gendarmes sent a bottle of Robitussin that they found on Arthur's bedside table out for testing…they found Ambien dissolved in the syrup."

"Yep, that's how she administered it, Sergeant. Muriel knew that if she just started plunging the knife into her victim, he'd likely cry out, raise the alarm with his screams, and thrash about…probably knock over lamps or whatever before he finally succumbed to his wounds…but knocked out cold with the Ambien he was defenseless, which is why no defensive wounds were found on his hands or arms."

"It certainly sounds plausible, sir. I also recall that both you and I observed Muriel's hands and arms on the day we interviewed her. She was wearing a short sleeve blouse, so we didn't even have to ask her to show them to us. Not a scratch on her."

"Very unusual in stabbing cases, particularly ones that are this vicious, that the killer does not sustain at least some minor wounds on his hands and arms due to slippage of the knife as he repeatedly plunges it into the victim, hitting not just soft tissue but bones and ribs."

"You said 'he', sir. Not a Freudian slip is it?"

"Don't be cute, Sergeant. I was talking about the usual case in which the killer is male. Granted that in this case the killer is female, which is why the Ambien evidence is so critical. If the victim here had not been so thoroughly sedated he would doubtless have been able to mount a more vigorous defense that would have forced his attacker to sustain at least some minor cuts."

"Of course…"

"Of course, what, Sergeant?"

"Of course…a competent barrister would point out that the lack of cuts on the attacker could also be explained by the fact that the defendant was not the killer."

"Sergeant, I realize that," Stone retorted, a little annoyed that so far his Sergeant had offered little support that he was on the right track. "In any case, keep reading…page three of the update."

"Yes, sir. It says that the cough syrup in question has now been turned over to their crime lab in Paris to test for fingerprints and DNA."

"That's correct Sergeant…and how much would you wager that our sweet little Muriel's fingerprints aren't all over that bottle…and her DNA too."

"She and Arthur were travelling together, so I wouldn't be surprised."

"Would you be surprised that a bottle of Robitussin was spiked and dissolved with crushed tablets of Ambien?"

"No sir. Would you like me to check with Arthur's doctor to see if he had come in with complaints of sore throat or cough?"

"I suppose you could do that, but I wouldn't expect much. Most people don't go to the doctor for a mild sore throat or cough. I believe Robitussin can be sold without a prescription. If Arthur's sore throat or cough had been serious, he probably would have cancelled his trip with Muriel."

Graham sat silent, but with a slight hint of a very smug smile.

"Yes, Sergeant, now if that's all…"

"Sir, I'm still not convinced we're on the right track, since we still don't have any motive, but I do have some information for you that I think you will find…interesting."

"Why didn't you say so, instead of sitting there like a….don't play games with me, Sergeant. If you've got something, give it to me. I see you have two files with you. Were you planning to share them with me?"

Graham now broke out into a broad smile, for she was sure that her boss's tone would change dramatically once she showed him the information she had discovered. She took out the first of the two files that she had brought, and handed it to her boss.

"You asked me to cover the pharmacies in a fifty mile radius of Newbury."

"Yes…"

"Read, sir."

After several moments of reading, Stone slapped the back of the document in the file with the back of his hand. "Excellent work, Sergeant!"

"That's a copy of the prescription Muriel brought to the Newbury Pharmacy…signed by Doctor Charles Gates… Ambien…sir…two whole packages of it. Each package contained ten capsules of full strength Ambien."

DI Stone sat back in his chair and looked up at the ceiling. "I take back everything I said, Sergeant. Good work. I'm going to the Chief Inspector with this information right now. The law is clear that if any part of an element of a crime is performed in this country, the crime may be prosecuted here. In our courts!

The French Police report is clear that Ambien played a critical role in Arthur Edgeware's murder. If Muriel bought the Ambien here in the UK, that means there is concurrent jurisdiction with France to try her for the murder of Arthur Edgeware."

"Of course…"

"Now what, Sergeant?"

"We'd still have to prove that Muriel used the Ambien she bought in the UK to sedate Arthur in order to facilitate the murder."

"And if the forensic tests on the Robitussin come back positive for Muriel's fingerprints and DNA on the bottle, do you think that would be a problem?"

"Probably not, sir."

"You're damn right, Sergeant!"

"But shouldn't we wait until we get those fingerprint and DNA results before you see the CDI?"

Stone sighed with disappointment. "You're right, Sergeant. What would I do without you? We'd better wait."

"Sir, you might not have to wait to see the DCI. I have another file here."

"So you do. Let's have it."

Graham stood and held out the second file. Just as Stone was about to take it, she pulled it back. "You'll take back your implication that I wasn't giving you sufficient support?"

"I never implied that, Leslie." Stone held out his hand. "The file, please." He took it and read.

It took only a moment for Stone to explode.

"Holy Crap, Sergeant! This is what we've been missing! Talk about motive, we've got it now in spades! We've got her now, Sergeant! We've got her!"

CHAPTER SEVENTEEN

*T*he phone rang eight times before Muriel picked up.

"Hello, Muriel?"

"Hello," came the voice that sounded more like low moan.

"This is Judy Alexander. How are you?"

Muriel sighed and finally said, "Not very good Ma'am."

"Are you still staying in the guest bedroom there at Samantha's house?"

"Pretty much, yes Ma'am."

"Look, Muriel, I understand your loss and I understand how things look now, but if I'm to help you I will need you to work with me. I think it would be good if you could get out of the house for a while, get some air, think about something other than the terrible events."

"I can't help it Ma'am. The man I loved has been murdered, and I know I'm a murder suspect and I understand why. The evidence is all against me. I was the last person to see Arthur and he was murdered just after I…"

"Muriel, first of all, the evidence is not all against you. The police have nothing but circumstantial evidence against you at this point. The fact that you were the last person to see Arthur before his death is not proof, and by itself, would never convict you of anything. I would not categorize you as a murder suspect at all. At most you are a person of interest, and even that only because you were the last person to see Arthur. True, that is most unfortunate, but…"

"Then why do the French Police want me arrested?"

"I think they really just want to talk to you."

"Should I just go back there and talk to them, then."

"Oh no, I wouldn't do that. They know they do not have sufficient evidence to make a case against you—at least not at this point. I think they also know that, given what little evidence they actually have against you, there would be little or no chance of getting a British court to extradite you. That gives us time to find who really committed this murder."

"What can I do?"

"First, I will need you to be alert and active. You are still spending most of your time in Sam's guest room?"

"I've been going down for meals, that's all. I don't feel comfortable around Sam's husband."

"Eddie?"

"Yes, Ma'am"

Judy resisted pursuing that line for the time being. Later, she would ask what Muriel's reasons were for avoiding Eddie, but for now it did not seem that any reasons Muriel might give would have any bearing on the case at hand.

"I see. Well, I was hoping you might consider joining me for tea tomorrow. I do have a few questions I'd like to ask you, but don't want to do so on the mobile. Could you possibly take the train from Reading and meet me at Paddington Station at, say 11 AM tomorrow morning?"

"I don't know..."

"It will get you out of the house, for one thing, Muriel, which I think would be good for you. I have a favorite place I go to for lunch—the delicatessen at Harrods—and I can go over a few things I need to discuss with you. After that, we could just take a walk, talk about anything but the current matter that weighs so heavily upon you, maybe do a little shopping..."

"I have no money..."

"We don't have to buy anything. How long has it been since you've have been to Harrods?

"Oh, a very long time. My parents took me there once when I was about seven or eight."

"You haven't been there since? "

"No Ma'am. My ex would never let me go there. Too expensive he always said—he didn't want me to get any ideas. I did go to the Savoy for one night with Arthur...before... before..."

"We don't have to talk about that now. So what do you say? Will you join me?"

"I guess I could..."

"Brilliant! You should probably check with Samantha— let her know you're coming to see me here in London. Tell her I'll put you on the 4:15 to Reading and ask if she can pick you up at the station at 5:35."

"Okay, I'll ask her now. I'm sure she'll say it's all right."

"Would you like me to talk to her?"

"No, I'll ask her now."

"Call me back if there's any problem. If I don't hear from you I'll meet you at the Paddington at 11:32 on track...let me see, I'm checking the schedule now on the internet...track nine, it says, but they often change it. Anyway, I'll be there."

"Yes Ma'am. Thank you Ma'am."

Judy stood on the exit ramp of track eleven, on which the Reading train would be arriving. Muriel was one of the last to disembark, but Judy recognized her immediately and waved.

Muriel, wearing black leggings, boots, and sweatshirt, caught her eye and waved back.

Judy took her by the arm and led her to the station exit. "So glad you could come, Muriel. I think we'll have a fine time, and get to know each other a little better."

"Thanks for inviting me."

Judy was gratified that Muriel's face showed the faintest hint of a smile.

"Come, we'll get a taxi and go right to Harrods."

"I'm afraid I'm not very hungry."

"I understand, and neither am I, but perhaps we could have tea and you could try the oyster and caviar bar and after that the Laduree Macaroon shop. Are you a vegetarian, Muriel?"

'Not really, but I don't eat a lot of meat."

"Neither do I, so we'll skip the Charcuterie, but you must visit the pastry bar. It's a delight to the eyes as well as to the taste."

The cab stopped at the front entrance of Harrods.

"This way, "Judy said, and led Muriel to the Delicatessen. As they entered, Muriel marveled at the variety of meats, fruits, pastries and cheeses.

Judy found a corner table just outside the Traiteur and Fromagerie Hall. "I'll order the tea and sit here to keep our table while you go look and see if there's anything you like. Perhaps you could bring back a selection of cheeses and maybe any pastry that catches your eye."

"Of course."

While she waited for Muriel to return, Judy opened her brief case and reviewed the notes of her most recent conversation with Jake.

"I hope you like this pastry," said Muriel when she returned with a plate of cheeses and two colorfully decorated pastries.

After Muriel had finished sipping her tea and began nibbling at her pasty, Judy said, "Muriel I'd like to relay to you certain information that I have received from my investigator, and ask if you could comment on it."

"I'll try. Go ahead."

"I know it will be difficult, and I wouldn't ask you if I didn't think it was quite important."

"I understand. I know you want to help me, and I'm most grateful. Please ask anything you like."

Just last night I received information that the autopsy on Arthur's death reported that Arthur had four to five times the recommended doses of Ambien in his system. Do you know anything about that?"

"Ambien? No Ma'am. I'm quite sure Arthur never used any kind of sleeping aid like that. At least he never mentioned it to me if he did. He always seemed to sleep quite soundly."

"I have to ask a delicate question, then. May I ask how many times you have slept with Arthur?"

Muriel hesitated uncomfortably before saying, "Just a few times…"

"How many times, Muriel?" Judy pressed.

"Before we went to Carcassonne together, you mean?"

Judy nodded.

"Only a few. My teaching job at Brianhurst required me to be in residence there. Arthur was also in residence at his school at St. Johns. So we didn't have much opportunity to find time together…you know, private time…that kind of time…"

Judy scrutinized Muriel's' expression as she gave this answer. Muriel was being evasive, and she couldn't help feeling that Muriel was holding something back.

Judy decided that now was not the time to press her on this point. "But you know what Ambien is, I take it."

"Yes Ma'am," Muriel said cautiously.

"Apparently, a bottle of Robitussin was found at the crime scene—on a bedside table. Do you know anything about that?"

"Why yes. The week before we left for Carcassonne, Arthur came down with a cold and a cough. He said it wasn't too bad, though. I asked him if he thought we should cancel our trip, but he said he would be fine. He said we had already spent the money on tickets, made arrangements for the time off, and we had to make those arrangements a long time in advance. Who knew when we might get another chance to take a trip like this again."

"So you went ahead despite his cold?"

"He said it wasn't that bad."

"Did he see a doctor…did he tell you?"

"He said he didn't need to. People get colds all the time and they don't go popping off to the doctor every time they get one. It's been a cold and wet winter, so lots of us have had them."

"Did the cold give him much of a problem during your trip?"

"Not really. While we were up and about...you know... taking in the sights during the day...his cough seemed to dissipate a bit. It was mainly at night that it would start up again. He took the cough medicine in the evening before he went to bed."

"After you and he..."

Muriel blushed but nodded.

"Weren't you afraid you might get his cold?"

"Arthur was always such a gentleman. He offered to... you know...not..."

"But..."

"I told him I didn't care about his silly cold...I mean we hardly ever had the opportunity to be with each other...I didn't want to let his silly cold get in the way..."

"So you never got his cold..."

"To be honest, the last day or so that we were in Carcassonne I did start to feel a little tickle at the back of my throat. I guess I tried to hide it from Arthur...I didn't want him to feel bad that he had given me his cold...but when I did start to cough a few times one evening, he offered to let me use some of his Robitussin. There wasn't much of a pharmacy to speak of inside the Walled City, and we would have to have walked down the hill to the main city below at that time of night...meaning we'd have to sign out at the gate...plus we weren't sure there would even be a pharmacy open at that hour...so..."

"You took some of his Robitussin..."

"Yes. I didn't drink from the bottle, of course...nor did he...we measured it out into a paper cup..."

"It wouldn't surprise you, then, if your fingerprints were found on that bottle?'

"Fingerprints? Why would..."

"According to the latest French Police report, that bottle was dissolved with Ambien, and they have sent out the bottle to check for fingerprints and DNA on the bottle."

"DNA, fingerprints…but why?"

"Apparently the police believe that the murderer sedated Arthur before stabbing him to death so that there would be a minimum of thrashing and outcry during the stabbing that might awaken the other hotel guests."

Muriel held her hand to her mouth as she began to realize the implications of the Ambien in the Robitussin, and the fact that her fingerprints were almost certainly on the bottle. "You mean…and they think I…"

"Muriel, I have to ask you, have you ever bought or been prescribed Ambien?"

Muriel seemed stunned by the question, and for a moment her face went blank.

"Muriel, I have to ask you this, because I have no doubt that the police—either French or Thames Valley—if they have not already done so, are surely seeking court orders to examine the records of all pharmacies in the St. Johns and Newbury area."

Muriel began to shake her head, but then stopped.

"Muriel…think…"

"I think…yes…Doctor Carter did prescribe some Ambien for me…some months ago."

Judy sighed. "Tell me about it, Muriel. Why did he prescribe Ambien for you?"

"It was while I was staying at Samantha's house after my divorce from Norman, before I got the teaching job at Brianhurst. I had no money at that time and no place to stay. What money I had, I spent on a solicitor to obtain a restraining order. Norman had been stalking me. When I went out to interview for jobs, Norman was always there—at the grocery stores, at the bus stop, I was afraid for my own sanity. Samantha suggested that I stay at her home until the police did something about Norman. She said that Norman wouldn't dare to enter her grounds to bother me. That even if he did, they would be witnesses for the police, and that I should stay at her home all the time except when I absolutely had to go out for job interviews, which I did. I stayed at Samantha's all day and night every day, but then…"

"Then what, Muriel?"

"I did think I would be safe at Samantha's, but then one night Norman did come onto the grounds nosing around—it's about four acres. It was only when her dogs began barking that Samantha called the police, and Eddie went out with his shotgun to investigate. Eddie found Norman snooping around and they got into an altercation until the police arrived."

"Go on…"

"I was so frightened, Ma'am. I think that if he had somehow found a way inside the house he would have…"

"I'm sure that intrusion shattered your confidence that you could at least feel safe at Samantha's."

"It did. It did! I was so stressed. I couldn't sleep at all. I was up on her third floor guest room every night pacing back and forth. It was then that Samantha insisted on taking me to her doctor—that's Doctor Carter."

"And he prescribed the Ambien so you could sleep?"

"Yes Ma'am."

"Did it help?"

"It did, but just for one night. The next night I awoke in the middle of the night and blacked out while I was shuffling to the loo. I ran into a lamp and knocked it over. Samantha and Eddie heard the noise and came up to find me find me lying on the floor. I wasn't badly hurt—just a few cuts and bruises, but it could have been much worse if I had hit my head on the corner of the dresser or something."

"So you stopped taking the Ambien?"

"Samantha had me call the doctor for advice. He told me that I should stop taking them, and that he would recommend something different for me."

"I think he advised me to get some less effective non-prescription sleep aids, but I was frightened by my fall and decided to just live with my insomnia. It was shortly after that I got the teaching job at Brianhurst. I slept much better there, and without the pills, though even at Brianhurst, Norman was caught on the premises trying to find me."

"I'm so sorry, Muriel. I will see what I can do about getting a good solicitor to ride herd on the police to enforce your restraining order."

"Thank you Ma'am, though I'm not sure it will do any good."

"Muriel…the Ambien…you said you only used two of the tablets before you stopped using them. How many Ambien tablets were you prescribed? Do you still happen to have the tablets that you did not use?"

"How would that…"

"How many tablets were there on the prescription?"

"I think twenty."

"That can be easily checked…and you used how many?"

"I only used two before Doctor Carter advised me to stop using them."

"So there should be eighteen left. Ambien is a prescription drug, so if we could show the police those eighteen unused tablets, it would be evidence that you would not have had enough prescribed Ambien tablets to account for the Ambien found in both the Robitussin bottle and in Arthur's body. If you never had any other prescriptions for Ambien, and the police would check all the prescriptions for Ambien in the UK, the police could never prove that you had sufficient Ambien to sedate Arthur."

Muriel shook her head.

"You didn't keep the unused Ambien tablets?"

"No…I didn't want to be tempted to use them again. I threw them away."

"Oh, well—certainly understandable."

"I should have kept them."

"How were you to know? Anyway, the idea that the murderer used Ambien to sedate Arthur as a prelude to the stabbing attack is just a police theory. The autopsy does not suggest that the Ambien itself contributed to Arthur's death."

"I don't see how it could. Surely it was obvious what killed him."

"How many people knew that the doctor had prescribed you the Ambien?"

Muriel thought for a moment. "I don't know…besides me…I guess Samantha, Eddie, and Doctor Carson of course."

"Did Arthur know?"

"I think I did mention it to him. He was concerned that I had felt the need to get such a prescription."

Judy could see that Muriel was becoming ashen-faced as she realized the implications of her purchase of the Ambien.

"Muriel I'm sorry to be asking all these questions, but it's better that I ask them now rather than for you to have to answer those same questions later when posed to you by those who do not have your best interests at heart."

"You mean the police. Everything seems to be working against me."

"What evidence the police have is very much circumstantial. They still have to fill a gaping hole in the evidence."

Muriel eyes began to water as she held back tears. "Why would I ever want to kill Arthur? How could I?"

Judy took her hand and handed her a tissue. "Precisely, Muriel. You would have no reason to do such a thing. You have a spotless record…I've checked of course…you know I had to… and I cannot believe anyone could ever believe you capable…"

Muriel tried to dry her tears, and looked around to see if any of the patrons from nearby tables was watching. They were not.

"Muriel, I'm so sorry I've caused you any distress, but I must ask you one more question. "Can you think of any reason why anyone might discern a possible motive for you to kill Arthur?"

Muriel let out a deep breath and seemed to be about to say something when she suddenly shook her head in distress, rose from the table and lurched toward the exit without picking up her purse. "I can't talk about it right now! I can't...I can't... please get me a cab...I have to go."

"Muriel, wait!" Judy picked up Muriel's purse and followed her out to the street. "Muriel, please wait. You left your purse."

Muriel turned and took the purse. "I'm sorry. I...I..."

Judy flagged down a taxi. "We'll go back to Paddington together. I'll call Samantha and let her know you're on your way and she needs to pick you up in Reading."

Muriel got in the cab, but as Judy followed, Muriel said, "Judy, I'm so sorry. Would you let me go to the station by myself? I have my return ticket."

"Of course." Judy handed the driver a twenty-pound note. 'Paddington Station," she told the driver.

"I'll call you tomorrow," said Muriel. "Thank you for everything. Thank you for your help. I'll call you tomorrow... promise..."

As Judy watched Muriel's taxi disappear into the traffic of Brompton Road, she could only wonder what Muriel was about to tell her, but then could not.

CHAPTER EIGHTEEN

*J*udy picked up her mobile. "Hi Jake, what's up?"

"Got some interesting information, and wanted to give it to you right away. Do you have a few minutes?"

"For you, always, Jake. Give it to me fast if you can. I promised Braxton I'd go to lunch with him."

"First, I wanted to let you know that we're all set up here at the Enterprise Building, and we've integrated our data base completely with NXR."

"Glad to hear it. Did I mention that Amber and I bought NXR?"

"You're kidding!"

"It turns out we both need a reliable investigative service capable of giving our cases top priority. Consider your annex here in London as a wholly owned subsidiary. I would have asked you to serve as the Chief Operating Officer of NXR, but I need you here near me in London. Is that still good for you?"

"Absolutely. I've already found a nice flat here in Knightsbridge near our new offices. Not cheap, but as a confirmed old bachelor I don't need a huge layout."

"Are you saying you need a raise?"

"No at all, Judy. You pay me well. And I like the work."

"Glad to hear that...now, your news?"

"First, the French Police finally released Arthur's body. His brother Chester went to pick him up two days ago, and brought him back to St. Johns. He's scheduled a funeral service for next Thursday at Brookwood Cemetery, which is adjacent to St. Johns Village. You might want to let Muriel know. It would probably be a good idea for her to go. It might not look good if she doesn't go. From what my agents have been able to ascertain, word of Muriel's status as a murder suspect has not yet made the rounds…at least not in the local papers."

"That's good. Muriel will be glad to hear that, though it won't get her job back at Brianhurst. I'll let her know about the internment ceremony. I'm sure she'll want to go…if I can get her to leave Samantha's guest room again. I had lunch with her yesterday, and she's in pretty bad shape as you can imagine."

"You might want to go to the internment as well, even if Muriel doesn't."

"Really? Why?"

"You know from all the cop shows on TV, they always have an officer go to the funeral of a murder victim to see if they can spot any suspicious characters who might be attending out of curiosity—like maybe the murderer himself."

"Is there anything to that?"

"Maybe. I haven't been to many funerals of murder victims, but it sounds plausible."

"Fine. I'll plan to go. Is that it?"

"I have a lot more."

"Oh…then I'd better tell Braxton to go ahead to lunch without me. I'll be right back."

Moments later Judy returned. "All right. I'm here for as long as you need me. Go ahead."

"Have you interviewed the Thames Valley Police yet?"

"No, I decided to wait until I got more information from you so that I'd be less at their mercy when I do go there to see them."

"Probably a good idea, because I have a lot more to tell you. The test results came back on the bottle of Robitussin found at the crime scene."

"And?"

"Muriel's fingerprints were all over the bottle. Their lab can't confirm that her DNA is on the bottle until they get a DNA sample from her, but I would guess that they will find her DNA as well."

"How did they get her fingerprint sample then?"

"I'm not sure, but I assume that the Thames Police were able to get her fingerprints from one of Muriel's previous job applications and sent it to the lab at the request of the Gendarmes."

"She doesn't have much of a work history—she didn't work during her marriage she told me."

"Well, I assume she must have, or maybe they got a sample when they interviewed her at Brianhurst. Did she get a glass of water or anything during the interview?"

"I don't know, Jake. I guess I can ask her the next time I see her, but somehow the French got her fingerprints and made the match, so that's that. What's important, though, is that Muriel has a very credible explanation for why her fingerprints might be on the bottle. She and Arthur bought the bottle at a small pharmacy in the Walled City because Arthur needed it for his cold and sore throat. Muriel may have held the bottle while she measured out a dose on to a spoon or small cup. So is that all you have for me?"

"I have more. I intercepted a follow-up report from the French pathologist who believes that Arthur's throat was cut first—presumably to insure that he could not cry out and alert guests in neighboring rooms. The subsequent stab wounds were not random, but aimed at the heart for a quick kill. Several hit a rib, or missed the heart, but one finally hit its mark."

"And that's significant because..."

"The Gendarmes have concluded that it may not have been a crime of passion, but rather deliberate and premeditated— that Arthur was targeted."

"If so, wouldn't that be good for Muriel? I've always thought that the only way a prosecutor could convince a jury that a sweet and law abiding woman such as Muriel could have committed such a crime would be to suggest that it was a passion killing, sudden anger, jealousy."

"I don't think so—not if she had a very powerful motive, unrelated to anger, revenge or jealousy—to kill him in a very deliberate manner."

"What other motive could she possibly have had?"

"Judy, you told me that Arthur's father was a billionaire, owner of a controlling interest in Edgeware Industries."

"Yes, that is what I gathered from talking with both Samantha and Muriel, but why would that provide any motive for Muriel to kill Arthur? She was just his girlfriend. She could not possibly profit from his death."

"Okay, hear me out now. I took the liberty of checking recent Probate Court filings. Arthur's father, Lord Edgeware, passed away at the Parkington Abbey Retirement Home on March 27 of this year. Lord Edgeware's death had been considered imminent for some weeks before that. For some period of years before his death, all Edgeware's financial affairs were handled by a court-appointed solicitor by the name of James Holliston."

"I didn't know that."

"That's what you pay me the big bucks for."

"You still haven't told me how any of this is relevant if Muriel didn't stand to profit from Arthur's death."

"Hang with me. Arthur was murdered on March 29."

"That I know."

"Yesterday, I obtained a copy of Lord Edgeware's will which leaves his entire estate to his eldest son."

"According to Muriel, Chester was the eldest son."

"But is he?"

"What do you mean?"

"Chester and Arthur are fraternal twins. According to the medical documents and letter signed by the doctor who delivered the two boys, Chester was born fifty-seven seconds before Arthur. Since Lord Edgeware died while Arthur was still alive, those documents will be critical in establishing Chester's right to inherit as the eldest son."

"So why would those documents not have been critical if Arthur had predeceased his father?"

"Because if Arthur had predeceased his father, Chester would still inherit, just without the need to have to establish that he was the eldest son. Since Arthur would no longer have been alive, Chester would instead inherit by intestate succession as Lord Edgeware's sole surviving son, regardless of whether he was the eldest or not. Get it?"

"I think so. So what will happen in Probate Court now?"

"Chester will simply ask the Probate Court to accept the authenticity of the attached medical report and letter, and award him the entire estate based on the fact that at the time of his father's death, the estate passed to him in accordance with the will leaving the entire estate to him as first born son."

"What if, for any reason, the Probate Court were to reject the authenticity of the medical documents and letter, and instead find that as of the date of Lord Edgeware's death, Arthur was actually the eldest son?"

"In that case, the Court would of course determine that as of the date of the father's death, the entire estate passed to Arthur who was still alive on that date. When Arthur subsequently died two days later, his estate would then pass to Arthur's closest living relative…"

"Chester, then?"

"Probably, though we'll need to check with a solicitor on whether Arthur's estate would then pass to a sole surviving brother if he has no closer living relative."

"If not to a brother, then to whom?"

"Just before calling you, Judy, I checked the British law on this point. If a man dies intestate, his entire estate goes to his spouse."

"Then where is all this going, Jake, and why are you telling me all this? Arthur was not married, so what is the relevance?"

"Judy, I had my staff check the marriage records of every county in the UK. Have you heard of the county of Berwickshire in Scotland?"

"No, should I have?"

"Not necessarily, but I think perhaps you will."

"Stop teasing me, Jake, and just tell me about Berwickshire."

"According to their county records, Arthur was married there on the eighth of September last year."

"Oh my God! To whom?"

"Hold your breath, Judy, because in one way it's good news, but in another way it's very bad. Which do you want to hear first?"

"Stop it, Jake…okay give me the bad first. Why is it bad?"

"Because the Police will no doubt see this as providing your client with a very big motive indeed."

"What are you talking about? "

"Are you sitting down?"

"Stop it."

"Judy…Arthur married Muriel Wright."

CHAPTER NINETEEN

*J*udy took a table in the far corner of the Lock, Stock, and Barrel, and waited for Muriel to appear.

The night before, she had called Muriel to let her know that she had discovered the records of her secret marriage to Arthur Edgeware and needed to talk to her about whether it would be possible to continue working on her case. Judy had been inclined to simply let Muriel know that, in light of Muriel's failure to advise her of such an important matter that she was withdrawing from the case. However, she had decided that it would be unfair to do this without giving Muriel an opportunity to explain this glaring omission.

Judy saw Muriel enter and scan the dining area. She waited for Muriel to look in her direction and then held up her hand.

Muriel, looking much distressed, approached apprehensively and sat.

For several moments, the two simply looked at each other.

"Samantha dropped you off?" Judy finally asked.

"Yes Ma'am. I'm to call her when we've finished talking."

Judy took in a deep breath, and then said, "Muriel…you remember when we first talked I told you how important it was that you confide in me completely about anything relating to this dreadful matter? If you cannot trust me, then I cannot help you."

"Yes Ma'am."

"Do you recall that I also told you I would not be able to help you in any way if I found that you were holding back anything?"

Muriel hung her head. "Yes, Ma'am."

"If I were representing you in my capacity as a barrister… that is, if you were already charged and I was defending you in court, your failure to confide in me would certainly undermine your defense, but that omission alone would not necessarily oblige me to withdraw from the case. Several of my clients have withheld information from me in the past, and I did not petition to the court to withdraw, despite the harm it did to my ability to defend them."

"And now…"

"Now, I am not representing you in my capacity as a barrister, or even as your lawyer of any kind. If I were, I would have you sign a retainer agreement. Rather, your very good friend, Samantha, asked me to help you find out who killed Arthur. I agreed to do so because I have access to investigative resources that might help me in forestalling a great injustice that might be inflicted upon you."

"I am grateful."

"And you repay me by failing to tell me about something as important as your marriage to Arthur—a marriage that may prove to be a critical piece of evidence in the case now being compiled against you by the police both in France and here in the Thames Valley."

"But Ma'am, I don't see how that would have anything to do with…"

"If you don't see that, I can explain it to you…but before we get to that, I need to hear why you entered into this marriage so secretly. I take it that you and Arthur both meant this marriage to be secret, and that you told no one?"

Muriel shook her head. "No, Ma'am. I mean, yes Ma'am. We both meant our marriage to be a secret."

"Tell me why, Muriel."

"Arthur was afraid…"

"Afraid of what?"

"Arthur and his brother rarely had contact with each other, at least not after they went their separate ways and attended separate boarding schools. They were so different, and had so little in common. Chester wanted to be like his father, take over his father's business someday, and be as rich and powerful as his father."

"And Arthur?"

"Arthur had no such pretensions. He loved his studies in the classics at school. He wanted to be a teacher—that was his sole ambition."

"So he accepted that he was not the first born, and would inherit little or nothing from his father?"

"His father never told him that explicitly, but it was understood. I think Arthur knew that his father was deliberately withholding that information from his sons."

"For what reason?"

"Arthur thought it was because his father wanted to wait, observe them as they grew up, until he was sure which of his sons would be the best to take over his company. He didn't want to break up the company, but he also didn't want there to be any animosity between his two sons that would create a situation where one might threaten to sue the other later on or cause trouble."

"Arthur understood this."

"Oh yes. Many times he said he tried to convince his father that he was quite satisfied to be the second son and that he had no ambitions to inherit or run his company."

"So why didn't Lord Edgeware just go ahead and declare which son was the first born and resolve any and all uncertainty in that regard?"

"Arthur thought that his father nursed some reservations about Chester, and just wanted to wait and see how each son performed in life before making any such declaration about which son was in fact the first born."

"What reservations?"

"I don't know. Arthur and I didn't talk about that very much, but I think Arthur was aware of a character flaw in his brother, and that his father saw it too."

"He didn't say what that was?"

"No. I don't think he wanted to say, but I think he knew it was a serious enough character flaw that it might cause his father to have second thoughts about bequeathing the entire company to Chester. The irony is that Arthur didn't want to have anything to do with the company, and tried to convince his father of that."

"And his father wouldn't believe him?"

"No. Apparently Lord Edgeware couldn't even imagine the possibility that anyone, least of all one of his own sons, wouldn't want to be a billionaire."

"I suppose I can see that, but I'm left wondering why Lord Edgeware didn't just rewrite his will to leave it to the son whom he thought most worthy—regardless of which son was the first born."

"Arthur said his father was old school—believed in primogeniture, and wanted to leave his company to the first born—that way there would be no animosity between the brothers. Who inherited would then be the result of which son was actually first born, and not because their father favored one son over the other which could only create animosity between the two brothers and lead to a rivalry that might threaten the company that their father had spent a life creating."

"I don't understand, Muriel. How could Lord Edgeware control a fact? A fact is a fact. How could he determine who was first born? I mean, either Chester was born first, or Arthur was born first."

"That's just it, Ma'am. Arthur thought that Chester was convinced that his father did somehow have it within his power to determine who was first born."

"How?"

"There was a doctor's report, and letters. Arthur was convinced, that Chester was convinced, that their father had the delivering doctor prepare two sets of reports and letters—

one stating that Chester was first born, and the other stating the Arthur was first born. Then, at a time of Lord Edgeware's own choosing, he would produce the set which matched his choice of which son should inherit."

"Muriel, all this seems so...I have a problem wrapping my head around all that. I mean, surely, there must be some objective way to determine who was first born, regardless of these two sets of medical reports and letters. What about the doctor who delivered the two sons...were there no other witnesses?"

"There was their mother, of course, but she was heavily sedated and did not see who was born first. Apparently there was also one nurse, but that's all."

"Are either of them still alive to testify? Did Arthur or his brother know the name of the doctor and the nurse who delivered them?"

Muriel shook her head. "I'm sure Arthur did not know, and I don't think he wanted to know. That's the thing, Arthur didn't care! He wanted nothing to do with his father's company. The one thing that Arthur knew for sure was that his brother was paranoid."

"Paranoid about what?"

"That somehow Arthur might produce a second set of medical reports and letters to prove that he was first born."

"Did Arthur have any knowledge of any such second set of reports or letters?"

No, none! That's why he thought his brother was paranoid."

"Did Chester ever tell Arthur why he thought there might be two sets?"

"No. That's another reason why he thought Chester was being paranoid."

Judy paused to think before she asked, "All right, Muriel, what does all this have to do with why you and Arthur kept your marriage a secret?"

"As far back as last August, Arthur and I knew we loved each other and wanted to get married. So we did. However, we soon realized we couldn't live on Arthur's meager salary alone, so I started looking for a job. I finally found a job opening to teach French at Brianhurst School for Girls. However, when I found out that the job opening was for an unmarried woman with no children who would live at the school in residence, I almost decided not to apply. That's when we decided that I should go ahead and apply, but keep our marriage secret. We didn't see any harm in it, but of course Arthur and I could only see each other on holidays after that."

"You couldn't have just gotten married and lived on Arthur's salary until you found a job?"

"We thought about that, but Arthur was in residence at Coldbridge as well. Our plans were to find a co-ed school that could provide us with a cottage on the premises and offer teaching positions to both of us. Several schools do provide such cottages for married teachers. So we decided to wait, and just see each other when we could."

"Why didn't you?"

"Why didn't we what?"

"Why didn't you wait?"

"It was in early September that we decided we couldn't wait. Chester made an unexpected visit to Coldbridge School and asked Arthur if they could have a talk about their father's failing health, and if they could agree on certain matters before their father passed away. Arthur agreed to discuss such matters, and the two took a walk around the school grounds, but the conversation didn't go well."

"How so?"

"Well, while they were discussing financial matters, the coming probate and the like, Arthur happened to mention that he was planning to get married. All of a sudden, Chester went into a rage. He told Arthur that under no circumstances must he get married prior to their father's death."

"Did he say why?"

"No, that was the thing. Arthur asked Chester why he couldn't get married before his father passed away, and Chester couldn't really give a reason—other than to say it would complicate probate matters unnecessarily. Maybe he just didn't want a third party—like me—complicating the probate. When Arthur demanded a better explanation, Chester lost his temper, and basically just tried to order Arthur to wait until their dad passed, and that if he didn't do so he could make things very difficult for him."

"How did Arthur take that advice?"

"He didn't…and he didn't like Chester's threats, which frightened him. Arthur was very non-confrontational, and was not inclined to get in a dogfight with his brother over something he didn't understand anyway. In the end, he just thought it prudent to pretend to agree not to marry me until after his father passed away."

"So you and Arthur decided to marry despite Chester's objections."

"We thought it solved several problems. If we married, but kept it secret, I could keep my job at Brianhurst, and Arthur could avoid a nasty confrontation with his brother. Also, Arthur knew I was Catholic, and that delaying our marriage would mean foregoing conjugal relations for an indefinite period of time. I mean, why should we have to wait until we get married just because his brother demanded it? Who knew how long it would be before his father passed away anyway? I mean were we supposed to wait, maybe years, to get married? It made no sense to us."

Judy shook her head. "Muriel, what possessed you and Arthur to think you could keep such a marriage secret?"

"That's why we looked for the most far out place we could find to get married—a little town called St. Abbs in Berkwickshire."

"Muriel, surely you know there's such a thing as a national data base of marriages."

"We couldn't imagine who would spend time looking for it. Who cares, and how could it have anything to with Arthur's murder."

"It could have a lot to do with Arthur's murder. Do you not see that if it is ever determined that Arthur was the first-born, it would mean that Lord Edgeware's entire estate passed to Arthur upon Lord Edgeware's death, and upon Arthur's death, Arthur's entire estate would pass to you by intestate succession?"

"To me?"

"Muriel, I'm sure the police are looking for a motive for you to kill Arthur. Do you think any prosecutor can come up with a better motive than inheriting an estate conservatively valued at two and half billion pounds?"

"Oh my God! But I had no idea!"

"I'm sure you didn't. The irony is that whatever Chester's motive was in trying to get Arthur to forego marrying you until after his father's death—fear, perhaps, that a probate court might look unkindly on leaving Lord Edgeware's daughter-in-law destitute—it is likely that Chester could very well end up being hoisted by his own petard if it turns out Arthur was indeed the first-born."

"I'm Lord Edgeware's daughter-in-law!"

"No question about that, now."

"But Arthur wasn't the first-born! Arthur said that Chester told him that Lord Edgeware's Conservator has the doctor's medical report, letters, proving that Chester was first-born."

"We shall see. Right now I have a lot on my plate to investigate."

"So you'll stay on this case, then? You won't desert me, will you Ms. Alexander?"

"Okay, Muriel, I guess I can understand why you kept your marriage secret, but you must promise me that from now on you will not keep any evidence from me. Will you do that?"

"I promise, thank you, thank you!"

"All right, Muriel, go ahead and call Samantha to pick you up. I will be looking into all this, and get back to you. Before

I go, I will ask you just one more very important question, and you must promise to answer truthfully. Before Arthur's murder, did you have any information, anything at all, that might have led you to believe that Arthur might be first-born? Think hard before you answer, Muriel. Forget the two and a half billion pounds you might inherit. Your life is more important, and your answer may depend on it!"

Muriel shook her head vigorously. "No, nothing!"

Judy got up and extended her hand. "All right. I'm rushing back to London. Wait here until Samantha comes to pick you up.

Suddenly, Muriel put her hand to her mouth.

"What is it, Muriel?"

"Oh my God! I just remembered something!"

Judy sat. "You'd better tell me. Good or bad, you'd better tell me. Take your time."

"I didn't think anything of it at the time, but now..."

"Just tell me. I'll tell you if it's anything important."

"Well, it was during a picnic Arthur and I were enjoying one afternoon last September on the Coldbridge grounds. For some reason we got to talking about his childhood. He told me about a time when he was seven years old or so, his father called him into his study one day and scolded him about something."

"Go on..."

"He said that his father took him in his lap and said something like 'I have high hopes for you, son. Some day you may turn out to be my first-born.' Arthur said he asked his father 'but how will I know?'"

Judy said nothing but held her breath waiting for Muriel to continue.

"He said his father told him, 'I told the doctor who delivered my first-born to put an indelible mark upon his body so that there would never a be question as to who was first-born."

"Like what, a tattoo or something?"

"Arthur couldn't remember. He just remembers his father saying it was like a tiny eclipse."

"An eclipse? Like a tiny dark dot maybe?"

"That's all he remembered. What do you think?"

"Well, since Lord Edgeware was not present at the birth, it would make sense that he would want to be able to satisfy himself at some later date as to who was the actual first born, so having the doctor make a small mark on the first-born..."

"Arthur thought nothing of it at the time, and so did I when he told me that. I mean, Arthur was only seven years old."

"Arthur said his father never mentioned it again?"

"That was the only time."

"I doubt if it means much, unless there exists somewhere a letter or document confirming what such a marking indicates. Without such a letter, any marking found on Arthur's body would be meaningless to anyone but Lord Edgeware. I'll make a note of it, however. Now are your sure that is all Arthur ever said to you about whether he might have been the first-born?"

"That's all I remember Arthur telling me. Promise."

Judy decided that now was not the time to tell Muriel that any competent prosecutor would be likely to make hay out of Muriel's recollection.

"Alright, Muriel, I'll go ahead. I'll call you tomorrow. I take it you're still planning to go to Arthur's funeral on Friday? You're going home with Samantha?"

"Yes Ma'am."

"I'll see you both at the funeral."

CHAPTER TWENTY

*J*udy checked her iPhone and realized that she had missed several calls during the time she had turned off her phone while talking to Muriel. She had also neglected to turn her phone back on after returning to London, and now saw she had missed several calls from Jake.

"Jake?"

"You rang, mistress?"

"Sorry I missed your calls. What's up?"

"I wanted to ask you the same thing, but I also have some information. I wanted to ask your permission before seeking it, but you didn't answer."

"I know, I'm sorry. So what did you do without my authorization?"

"As soon as I learned that Muriel and Arthur were married, I thought it would be best to visit Parkington Abbey as soon as possible after Lord Edgeware's death, and see if he had left any papers or documents there."

"How did you do that?"

"I simply went to the reception desk and introduced myself as acting on behalf of Lord Edgeware's daughter-in-law."

"Jake, you can't go around misrepresenting yourself like that."

"I assumed you would want me to pursue that avenue, and you are acting on behalf of Muriel Edgeware are you not, now that we know that Muriel was married to Arthur Edgeware."

"All right Jake—my fault, and yes I would have authorized you to check that out, so did he leave any documents there?"

"Apparently Lord Edgeware did leave a file cabinet behind in his private room there at Parkington. However, the receptionist said that Arthur Edgeware had already come to retrieve any belongings that might have been left behind after they took Lord Edgeware away for the funeral."

"When was his funeral?"

"There was no autopsy?"

"Apparently not. His death had been anticipated by his doctor for some months."

"So Chester took the file cabinet?"

"Actually, no. I guess he didn't want the hassle of trying to load the file cabinet in his car, so he just took out all the documents in the cabinet, put them into several cardboard boxes the staff provided for him, and left."

"Hmmm…so is the file cabinet itself still there?"

"Yes, the staff had put it into their storage room until it could be disposed of. I asked if I could look at it to see if Chester had missed any documents. They said I could, and led me to the storage room."

"You looked in the cabinet, then?"

"Yep, but it was completely cleaned out. Nothing left in it."

"That's too bad."

"Why?"

"It was something Muriel mentioned to me yesterday when I spoke with her."

"I thought you might have told her you would withdraw from her case because of her failure to tell you about her marriage to Arthur."

"I was planning to do just that, but she had a fairly good reason for not telling me. I agreed to stay on if she promised not to keep anything from me."

"Did she?"

"Yes. I'll tell you about that later. The reason I was hoping you might have found something is because of what Muriel told me about a conversation she had with Arthur back in September. Muriel said that Arthur told her about a conversation he had with his dad when he was just a child of about seven. He told her that his father had told him that he had instructed the delivery doctor to place some kind of small indelible mark on the first born child."

"Like what?"

"Arthur said he didn't know. He only remembers that his father said it was some kind of an eclipse."

"Eclipse?"

"That's all Arthur remembered, but it wouldn't matter even if he had known, because any mark found on the first-born would be meaningless without a some kind of documentation showing the purpose of any such mark, and what it signified."

"I'm not sure I'm following you."

"Well, if Lord Edgeware had, say, written a letter to the doctor instructing him to place a mark on the first born…"

"…so that Lord Edgeware could later confirm to his own satisfaction who was in the fact the first born."

"Exactly…but if any such letter actually exists, it probably would have been among the documents Edgeware so closely guarded in that file cabinet in his room. And apparently, Chester now has all the documents in the file cabinet."

"Edgeware had Alzheimer's, didn't he?"

"Yes, but that doesn't mean he wouldn't have understood the importance of such a document. In his later years he might not have remembered why he had kept such a document, but he might have nevertheless—jealously and the staff say obsessively—guarded all the contents of that file cabinet during his entire time at Parkington. All his visitors were not allowed to touch it."

"Well, I suppose it's all moot now since Chester is now in the possession of its entire contents."

"Perhaps it's not moot, Jake."

"What are you thinking?"

"You said you saw the cabinet?"

"Yes."

"Can you describe it? Was it just an old metal-style cabinet?"

"Oh no. I think it was originally a very fine piece—mahogany perhaps—but now pretty scratched up and unsightly even."

"How many drawers?"

"Five, I think, and there were a number of separate compartments in each drawer."

"You looked in each compartment?"

"Yes…nothing."

"And each drawer had a separate lock?"

"Yes, but only one or two of the compartments within each drawer has a separate lock."

"Were you able to look in each drawer and each compartment within each drawer?"

"Yes. When Chester asked the staff for a key, they said they did not know of any key, and had never seen Edgeware in possession of any kind of key. I think the staff just dismissed the cabinet as some kind of obsession of Edgeware's. But of course they didn't want to get crossways with him, so they never messed with it while he lived there."

"How was Chester able to access the documents in the cabinet?"

"At Chester's request, the staff broke open each drawer and compartment with a crowbar so that Chester could retrieve the documents within."

"What did the staff say they intended to do with the cabinet?"

"Just call some service to take it away. It was pretty much a shambles after they broke open all the locks and drawers."

"Hmmm…Jake, I'd like you to go back there and tell them that Lord Edgeware's daughter-in-law would like to have that cabinet and ask if you could…"

"What if they later mentioned to Chester that someone on behalf of Muriel came to pick up the chest?"

"You're right. That's a bad idea. It would just alert Chester…and…which reminds me…does Chester even know yet about Arthur's marriage to Muriel?"

"I don't know. If Arthur has been in touch with the Thames Valley Police, they might have told him."

"You think the Thames Valley Police know about the marriage?"

"Yes, Judy…they know…"

"Okay, Jake. Enough of that. No more interceptions. I told you that."

"I made that interception before you told me not to…"

"All right. From now on, you play by the rules. Promise me, Jake."

"I promise."

"Nevertheless, you're right not to purport to act on Muriel's behalf. How about if you go back to Parkington in your own right. Just say that you were thinking about that cabinet. That one of your hobbies is restoration, and ask if they'd be willing to sell it since it had been abandoned by Chester."

"Sure, I could do that. They'd probably let me have it in return for just hauling it away. But…can I ask why you want it, and where you want me to stash it?"

"I'd think it might be worth taking it apart and see what we can find. If Lord Edgeware really was that obsessive and paranoid about anyone messing with this cabinet, maybe there's something imbedded in some secret compartment that would be of some interest."

"It's your money. I'll call a moving service and see if Parkington will sell or give it to me."

"Right away, Jake…before they let someone else take it away."

"Done…and what should I do with it after I get it?'

"Rent a warehouse somewhere and just stash it there for the time being."

"Okay…done."

"Jake, I suppose you know how this marriage will affect the case that the Police are massing against Muriel?"

"Oh yeah. They now have the one piece of evidence they've been lacking up to now—motive, several billion motives to be precise. Add that to opportunity, which they obviously have, and means, which they also have with Muriel's purchase of the Ambien and her fingerprints all over the Robitussin bottle and they may just have her dead to rights."

"Of course, this motive only holds up if they show that Muriel knew there was a chance that Arthur might inherit."

"Yep. In the end, it all comes down to which of the two sons was actually the first-born."

Both paused for the moment, while Judy thought for several minutes.

"Jake, I guess there's no way we can take a look at Arthur's body before his burial at Brookwood next Friday?'

"You're the barrister, Judy…but I don't see how. All you've got is Muriel's hearsay about what Lord Edgeware told Arthur when Arthur was seven years old, and like you said, any mark found on his body would be meaningless without a document verifying the meaning of any such mark."

"I know. I was just musing. Look, I'm going to Arthur's funeral, as are Muriel and Samantha. I'd like you to go too—get a good look at everyone who's there, take pictures if you can do so without anyone knowing."

"My specialty, Judy."

"Don't stand anywhere near me or the girls."

"Of course. Anything else?"

"Get me all on the information you can find on this Brookwood cemetery. I've heard a lot of rumors about it. Muriel thinks that Arthur is to be buried in a family plot there…a plot that goes back a couple of hundred years….this cemetery seems to be the source of a lot of very strange tales."

"Done."

"I need more than googling. Everything you can find, including what you can find off the grid."

"Done."

CHAPTER TWENTY-ONE

Although Jake had proven himself invaluable to Judy in gathering information, his services were no substitute for conferring with a colleague on legal questions and strategies.

She considered conferring with Braxton, but feared that doing so might compromise their commitment to keep their private and professional lives separate.

Accordingly, Judy called Amber the day before their scheduled transatlantic call. For the first half hour, she reviewed the swiftly mounting evidence against Muriel Wright. This included not only the evidence of Muriel's purchase of Ambien at St. John's Pharmacy and the toxic levels of Ambien found in Arthur's body, and the fact that Muriel's fingerprints were all over a bottle of Ambien-laced Robitussin found at the scene of the crime. Most incriminating of all was the fact that Muriel, having kept her marriage to Arthur a secret, now stood to inherit several billion pounds if it could ever be determined that Arthur was the first-born son of Lord Edgeware.

"Wow," said Amber after hearing this litany of mounting evidence.

Judy sighed. "It's getting to the point where I'm afraid to answer Jake's next call for fear that he will unload yet another bombshell on me."

"I thought Jake was supposed to be so good at finding evidence that would help your clients, not do them in. Are you having second thoughts about taking on this cause…I mean not even confiding in you that she and Arthur were married?"

"I did have second thoughts, yes. Yesterday I came very close to terminating our relationship."

"Why didn't you?"

"She came up with some reasonable explanations for why she bought the Ambien, and why her fingerprints were all over the Robitussin bottle. I couldn't really fault her for not telling me about those things, because if she's innocent she would have had no reason to think that her one time use of Ambien or purchase of Robitussin would be at all relevant."

"And not telling you about her marriage to Arthur?"

"She said she kept it a secret because if the school found out she would lose her teaching job. She also said Chester Edgefield had threatened Arthur if he got married before their father died."

"Threatened what?"

"He didn't say, but it was enough to scare Arthur."

"But not enough for Muriel and Arthur to wait to get married?"

"Apparently not. It was true that Lord Edgeware was ailing, and might not live much longer, but neither Muriel nor Arthur could be sure of that, and they weren't prepared to wait an indefinite period of time and forego marital relations while they waited."

"Whoa! It is the twenty-first century. Since when do couples their age worry about foregoing sex until marriage?"

"She's Catholic."

"Uh-huh. Do you buy that?"

"I'm willing to give her the benefit of the doubt on that one."

"It might be worth checking."

"I suppose…"

"So, sister, it sounds like you've already made up your mind to continue with this case."

"I still could terminate if you thought I should."

"No, I think it's just the kind of case you're so good at. I agree that you should continue with it."

"Even if the evidence keeps mounting against her?"

"All the more reason to stay on the case…if you still think she's innocent. Do you?"

"I think I do."

"Why?"

"I can't say really, other than I just do."

"Intuition? Go for it girl. At this point, in for a penny, in for a pound. My only suggestion is that you make clear to this young woman that you're going to seek the truth…wherever it leads you. At this point, you've only agreed to help her find out who really killed her husband. If the evidence becomes irrefutable that she killed him, there's nothing to oblige you to represent her in court as a barrister."

"If it came to that, I don't think I would be the best person to represent her. She deserves a barrister with far more experience than I."

"Fair enough. Now what can I do to help you?"

"I need to ask you a question. I think it's primarily a legal question—or at least a strategy question—but it may be an ethical question as well."

"I'm always here for you, sweetie. Give it to me."

"Well…I didn't mention that Arthur told Muriel a story about what his father told him when he was a young boy—that at the appropriate time, he would decide who was the first-born."

"The father would 'decide' who was first-born? How could he possibly decide that one way or the other?"

"Apparently Chester was paranoid that his father kept two sets of medical records and letters…both written by the doctor who delivered the boys at the hospital."

"How could there be any question about that?"

"I think I mentioned that the boys were fraternal twins, and were born only fifty-seven seconds apart. Only the doctor and the assisting nurse witnessed which son came out first. It would have been very tempting for the doctor to accept a payment of, say, a million pounds, to create two sets of records."

"For what possible purpose?"

"…to give the father the option of later deciding which son was most deserving of being declared first-born."

"…but why go to all that trouble…why not just wait until he decided which son proved most worthy, and just name that son as his heir in his will?"

"What Lord Edgeware feared most was that leaving the entire estate to a single son would cause the disinherited son to challenge the will and thereby jeopardize the integrity of the company he had spent a lifetime building. Apparently that was the rationale for the ancient law of primogeniture."

"…but he was planning to do that anyway by leaving everything to the first-born."

"…only if he left it to the true first born…the second son would have had no complaint or ill feeling that his father had favored one son over the other."

"All right, Judy…so what is the advice you seek?"

"It is this: should I seek to find the truth of which son was the first-born?"

"Why would you not?"

"For Muriel, it would be a double-edged sword. Let's say I uncover evidence that Arthur was the true first-born. Yes, that would make Muriel a billionaire, but it would also give police the very motive they need to convict Muriel. By finding such evidence I might be sending Muriel to the gallows."

"Not the gallows, sweetie. The UK abolished the death penalty."

"Okaaaaay…life in prison, not much better. Not much you can spend your billions on if you're in prison for life."

"I see what you mean…but who's to say that even if you do find such evidence, you'd have to fork it over to the police. They do have something like our Fifth Amendment over there don't they."

"Something like it, yes, but that's not the point. You made the point yourself, that if I'm to help Muriel find out who killed her husband, she has to understand that I will pursue the truth, regardless of where it leads. Without that understanding,

I'm out. I'm not her barrister. I'm not acting as her lawyer. I have no fiduciary duty to her."

"Even if the evidence you find helps convict her?"

"Yes. That's the deal. Do you agree? Would I be unethical to do that?"

"No, I don't think it would be unethical as long as Muriel understands that finding the truth with regard to which son was first-born may not help her, and in fact may increase the chance of her being convicted."

"Okay. That was my ethical question. But now my question as to strategy. Would it be a sound strategy in terms of tracking down the true killer to spend my time and resources trying to find the truth as to which son was the true first-born."

"Judy, I think it would. Granted, such evidence, if you found it, would be a double-edged sword—the other side of the sword being that if you found evidence that Arthur was first-born, that would give Chester a huge motive to kill Arthur himself, or more likely, hire someone else to kill him."

"I'm not sure that just showing that Chester had a motive would be sufficient to exonerate Muriel. It is still Muriel who had the opportunity and means, and it wouldn't detract from the fact that Muriel still has a motive as well. Chester was five hundred miles away when someone murdered Arthur in Carcassonne. Granted, it's a common defense tactic to raise reasonable doubt in court by pointing the finger at someone else, but in my experience it rarely succeeds."

"Well, that's true, of course but I wonder if all this is really moot. I mean do you really have any idea how to go about finding who the true first-born was?"

"I suppose the most obvious course would be to try to track down the doctor and nurse, if they're still living, and just ask them."

"As if, after receiving the bounteous bribe you hypothesized, they would just pony up and tell you the truth… and if either, or both did take a bribe, they might be living it up on the Riviera by now."

"There's that, of course, but I have confidence in Jake. If either of them is alive, I'm sure he can find them."

"…and if they're both dead do you have a Plan B?"

"…there's a Conservator, a Mr. Holliston, who might have some useful information if pressed, though he might have been bribed as well…"

"By Lord Edgeware or his son?"

"Either, I suppose."

"I don't know, Judy…how about a Plan C?"

"I do have a Plan C, actually, though I confess it's the most far-fetched."

"…bated breath here…"

"It seems that Lord Edgeware also mentioned to his seven year old son Arthur that he would always be able to prove which son was first born."

"…how?"

"Lord Edgeware told Arthur that he instructed the delivering doctor to make a mark on the son who was delivered first—some kind of 'eclipse'…more likely a tiny black dot… maybe a tattoo of some sort…imperceptible to the naked eye but visible under some kind of ultraviolet light."

"…but without a letter in which the significance of the 'eclipse' or dot is specified, how would anyone viewing the body know that the dot indicated first-born, or second-born?"

"You're right, we'd need a letter specifying the significance of the dot."

"…any leads on that?"

"Only a very thin one. Apparently, Chester went to his father's nursing home, Parkington Abbey, shortly after his father's death, and retrieved some documents from a heavy wooden file that Edgeware guarded in his apartment for many years. If such a letter exists, Chester probably has it now… perhaps to use as a back-up if the Conservator's set of medical reports and letters were ever challenged in Probate Court."

"You said you had a thin lead, not a non-existent one."

"On the off chance that Chester might have missed such a critical letter in some kind of secret compartment in the file cabinet, I had Jake go to Parkington and either buy or offer to cart away the cabinet."

"Where is the cabinet now?"

""I had Jake find a warehouse or storage locker to store it until we can have the file cabinet taken apart piece by piece."

"Well, good luck on that."

"We'll need it, that's for sure."

"Any other leads you're following?"

"I do think I need to visit the scene of the crime."

"You mean go to the hotel. What was it the Hotel Ville Fortifiee...there in Carcassonne?"

"Yes, Room 213. I'd like to have Muriel take me through, minute by minute, everything that she did on Wednesday morning, March 29...but much as I'd like to have Muriel accompany me...of course I can't."

"...because the local Gendarmes might take advantage of her presence to arrest her there in France."

"Yep. I can't take that chance. So I guess I'll have to go alone."

"What will you be looking for exactly?"

"For one thing, I'll want to try and get the names and addresses of everyone who was a guest in the hotel that night."

"How do you propose to do that?"

"Well, I'd..."

"Don't tell me...you have your ways. I'm sure you'll have them eating out of your hand to help you."

"I'm not counting on that."

"How will you know who to look for?"

"Well, Jake is going to Arthur's funeral tomorrow at Brookwood Cemetery, and will take pictures of everyone who is there. Jake is good at that—tiny cameras on his lapel the size of a pin. I'll be there as well, and so will Muriel and Samantha. I told Muriel I want her to keep a lookout for anyone at the funeral whom she recognizes as someone she might remember seeing at the Hotel Ville Fortifiée."

"Sounds like you've got your bases covered—Brookwood Cemetery—seems like I've heard of it before. Isn't it one of the largest cemeteries in the world?"

"It was at one time. Pretty much fallen into disrepair and overgrown in recent years—supposed to be the most haunted. The Edgeware family has quite a family plot there as well as a mausoleum. It's at the end of the Necropolis Railroad Line."

"Necropolis Railroad?"

"Yes, it was called the death train. Jake has been sending me info on it. It seems that back in 1852, London was running out of burial grounds, so promoters formed the London Necropolis and National Mausoleum Company to carry as many as 2000 bodies a day to be buried at Brookwood. I definitely want to scout it out…in case I ever need to petition the court for an exhumation."

"Exhumation?"

"Arthur's being buried today."

"Okay, babe. Explain all that later. Is it my turn to tell you what's happening with me?"

"Oh, Amber! I'm so sorry! What's the latest with Harvey?"

"We've set a date!"

"Before the election?"

"The week after."

"Amber, I've been so self-absorbed! Tell me all about it!"

CHAPTER TWENTY-TWO

As she entered Waterloo Station, Judy scanned the electronic billboard to look for the platform number and departure time of the next train to the village of St. Johns in the parish of Woking. Brookwood Cemetery was within a short walking distance of St. Johns, and she planned to arrive at Arthur's burial site well before the funereal party arrived.

She had asked Braxton if he might be free to drive her to Brookwood Cemetery in his Spitfire, but he had reluctantly begged off due to a pretrial hearing in Crown Court that morning. Although he had offered to let her drive his car, she decided it would be less hassle to take the train to St. Johns and walk to Brookwood from there.

Seeing that the next train to St. Johns was on platform twelve and would leave in the next fifteen minutes, she quickly boarded the train and settled into a vacant window seat. Tucked under her arm was an old out-of-print copy of John M. Clarke's book *London's Necropolis: a Guide to Brookwood Cemetery.* Jake had found the book in a small used bookstore in SoHo, and hand-carried it to Judy the previous morning. Judy had spent the rest of the day, and all but a few hours the night before, reading it with great interest. She now hoped to finish the book in the next forty-five minutes on the short thirty-one mile rail journey to St. Johns.

Each chapter of the book contained maps and trail guides of the Brookwood, which would assist her in locating the Edgeware Mausoleum and family plot. A hundred and forty black and white photographs illustrated the most intriguing memorials and cemetery structures that would serve as guideposts as she navigated the two hundred and twenty acre Necropolis to find the Mausoleum.

Although the photographs of the many crumbling and deteriorating mausoleums, obelisks, and gravestones were spellbinding—reminding her of a setting for a Stephen King horror novel—it was the history of Brookwood which she found most fascinating.

Brookwood Cemetery was the inspiration of Sir Richard Broun and Richard Sprye who claimed to have found the solution to a severe shortage of burial space in London. From 1800 to 1850, the population of London had almost tripled to over two and a half million inhabitants. Despite this rapid growth in population, the land set aside for burials during this period had remained fixed at no more than 300 acres spread out over 200 small sites—mainly church graveyards. As a result, graveyards became so congested that decaying corpses contaminated the water supply, which in turn caused widespread and recurring epidemics of typhoid, measles, and cholera.

In 1849, a single Cholera outbreak killed almost 15,000 people, and left thousands of unattended corpses piled in huge stacks awaiting burial. In desperation, loved ones resorted to exhuming recent burials to make room for new burials.

It was in the aftermath of these ongoing catastrophes that Broun and Sprye conceived of a 1,500 acre Necropolis to be set aside some thirty miles west of London in what was then the sparsely populated countryside of Sussex. In order to transport the dead to this new cemetery, they proposed building a special railroad line on which a train might carry both bodies and mourners to the Necropolis for burial on a daily basis.

In pursuit of this scheme, the two promoters formed the London Necropolis and National Mausoleum Company. The designated train to be built by this company was later referred to simply as the "death train."

Despite the vociferous objections of Christian prelates who protested that carrying both bodies and mourners on the same train was incompatible with the solemnity of Christian burial, the severity of the London burial crisis was simply too severe to lend itself to any other alternative proposal.

Accordingly, Parliament approved the scheme, and the London Necropolis Railroad Station was duly built adjacent to the Waterloo train station in London. (This building, though later remodeled for a different purpose, still exists and can be seen today at its original location on the Westminster Bridge Road). It was from this station that mourners boarded the death train, and the bodies, hoisted by steam-powered hydraulic lifts, were placed in specially outfitted railcars that were linked behind the death train's passenger cars.

At the other end of the line, two separate Brookwood Cemetery train stations were built—one on the north side, and the other on the south side. On arrival at the proper station, the bodies were unloaded on to a hand-drawn cart and pulled by railroad staff to the appropriate chapel on the cemetery grounds. The south side station was reserved for Anglicans, and the North side was set aside for Jews, Roman Catholics, and 'Nonconformist' Christians.

The site of the northern station serving Non-Conformists is today heavily overgrown and ill-maintained, giving it a gloomy, misty, and shadowy appearance. The site of the southern Anglican section is somewhat better maintained, and is the location of the shrine of King Edward the Martyr.

Each station held separate first-class and second-class reception rooms that served the mourners. A third set of apartments was set aside for train staff who waited until the train was ready to return to London. Railroad staff irreverently referred to the death train as 'the dead meat train', or 'the stiffs.'

Although all three reception rooms were licensed to serve alcohol, the license for the rail staff was soon revoked after the train engineer became drunk one morning, and the fireman had to drive the train back to London.

On November 13, 1854, the first scheduled death train left the London Necropolis Train Station for the newly opened

Brookwood Cemetery, where Mr. and Mrs. Hore of Ewer Street, London, buried their stillborn twin girls.

The Necropolis Railroad offered three classes of funerals. A first class funeral, costing two pounds, gave the purchaser the right to choose any plot on the cemetery grounds and the right to build any kind of mausoleum or memorial. As second class funeral cost one pound, and the right to build a memorial for an extra ten shillings. Third class funerals were available for the poor, provided their parish sustained the costs of burial at the section set aside for the parish.

The death trains themselves had separate cars for each class, and separate compartments for Anglicans of the Church of England, and for 'Non-Conformists' (those of any religion other than Anglican). This separation by class and religion applied both to the mourners in the passenger cars as well as to the dead bodies in the coffin cars. The Necropolis Railroad owners considered this separation necessary, not only to avoid unduly distressing mourners by having them mix with persons of a different social class, but also to avoid subjecting the dead to having their bodies mixed with those of a lower social order.

Although Broun and Sprye had high hopes for the economic success of Brookwood, it never quite lived up to their expectations. The pair expected that within the next hundred years, their death train would be delivering 50,000 bodies a year, and eventually accommodate as many as twenty-eight million dead bodies. Brookwood did in due course become the largest cemetery in the world, and to this day is the biggest cemetery in the UK. However, a series of catastrophes would soon dash the much higher hopes of both Parliament and its original promoters. By 1941, eighty-seven years after opening, only 200,000 had found peace in Brookwood.

During the 1930s and 1940s, the increased ownership of private cars decreased the cost of transporting bodies by hearse and private transport—all at the expense of the profitability of the railroads, including the Necropolis Railroad.

World War II also delivered a body blow to the London Necropolis Company. Waterloo Station became a prime target of the Nazi bombing. On April 17, 1941, German bombs destroyed and burned all the Necropolis rolling stock. This attack was followed by an attack with multiple incendiary devices that destroyed the Necropolis buildings. On May 11, 1941, the station was closed.

The last recorded funeral party carried on the London Necropolis Railroad was that of a Pensioner named Edward Irish, who was delivered by the death train to Brookwood and buried on April 11, 1941.

The nationalization of the railroads in 1947 delivered yet another body blow to the death train as new regulations made it impractical to deliver bodies by rail except by special charter. By the 1950s, most visitors to Brookwood travelled by automobile. The last funeral party transported by rails was that of Lord Mountbatten in 1979, and by 1988 British Rail ceased carrying dead bodies altogether.

Today, the rare visitors to what remains of Brookwood are treated to a setting of great beauty, stillness, and tranquility. The decaying and collapsing monuments remind one of a long lost civilization. However, few actually visit Brookwood after hearing accounts of it being haunted. Stories abound of people hearing strange sounds coming from its many tombs, along with visual sightings of spirits and ghosts, shapeless mists and shapes looming over graves. Police field countless and relentless reports of grotesque rituals and pagan worship conducted by chanting and black-robed figures, particularly on unholy days celebrated by devil-worshippers. Others claim to hear the screams and sobs of mothers and their babies that emanate from within the overgrown trees and foliage surrounding the many paths and trails through the cemetery.

Not surprisingly, Brookwood is often compared to the Bonaventure Cemetery in Savannah, Georgia, reputed to be America's most haunted, and the setting of John Berendt's 1994 novel, *Midnight in the Garden of Good and Evil*.

The few books written about Brookwood rarely fail to mention some of its most notorious inhabitants, such as Robert Knox, the Scottish Doctor who, when bodies for his practical medical dissections became scarce, resorted to the use of body-snatchers who stole them from graves; and who allegedly later aligned himself with William Burke and William Hare who became famous for not waiting for the victims to die of natural causes before supplying them to the good doctor.

Others mention Styllou Christofi who in 1954 became the last woman in the UK to be executed despite the fact that she spoke not a word of English and was obviously insane.

The cries of Edith Thomason, executed for murder despite conclusive evidence of her innocence and the pleas of millions who called for her exoneration, are also often mentioned in the books on Brookwood.

For those who want to experience the eeriness of Brookwood, but may not be inclined or brave enough to actually visit there, the London Dungeon, on London's South Bank, close to the London Eye, provides a vicarious experience for its paying guests. Among other horrors, it includes a funeral party at a replica of the Brookwood Cemetery Station, with cakes and ham sandwiches thrown in for good measure as they await an account of 1,000 years of London's dark history.

Judy sat back in her seat as she closed the Brookwood Guide as the train approached the St. Johns Station. She looked out the window for any sign of the whispering vines, gray mist, gravesite images, or monuments of the cemetery that loomed some three hundred yards in the distance.

Locating her position on the guidebook map, she traced out the path to the Edgeware Mausoleum and family plot which Jake had so kindly highlighted for her.

She looked at her watch. She would have a full hour to experience Brookwood before finding her way to Arthur's gravesite.

CHAPTER TWENTY-THREE

*J*udy sat on a bench next to the entrance to Brookwood, took off her heels, and extracted a pair of tennis shoes from her bag. She then slipped them on while studying a map from the clerk's guide. She calculated that if she walked briskly, she could navigate most of the paths within the cemetery and arrive at the Edgeware Mausoleum within the hour.

Passing the Remembrance Gardens and lake on her right, she proceeded down the path of St. Barnabas past the first group of Redwood trees, and took a quick photo of the water features. Ignoring the many side paths through the forest on her left, she passed the path of St. Phillips until she reached the T-junction with the path of St. Cyprian's.

Following that path she turned right on the Path of St. David, and stopped to admire the elegant but crumbling Columbarium holding in its cavities the urns of hundreds of cremated remains. Fifty yards further through the Redwoods, she came across the crumbling gothic memorial to the Bent family. She would have entered this stately miniature cathedral, but its gates were locked tight.

She had better luck at the St. Edward Brotherhood Orthodox Church another twenty-five yards down the lane. There she was able to enter and marvel at the artistry of the interior before exiting and continuing her trek down the Path of St. David's. As she stopped to read the memorial engravings on the stately mausoleums that lined the path, each one of which told a story, she realized that an hour was not nearly enough time to gaze upon and appreciate these cathedrals of death. Nor did it give her sufficient time to take in the picturesque woodlands, vistas, and heartland trails that weaved through the 200 acres that encompassed the Necropolis. She resolved to return some day and give this garden of remembrance the attention it deserved.

Aside from the magnificent but crumbling crypts, vaults, Gothic revival chambers, charmel houses, and tombs that lined the pathways, what amazed Judy the most was the Victorian arboretum with its impressive range of California Redwoods and Wellingtonias.

Realizing that she had only fifteen minutes in which to arrive at the Edgeware Mausoleum, she quickened her pace toward the plot that Jake had marked for her on the Clarke map. Thus far, she had come across only a single other visitor along the paths, an elderly woman, head covered with a shawl, pushing a two-wheeled walker.

Now as she approached the plot she began to hear voices of children. Soon a contingent of uniformed boys from Coldbridge School for Boys came into view, followed by a hand-pulled cart containing a casket and a somber procession of adult men and women in appropriate funereal attire. Slipping in behind this entourage at a distance of about twenty-five yards, she followed it to the Edgeware family plot.

The Edgeware Mausoleum was a granite edifice built in the style of the Parthenon in Athens. Four white Doric columns supported the frontage of the structure, within which was a heavy iron gate. The whiteness of the granite and columns stood in contrast to the gray and weathered exteriors of the tombs nearby, suggesting that the Edgeware Parthenon had been well maintained and perhaps recently sandblasted to maintain its original character and tone.

Judy quietly dipped behind a Redwood to change back into her black heels, and lowered her black fedora to hide her face as much as possible. She then approached and joined the funeral party.

Mingling, and trying to find a position in the party in which she could see most of the others, she scanned their faces— hoping that the favor would not be returned. She saw Muriel and Samantha standing together near the uniformed little boys who she assumed were Arthur's Latin and Greek students who had been granted permission by Coldbridge to attend the funeral of their beloved schoolmaster. When Muriel caught her eye, Judy shook her head slightly to indicate that, as agreed, they would not acknowledge each other at the funeral.

Nearest to the cart holding the coffin, Judy saw a man in his forties standing next to an attractive young woman in her early twenties, and assumed, based on the description Jake had provided her, that they were Chester Edgeware and his wife Madeleine. Judy did not recognize anyone else, but assumed that, other than friends of the Edgewares, most of those in the party were Arthur's friends and fellow instructors at Coldbridge.

Judy was sure that Jake was present, but could not immediately pick him out of the entourage numbering about twenty-five to thirty adults, not counting the thirteen or so boys. Presumably, he had positioned himself to take photographs of as many of those in the funeral party as he could without being observed doing so.

Looking at the Mausoleum, and judging its interior size, Judy guessed that it was high enough to accommodate as many as eight coffins within sarcophagi stacked one upon another on each side of an aisle, for a total of sixteen in the edifice.

The Anglican priest, arrayed in full ornamental attire of alb, chasuble, and stole, looked disapprovingly at the coterie of boys who were whispering among themselves. He waited until they were silent, and then initiated the Burial Rite from the *Book of Common Prayer,* reading first the Resurrection Prayer, followed by the Twenty-Third Psalm and the Serenity Prayer.

When the Priest had finished, he motioned for the Brookwood Funeral Attendants to unlock the Iron Gate to the Mausoleum. He then gestured to Chester and a man whom Judy could not identify, but guessed it might be Lord Edgeware's

Conservator, James Holliston, to draw the cart into the interior of the tomb. From the angle in which she was standing, Judy could see that an apparatus consisting of crane, winch, and tackle had been pre-assembled in the interior to lift the coffin to a sarcophagus on the fifth tier.

There was a long silence as a crew of four workers, who had been waiting a discreet fifty feet or so from the funeral party, were summoned to enter the tomb, hoist and insert the coffin into the waiting sarcophagus, and finally to seal and tighten it with all manner of rivets, screws, and bolts.

Members of the funeral party slowly maneuvered to get a view into the interior of the tomb to watch this task being accomplished before their eyes. The operation took over an hour, and not all in the party, including the schoolboys, stayed to see it completed. Chester and Madeleine Edgeware were among those who left after less than ten minutes.

With the funeral party thus thinned, Judy finally identified Jake, who was sporting a goatee and heavy glasses. As previously agreed, they did not acknowledge each other and each left the Edgeware plot by separate paths.

Judy took a different path back to St. John's Station. She was tempted to stay and use the rest of the afternoon to explore the parts of Brookwood she not yet experienced, but decided she needed to get back home as soon as possible to engage with Jake about where she should go from here in her quest to find Arthur's killer.

As Judy settled back in her window seat on the return to Waterloo, a single thought predominated in her mind: the key, and indeed the only key to finding Arthur's killer would be to find which of the sons was truly first-born. She was now convinced that greed, money—an unbelievable amount of it, enough to satisfy anyone's desires—was the true motive. She could see no other.

It also was becoming clear to her that the only proof of which brother was first-born would be found somewhere on the body of Arthur Edgeware. She tried to put herself in the shoes of

Lord Edgeware. It now made perfect sense to her that he would never have left to chance the means to satisfy himself, without any doubt, which of his sons was first-born. What better way to insure this than to have the doctor make some indelible mark on the first-born—a mark of which neither son would ever be aware except when the father was prepared to reveal the truth for his own purposes?

Judy's thoughts now turned to what she had observed at the burial site. Some way, somehow, she had to find a way to convince a court to order Arthur's exhumation. Obviously she would need more than Muriel's recollection of Arthur's recollection of what his father had told him when he seven years old.

She would need more.

Much more.

CHAPTER TWENTY-FOUR

*M*uriel answered her mobile after the first ring. "Hello."

"Muriel?" Judy asked.

"Yes Ma'am."

"How are you?"

"It was hard. The funeral I mean…to think he's there… in that…I still just can't believe that all this is…"

"You've been very brave up until now, Muriel, and I will need you to keep being brave as we try to find the one who did this."

"Are they going to arrest me now?"

"I don't know, Muriel, but I do think it's time that I meet with the Thames Valley Police."

"You'll be my lawyer, then?"

"Muriel, we talked about this. At this point, I don't think I should represent you in that capacity. For one thing, I think I know the police well enough by now to know that they are always wary of a suspect's lawyer. They assume, rightfully of course, that any competent lawyer will always put their client's interest first even if the lawyer thinks their client is guilty."

"Do you think I'm guilty, Ma'am?"

"No, I don't. I wouldn't have offered to help you if I did, but I do think I'll have a better chance of finding your husband's killer if I have a free hand to go where the evidence leads me without worrying about whether any evidence I find will hurt or help you in a court of law."

"So if you found such evidence, you would report it to the police?"

"Let's be very clear about this, Muriel. The answer to that question is yes, I would. If I can convince the police that I'm willing to work with them in finding Arthur's killer, and not against them, I'll have a better chance of gaining their cooperation—at least that's what I'm hoping."

"And if you don't get their cooperation, would you represent me then?"

"No, and let me tell you why. You do need representation at this point, as I believe the police will very soon be asking you to come to the station and answer questions while under caution."

"But I've already talked to the police."

"That was at the school under very informal circumstances. At that point, I believe you were only a person of interest, and the police were simply responding to a request from the French Gendarmes to contact you and confirm your presence in Carcassonne with Arthur at or about the time of his murder."

"They told me that I didn't have to say anything."

"I'm sure that was only out of an abundance of caution, in case you did say anything to incriminate yourself, but they obviously did not believe that they had enough evidence to arrest you or they would have. Even if they did have enough evidence at that time, it was not clear that any crime you might have committed was within the jurisdiction of the UK."

"And now?"

"Now, the police know that you bought Ambien at the pharmacy in St. Johns, and that Ambien was found in a bottle of Robitussin at the crime scene in Carcassonne. If the Thames Valley Police can connect your purchase of Ambien in St. Johns to the murder in France, they may be able to establish that the UK has jurisdiction to indict you for murder."

Muriel now broke into tears. "Oh my God! They really can arrest me then? They can try me for murder here in the UK?"

Judy waited for Muriel's sobs to subside, and then said, "Muriel, it's important that you focus now. Please listen to me."

"Yes Ma'am, what do you want me to do?"

"For now, just listen. I have to be honest with you. The fact that you were married to Arthur at the time of Lord Edgeware's death, and then kept your marriage to Arthur a secret, gives you a powerful motive. You understand that, don't you?"

"Because if Arthur inherited from his father, I would then inherit from Arthur."

"Yes."

"But Arthur wasn't the first-born...he wouldn't inherit..."

"We don't know that for sure, Muriel. That is the problem, and that's the problem the police will surely have as well. You told me that Arthur told you that."

"Yes, he told me that his father instructed the doctor to place a mark on the first-born."

"So you understand, then..."

When Muriel did not immediately respond, Judy said, "The only way that the identity of the first born son can be confirmed is if Arthur's body can be examined."

"You mean...you mean..."

"Exhumation, yes. I believe that's the only way the identity of the first-born can be confirmed."

"Oh, no. I could never agree to that."

"I understand, and that's precisely why I can't represent you, Muriel. If I were ever able to obtain a court order to exhume your husband, and a mark was found, it would greatly harm your defense. That is why as your lawyer I would never pursue that course."

"But if a mark was found, I might inherit from Arthur's estate?"

"There's no guarantee of that either. First of all it is doubtful that I could even get a court order for exhumation without some kind of authenticated document confirming that Lord Edgeware did indeed authorize the delivering doctor to make such a mark on the first-born."

"But if such a letter were found, and such a mark were also found on Arthur, I would then inherit?"

"Probably, yes. So you can see why as your lawyer, I would never advise you to either seek to find such a letter, or to have your husband's body examined. And I certainly wouldn't advise you to admit to the police what Arthur told you about Lord Edgeware instructing the delivering doctor to make such a mark on the first-born."

There was a long pause before Muriel finally said, "Then what is it that you want me to do?"

"I want you to give me an instruction, here and now. I may also ask you to confirm that instruction in writing. If you wish to retain me for the sole purpose of finding your husband's killer, even my attempt to do so may harm your case in court if the police charge you with murder, I will do everything in my power to find the killer. Because I believe Lord Edgeware's inheritance is the key to finding that killer, I would then meet with the police and tell them about what you told me about Edgeware's directive to the delivering doctor. I would also seek to find documentary evidence of that directive, and petition the appropriate court to authorize your husband's body to be exhumed."

"And if I do not retain you for the sole purpose of finding Arthur's killer?"

"Then you and I will part ways, Muriel. However, I will consider all the information you have given me about what Arthur told you to be confidential, and will not divulge anything you have told me to the police."

"And you would leave me without legal representation?"

"Not at all. I would refer you to an excellent solicitor, Peter Mayfield, to represent you if the police arrest you or ask you to go to the station to make a formal statement; or, you would be free to seek a solicitor of your own choosing."

"And if I do retain you for the sole purpose of finding Arthur's killer, I would then be left without legal representation?"

"Not at all. Indeed, I would insist that you have the best legal representation. Again, I could refer you to Peter Mayfield, or you could retain your own solicitor. Regardless of whether you retain me for the sole purpose of finding Arthur's killer, you will need a solicitor by your side when the police call you for further formal questioning."

"You couldn't be there when I'm questioned?"

"No, that wouldn't be appropriate, nor would the police permit me to be present if I'm not representing you."

"I see."

"Perhaps you should take some time to think about it."

"No. I want you to find who killed Arthur. Nothing else matters. Do whatever you need to do."

"Perhaps you should talk it over with Samantha."

"No, I want you to do whatever you have to do to find Arthur's killer."

"You understand that if I ever find evidence that convinces me that you have been hiding anything…"

"I understand…but you won't. I had nothing to do with Arthur's death. I loved him."

"I believe you. Very well, if you're sure, and understand fully that I do not represent you in any legal capacity. If anything I represent Arthur."

"I understand."

"I think you should contact a solicitor right away. Would you like me to text you Peter Mayfield's number, or would you like to contact a solicitor on your own."

"No, please send me his number. I'll contact him."

"I'll also fax you a letter to sign in which you retain me solely as an investigator to find Arthur's killer, and acknowledge that I do not represent you in any legal capacity. You're still living at Samantha's, right?"

"Yes, though I still feel bad about imposing on her."

"She's the kind of friend you need right now, and from talking to Samantha, I gather she is most willing to help. Do you know if she has a fax?"

"Yes, I think I saw one in her downstairs office."

"All right, text me her fax number, and contact Peter right away. As soon as this is done, I plan to visit the Thames Valley Police. I'll keep you posted."

"Thank you so much, Ma'am. If I ever do come into money, I want to pay you."

"Don't worry about that. Bye for now."

CHAPTER TWENTY-FIVE

*A*fter tightly shutting the window divider between the front and back seat of the taxi, Judy settled back and called Jake on her mobile.

"You rang M 'Lady?'"

"Hi Jake. It's me. Sorry we didn't get a chance to hook up at the funeral, but..."

"It was better that way. Best not to advertise our connections at this point."

"You pretty much had me fooled with your pince-nez and goatee. I suppose everyone who saw you assumed that you were a friend of another branch of the family and friends. Were you able to get pictures of everyone?"

"Most of them, yes...not of the schoolboys of course. I doubt if you'll need to track any of them down. I'm having my digital pictures developed into hard copies, and will hand carry them to you. Until we get a more secure line between your mobile and my new office here in Knightsbridge, I thought it better not to send them to your mobile."

"I'm not sure we're quite ready for that degree of cloak and dagger, but that's fine. Let me know when you're ready to bring them. How many of them could you identify?

"Chester and Madeleine Edgeware, of course...Muriel and Samantha, based on your descriptions, though I will need those more than you...a man I assumed to be James Holliston, though that was somewhat of a guess...a couple of younger men who looked like schoolmasters , probably friends of Arthur..."

"Any 'suspicious characters' as they say in the crime novel potboilers?"

"Not really, but you can judge for yourself when you look at the pictures."

"You're pretty sure that no one could have seen you taking the pictures."

"Oh, yes. The camera is the size of a pin imbedded on a button, and I snap the pictures with a small clicker in my shoe."

"Amazing. All right, I take it you got pictures of, and a good look at the Edgeware Parthenon…were you able to get a shot of the interior at all while they were hoisting the coffin?"

"From several different angles, yes, but having to take the shots from the outside I wasn't able to get a full frontal shot. There was no way for me to get entry into the interior itself, of course, at least not in a way that would be inconspicuous."

"How about the lock mechanism on the iron gate doors to the interior?"

"Yes, I did get some close-ups of that, though you haven't really explained why I needed those."

"Jake, I've come to the conclusion that the key to solving this murder is to discover which of the two Edgeware sons was in fact the first-born. My experience is that in such matters, the truth ultimately comes out one way or another."

"…and what does that have to do with the Parthenon lock?"

Judy explained in further detail what Arthur had told Muriel about his father's instructions to the delivering doctor to mark the first-born.

"That seems like a rather thin reed upon which to…"

"Thin or not, it sounds not only credible to me, but rational and predictable that Lord Edgeware would have taken such a precaution to insure that he would know the truth, should he later find it suited his purpose to either reveal it, or to conceal it."

"Since the Lord fell into senility long before he had reason to…"

"Here's the thing, Jake," said Judy interrupting. "We have to remember how much money is at stake here. Of course I could be wrong, but someone—whether its Chester, his wife, the Conservator who has a reputation at stake, or even Arthur, and now of course Muriel herself—has a motive to either find or hide any evidence that might prove who was first born."

"So you're saying that such evidence may currently be found on the body of Arthur?"

"That's what I'm saying, Jake…and if I'm barking up the wrong tree, so be it. The great thing about Timothy's legacy to me and Amber is that we can afford to bark up the wrong tree and still have the resources left to bark up another tree."

"Have you consulted with Amber on this matter?"

"Yes, though not yet in detail. It is true that Amber and I have somewhat different agendas as to how to employ our joint legacy, but out of both mutual respect and respect for our godfather, we long ago agreed and resolved to support each other's decisions on a 50/50 financial basis, no questions asked."

"Do I hear an instruction coming on how to use the resources at your disposal in this matter?"

"Yes, and it is simply this. I want the Edgeware Mausoleum watched for any attempt to remove Arthur's body from his sarcophagus."

"Watched, 24/7? Really? For how long?"

"For as long as it takes me to compile evidence sufficient to convince a court to order a supervised exhumation."

"What kind of court are we talking about?"

"I don't know yet. It could be in Probate Court when it comes time to probate Lord Edgeware's will, or in any UK court hearing a request from the French Police or government to extradite Muriel to France or, God forbid, in the Crown Court hearing a prosecution against Muriel Wright for Murder in the First Degree."

"Whoa…Judy…that's not the kind of assignment for which I'm likely to find many qualified and reliable applicants, although I suppose for the right remuneration…"

"I know it could be expensive. I don't think it would be necessary to have it watched 24/7. Aside from that being impractical, I don't think it would be necessary. I don't see anyone trying to break into the Mausoleum during the daylight hours when the grave robbers would be easily observed by cemetery visitors or staff. I think surveillance from dusk until dawn would be sufficient. That could be done, couldn't it?"

"I suppose anything can be done for the right remuneration. Of course, we couldn't have any observer simply take a position in front of the tomb and watch it all night— that would be too conspicuous. He'd have to make a number of inconspicuous circuits of the area around the tomb, perhaps in different dress on different nights. Also, we'd probably have to use several different watchers as well to reduce the chance that any particular watcher might be identified. I'd also have to check the Brookwood rules to see if there are visiting hours, and if so, how and if they are enforced."

"Great. I'll leave all the details to you. Now, about the lock on the front gate. Can you tell from the pictures how secure it is?"

"I can check that out from the pictures and let you know. I'm not a lock expert, but it looked solid to me…but even if it isn't, we can't very well replace it without breaking the current lock. Maybe we could just secure an additional lock."

"No, you're right. Anything we did to increase the security of the doors would alert and bring unwanted attention from whoever might want to remove Arthur's body. Of course, the more secure the lock, the longer the time one of our roving watchers would have to catch them in the act."

"We should probably leave it, Judy. Anything else you want me to do?"

"If possible, try to track down the names of all those whose pictures you took at the funeral and whom you couldn't identify. I want to have those pictures, as well as the names that go with them, when I go to Carcassonne. I want to conduct my own examination of the crime scene in room 213 at the Hotel

Ville Fortifiée. By now that room should have been released by the Gendarmes. I also want to talk to any of the staff or guests who were staying at the hotel on the morning of the murder."

"You are going alone?"

"Yes, but I need you to be available by phone 24/7. I'd like to take Muriel with me, but that would risk her arrest by the French Police if she sets foot in France."

"When are you going?"

"I need to conduct a few more interviews before I go. In fact, I'm on my way now to the Thames Valley Police Station. I have an appointment in an hour with..." Judy checked her notes..."with a DI Stone and a DS Graham."

"You really think they'll give you any information about the case?"

I'm hoping they might cooperate with me if I can convince them I don't represent Muriel in a legal capacity, but only as an investigator she retained to find Arthur's murderer."

"Good luck. Anything else you want me to do?"

"I'd really like to track down the hospital where Chester and Arthur were delivered."

"Done. I already have that information for you—hold on while I check my notes—the twins were delivered at a luxurious private clinic called Ashland Maternity, located outside Oxford in Oxfordshire. Private patients pay 48k to have their babies delivered there. It was 34k back when the twins were born. A consultant obstetrician, gynecologist, and physiotherapist are on site 24/7. All mothers are provided a private ensuite, including big screen televisions, toiletries, dressing gowns, and slippers. All meals are cooked to order by a team of ten gourmet chefs."

"Wow."

"It's billed as providing expectant mothers with 'flexibility and control over their pregnancy', and a 'truly individual experience'...the 'it' girl from China, Li Ma is quoted as saying that the birth of her child there was 'the most marvelous experience in childbirth that any mother could ever have'…the clinic was featured on the BBC show 'Five Star Babies' as the 'ultimate maternal experience.'"

"No wonder it costs 60k American."

"Let's see…it's run now by a Doctor Elisa Hart, an obstetrician, who also happens to be a Duchess of Brent."

"Enough. Send me the address. Have you also found the doctor and nurse who delivered the twins?"

"Yes, I've tracked down the name of the doctor… Jeremiah Jones…obstetrician…retired from Ashland Maternity about sixteen years ago."

"Jeremiah Jones? Really? Sounds like a fictional character."

"Oh, he's real enough…or was."

"Is he still alive, and if so have you found an address or telephone number?"

"I've been scouring the database on deaths, but haven't found anything yet, so I assume he's still living. I called the Ashland Clinic to see if they had any information on him or where he lives, but they didn't. I'll keep looking for an address."

"And the nurse?"

"Yep, got a name for her as well—Heidi Wentworth. She actually still works there as a nurse."

"Great work, Jake. Fax me everything you've got—or, better, just bring it all with you when you come to give me the photographs."

"Right. Anything else?"

"None that I can think of…just get me those funeral pictures, sign up the tomb watchers as soon as you can and keep looking for the whereabouts of this Doctor Jones. I think I'm just coming up to the Thames Valley Police Station, so I'll sign off."

"Bye, Judy. Good luck at the Police Station."

CHAPTER TWENTY-SIX

"*T*he station is just down on the corner, Miss."

Judy paid the driver and headed toward the Thames Valley Police Station.

"I have an appointment with DI Stone and DS Graham," Judy announced at the police reception desk.

Asked to take a seat, Judy sat and reviewed the notes she had made of how she might best direct the interview; or more likely, how she might allow herself to be directed.

It was twenty minutes before she was shown down the hall to DI Stone's office. The door was open, and Judy tapped on the open door. DS Graham was seated across from a middle-aged male plain-clothes detective with a shock of unkempt hair.

"Come in," Stone said amiably. "You are Ms. Alexander I take it?"

"Yes, detective."

"Please come in."

Judy smiled and entered.

"I am Detective Inspector Stone, and this is Detective Sergeant Graham."

DS Graham smiled, but did not rise. "Please have a seat, Ms. Alexander."

Judy took a seat and placed her brief case down beside her. "Thank you for seeing me."

"Now, how can we help you?" asked Stone. "I must say it isn't every day that we have the pleasure of being visited by a London barrister."

"Actually, I'm not here in that capacity, detective."

"…solicitors yes, quite often." Stone turned to Graham. "This is our first visit from a barrister, wouldn't you say, Sergeant?"

"Yes, sir," replied Graham compliantly.

"Now, you were saying, Ms. Alexander…"

"I am a barrister, yes, from the Quadrangle in London, but I am not here today as anyone's legal representative."

Stone looked down at some notes. "I have a message here that you wanted to meet with us on behalf of Ms. Muriel Wright."

"In a way, that is correct, detective, but not as Ms. Wright's legal representative."

"Then I'm confused. Perhaps you could enlighten us."

"I understand that Ms. Wright is currently suspected of a murder that occurred in Carcassonne, France, several weeks ago."

Judy paused for several moments, but getting no reaction, continued, "She has retained me for the sole purpose of finding out who killed her husband, Arthur Edgeware, of St. Johns in Sussex."

At this, Stone and Graham exchanged puzzled glances.

After several moments of silence, Graham finally said, "May I ask how you came across the information that at the time of Arthur Edgeware's death…"

Graham turned to Stone, who glanced at a file and said, "…that would be March 29 of this year…"

Graham continued, "…that Muriel Wright and Arthur Edgeware were in fact husband and wife."

Judy replied without hesitation, "Very simply, detectives. Muriel Wright told me."

Stone picked up a file and thumbed through several pages. "I find that very interesting, Ms. Alexander, because on March 31 we had occasion to visit Muriel Wright at her residence at…"

"Brianhurst School," Judy said helpfully. "She's a teacher in residence there."

"Yes, at Brianhurst School. We spoke with her…" Stone flipped another page in his file. "…we spoke with her at or around 10:30 AM on Saturday April 1. At that time, she advised us that she had indeed left Reading with Arthur Edgeware on Friday, March 24…that she had arrived in Carcassonne on Sunday, March 26, and left Carcassonne in the early morning of Wednesday, March 29, and arrived in Reading on Friday, March 31."

"Yes," said Judy, consulting her own notes, "where her friend Samantha picked her up and then dropped her off later that afternoon at Brianhurst. You and Sergeant Graham visited her the next day, Saturday, April 1 at Brianhurst."

Stone now fixed his gaze at Judy and with a frown intoned, "At which interview she never happened to mention that she was in fact Arthur Edgeware's wife."

Judy sighed. "Yes, that was a mistake on her part, and I have told her so, but keep in mind that she had no idea at that time, at least not when you initiated the interview, that she might be suspected of Arthur's murder, or even that Arthur had in fact been murdered. The only reason she had kept her marriage a secret was that she was afraid that she would lose her job at Brianhurst if it became known since she had been hired as an unmarried instructor in residence."

So far, Judy was pleased with the way the interview was going. She had already engaged the investigating officers, perhaps without them fully realizing it.

Detective Stone now turned to his Sergeant with a look of what appeared to Judy to be a look of displeasure. Stone had previously heaped high praise on his Sergeant for discovering that Muriel had a possible strong motive for killing Arthur. As Arthur's wife at the time of Lord Edgeware's death, Muriel stood to inherit a substantial fortune. A jury might see Muriel's failure to disclose this critical fact during her interview as a strike against her in evaluating her credibility if she took the witness box to testify in her own behalf. The fact that Muriel might now have a perfectly understandable, if not entirely honest, reason for keeping her marriage secret would detract considerably from the force of prosecution evidence that she kept her marriage a secret for so long.

Judy now realized that neither detective was yet aware of the terms of Lord Edgeware's will in which he left his entire estate to the first-born son. The detectives had simply assumed that the sons would inherit equally. Judy now saw that she might ingratiate herself with the detectives by giving them information about which they did not yet appear to be aware. In return, they might trade information with her.

"Inspector Stone, are you aware of the terms of Lord Edgeware's will?"

Sergeant Graham cleared her throat and began to say something before Stone cut her off. "No, Miss Alexander... we are just now in the process of preparing a subpoena to obtain that information from whoever is to be the executor of Lord Edgeware's estate...are you saying you are aware of the provisions of that will?"

"I do have such information from a source which I believe to be reliable, though I have not yet seen the will itself."

"I don't suppose you would be willing to give us what information you have."

"I could do that, yes. I'm sure you understand that if I were representing Muriel Wright in a legal capacity, it would not be proper for me to provide you with information that might harm my client's defense, but if you are willing to work and engage with me in my capacity as one who has been retained by Muriel Wright for the sole purpose of finding the real killer of Arthur Edgeware, I believe we can help each other. I'm assuming, of course, that you want to find the true killer, and are not bent, at this stage of your investigation, on excluding from your inquiries any others to whom more evidence might point."

Inspector Stone sat back in his chair and considered for some moments before saying, "Miss Alexander, I wonder if you might excuse us for a few minutes while I have a word with my sergeant?"

Judy picked up her briefcase and rose from her chair. "Of course, Inspector. I shall go powder my nose while you consider my proposal."

"Give us twenty minutes?"

"Of course." Judy left.

"Close the door, Sergeant."

"What do you think?" Stone asked after Graham closed the door and lowered the shades.

"I don't know, sir. It's highly irregular. How do we know we can trust her? I mean how do we know she isn't really acting for Muriel in some kind of legal capacity? She is a barrister, after all. Since when do barristers spend their time engaging in investigations as she claims she is doing? And how can our supposedly penniless Muriel afford her? There are plenty of private investigators out there, not to mention solicitors. Perhaps we should ask the Chief Inspector what he thinks."

"Oh no, I think not. That would just get us embroiled in a lot of red tape."

"So what are you thinking, boss?"

"I don't see how it would hurt to engage with her. She seems to have sources of information that go beyond simply what Muriel Wright has supposedly told her."

"Should we contact the Quadrangle chambers and check on her? I do know a couple of solicitors who refer cases to that chambers."

"No, let's see what information we can get out of her for now—the kind of information she'd never give us if she's actually representing Muriel Wright in a legal capacity."

Graham knew her boss only too well, and wanted to insure that he didn't have an alternative motive in wanting to work with Judy. "Sir…she's very good looking, isn't she."

"Really, Sergeant? I hadn't noticed…and thank you very much for not…"

"Sorry, sir. Just asking. So…"

"Well don't, and get her back in here. Let's see what she's got."

"Are you going to tell her about Muriel's Ambien purchase in St. John's, and the Ambien found in the Robitussin bottle at the crime scene?"

"Not yet."

"If Muriel does retain counsel, you'd have to fork over that information in any case."

"Yes, but not at this early stage of our inquiries. In the meantime, we need to see what information she has that can help us. Go out and get her Sergeant."

Moments later Graham returned with Judy.

"All right, Ms. Alexander, I think we'd be willing to trade some information with you, on a proportional basis, if you get my drift."

"I think I do, Inspector, yes."

"So for starters, how do you know the contents of Lord Edgeware's will?"

Judy held out the palms of her hand. "Muriel told me."

"And how did she know?"

"Arthur told her."

"So your information is basically double hearsay, then?"

"Not entirely. I have my own independent sources of information."

"Which are…"

"I believe you mentioned proportionality, Inspector?"

"All right…so that's it, then. That is all you can give us now…how you got information about the will, but you can't tell us what's in it. I don't know that's particularly helpful if you can't tell us what's in the will."

"Actually I can. In due course, I know you will find this out yourself, but I can give you now some important details about Lord Edgeware's will."

"Go on…"

"Lord Edgeware left his entire state to his first-born son."

"Who is…?"

"That's the question inspector, but I can tell you how I think we can find out."

"I'm all ears."

"Arthur and his brother Chester are fraternal twins, born fifty-seven seconds apart. I believe that Lord Edgeware instructed the delivering doctor to make a permanent mark, visible only under ultraviolet light, upon the body of the first born son."

"What kind of mark?" asked Graham trying not to gasp in amazement.

"Proportionality, Sergeant…but I can tell you that it is possible to examine the body of at least one of the sons in order to search for that indelible mark."

Both detectives waited for Judy to finish her sentence.

"…and that body was just buried in a Mausoleum at Brookwood Cemetery. I can also tell you that I believe that the key to finding Arthur Edgeware's murderer lies in finding which brother is the first-born."

CHAPTER TWENTY-SEVEN

Braxton Thomas tapped lightly on Judy's Quadrangle office door.

"Door's open," said Judy as she continued poring over the file which Jake had hand-carried to her flat earlier that morning.

Braxton entered looking a bit on the sheepish side.

"I've missed you the last couple of days," he said. "Been busy on a case?"

Judy quickly put aside the file and smiled. "Oh, Braxton, hi...yes...sorry. I guess you could say that. Just not a case that came from Archie...wait, I take that back. It is a case that Archie referred me to...indirectly."

"Care to talk about it?"

"Let's just say that it turns out the case is not ready for prime time."

"Meaning?"

"There have been no criminal charges yet filed against the person with whom Archie indirectly put me in contact, so at this point I'm just doing some preliminary investigation to help me decide whether or not to take this person on as a client."

"So...so far no actual client."

"That's right. No actual client yet, and there may not be."

"Which investigator are you using?"

"I have my own investigator."

"Oh, yes. You mentioned something about having your own investigator on call...very mysterious."

Judy laughed. "Nothing mysterious I assure you. Just someone I've used in past cases and whom I trust."

"I take it that this potential client didn't come through Mayfield, but directly through Archie."

"Yes. Archie didn't much like it, but as you know I am on the Direct Access list."

"I knew that, but can't imagine why you'd want to be."

Judy got up, approached Braxton, and with a broad smile adjusted his collar. "Sweetie, I'm sorry I've been a bit incommunicado of late. How about this. Give me a week—I don't think much longer than that—to do my own thing investigating what the police have against this potential client, if charges are ultimately filed against her."

"Oh, it's a her, is it?"

"Yes, darling it's a her. Now listen. If charges are ultimately filed against her, I may ask you to defend her. You have so much more experience in serious cases."

"So a Crown Court case, then?"

"It could be, yes."

"Maybe you could sit second chair."

"No. Remember our agreement—we keep our private lives and professional lives separate."

"Well, then, maybe the CPS might ask for me to prosecute."

"That would be something. God, I hope you'd refuse the case."

"You and I going head to head in the Crown Court. Hmmmm. You'd have to get a waiver from your client—conflict of interest and all that—but at this point I'm not sure I'd know enough about who this mysterious potential client even is to refuse it if you can't tell me more about it."

"Give me a week."

"Sure, whatever you say."

"Wanna take me to lunch?"

"An hour?"

"Give me two hours. We'll make it a late lunch. I've got some calls to make."

"Right. I'll come by at two. The Monkey is ok?"

"Fine, come back at two."

Judy waved as Braxton left.

Judy called Peter Mayfield.

"Hi Peter, Judy Alexander."

"Hi Judy. I've been in touch with Archie. I'm hoping you could take on an assault and burglary case."

"I told Archie I'd be out of commission for a week or so, and to hold off for a while."

"Yes, I wasn't sure what was up with that."

"I've been working with a Muriel Wright. I was just wondering if Muriel Wright called you."

"Ah yes, she did, and said you referred her to me."

"Did she say whether the Thames Valley Police had called her in for a formal interview?"

"Yep, tomorrow as a matter of fact."

"I assume she filled you in on the details of her situation."

"Yes, unbelievable. I feel for her. "

"So you'll represent her—be there when they interview her?"

"Yes, I'll be there. She says she retained you for the sole purpose of tracking down her husband's killer."

"That's correct."

"I assume you'll fill me in on what you find out."

"Absolutely. Let me know how the interview goes. You're representing her now, but just to let you know, I met with the Thames Valley Police and assured them that Muriel would cooperate in any way she could. It would help me to find Edgeware's killer if she didn't hold anything back. I've told her that if she does, she and I will have to part ways. Of course, as her legal counsel you've got to look at her case from a different angle. I assume she told you about keeping secret her marriage to Arthur Edgeware."

"She did. She knows it doesn't look good—gives her such a huge motive—though she had an innocent reason for hiding it."

"So she says, and I'm willing to take her at her word for now. Has she also filled you in on what Arthur told her about Lord Edgeware's will—his instructions to the delivering doctor—the mark on the first-born?"

"Oh yes, pretty thin evidence...but yes, she filled me in on all that."

"The eclipse tattoo?"

"Oh yeah. That's really a long shot as an avenue to pursue. Sounds crazy, to be honest. I certainly wouldn't have the wherewithal to pursue it."

"Peter, let me handle that angle and also pay your fee. I've basically taken a leave of absence from the Quadrangle, though I might need your assistance if it ever comes down to having to file a petition for exhumation."

"Whoa! Are you serious? Exhumation, really?"

"I don't yet have enough evidence to justify filing such a petition, but would like to know that you'd be on board if I do."

"If it would help my client, and you'd take care of the expense, but I can't commit to that right now."

"Understood. I'm working now on tracking down the doctor who delivered the Edgeware twins—if he's still alive and still living in Britain—which he may not. I want to see what he has to say. If he denies receiving any such instructions from Lord Edgeware, I know I'd probably have to drop the whole idea."

"Well, good luck."

"You'll let me know how the interview goes."

"I will. Talk soon."

Judy hung up and immediately called Jake.

"Hi Jake...me again. Thanks for bringing over those pictures this morning"

"See any faces of interest though there's several I didn't recognize?"

"Not really, though I didn't expect to. Have you been able to line up watchers for the Edgeware tomb?"

"I've lined up a couple. None of those working here in my office or at NXR are willing to do it. Don't blame them, but I've contacted several outside agencies. I screened out all but the most reputable candidates for such a job, and of course the most reputable ones want to know why they're being asked to roam about a creepy cemetery at all hours of the night."

"As long as you're satisfied they're reputable, go ahead and increase the fee you offer, but only tell them the least they need to know."

"OK, Judy. It's your money."

"How about tracking down Doctor…Jeremiah Jones… sorry just sounds like a funny name for a doctor."

"You called at just the right time. Just got a lead from one of my most reliable stalwarts out at NXR. The good doctor is definitely alive and kicking. My man says he's tracked him down to a seaside town in—you won't believe this—Wales."

"Wales? Well that shoots down my theory about the doc living it up in the Riviera on Lord Edgeware's bribe money."

"Oh, some of the locals I've hired here tell me you can live quite regally in many places in Wales—if you have the money. Not every millionaire wants to leave the good old UK and be an expat abroad."

"No address yet, though?"

"He thinks he'll have one within the next couple of hours. How soon can you get out there?

"I'll see what I can work out. Maybe Braxton could take me. He feels like I've been ignoring him lately, and I guess I have. How long does it take to drive out there?"

"Three or four hours. You'd probably want to go by car rather than train and have to mess with getting a car or taxi once you get to Wales.

"I'll ask Braxton if he can drive me. Otherwise I'll rent a car."

"I'm sure you'll love Wales."

"I can't tell if you're being sarcastic."

"Have you ever been there?"

"No, haven't had a chance, but I'd like to."

"Well, being a newcomer to the UK, I knew that after I told you that Doctor Jones lives in Wales, you'd probably want to go out there and interview him, so I had Smithy—he's one of the locals I just hired in my office here—he's from Wales and says that before you go you should be prepared for some antipathy between the Welsh and the English."

"How so?"

"He gave me some clippings. Here's one from the Sunday *Times*, which described the Welsh as 'loquacious, dissemblers, immoral liars, stunted, bigoted, dark, ugly, pugnacious little trolls'."

"Oh wow. I think I like them already."

"Here's another from the *Evening Standard:* 'The Welsh have never made any significant contribution to any branch of knowledge, culture, or entertainment...' No wonder that in 2000 the National Assembly of Wales called for an end to the 'persistent anti-Welsh racism' in the UK media."

"I can see why."

Smithy told me he considers the ultimate put-down of the Welsh a line from the British play *A Man for All Seasons* which later became a Hollywood blockbuster movie which won the 1966 Academy Award for Best Picture. In the play, based on the actual trial of Sir Thomas More in 1535, Henry VIII had initiated a treason trial against More for refusing to acknowledge him as the Supreme Head of the Church of England—you know, so he could get an annulment from Queen Katherine and marry Anne Boleyn."

Judy looked at her watch and realized that Braxton would be coming in a few minutes to take her to lunch.

"Jake, is this going to take long? I need to get going."

"During the trial," Jake continued, eager to show off to his boss how much he had educated himself on British history since arriving in the UK at Judy's behest, "Henry's prosecutors trotted out a parade of witnesses prepared to perjure themselves in return for bribes and favors from the king. One of the witnesses, a down and out duke of some sort, had been promised a prefecture in Wales in return for perjured testimony which would insure More's conviction for treason. As the witness left the courtroom, More cried out in a booming voice for all to hear, 'I can understand you, sir, for selling your soul to the devil...but for *Wales?*"

"Okay. I get it. No love lost. Tell your Smithy I sympathize with him, and I will keep all that in mind when I head out to Wales. I'm sure I can handle it."

"I'm sure you can."

"By the way, was Thomas More convicted?"

"Oh yes. The jury came back in twelve minutes flat. The sentence was—here, the article Smithy gave me cites the actual trial transcript: 'To be drawn on a hurdle through the City of London to Tyburn, there to be hanged until he should be half dead; then he should be cut down alive, his privy parts cut off, his belly ripped, his bowels burnt, his four quarters spit up over four gates of the City and his head upon London Bridge...'"

"Enough!" cried Judy. "Sorry I asked."

Braxton tapped on the door and peeked in. "You okay? Ready for lunch?"

Judy held up her hand, and signed off. "Bye, Jake. Call me the moment you get that address." She turned to Braxton.

"Sweetie, change of plans. How would you like to drive me to Wales?"

CHAPTER
TWENTY-EIGHT

"**W**ales? Why on earth would you want to go to Wales, Meow?" Braxton asked.

Judy folded her arms. "There's a witness there I need to talk to."

"You mean on this non-case of yours, with a potential client, whom you may or may not represent, depending on whether charges are ever lodged, and only if…"

"…you don't have to take me. I can rent a car."

Braxton sighed in resignation. "So it's Wales or nothing for this weekend, then?"

"I'm afraid so. Take it or leave it."

"Well I guess I'd better take it, or I might not see you again for who knows how long."

Judy smiled, batted her eyes, kissed Braxton on the cheek, and said in a high-pitched mock southern American accent, "Why yes, my darling Brett, I'd be so grateful if you'd accompany little ole' me."

Braxton looked both ways down the hallway and tried to return the kiss.

Judy backed away. "Not here, sweetie. But we'll probably have to stay overnight somewhere in the wilds of Wales."

"Damn you drive a hard bargain. Okay, when do we need to leave?"

Judy looked at her watch. "How does ten minutes sound?"

"Ten minutes?"

"Unless you've got something better to do this weekend. I want to get there before dark if possible."

"I did have an appointment with a solicitor this afternoon, but I can re-schedule for Monday. Will we be back by Sunday night?"

"Yes, we should. I need to be back by then as well. If we can get there tonight, my interview shouldn't last more than an hour if I can meet this person tomorrow morning. That will give us the rest of the day on Saturday to see the sights of Wales, and we can drive back at our leisure on Sunday."

"Do you need to go back to your flat to pack for overnight?"

"Nope. I happen to have an overnight bag in my office for just such contingencies. And you?"

"I'll have to stop at my flat on the way—won't take more than a few minutes. Why don't we go to the garage now, get my Spitfire and we'll drive to my flat, if you can wait in the car for me—there's no parking there."

"That's fine. While I'm waiting I'll get the address we're going to."

"You don't have it yet?"

"I will by the time you get back with your bag…I hope… if not I'll have it before we get out of London."

Thirty minutes later, Judy called Jake as she sat in the car waiting for Braxton to get his overnight bag.

"Jake, do you have the address of Doctor Jones?"

"Hold on…just came up a few minutes ago, so your timing is great. Here it is. Ready?"

"Yep. Go ahead."

"It's 16 Brigffordd Lane, County of Gynedd. About eight miles north of the Village of Porthmadog, about two miles off the A-487. Porthmadog is one of the top resort destinations in Wales. Should I repeat that? "

"Uh-oh. You'd better spell those names out for me if I'm going to be able to use my GPS."

Jake spelled out each of the names on the address.

"Got it. Anything you can tell me about the house?"

"Oh, it more than a house, Judy. It's a palatial estate, complete with stables, indoor pool, seven bedrooms—it's a manor house."

"I get it—the closest place in Wales to the Riviera—sounds like he lives like a Duke. I guess obstetricians make a good income in the UK."

"Generally, no, but like you said…"

"Uh-huh."

"I can't guarantee he'll be there when you arrive—hope you're not going on a wild goose chase."

"I didn't want to call ahead and alert him that I was coming. It would give him too much time to prepare himself for how to react when he's suddenly confronted about his delivery of the Edgeware twins. I hope to ask him about that when he least expects it."

"I supposed that's why you didn't send me or one of my minions out to interview him."

"You got it."

"I'll never forget how Timothy cited Aristotle to you when he explained why he chose you to find his daughter: 'Beauty is a better recommendation than any letter of introduction'."

"That was some years ago, Jake, so I'm not counting on that."

"If anyone can get anything out of this guy…"

"Okay, Jake. Get back to work on lining up the tomb watchers. I just hope we're not too late. Also, see if you can conjure up the address of Madeleine and Chester Edgeware. I'd like to talk to them as soon as I can."

"Good idea— to get the measure of them."

"Precisely."

"Do you plan to just drop in on them too and surprise them?"

"No, that's a different situation. I think it would be better if you called them on my behalf and made an appointment, if you can. Just be up front, tell them you're my secretary—that

I'm a friend of Muriel's and that she has retained me to find her husband's killer. That should arouse their curiosity if nothing else."

"Your secretary, huh? Okay, will do. When will you be back?"

"I think they live in Surrey, near St. John's—near Brookwood, in fact. It may be possible for me to stop by and see them on my way back to London."

"So set up a time for you to visit...when, then?"

"Sunday if possible. I'll have to convince Braxton to either let me off there or wait for me while I visit the Edgewares. If you can't arrange for me to see them on Sunday, as soon thereafter as you can."

"Anything else?"

"I need to get to Carcassonne as soon as possible to check out the crime scene and interview any witnesses who may have been there on the night that Arthur was killed. Make a reservation for me at the Hotel Ville Fortifiée."

"For what nights?"

"Hmmm. Depends on how soon I can visit the Edgewares. Go ahead and make a reservation for Tuesday and Wednesday. That will give me time to prepare for that trip—and get me as much information as you can about Carcassonne."

"Do you want me to line up the G-500?"

"No, I'd rather go like any other tourist, so just get me a train ticket leaving next Tuesday morning from St. Pancras. I'll follow Muriel's steps as much as I can, except I won't stay overnight in Paris unless that's the only way to get to the Hotel Ville by Tuesday evening."

"Shall I get a return ticket as well?"

"No. I don't know how long I'll be there...oh, I have to sign off, Braxton's here. I'll call you back later."

Braxton threw his bag in the boot and took the driver's seat. "Okay, where to?"

Judy activated the GPS. "First, get on the A-4, and I'll guide you after we're on it. We're going to a village called Porthmadog. Have you heard of it?"

"Rings a bell. A resort town, right?"

"Yes, apparently. I'll see if I can make a reservation at a hotel there. We can have a nice dinner in town tonight. It's not high season yet, so that shouldn't be a problem, and then we can get an early start tomorrow morning to find the man I want to interview. He lives about eight miles from Porthmadog."

"Does this person know you're coming?"

"Nope. It could be a wild goose chase."

"Great. That will give us more time together."

"Brax," said Judy after they were on the A-4, "I have a favor to ask you."

"Of course."

"I know you're probably curious about who I'm going to interview, and why."

"Not really. I'm thinking more about our dinner and time together this evening."

"I'm thinking of that too, but not sure I buy that you're not curious about my mission here."

"You'll tell me when you're ready, and I'm good with that."

"Thanks. So when we go tomorrow, I'm going to ask you to stay in the car while I go up and try to engage this Doctor Jones—if he's even at home, that is."

"Agreed, no problem. So now, what hotel have you found in Porthmadog?"

Judy scrolled down the Porthmadog website on her iPhone. "Wow! They've got a number of four and five star hotels. Very reasonable rates too. Here's one, the Maelgwyn House, five star—looks like a beautiful castle on a hill overlooking the village—only 185 pounds."

"It's the low season, and it's still Wales of course."

"Actually I think I'd prefer a little bed and breakfast style hotel in the middle of town—here's one, the Tudor House. Looks quaint and charming—only 119 pounds."

"Fine with me. You choose."

"I'm going with the Tudor House. I'm making the reservation now."

Within the hour, the Spitfire swung into the small lot behind the Tudor House at dusk. After settling in, Judy and Braxton enjoyed a quiet candlelight dinner of Welsh rarebit, ribs, patatas bravas, and block pudding, along with a fine bottle of Welsh wine.

"I didn't know they had a wine industry in Wales," said Judy. "It's good."

Several glasses later, they retired to their bedroom on the second floor overlooking the downtown area of Porthmadog.

After rising for an early breakfast of laverbread, block pudding, smoked fish, and fried mushrooms, the two set out for 16 Brigffordd Lane. They arrived at Doctor Jones' impressive manor house at approximately 10 AM.

"All right, you'll wait here while I go see what I can do?"

"Yep, I can see you from here."

"You'll be fine?"

"Yes! Go! I have the local paper and hopefully I can get internet on my phone to amuse myself. Wave to me if for any reason you need me."

"Right," said Judy. "Wish me luck!"

"You got it."

Braxton watched as Judy approached the long pathway to the front door of the manor and rang the bell.

It was several minutes before a matronly figure answered the door. He noticed that the figure began shouting and gesticulating in frantic fashion. Concerned, he watched closely as Judy and the woman engaged in what appeared to be a heated exchange.

Judy turned away from the door and ran back toward the car.

"Quick, go back to Porthmadog! Go to the Police Station there. Now!"

"What? What happened?'

"Just go! Yesterday morning Doctor Jones went into town to meet some friends. Just as he was crossing Pennsyflag Street, a hit and run driver deliberately mowed him down in broad daylight—right there in the middle of town. He's dead!"

"What the hell!"

"I'll get the directions to the station. Just go! We've got to find out what happened!"

CHAPTER
TWENTY-NINE

As the spitfire careened down Baker Street into the middle of Porthmadog, Judy scrutinized her GPS.

"Turn left here in Pennsyflog on to High Street. The police station is six blocks down on the right! Hurry!"

Braxton stopped at a traffic light.

"Meow," Braxton pleaded. "Please! Whatever happened has already happened. I doubt if the police will give us any information anyway. Do you really want to put yourself on their radar anyway? Can we stop for a moment and talk about this?"

Judy put down her iPhone.

"You're right. I'm sorry," she said. "Let's go back to that park we just passed. I need to think about this."

Braxton resisted the inclination to make an illegal U-turn, and instead made three left turns to return to the little village park they had just passed. He found a parking place in the small park lot, and turned off the engine. He waited, as Judy got her breath.

Judy ran her hand through her hair and laid her head back on the back of her seat. Braxton waited for her to say something.

Finally, Judy said, "They know…they knew I was coming here to talk to Doctor Jones. It's my fault. They've known from the very moment I got involved in this case—from the very beginning!"

"Judy, who is 'they'? Who are you talking about? *What* are you talking about?"

Judy sighed and shook her head. "I shouldn't have involved you. This is all on me."

"Meow, please! You haven't involved me in anything. All you told me is that you wanted to interview a witness in this mystery case you're working on, and asked me to give you a ride"

"I should never have taken on this case—certainly not as an investigator—I'm a barrister. This is not what I'm trained for. I'm out of my depth."

"Well, I'm still in the dark, but I know how you solved that murder on the Concorde when you first came to the UK four years ago."

"I was an American lawyer at that time. I acted as an associate of Amber Hartman to help her solve a murder case in Houston. I wasn't acting as an investigator on my own. I got involved here in a matter I had no business getting involved in, and now a witness has been killed because of my blundering."

"First of all, we don't know that. All we know is that someone you wanted to talk to was killed in a traffic accident."

"No, the housekeeper at Doctor Jones' house said he was deliberately run down."

"She's not the police! Rumors run rampant: small towns. Even if it was a hit and run, that doesn't mean it was deliberate, and it certainly doesn't mean that there's any connection between this Doctor's death and your coming out to interview him."

Judy was silent for another five minutes before Braxton finally ventured, "Sweetie, maybe it's time you let me in on what's happening—let me help you."

Lost in thought, and locking her gaze out the window at the children playing in the park, she said pensively, "our agreement...our agreement to keep our private and professional lives separate...we've done that up to now."

"Look, the hell with our agreement. I never thought it was necessary in any case. As long as we don't represent co-defendants with different interests in the same case, there's no danger of a conflict of interest."

Judy turned to face him. "What about us ending up on opposite sides of a case, like you said."

"Okay. I shouldn't have mentioned that possibility. First of all, it wouldn't happen because I wouldn't ever take a case to represent the Crown opposite you on the defense, and second, I said that even if I did there would be no conflict if your client waived any objection."

"Our fellow barristers, they'd always be suspicious that we were acting in concert and not as independent barristers."

"Look, if we were married that might be different, but as far as our colleagues are concerned we're just casually dating."

"I think most of them know it's more than that—certainly Hodges does."

"Meow. We're not the only barristers in the Quadrangle who are dating each other. Hell, we spend most of our time in chambers with each other."

"You forget, there's only three other female barristers in the Quadrangle."

"You didn't know that Jeanette and Robertson were dating? We went to see Hamilton with them, remember?"

"They really were casual."

"We don't know that…who's to say what is casual, anyway."

"I don't know. We had our own reasons for not mixing our personal and professional lives."

"Mainly your reasons. I really didn't see a problem."

"Maybe we should think about it."

"Look, how about this. Let's forget about this silly agreement for the time being. If it ever gets to the point where our personal relationship shows signs of interfering with our professional relationship, I will leave the Quadrangle."

"I'm sure it won't come to that."

"All right. So why don't you tell me what's going on with this case you're involved in."

"Whew. Well I could certainly use some help. I've been consulting with Amber, of course, but she's so far away in Houston."

"Try me."

"First I need you to promise something."

"Anything."

"I've gotten myself in the middle of something and I think it's too far along for me to extract myself from it. I'm afraid it wouldn't be fair to drag you into at this late stage when I may have already bungled it."

"I'll be the judge of that. Now what do I have to promise?"

"Promise me that if it comes down to having to make a difficult decision as to how to proceed, you'll let me make that decision."

"It's your case. Agreed. I'm only offering to help, that's all."

"Before I give you all the details of the case, I need to explain why I need to find out the details of the death of Doctor Jones. If the police really have chalked this case up to nothing more than a negligent driver who hit Jones and then, because he was drunk or didn't have insurance, or whatever, cowardly fled the scene..."

"Then it would put your mind at rest?"

"Well, yes, it would be tragic, but there would be no reason to think it was related to my case; but if the police believe there is evidence that Jones was deliberately struck, then I need to gain access to that evidence—what was the make of the car that hit him, did any witness catch any or all the license plate numbers, did anyone get a description of the driver?"

"...and that's why you want to visit the Porthmadog Police and ask to see their report?"

"Yes, but you made a good point. If I go to the station, of course they'd want my name and what my interest in the matter was."

"...and you're concerned that you might then be putting yourself on the radar of the same person who took out Jones?"

"Exactly."

"Hmmm, I see."

"Fortunately, I have access to a source that might be able to get that same information without me having to present myself to the Porthmadog Police to get it."

"Which is…"

"I'm afraid that before I answer that question, I'm going to have to extract another promise from you."

"Well, okay…extract away."

"I have to keep that source confidential."

"Even from me?"

"Yes. I'm sorry…and please don't ask why. It's for your protection—you know, plausible deniability if it ever comes to that."

"Okayyyy, whatever you say."

"As a matter of fact, I'm going to have to ask you to honor that promise at this very moment."

"So it's Amber."

"No, it's not Amber…and I'm calling that source right now."

Judy grabbed her iPhone which she had dropped in her lap, and dialed Jake.

"Mr. X?" Judy asked as soon as Jake picked up.

"Mr. X?" Jake asked, perplexed.

"Mr. X, this is Judy. Don't talk, just listen. I'm here in Porthmadog. I came here to interview Doctor Jones. Braxton drove me here last night, and he's here in the car with me right now. We just found out that a hit-and-run driver struck and killed Doctor Jones yesterday morning.

"Holy shit!"

"Mr. X! I said don't talk…just listen."

"Okay," Jake whispered. "Sorry…but holy shit anyway."

"I think I may have gotten in over my head on this case, and I agreed to let Braxton help us."

Judy could barely hear Jake whisper, "Is that wise, Judy?"

"It's my decision, X. I'm going to fill him in on everything we know about the matter we've been working on."

Jake kept his mouth zipped.

"I'm not telling him who you are...I think its best that way, given that..."

Judy didn't complete the sentence, but continued.

"I need you to find out the circumstances of that hit-and-run...for obvious reasons. I'm not going to ask you how you plan to get that information...just get it. Now I have two questions. First, have you lined up the tomb watchers? Cough if the answer is yes."

Jake coughed.

"Now, if you've arranged for me to have a chat with Madeleine and Chester Edgeware, text me the address and the time you arranged for me to visit. If you haven't managed to make that arrangement yet, text me that as well. I'll wait, and I'll tell you when I get your text."

Judy switched to her text app.

"Okay, great...got it...tomorrow afternoon at 3 PM, and I have the address. Perfect. Now text me if you made reservations for me at the Hotel Ville Fortifiée—dates, time, the train tickets if you have them."

Judy turned to look at Braxton and held a finger to her lips as she waited for the text.

"Got it, X, thanks. Talk later."

Judy signed off and placed the iPhone back in her purse.

Braxton looked at her with a look of curiosity and said, "What on earth have you gotten yourself into?"

Judy put her hand on his, squeezed it, and said, "Braxton, love, you ain't heard the half of it!"

CHAPTER THIRTY

As the Spitfire sped down the A-4 toward St. Johns, Braxton said, "So what did Jake say about what happened with that hit-and-run back in Porthmadog?"

Judy turned to him with a look of surprise. "So you caught his name."

"Not when you were talking to him a couple of hours ago, but I heard you say his name when you were on the phone in your office."

"Okay, so his name is Jake, but that's all you need to know about him."

"That's fine...so what did he say?"

Judy turned to her text app. "It happened early yesterday morning about 6:30 AM, so there was hardly anyone about on the street at that time. The only place open at that time was a coffee shop—not Starbucks, a local shop—where, apparently, Doctor Jones was going to meet someone."

"Do the police know who he was going to meet?"

"No. The only employee in the shop, a guy named Matt Schneider, said he didn't really notice. The customer was just a man who came in a few minutes before and sat at a window table looking out—presumably just waiting for someone."

"No description, then?"

"Not much middle aged man in jeans and brown jacket."

"And what happened?"

"A brown Vauxhall Corsa—apparently the sole witness, Schneider, knew his cars."

"Not necessarily. That's one of the most common cars in the UK…and what about the customer?"

"According to Jake, the mystery customer took off as soon as Jones was hit."

"That's interesting—and what did Schneider see?"

"He said he saw this Vauxhall come down Pennsyflog at a high rate of speed and run over Jones as Jones was crossing the street to the coffee shop."

"That's it? No one else on the street saw anything?"

"That early in the morning none of the other shops are open, so apparently not. Schneider was the only witness, and even he just caught a passing glimpse of what happened."

"No license plate, no description of the driver?"

"Nope—wait a minute—there was one other witness, an elderly gentleman out taking a walk, who said he saw a car similar to the one Schneider described speeding down Baker Street before it turned down Pennsyflog, but he didn't see the hit on Jones."

"Anything else?"

"Schneider called an ambulance right away. They came and took Jones to the hospital, but he died of internal injuries about three hours later."

"The police never found the car Schneider described?"

"The police immediately put out a bulletin. They found the car in a ditch a couple of miles out of town. A preliminary examination of the car—blood all over the bonnet, paint matches to the victim—confirmed it was the murder car."

"So the police are calling it a murder?"

Judy's expression revealed her anxiety. "Just what I was afraid of…yes. The witness said the car deliberately veered over the center line to make the hit before speeding off."

"No word yet on who the car was registered to?"

"They're still checking on that, but they're assuming it was stolen earlier that morning from somewhere in the area. Obviously, an accomplice picked up the driver. It was still early in the morning, and no one's yet been found who might have seen that."

"A clean kill, as they say. Dare I ask how your Mr. X obtained this information so quickly?"

"Jake? No you may not dare."

"Amazing. I'd love to know how it's done."

"So would I. Maybe someday I'll ask him."

"Plausible deniability?"

Judy did not answer, but instead changed the subject. "We're about forty minutes from Madeline and Chester's house. Do you mind waiting for me while I meet with them?"

"I don't suppose you'd want me to come in with you?"

Judy thought for a moment. "Well…now that you're in this with me…maybe."

"It's up to you."

"I could use the support."

"I do have some experience in conducting interviews, you know."

"I know, but here's the thing. Jake set up this meeting with the Edgewares with the understanding that only I would be coming to visit. I suppose I shouldn't arrive with another person under those circumstances."

"No problem. I'll be happy to wait for you in the car."

"Thanks for understanding. We're coming up on the turn-off now."

Braxton stopped the car at a large locked iron gate that blocked access to a path leading to the Edgeware estate.

"Is this it?" he asked.

"I think so…yep, this is it. It looks like it may be a way up this driveway. Maybe you should let me drive in. It might look funny to leave the car in front of the house with a person staying in the car while I go in."

"You want me to get out here and take a walk?"

"Would you mind?"

"No, it's okay. I can use the exercise."

Braxton got out, and Judy took the driver's seat. She reached for an intercom attached to a brick column and pushed the red button. "Hello. This is Judy Alexander, here to see Lord and Lady Edgeware."

The intercom cackled, and then came a voice, "Please wait for the buzzer and the gates to open. Lord and Lady Edgeware are expecting you. They will greet you at the front door."

"Thank you." Judy waved to Braxton, put the car in gear and slowly drove up the long driveway. After several twists and turns through a forest landscape, Judy came up to a large Victorian manor house. Chester and Madeleine stood at the entrance to welcome her.

"Hello!" called Judy as she herself extracted herself from the spitfire cockpit. "I'm Judy Alexander."

Chester came down the steps and extended his hand. "Please come in. We have a low tea spread in the back if you will follow us."

Judy shook hands with Madeleine and followed the pair on a path that led to the rear of the manor.

"Please have a seat," said Madeleine as she pointed to a comfortable lounge chair on a wide patio with a fountain in the center. "Do you take sugar and cream with your tea, Ms. Alexander?"

Judy sat. "No just tea, thank you."

"Now, Ms. Alexander," said Chester as he and Madeleine sat, "your secretary said that you are a friend of Muriel Wright."

"Yes, sir…your sister-in-law as I understand it."

Judy watched Chester's expression closely as she mentioned Muriel's familial relationship to the Edgewares. She noticed only a slight grimace.

"I seem to recognize you, Ms. Alexander. Were you not at my brother Arthur's funeral last week?"

"Yes, sir. I was, as was Muriel and a friend."

"I thought so. Well, Ms. Alexander," Chester said in a broken voice, "I must confess that it is only very recently that we had any idea of Arthur's marriage to this young woman, Muriel Wright. For whatever reason, he kept that marriage a secret. Perhaps you are in a position to enlighten us?"

"Muriel has told me that it was necessary to keep secret her marriage to your brother Arthur because revealing it would have caused her dismissal as a schoolteacher at Brianhurst School for Girls."

"We were heartbroken to hear of her secret marriage," said Madeleine. "You have no idea how much pain it has caused us."

"I strongly advised against such a marriage," said Chester, interrupting his wife. "It has also caused many legal complications, especially after the passing of my great father, Lord Edgeware. The deceit, which my brother exhibited in going along with this secret marriage, has us all mystified. If Arthur and this woman were in need of financial assistance, I would have been glad to provide it."

Judy, aware of at least one falsehood in this assertion, nevertheless resisted the urge to respond in argumentative fashion, and instead changed the subject.

"Lord Edgeware…I understand that is your formal title…"

"That is correct," Madeleine chimed.

"And Madeleine is now Lady Edgeware," said Chester. "Now, how can we help you? We are told that you are a barrister… and an American."

"Yes, sir."

"Extraordinary," Chester replied. "I have never heard of an American barrister practicing in the courts of the UK."

"Yes, Lord Edgeware. I understand there are not very many of us. However, I have not come as a legal representative for Muriel Wright. Rather, I have come to let you know that Muriel has retained me for the sole purpose of finding the true killer of your brother Arthur."

"The true killer? Ms. Alexander, surely you know that it is Muriel herself who is suspected of this killing, and forgive me for asking, but if Arthur and this woman were so destitute that they could not afford to live without her income as a schoolteacher, how could she possibly afford to retain your services for such a task—and would she not have been better off to hire a seasoned investigator?"

"Sir, I have frequently taken cases on a pro bono basis where I think there is a risk of injustice, and in this case I was asked by a friend of Muriel's, Samantha Sterling, to assist Ms. Wright."

"I find all this very curious, Ms. Alexander. I have heard of this other woman as well," Chester's voice rose. "I can assure you that there is very little chance of injustice in this case, unless the case against this young woman is not pursued because of some misguided sympathy for her, or some political or legal technicality."

"You are convinced of her guilt, then?"

"Of course I am convinced of her guilt! As a barrister, surely you must see that. The evidence against her is overwhelming!"

"There is circumstantial evidence, yes sir."

"It is more than circumstantial!"

"I take it that you have been in touch with the Thames Valley Police, then."

"Ms. Alexander, I do not wish to be rude, but I think it entirely inappropriate to talk of any contact I may or may not have had with the police. I can only tell you that if you have any doubts as to this evil woman's guilt—any doubt at all—that you yourself take it upon yourself to see the Thames Valley Police. They can tell you what you wish to know. Now, is there anything else you wanted to discuss with us?"

"Yes, sir. In the course of my inquiries, it has come to my attention that it was your father's desire that he leave his entire estate to his first-born son."

Chester's face flushed. "How dare you talk to us of such matters? And how could you possibly come across such information unless you are…"

Madeleine now looked at her husband with an iron gaze.

"Ms. Alexander, "said Chester, "I do not wish to be inhospitable, but I do think it would be best if we terminated this interview at this time. You may address any questions about my father's estate to my solicitor at the proper time." Chester rose from his chair. "Now, my wife and I have an engagement this evening for which we must get ready. Now is there anything else I can help you with?"

"No sir, "said Judy, also rising. "I thank you for seeing me."

"Before you go, Miss Alexander, I should tell you in no uncertain terms that I am my father's first born son and my solicitor has absolute proof of this, so you might tell Muriel Wright that there is no way in hell she will inherit a single penny of my father's estate!"

The gates opened as Judy exited the Edgeware manor estate. She looked both ways down the lane in front of the gates. She stopped the car, saw Braxton walking toward her in the distance, and waved.

Braxton broke into a run. Judy traded seats.

"Well, "Braxton said breathlessly, "How did it go?"

CHAPTER THIRTY-ONE

*R*andy Orbison of the Stanford Agency checked his watch. It was 3:20 AM, only four hours before his shift would end and he could go home to sleep it off.

Since the London branch of American NXR had hired him to wander the byways of Brookwood Cemetery in the dead of night to look for any suspicious grave robbers in the vicinity of the Edgeware Mausoleum, he was ready for a new assignment to operations more suitable to his skills and training.

Still, there had been compensations. He had agreed to let his boss at the Stanford Agency farm him out to this new American Agency for only one reason—a thousand dollars an hour for a twelve hour shift. For such a fee, he could buy that new Range Rover his wife had been nagging him to buy—or at least make a down payment on one. If only the kids were back in school, so he wouldn't have to worry about them keeping him up during the day when he tried to sleep after an all-nighter mingling with the ghosts of Brookwood.

He had also found the twelve-hour nightly walk to be beneficial to his health—he would brag about it to his doctor when he went in for his next physical. He estimated that he had walked over twenty miles a night after accounting for several rest stops along his chosen route around the cemetery.

Thankfully, he was in reasonably good shape. Listening to music or an audio book on his headphones had made the time pass more pleasantly, but he had taken care to keep the volume low so that he could still hear any unusual sounds that might reveal the approach of any grave robber.

His chief had not told him much about the purpose of his assignment—just that a client was involved in a probate matter in which the body of a resident in the Edgeware Mausoleum, if legally exhumed for examination, might play an important part. If it sounded a bit hokey, it was not for him to reason why—at least not when the client was willing to pay him well. It must be some probate case.

He had been warned that his assignment might carry some risk. While it was probable he would not encounter any dangerous grave robbers, neither the client nor his chief could guarantee what might happen if he did. If he encountered anyone attempting to steal a body from the Edgeware Mausoleum, he was not to confront them, but instead should call the police. If it appeared that grave robbers might accomplish their task before police arrived, he was to do what he could from a distance to scare them away with shouts and warnings.

Jake had kindly provided Randy with Judy's copy of Clarke's *London's Necropolis: a Guide to Brookwood Cemetery Guide*.

This copy had not only assisted Randy in finding the Edgeware Mausoleum on the guide's map, but also in planning his various routes around the Mausoleum. Now on the seventh day of his surveillance, Randy was familiar with seven different routes—all of which came within hearing distance, if not sight, of the Mausoleum.

On the first night of his surveillance, he had taken close measure of the Mausoleum itself. Supplied with Jake's picture of the lock on the inner Iron Gate to the entry, he had calculated how long it would take a skilled intruder to crack the lock, either by picking or breaking it with brute force.

After entering the crypt, the process of exhuming the body from the Mausoleum would be the reverse of entombing it. The robbers would need some kind of a hoist to reach the fifth level of the eight level crypt along the north side of the tomb. This would require power tools to unscrew the nuts and bolts of the outer shutter (made of marble), and then remove it. A different set of tools would then be required to remove the inner shutter made of sheet metal. Finally, they would have to remove the casket from the vault, and lower it to the floor by hoist. For ease of exit and escape from the cemetery without being seen, they would likely pry open the casket with a crow bar or chisel, jam the body in a bag that might pass for an item of cemetery or landscape maintenance, and carry it out as quickly as possible to a waiting car

Randy had calculated that a team of two or three skilled robbers could scarcely complete the entire process in less than an hour. To be on the safe side, and to increase his odds of catching any robbers in the act—for which he was promised a bonus of five thousand pounds if he did so—he decided not to let any route take him out of sight of the Mausoleum for more than a half hour—forty minutes at most.

Accordingly, he planned all seven separate routes through the maze of Brookwood pathways so that each route passed within sight of the Mausoleum at least once every half hour.

As the hour now approached 3:30 AM, Randy began to relax. Although the sun would not rise until 6 AM, there would be sufficient light by 5:30 to see any human figure rushing about in the twilight. If any robbers were going to make their move, it was likely to be within the next half hour.

With his pen-flashlight, Randy checked his location on the Clarke map. With the St. Edward Brotherhood Orthodox Church on his right and the Remembrance Gardens in clear sight down the path of St. Barnabas, he calculated that by taking the trek of St. David on his left, he would arrive within sight of the Edgeware Mausoleum within seven minutes.

Up until this moment in his twelve-hour shift, Randy had observed only five human beings. The first, at about 10 PM, had been an elderly man with a gray beard carrying a walking cane, and with whom he had a short conversation. From this short conversation, he learned that man was a war veteran who took this walk every night at the same time—both as a constitutional, and to visit his wife at her grave. It was the third time Randy had crossed paths with this fellow since he had begun his surveillance walks seven days before. He had no reason to regard him as a suspicious person.

The second person with whom he had crossed paths around midnight was a police constable. The constable's beat included a stroll through the cemetery every week to look out for such illegal activities as pot parties, or rituals of a dubious nature. When the constable had stopped to inquire about his business, Randy had satisfied him that he was taking his exercise. Randy assumed that the constable had completed his beat, for he had not seen him since.

At 1 AM, Randy had seen two heavily tattooed young men and a woman sitting under a Redwood tree exchanging reefers. He ignored them. Minding their own business and obviously not equipped to conduct an exhumation, they were not there when he went by again at 2 AM.

Just as the Mausoleum came within sight through the Redwoods, Randy heard a rustling in the underbrush. Turning, he saw the silhouettes of two figures carrying long poles and bags of equipment and making a beeline for the Mausoleum.

"Hey!" Randy shouted. "Stop!"

The pair continued running.

Randy took out his iPhone to call the police, when suddenly one of the figures, his face covered with a ski mask, suddenly turned toward Randy and pointed a handgun at him. This being more than Randy had bargained for, Randy fled.

The sound of three muffled shots from a silencer disturbed the sulky stillness of the night.

CHAPTER THIRTY-TWO

"**W**here to now, babe?"

Judy had tried to relax and shut her eyes after her unsettling conversation with Chester and Madeleine Edgeware. In response to Braxton's question, she perked up and looked at her watch.

"There's a petrol station up ahead. Can you turn off for a minute? I want to check my GPS and see how far it is to the Ashland Maternity Clinic."

"Sure. Something you want to tell me? You've been making me use protection…over my protests I might add."

"Hmmm…that would be something…but no, honey… after what's happened the last few days I want to check in with a certain nurse before something happens to her as well."

"Don't tell me…"

Judy consulted her notebook. "Heidi Wentworth, the nurse who assisted Doctor Jones in the delivery of the Edgeware twins."

"You're kidding me!"

Braxton swung the spitfire into a parking spot and turned off the engine.

"Do you think she's still working there? I mean it's been…what, how many years since then?"

"I know it's a longshot, and she's probably ready for retirement if she's still there…but according to Jake she was still on the payroll as of a couple of months ago."

"She must have been pretty young when she assisted in the delivery."

No doubt…young and impressionable… just the sort to obey orders and not to question why…or maybe she didn't think it was unusual to make some kind of weird tattoo on a newborn baby. Must have hurt, poor thing."

"Compared to circumcision, maybe not that bad. Have you ever had a tattoo?"

"You would know, darling…"

"You could have one hidden away I haven't seen."

"No I've never had one, but like you said, compared to circum…"

"Ouch! Let's change the subject. What I'm really getting at is this…based on what you've told me…I mean the only evidence you have that any baby tattooing even took place is Muriel's second hand hearsay about what Arthur said that his father may have said or implied."

"I know. That's exactly why I'd like to get confirmation from another source."

"And you really think that after all these years…"

"Like I said, it's a longshot. Now hold on while I check the GPS…okay, it's in Sussex, only forty-five minutes from here. Turn south on the A-339, and take that to the M-3. Then turn off to get on the A-33 to Farnborough. The clinic is just outside Farnborough."

Braxton turned on the engine. "Okay, I know how to get to Farnborough. Can I get some petrol first?"

The Ashland Maternity Hospital and Clinic looked more like a vast royal estate than any kind of hospital or clinic. The entry road weaved through rolling green hills before coming to a gate manned by a guard.

Judy had not anticipated this nor had she prepared a cover story to obtain entry.

Braxton rolled down the window.

"Welcome to Ashland Clinic," said the guard with a friendly voice. "Are you coming to visit a mother?"

Judy leaned over and said, "Sir, I just found out I'm pregnant. My friends have told me so much about Ashland.

We were just driving by and I was hoping I might view your facilities and perhaps talk to someone about how I might get maternity care here."

"Of course, Ma'am. Please give me your names and addresses."

Braxton and Judy gave their names and noted that the guard wrote down the license number of the Spitfire.

"You can park in the visitor's lot just off to the right. Be sure to check in."

"Thank you, sir."

There were nine or ten cars in the visitors' lot, including an assortment of Rolls Royces, Bentleys, BMWs and Porsches.

"I suppose I'm to wait here again," Braxton asked resignedly.

"Actually, it might be good if you came in with me…the expectant father…might lend some credibility to our naughty little cover story for why we're here."

"I see. A good prop, am I? Well, I do like the story— better than sitting out here in the car twiddling my thumbs."

Judy took his hand and kissed him. "Thank you."

She sat back and picked up her purse; but then paused before opening the door."

"Well, are we going in?" Braxton asked.

"I was just thinking…"

"About what you're going to say to this aging nurse who might, or might not, confirm your little tattoo theory?"

"No, I was actually thinking about the story I just told the guard. If I were to have another child, this looks like the place for a mother to be."

"Wow …really?"

"How would you feel about that?"

"I think you already know. It's always you that insists on guarding the door, not me."

"I know. I just need time."

Braxton breathed in heavily. "Time, Judy…the one thing in all of life that needs to be the most meticulously rationed.

There's only so much of it…and before you know it, we've used it all up and it's too late to get any more."

"Why Braxton…I didn't know you were such a philosopher."

He looked at her with his deep dark eyes, which now glistened.

"You're serious," she said.

"Very much so."

"Tell me…what are you really saying?"

"I'm not sure you want to hear it."

"What are you talking about?"

Braxton shook his head.

"Go on, Braxton…say it!" There was a disconcerting sharpness in her voice. "What are you talking about?"

So pressed, he risked saying, "It's your biological clock, dearest. That's what I'm saying."

Judy turned away and locked her view upon the rolling green hills on the horizon. She pursed her lips.

Finally, she said pensively, "I have several more years…"

"Sure. Plenty of time." He opened the door.

"Wait…"

He closed the door. "Yes?"

"What if I said I'd be willing to…to be a mother again?"

"In a few years, then?"

Judy shook her head. "Now."

"You mean…no more artificial barriers…no more pills?"

Judy nodded. "That's what I mean." She kissed him again, this time in a long embrace.

The attractive and smiling young receptionist gushed, "Hello, I'm Mara. Welcome to Ashland, Ms. Alexander…and is this the expectant father?"

Braxton blushed sheepishly and nodded.

"Sir," continued the receptionist, "Would you mind if I asked you to wait in our very comfortable Visitor's Lounge while I call one of our counsellors to show Ms. Alexander around our facility? It's just down the hall on the left, sir. Please feel free to partake of our excellent condiments and fine selection of coffees and tea."

Braxton nodded. "Thank you."

"Now," said the receptionist to Judy, "If you'll just wait a moment I'm calling our head counsellor to show you all that we have to offer our expectant mothers here at Ashland."

In moments, an elegant woman of about thirty wearing a white coat, black heels, and sporting fashionable dark rimmed glasses, appeared.

She held out her hand. "Welcome. I'm Julie Barnes. Ms. Alexander is it? Please follow me."

Judy followed Julie down a long skyway. They stopped at the door of a vacant room.

"Please come in. As you can see, there are skylights in every room…floor to ceiling windows, all with expansive views…sixty-six inch video screens which offer a wide variety of films or music. You can also connect this screen to your own laptop or mobile. A control panel here next to the bed controls all the window curtains, as well as your preferred temperature and humidity. An experienced obstetrician and gynecologist is on site 24/7. We also have two five-star chefs and full-time kitchen staff to serve you meals to order…either in the mother's room or the main dining room. We also have private dining rooms if you prefer."

Very impressive!"

"Now, please follow me and I will show you our theater, swimming pool, library, exercise facilities, and our main dining room—should mothers choose to take their meals with other mothers and socialize."

Next on the tour were the surgical and operating rooms. Julie pointed down another long skyway.

"This skyway leads to the doctors and nurses' offices, and also their private rooms and sleeping accommodations. As I said, there are always two doctors and six nurses on site twenty-four hours a day. In addition there are another twelve doctors and seventeen nurses on call should their assistance be required at any time."

The tour concluded with a walk around a large patio, beyond which were meticulously maintained grounds. These included a three-acre lake with ducks and a garden with paths that crossed several little stone bridges over a bubbling brook.

"Mothers can also take their meals out here on the patio when the weather permits."

"Beautiful."

"Now, is there anything else I can show you?"

"I think I've seen enough to know that I'd love to have my baby here."

"We do believe this is the finest maternity facility in the UK. Now, may I ask your approximate due date?"

"I only just found out that I am pregnant, but would like to make my plans now."

"Of course...most wise...we also offer the finest pre-natal care."

"Oh. There is one thing I wanted to ask."

"Of course."

"The friend who recommended Ashland told me she had a wonderful nurse who cared for her, but it was many years ago, so I doubt if she is still here."

"Many of our nurses serve their entire careers here. Do you have a name?"

"Yes. Let's see...it was Heidi...yes, that was it...Heidi Wentworth."

The Counsellor looked a little startled. "Why yes, we do have a woman of that name here on staff, but she's not a nurse anymore."

"Oh, maybe it's not the same woman."

"It may be the woman who nursed your friend. I know her well. I have only been at Ashland for six years, but I am told that Heidi retired from nursing some years ago. However, Ashland re-hired her as a counsellor. She is wonderful with the anxious mothers...counsels them...relieves their anxieties better than many other formally trained counsellors do. She actually lives on the premises in one of our cottages."

"Do you think I might be able to talk to her?"

"I don't see why not. Let's go back to the reception desk and see if we can find her. Of course, she might be with a mother."

"If you could check, I would love to see her. My friend would be most pleased if I did and let her know how she is doing."

Back at the reception desk, Julie asked Mara if she knew where Heidi was."

"Heidi?" said Mara. "Let me check…I think she may be in the Mother's lounge. Hold on, I'll check…yes that's where she is."

"Would you like me to take you to the Mother's Lounge?" Julie asked.

"No, you showed it to me on your tour. I can find it. Would it be all right if I went down by myself?"

"I think that would be all right. Mara?"

Mara nodded.

Julie held out her hand. "Then I shall go ahead. Please let Mara know if there's anything else you require. In the meantime I will say goodbye."

Judy walked down the corridor to the Mother's Lounge and looked in. There were several young women in the lounge, reading books or looking into their mobiles. The only older woman, who looked to be in her mid-sixties, was at a corner table talking to one of the younger women.

Judy approached the table. "Pardon me, but I was looking for a Heidi Wentworth. Do either of you know where I might find her?"

The older woman stood. "I'm Heidi Wentworth. How can I help you?"

Judy extended her hand. "Hello, my name is Judy Alexander. I just learned that I am pregnant. A friend of mine recommended Ashland so I came by to look. She also asked if

I might look up the nurse who took such good care of her when she gave birth here."

Heidi smiled. "Oh, I've taken care of so many beautiful young mothers over the years. I'm not a nurse anymore, but I guess I couldn't stay away from this wonderful place."

The younger woman at the table piped in, "Oh, yes. I don't know what we'd do without Heidi. She puts all us mothers at ease."

"Oh I'm sorry," said Judy. "I didn't mean to intrude."

"It's all right, Miss. We were just finishing up our little therapy session."

"You wouldn't mind if I stole her away for a few minutes?"

"Not at all," said the young woman, smiling.

Judy turned to Heidi. "Is there a room where we might talk in private?"

"Of course. Follow me."

Judy followed Heidi out the lounge and down an adjoining corridor to a small private room with a couch and two chairs.

"Now, tell me about your friend," said Heidi.

Suddenly, Judy realized she had not completely thought out how she would introduce herself to Heidi if she actually found her. After pausing, she realized that she probably had no choice but to be up front with her and hope Heidi would be willing to help her."

"Ms. Wentworth….I must confess to you that I have come to you for a particular reason…the friend to whom I referred has never met you, but she is in serious trouble and needs your help."

Heidi's expression now turned decidedly less amiable.

"What do you mean?"

"She's being accused of a serious crime which she did not commit."

Suddenly Heidi stood up and said, "You've come to ask about the Edgeware twins I helped deliver many years ago!"

"Well, yes…"

Heidi now looked around nervously as if someone might be spying on her.

"I've told you people before…I don't remember anything about that. I helped Doctor Jones deliver twins…that's all!"

"What people?"

"I can't talk about it…please!"

"Have other people told you not to talk about it?"

Now visibly shaken, and looking frightened, Heidi said in a hushed voice, "Please go Miss. I'm not allowed to talk about it…please understand."

Judy stood. "Of course. I'm so sorry."

Heidi opened the door and looked both ways down the hall. She then came back in the room and put her hands on Judy's hand.

"I'm so sorry, Miss. I can't talk about it…not here… please don't tell anyone you came to see me."

"I did ask Julie where you were, but only said what I first told you that a friend had asked me to look you up."

"Then maybe it's all right. You look honest, my dear. If I could talk, I would…but…but…"

Judy handed Heidi her card containing her phone number. "Okay, I'll go. I'm so sorry. If you ever feel you can talk, please call me."

Heidi took the card and put it in her pocket. "If I can… but please go now."

CHAPTER
THIRTY-THREE

*I*t was early evening when the Spitfire pulled up to the front driveway of Judy's condominium building.

Braxton asked, "Would you like me to come up for a while? It's still early."

Hold on," she replied as she flipped through the text messages on her mobile. "I don't believe it!"

"What?"

"Nurse Wentworth, the one I tried to interview this afternoon..."

"The one who said she was afraid to talk to you?"

"Yep...she just texted me and said she'll meet with me... but away from Ashland and in a private place."

"Whoa...so maybe she can give you a lead after all."

"Maybe...hold on...I'm googling up quiet little out-of-the-way pubs in or around Farnborough...here's one, the Frog and Wicket...I'll see if she can meet me there tomorrow."

"Any answer?"

"Actually, yes...she must have been watching her mobile. She can meet me at four tomorrow after her shift at Ashland."

"Great. I'm afraid I can't drive you there. I have a hearing tomorrow morning in Crown Court."

"No problem. I'll take the train and Uber it from the Farnborough Station to the pub."

"Sounds like she does want to tell you something that could be important."

"We'll see. I will let you know. I'll call you when I get back."

"So about tonight…I was thinking we might talk more about…you know, our…your maternal plans…"

Judy smiled and caressed his neck. "Sweetie, we will, I promise…but right now I'm exhausted. I'm going to go up, cuddle with Chloe, take a hot bath, and then call Jake to exchange intelligence. For one thing, I need to tell him about my short meeting with Nurse Wentworth, and that she wants to talk to me. After calling Jake I'm going to crash and get up early tomorrow morning to catch the train to Farnborough."

"Before you go, would you mind if I asked you something?"

"You got yourself into to this whole mess with me, so the least I can do is keep you informed about what I'm doing. Ask away."

"What's next on your agenda?"

"I have no hearings set for this coming week. I asked Archie to block me out."

"So…"

"I tried to set up an interview with James Holliston, the Conservator of the Senior Edgeware's estate."

"And…"

"He won't meet with me."

"Really? Did he say why?"

"I didn't get past his secretary. She only told me that it wasn't appropriate under the circumstances…whatever that means."

"You told the secretary who you were and why you wanted to meet with him?"

"Of course…I told her exactly what I was doing…that I was a barrister, but had been retained by Muriel Wright for the sole purpose of finding Arthur's killer…that I felt that his murder might have something to do with which of Lord Edgeware's sons was the first born…and that I was hoping that Mr. Holliston had any documents that might shed light on that."

"What did the secretary say?"

"Just that she would forward my request for an interview to Mr. Holliston. When I hadn't heard back from her, I called her back. She told me that Mr. Holliston didn't think an interview with me would be appropriate…and that was that."

"So what's next?"

"I think I've exhausted my avenues of inquiry here in England. As soon as I meet with Nurse Wentworth tomorrow morning, I'm coming home to pack…I'm going to Carcassonne, Braxton."

"Tomorrow?"

"That depends on what information Wentworth is willing to give me tomorrow. If she can point me in another direction here in England, I might stay to follow up before I go to Carcassonne. Otherwise…yes I'm going to Carcassonne… probably not tomorrow, but Tuesday at the latest. I need to see the crime scene and talk to whomever I can who was there the night of the murder."

"You really think you can get information from witnesses that the police over there haven't already gotten?"

When Judy paused before answering, Braxton continued.

"I get it. You can use your charms to elicit information that a bunch of hardnosed male policeman couldn't get."

Judy withdrew her hand and said sharply, "What are you saying?"

"I didn't mean…"

"I think I know what you mean, and I don't like it…and why do you think the Carcassonne Gendarme only consists of male detectives?"

Braxton realized he had stepped in it and tried to recover. "If you're really going to Carcassonne, why don't we go together? It would be a nice trip and we could have some time together."

Far from recovering, it was soon clear that he had succeeded only in getting himself deeper.

Judy opened the car door. "No, Braxton, I don't need a chaperone...look I'm tired and need to get some rest. I'll call you tomorrow."

"Wait! Please...I'm sorry...can you wait a minute?"

Judy shut the door. "Go on. What?"

Braxton slid his fingers through his hair. "Are we having our first fight? I'm sorry, okay? You need to do what you need to do. I respect that...it's just that it would be nice if we had some time together."

Judy softened. "I'd like that too. After this case is settled, we can plan something, but right now I need to focus, and I need to do this my way. Please understand."

"I do...I do."

"We'll talk tomorrow. I'll let you know when I leave for Carcassonne—probably Tuesday morning."

"I can take you to the airport."

"No, I'm taking the train. I want to retrace Muriel's steps all the way to Carcassonne."

Chastened, Braxton said, "Then I'll take you to the station. Pancras?"

"Probably...I'll let you know. Thanks."

"I'll get your bag."

As they met at the boot, he handed her the bag.

Judy said, "Thank you for taking me to Wales. If it weren't for the..."

"The murder of the witness you hoped to interview..."

"I know...so terrible."

"If it weren't for that damn iceberg, our trip on the Titanic would have been lovely."

Judy cracked a smile and gave him a peck on the cheek. "Yeah, except for that...Goodnight, Braxton."

Back in her flat, Judy was met by Chloe who purred loudly and rubbed against her ankle.

"There you are sweet puss! Did you miss me...Josephine take good care of you while I was gone?"

Chloe followed Judy in to the bedroom. Judy flung her bag on to the bed, undressed, retreated to the sanctity of her bathroom and took a long hot shower. After putting on her white towel robe, she retreated to her living room. Curling up on the sofa with Chloe, she gazed out at the lights of London below and called Amber. She could use her advice right now.

There being no answer, she called Jake.

"You rang, mistress?"

"Yeah, it's me…I just got back from Wales. Any news?"

"No more on what happened at Porthmadog…police still investigating, of course. I'll let you know if I get any more information, but it looks like your hunch about someone wanting to exhume Arthur was right."

"You caught someone trying to break into the Edgeware Mausoleum?"

"Not exactly, but we're pretty sure someone tried to."

"Who?"

"Unfortunately, we don't know…but the man I retained from the Stanford Agency definitely confronted two men carrying exhumation equipment making a beeline for the tomb."

"He got a good look, then?"

"Hardly. When our man tried to confront them, they fired shots at him."

"Oh no! Is he okay?"

"He's fine, but he definitely hightailed it out of Brookwood when he saw they had firearms and heard the shots."

"Were there any Brookwood staff around?"

"Oh no…they don't have the funds for anyone to patrol the grounds every night. They barely keep the grounds maintained as it is in the daytime."

"Did your man call the police?"

"Oh he did…after leaving the cemetery in a state of panic…and apparently a constable did get out there to check it out, but by that time our would-be grave robbers had long since left the premises."

"Was your guy sure that they were on the way to rob Arthur's grave?"

"He couldn't be absolutely sure, of course, but it sure looked like it. They were carrying scaffolding, lots of equipment and tools."

"Where was the nearest carpark for that area of the cemetery?"

"Only a hundred yards or so. We're pretty sure that's where they made their escape from."

"And they carried all their scaffolding and equipment there?

"Actually, they dropped some of the scaffolding— probably to make their way to the carpark quickly before any police arrived."

"You retrieved it?"

"The police did. I'm trying to persuade them to let me have it to see if I can track it to some rental facility or other.— though that's probably a long shot."

"Are the police really investigating the incident?"

"Not really. It's a fairly low priority for them. The only crime that was committed was discharging a firearm in a public area. There's no direct evidence that the two intended to rob a grave. Unfortunately our guy scared them away before we could catch them in the act of grave robbing, which would have been a much more serious crime."

"I see."

"Do you still want us to patrol the area around the Mausoleum? I think we can take this aborted attempt as confirmation of your suspicion that someone—very possibly the killers of Arthur Edgeware—had a motive, and now we know the means to exhume Arthur Edgeware. I'm pretty sure that the Stafford Agent won't be willing to continue with that operation— despite the exorbitant amount of money we're paying them."

"I guess we can terminate it."

"I doubt if they'd try again, knowing that someone is on to them. I'm satisfied that someone has a powerful motive to inspect Arthur Edgeware's body. Now I've just got to see what I can do to have his body exhumed by court order."

"Right. I'll tell Stafford that we won't go any further with this surveillance. Any other information for me?"

"On the way back from Porthmadog, we visited the Ashland Maternal Clinic and tracked down Nurse Wentworth."

"Wow. I thought that was a longshot too. How did it go?"

"She was scared, Jake. Didn't want to talk about what she remembered about assisting Doctor Jones with the birth of the Edgeware twins."

"So dead end anyway…"

"Actually, I got a text from Wentworth soon after we started back to London that she'd be willing to talk to me in private at a location away from Ashford. I'm going to see her tomorrow morning at a pub in Farnborough."

"Let me know what she says. In the meantime, anything more you want me to do?"

"You're still working on tearing down that file cabinet from Parkington."

"Yes, I found a warehouse to store it and found a master carpenter to dismantle it piece by piece."

"Nothing yet, but if there's something hidden in it somewhere, we'll find it. Is that it?"

"Jake, unless Nurse Wentworth tells me something earthshaking and sends me on a totally different line of inquiry, I'm going to Carcassonne on Tuesday. Were you able to get me a reservation for Muriel and Arthur's room at the Hotel Ville Fortifiée?"

"Yes, reserved it for the next two weeks since I wasn't sure what day you were going. I'll book you for the first Chunnel departure from Pancras on Tuesday morning and text it over to you within the hour."

"Great. One more thing. Between now and then I need to learn everything there is about Carcassonne—books, history, politics, anything you can get your hands on."

"I'm sure I'll find a number of books. Those would be hard to text. I'll have one of my staff put everything I find in a bag and leave it with the concierge at your condo building. You can pick it up after you return from Farnborough tomorrow"

"You're amazing. Talk soon."

CHAPTER THIRTY-FOUR

"**Y**ou didn't have to get up this early to take me to the station, but thank you."

"Happy to do it," said Braxton as he maneuvered the Spitfire around a bus in front of the entrance to St. Pancras Station. It was 5:30 in the morning.

"You're not still mad at me for not taking you with me, are you?"

"Maybe a little," said Braxton resignedly. "I understand... like the maverick cowboy in those old westerns who says to his besotted lady friend, 'I travel alone.'" He finished the sentence with an exaggerated imitation of an American western accent.

Judy hummed good-naturedly and caressed his neck. "I'm afraid that in this matter, I do need to travel alone. Thanks for understanding, but I promise I'll make it up to you. Tell you what...later this year, after this case is solved—and we will solve it—we can go on a trip together."

"To Carcassonne?"

"Maybe...if that's what you want. I'll show you all the places I scout out on this trip."

"Promise?"

"I do. Want it in writing?"

"Not necessary, but I'm absolutely going to hold you to it. I doubt if I'll want go to this Carcassonne place, though—much too medieval for me—how about the Galapagos Islands? We can watch the turtles together."

"Actually, I've always wanted to go to the Galapagos. So sure...sounds great."

"It's a date, then. You've solved a murder in Mont St. Michel; you'll soon solve this one in Carcassonne. Maybe next time in the Galapagos?"

Judy chuckled. "Maybe…"

Just then, a taxi behind them honked. The driver obviously was impatiently waiting for their juicy spot in front of the station.

"I'd better go, Brax." Judy opened her door.

"I'll find a garage to park and walk back to send you off."

"Don't be silly. I'll be in the secure departure area for the Eurostar in five minutes and you can't come in." She leaned over and kissed him. "I'll call you when I get to Carcassonne. I'm taking the 8:15 night train from Paris tonight, which arrives in Carcassonne at 7:30 tomorrow morning."

"Bye, Meow. Please be careful."

"You too." She blew a final kiss, and briskly walked into St. Pancras with her roller bag.

While she waited in the Eurostar Departure Lounge, Judy called Jake.

"Hi Judy. On your way?"

"Yep. The Chunnel train is leaving in a few minutes."

"Any news for me?"

"As I told you, Nurse Wentworth called me and agreed to meet with me."

"And…"

"She was scared to death, though she wouldn't tell me what she was scared of or who had told her not to talk about it, but she confirmed that Doc Jones did make some kind of mark on one of the twins."

"Wow! I'm impressed! So your hunch was right—a tattoo?"

"She wasn't sure exactly, and Jones didn't tell her anything."

"But she said he definitely made a mark of some kind?"

"Yep, she did."

"Did she see where Jones made the mark?"

"She thinks it was on the buttocks. From what she could see, it looked like a tiny little eclipse."

"A what?"

"Just a tiny little circle...half black, the other half white."

"Not a mark that could be mistaken for a birth mark, then?"

"Apparently not...at least she'd never seen a birth mark like it."

"Now, the $64,000.00 question: did she know which twin got the mark?"

"I'm afraid she couldn't remember. Jones didn't say anything to her except that the twins' father had asked him to make an indelible mark, visible only with some kind of special light."

"Infrared, or something?"

"She doesn't remember. He just said he had a special kind of light apparatus which he used to make the mark."

"And Jones never told her what the mark was for?"

"The only thing Jones told her was that the father wanted to be able to tell which twin was which. She knew they were identical."

"Unless we know which twin got the mark and what the mark signified, I don't see how that helps us much. We need to know, first, which twin got the mark, and second, whether the mark signified that the child who received it was first born or second born."

"You mean was the mark made on the first or second born twin?"

"Yes, but wouldn't it be more logical to mark the first born rather than second born."

Jake shrugged, though Judy could not see it. "Even if she didn't know the purpose of the mark, or significance, did she at least just happen to notice whether Jones made the mark upon the first twin to come out? The twins were born only a minute apart, and she was right there, watching. Right?"

"Yes, she says she was, but Jones only told her that the mark was to enable the father to tell which twin was which. As I said, Jones never mentioned that he was marking the first born, and of course she didn't follow the twins out to the maternity ward to see what name was attached to which baby. But yes I did ask her if she just happened to notice whether Jones made the mark on the first twin to come out."

"And…"

"She said she *thinks* Jones made the mark on the first twin to come out*.*"

"Thinks…?"

"Yes, *thinks*. I had to give her a break. It was over forty years ago, and she's assisted at hundreds of births since then."

"Not good enough, I'm afraid. So that's all we've got, then. At least you've confirmed the story that Lord Edgeware told Arthur about having a foolproof way of determining who was first born. That's something."

"I couldn't think of any other foolproof way that Lord Edgeware could know except by such a mark. Typical methods— bows, rings, and the like are never permanent, but I agree, what I've got doesn't get us very far and at least not without knowing what the mark signified, and which twin actually got the mark"

"Not enough to get an exhumation order, then."

"Probably not—well, maybe. If Muriel not only consents to the exhumation, but actively petitions for it."

"Why wouldn't she?"

"Maybe because I might decide to advise her that any exhumation might end up showing that she had a motive to kill Arthur—which the prosecution could use against her."

"What about Chester. Do you think he has any knowledge of this mark on the buttocks thing. I mean you figured it out from what Arthur told Muriel, but do you think he's figured it out too?"

"I don't know, Jake. I have no evidence that Lord Edgeware ever told Chester what he told Arthur about having the means to confirm absolutely who was his first born."

"But if Chester did know, and figured that only an indelible mark on the body of the first born twin would enable his father to confirm his first born, he might have good reason to oppose any attempt by Muriel to exhume his brother. To whom would a court give the most credence—Arthur's wife or his brother?"

"You've got me again, Jake. I just don't know. I would think that Muriel would take precedence if she files the petition. A spouse is closer kin than a brother, at least for purposes of inheritance, but exhumation is a different matter—at the very least a vigorous objection by Chester to exhumation would delay any court decision on exhumation. My guess is that any court considering an exhumation petition would want both spouse and brother to agree, especially since Muriel and Arthur were married for such a short time and in secret."

"Hmmmm…can we think of any reason why Chester might oppose exhumation?"

"Yep, a couple of billion of them."

"So you think we need more if we're ever going to get to the bottom of who is first born, and who had the motive to kill Arthur, not to mention who has the motive now to get rid of Arthur's body so that it can never be legally exhumed for examination."

"That's why I'm going to Carcassonne, Jake."

"One final thing bothers me, Judy. I think we've figured out that Lord Edgeware actually wanted to keep his options open. He wanted to be able, at the appropriate time, to 'prove' who was first born. He wanted to be able to prove it either way, which is why Chester told Arthur that he suspected that their father kept two sets of letters. Somewhere, there has to be something—a document, a letter, anything—*something* that proves absolutely who was first born."

"I agree Jake. I take it you are still working on that wooden file cabinet."

"Yes, but ever so delicately. We're slicing off wood with a razor blade. It takes time."

Just then, the loudspeaker crackled "Eurostar 741 to Paris now boarding on track fourteen. All passengers proceed with ticket and passport to the departure gate."

"Gotta go, Jake. I'll call you when I get a chance—and by the way, thanks for all the material on Carcassonne. I look forward to reading it on the way.

"Have a good trip. Bye for now, Judy."

CHAPTER THIRTY-FIVE

*J*udy was one of the first to board the Eurostar and took one of the four open seats around a table. While she waited for more passengers to take their seats, she took from her briefcase the file containing the pictures that Jake had taken of the members of the funeral party at Arthur's funeral.

Jake had been unable to identify the pictures of five men in the party, and had marked them with an "X." When Judy had shown these pictures to Muriel, she too had not been able to identify any of the faces marked with an X. Now as Judy again scrutinized these five faces, it occurred to her that at least three of them could have disguised their faces. Two of them in particular had ample beards that could have been fake.

Despite the early hour of the morning, Judy decided to call Muriel before incoming passengers joined her at the table.

"Muriel?"

Muriel sounded woozy. "Hello?"

"Muriel, this is Judy. I hope I'm not calling too early."

"Oh, hello Judy. It's okay. I was about to get up."

"I just wanted to let you know that I'm on my way to Carcassonne."

"Oh, you're finally going! Wonderful! Will you be looking for anything in particular?"

"I want to visit the scene of the murder. I'm booked in your room at the Hotel Ville Fortifée."

"Oh."

"If I am able, I want to talk to anyone who was present on that evening."

"You have the French police reports?"

Judy hesitated to answer. Jake had been able to obtain a copy, and had forwarded it to her, but Judy wasn't sure if she should confide this fact to Muriel.

"Muriel, the Thames Valley police told me what evidence the French Gendarmes sent them, but I need to see what witnesses I can find myself. Potential witnesses don't always come forward voluntarily to give statements to the police—for a variety of reasons."

"Like what?"

"Maybe they don't want to become involved, or they're undocumented and don't want to get on the police radar, or…"

"Yes, yes, I see. Well, I hope you find a witness who can help me. I really do. I wasn't even there at the Hotel Ville Fortifée when the police were called. The French police have never even heard my side of the story."

"Normally, I'd advise anyone in your circumstances to turn themselves in to the police as soon as possible and give them a statement, but in your case I couldn't suggest that you return to France because of the risk that you'd be immediately detained. However, I'm not sure that I gave you the best advice. The police often form impressions based on their first interviews at the scene, especially if the person whom they deduce is a prime suspect has already left the scene, and in your case, left the country. It's unfortunate that you never found out what happened to Arthur until you arrived back in England."

"I was so shocked when the police came to Brianhurst and told me."

"I know. I can hardly imagine. Listen, the train's about to leave St. Pancras and a couple of passengers look like they may sit at my table, so I need to ask you a question before they do."

"Yes?"

"Remember those pictures I showed you of those who attended Arthur's funeral?"

"Yes. Samantha and I identified most of them, but there were a few neither Samantha nor I could recognize."

That's what I'm calling about. I was just looking at the five faces that neither you, Samantha, nor my investigator could attach a name to."

"Yes?"

"As I'm looking at those pictures again, it occurred to me that several of them could be wearing disguises."

"Like what?"

"Beards, sunglasses, hat over the eyes…"

"You want me to take another look, then? Is there a particular person you had in mind that I might recognize if he wasn't wearing a disguise?"

Judy laid out her briefcase on the table and spread out her files in hopes that this would discourage any last minute passenger boarding the train from sitting down next to her. Fortunately it worked, as the train was less than half-full and she had already sat in the prime window seat.

"As a matter of fact, I do. Is there any chance that any of those pictures could be of your ex-husband in disguise?"

Muriel gasped. "Oh my God! You mean Norman! You think he could have been there? Why would he ever…I can't believe…"

"I know it's unlikely, but I need to be sure. One thing I plan to do when I get to Carcassonne is show these pictures to anyone who was there on the night of the murder. If your ex was at the funeral—well, murderers have been known to attend the funerals of their victims."

"I don't know, Judy. I mean Norman was a despicable human being who abused me horribly, but murdering my husband?"

"Jealousy is a powerful motive, Muriel."

"I'm sure Norman didn't even know I was married."

"Apparently almost no one did, but that doesn't mean he wouldn't have been jealous all the same—you know, travelling with another man, whether you were married to him or not, on an overnight trip."

"But if he was that jealous, why not murder me?"

"Who knows? By murdering Arthur, he might believe he's killing two birds with one stone—getting rid of a rival, and getting rid of you by framing you for Arthur's murder.

"It's true, Norman almost killed me once—threw me against the wall one time so hard it knocked me unconscious and sent me to the hospital."

"So he is capable of something like this."

Muriel blew a deep breath. "Whew. Yes, I do think he's capable of it."

"Even if he killed Arthur it doesn't mean he would have attended his funeral, though. If I send these pictures to your mobile, could you take another look?"

"Yes, but I'm sure I would have recognized him even with a fake beard."

"All right, but I'd still appreciate it if you could take a final look. If I'm going to show a picture of Norman to any witnesses I find in Carcassonne, I'd like to show a picture of him in disguise since he may have been using the same disguise that he would have worn at the Hotel Ville Fortifée on the night of the murder."

"I'll look, Judy, and let you know."

"Of course, I'd also like a picture of Norman without a disguise as well. Do you have a picture of Norman?"

Muriel paused before saying, "I think I threw out all my pictures of him after I was divorced. Let me think...I believe I may have kept one picture of Norman and me together with Samantha when we were at school. I think I kept it because it was a good picture of Samantha and me."

"All right. See if you can find it and send it to me on your mobile."

"Sure. I'll look in my things right away."

"That would help. Muriel, here's the thing. If, God forbid, either a British or French Court ends up prosecuting you for this murder..."

Muriel let out a low groan.

"…I hope not, but *if* they prosecute, we have to be prepared. Our best defense may be to show that someone other than you had a better motive, means, and opportunity to carry out such a dreadful crime. It could raise a reasonable doubt if we do that. "

"Like who…I mean other than Norman?"

Judy considered telling Muriel that her list of potential suspects included:

1) Chester Edgeware, whose inheritance would be ensured if Arthur were out of the way;

2) Lady Madeleine Edgeware, whose gold-digging tendencies may have led her to undertake extreme measures to preserve her marriage, wealth, and status—though almost certainly through the offices of a hired killer, and who may have acted alone or in connivance with her husband;

3) James Holliston, whose professional reputation, livelihood, and perhaps even personal liberty would be at stake if convicted of the forgery of legal documents or letters—though this motive alone seemed somewhat less than the other suspects;

4) Doctor Jeremiah Jones, who though he was deceased, may have received bribes or other incentives to falsify medical reports, and who until his death had both a reputation and wealth to protect;

5) Nurse Wentworth, who Judy was not sure had told her the entire truth about her part in whatever happened while she was present during the birth of the Edgeware twins, and who may only have confided out of extreme fear;

6) Norman Yates, for the reasons that Judy had just explained to Muriel; and

7) Unknown persons, who may have had some stake in the outcome of the Edgeware inheritance. This would include those whose expectation of largess may have depended on which twin inherited from Lord Edgeware.

Instead of informing Muriel of her list of suspects, Judy said, "Muriel, I will keep you apprised of what evidence I discover in Carcassonne. You retained me to find who killed your husband, and that's what I'm going to do. Send me the picture of Norman Yates as soon as you can. I'm sending my pictures to you now."

Judy signed off.

As the Eurostar left St. Pancras, she returned her file of pictures to her briefcase, and extracted her Carcassonne Tourist Brochure and two books on the history of Carcassonne.

CHAPTER THIRTY-SIX

As the Eurostar entered the Chunnel, Judy sat on the bar stool in the lounge and sipped on a Cappuccino.

She felt strongly that her visit to Carcassonne would be the key to finding the person who had murdered Arthur Edgeware. She was hopeful that someone who was present or near the scene of the crime when the murder occurred would know something that had thus far eluded the French police. She also realized that without some knowledge of the history of Carcassonne she would not be able to navigate the maze of byways in the ancient city that might lead her to such a witness.

Having less than twenty-four hours in which to immerse herself in that critical history—and even that number of hours depended upon her allowing herself only a few hours of sleep on the night train to Carcassonne—she opened the book which Jake had recommended that she read first as an initial introduction. Its title was *Carcassonne: a Romantic History of the Legends of Medieval Carcassonne.*

Perusing the table of contents, her eye was drawn to the chapter entitled "How a Heroine and a Pig Saved the Sacred City of Carcassonne." Intrigued, she flipped the pages to this chapter, which told the following story:

It was the year 758. A young Charlemagne, acting to prove his worth to his father, Pepin the Short, had led an army that besieged the City of Carcassonne, a fortified City nestled at the strategic crossroads between present day France and Spain.

For five long years, the City, had withstood the siege because of the fierce defense mounted by Lady Carcas, the wife of Bulcak, the reigning Prince of Carcassonne. When Bulcak proved ineffective in marshaling the City's inhabitants to resist, Lady Carcas stepped forward to inspire the City's citizens to fight to the death in defense of their beloved City.

After assuming command from her ineffective, vacillating, and faint-hearted husband, the first strategy Lady Carcas employed was to deceive the besiegers into believing that she had far more defenders than she actually had. She did this by ordering the construction of hundreds of dummy figures made of straw. She then had all the figures dressed in armor and placed all along the City's high ramparts. From behind these figures, she had crossbows fired at the besiegers. This fooled Charlemagne, the future Holy Roman Emperor, into believing that a frontal assault would be too costly in men and material.

Instead, Charlemagne settled in for siege, expecting that the City's inhabitants would soon run out of food and capitulate without a fight.

Lady Carcas ordered strict rationing of the food supplies available in the City. When the inhabitants had consumed most of the limited number of livestock within the walls, men, women, and children were reduced to scavenging for rats, and eating straw. In order to camouflage the skeletal states of her dwindling defenders, she ordered all her citizens to wear thick clothes stuffed with straw to give the appearance of robustness when they manned the ramparts.

After five long years of privation and starvation, Lady Carcas realized that the City could not hold out much longer. She began to abandon all hope of saving the City.

However, she also realized that the besieging army too was suffering from lack of food and supplies. For five long years that besieging army had laid waste the fields and countryside for food, but now there was no agricultural produce or livestock to be had for a radius of fifty miles. She could see that many of the besieging soldiers were also on the verge of starvation, and that some were even deserting. The young Charlemagne was on the verge of reporting to his father that his mission to conquer Carcassonne had failed.

It was at this critical juncture that Lady Carcas called upon the City Fathers to provide her with a complete inventory of all available foodstock in the city. The depressing tally was that a single half-starved pig and one sack of grain remained to feed the inhabitants of the City.

Upon hearing this, Lady Carcas retired in anguish to her chambers. By the next morning, she had decided upon her next course of action. She once again summoned the town fathers who expected that she would announce a capitulation. To their dismay and shock, however, she announced no such surrender. Instead, she decreed that there would be a celebration of feasting on the following day, and that all citizens would be required to attend. She also ordered that the last sack of grain be sewed into the belly of the pig.

Shocked by this decree, the City Fathers protested, arguing that a single pig and one sack of grain would never be sufficient to feed all the inhabitants even on a day of rationing and privation, much less on a day of feasting.

It was only when she explained her plan that the Fathers carried out her decree. On the appointed feasting day, every starving citizen in the City manned the ramparts alongside the armored dummy warriors. Using their last reservoirs of strength, they waved banners and flags and let out shouts and hoops of joy and celebration on this their day of feasting. Seeing so many of the soldiers below them looking so desperate and forlorn, they followed up the shouts of joy with expressions of heart-felt sympathy for their distress.

"You look so hungry and in such distress!" they cried. "Even though you are besieging us, we cannot bear to see you in such a state. It is only right that we should share our bounty with you."

As Charlemagne's soldiers looked on in amazement, Lady Carcas ordered that the pig, whose belly she had filled with the last remaining sack of grain, be thrown off the ramparts to the starving soldiers below.

As the pig bounced off the walls on the way to the ground, its belly ripped open, showering the starving soldiers with the precious grain.

Like a ravenous pack of wolves, the soldiers below attacked the bounty, scraping and licking the grain from the ground and in a frenzy tore off pieces of the pig's flesh to take to their fires for cooking.

That evening, a terrible realization came upon Charlemagne's men. Somehow, someway, the citizens of Carcassonne had so much food stored within their City that, even after five years, they could afford to share their bounty with their enemy.

The next morning, Charlemagne's demoralized soldiers demanded that they give up the siege. A courageous woman had defeated

Charlemagne, the future Holy Roman Emperor. He reluctantly agreed to give up the siege.

As the citizens of Carcassonne saw their hated enemy army retreat, all the bells in the City rang out, and the citizens shouted *"Carcas sonne"*— meaning, "Carcas is ringing!"

Judy smiled as she read this wonderful tale of the courageous Princess who defied Charlemagne and saved her city. She wondered if it was true, or just a legend. She put aside the book for a moment and opened the most recent edition of the Carcassonne Tourist Brochure. On the cover of the magazine was a picture of the Narbonne Gate to Carcassonne. In front of the Gate was a magnificent five-meter high-carved stone bust of...Lady Carcas.

CHAPTER
THIRTY-SEVEN

Shortly after Judy finished reading the Carcassonne Tourist Brochure from cover to cover, the Eurostar arrived at Gare du Nord in Paris. Gathering her briefcase and roller bag, she quickly departed the train and walked directly to the front entrance. From there she took a cab to the Paris Austerlitz Station. As she still had several hours to kill before boarding the night train to Carcassonne, she found a Starbucks and nestled into second floor table overlooking the Quaid'Austerlitz below. She ordered a cappuccino and a petit pain, slowly opened *A Short History of Carcassonne*, and began to read.

Engrossed in the introductory chapter, Judy did not particularly notice the man seated at the table next to her. He was a distinguished looking man in his mid to late forties with a wide bohemian beard with soul patch, eloquently dressed in a business suit, smart jacket, and an understated bow tie. He reminded some people of the visage of Johnny Depp.

"Pardon, Madame," he ventured in French. "Are you by any chance waiting for the 8:17 night train to Carcassonne?"

Judy looked up, and attempted to answer in French, but with an accent and hesitancy that instantly gave away her status as a foreigner. "How did you know?"

Reverting to crisp and almost fluent English, the man said with a flirtatious twinkle, "I saw your books, Madame."

Judy was used to being approached by men in public places, and had long learned the art of gentle rebuff. Nevertheless, his interest in her books intrigued her, and he seemed genuine and presentable enough.

"I suppose my accent gave me away," she said.

"Not at all, Madame, and you must forgive me for assuming that you were French, but your face most reminded me of Marianne."

With the flirtation now underway, Judy considered professing ignorance of who Marianne was, thereby giving him the opening to elaborate on the compliment. In fact, Judy knew very well that since the French Revolution Marianne had become the beautiful and iconic symbol of France, personified in recent years by the images of Catherine Deneuve and Sophie Marceau. Instead, she attempted to shut it down by relying diffidently:

"You are kind to say so, sir." She returned to her book.

Undaunted, the man continued, "You are reading *A Short History of Carcassonne,* n'est-ce pas?"

Judy held up the book, and said with a slight tone of irritation, "Yes, sir, you are correct."

"Then please allow me to introduce myself, for it is you who have given me a compliment."

If this was the man's idea of a come on, Judy realized it was finally working, and said, "How so may I ask?"

"I wrote that book, Madame, and I too am heading to Carcassonne."

Now drawn, Judy revealed her skepticism by sitting back, smiling, and crossing her arms. *"Really."*

"Mais oui."

She closed the book and held it to her chest.

"Bernard Laurent, Madame. At your service."

Judy checked the back cover, which included a picture. After scrutinizing the picture, she looked up and then back at the picture. Then she bowed her head, and said, "I see. My. What a coincidence that you have occupied the seat next to me. You really did write this book."

"Yes, it is indeed a very pleasant coincidence. I hope you enjoy it."

"I'm sure I will." She read his biography. "It says you are a history professor."

"For some years I taught French history at the College de Bastion, which is just outside Carcassonne. For the last year I have been giving monthly lectures at the College de France here in Paris."

"Interesting. Where is that exactly?"

Professor Laurent stood and pointed to the chair at Judy's table." "May I?" he asked.

"Please."

Laurent sat and pointed out the window at a spire in the distance. "The College is just a short walk from here, on the 5th Arrondissement, across the street from the grounds of the Sorbonne, near the Pantheon."

"You are a Professor there as well?"

"Yes, but the College is a research establishment. We don't grant degrees—that is for the Sorbonne—but we are required to give lectures, which are free to the public. The motto of our College is *Docet Omnia*—we teach everything... chemistry, physics, social sciences, humanities..."

"And history, I assume."

"Indeed, that is true, Madame. To date, twenty-one Prizewinners and nine Fields Medalists have been affiliated with the College. I am presently one of fifty-one professors there."

"I had no idea. What do you teach there?"

"I just finished a series of six lectures on the history of the Occitanie region of southwestern France."

"Carcassonne is in that region?"

"Yes. A paper I wrote some years ago was cited by UNESCO in its decision to make Carcassonne a World Heritage Site back in 1997...but enough about me. Might I prevail upon you to indulge my curiosity to tell me what brings you to wish to visit this ancient City of Carcassonne?"

"Of course," she said, though she debated with herself how much to tell the good professor—assuming he really was one. If he was telling her a tall story—and she had heard most of them—this was certainly the best she had heard.

"I am Judy Alexander," she finally offered. "I am a London barrister, and I am visiting Carcassonne on a case."

As Laurent began to inquire about the nature of her 'case', Judy quickly changed the subject.

"On the Eurostar this morning I read the Carcassonne Tourist Brochure from last year...about the legend of Lady Carcas and the famous pig thrown over the ramparts. Is that a true story?"

Laurent flashed a broad smile. "Not really," he said sheepishly. "As an historian, I'm afraid there is very little in the historical record to validate that legend, though my good neighbors in Carcassonne would never admit it. It is a bit like your legend of King Arthur. Although most of what we know today as the Arthurian legend was concocted, and certainly fictionalized many centuries later by such writers as Geoffrey of Monmouth in the 12trh century and by Thomas Mallory in the 15th, what little we have of real history does record an historical Artorius, a Roman General first or second century AD. I would therefore concede that many legends may ultimately be sourced to actual historical events—including that of Lady Carcas."

"But the City is not really named after Lady Carcas?"

"Yes and no. Certainly, the City was not originally named after anyone by that name as late as the eighth century. What little we have in the historical record is that the Romans first fortified the hilltop on which the City now stands around 100 AD, and named it the *colonia of Julio Carasco*—presumably after the Roman General who first fortified it. Rome did not relinquish the City until 476 when it was forced by military weakness to formally cede the City to the rampaging Visigoths."

"So Carcassonne got its name from a Roman General and not from a 'Lady Carcas' in 758."

"Even assuming that the Romans first gave that name to the City, who is to say that sometime in the eighth century, the City's besieged inhabitants didn't call their heroic savior—whatever her actual name—'The Lady of Carcas'."

"Yes, I see what you mean...but what of the story that Charlemagne actually besieged the City in 758?"

"It's true that Charlemagne's father, Pepin the Short, was unable to conquer Carcassonne even as he conquered most of Southern France in the mid-750s, though we have no reliable historical details as to how the City was able to repel him. Charlemagne could not have besieged Carcassonne in 758, however, as by that time his father had managed to finally negotiate a ceding to him of the City. Charlemagne was but a boy of sixteen or seventeen at that time; he certainly wouldn't have commanded any of his father's armies. No doubt, the name of Charlemagne was later added to the legend as a way of giving it more gravitas. Charlemagne was not crowned as Holy Roman Emperor by the Pope until many years later on Christmas Day in the year 800."

"Fascinating. Are there any more momentous events in Carcassonne's history that I should look for when I read your book?"

"You might be interested in my chapter on the religious crusade against the Cathars."

"Cathars?"

"They were a Christian sect whose adherents were concentrated in the Carcassonne region in the middle of the Thirteenth Century. The Catholic Church considered them heretics for believing that there was no need for churches or buildings. All that was needed was the power of the Word as set forth in the Gospels. Among other heretical beliefs, the Cathars were vegetarians (although they ate fish), and had female as well as male priests."

"Female priests...ahead of their time...the Church of England is dealing with that issue even today."

"Perhaps most abhorrent was that the Cathars were relatively tolerant and accepting of other systems of belief."

"Horrors!"

"It was enough to motivate Pope Gregory IX to establish the Inquisition in 1233 for the express purpose of exterminating the Cathars and their heresies. The Inquisition tracked down and burned the last remnants of them at Montsegur in 1244. Once the Cathars were wiped out, the Church found other uses for the Inquisition which reached its zenith in Fourteenth Century Spain."

"I fear my history education has been deficient. I didn't know that."

"Have you by any chance read Kate Mosse's popular novel, *Labyrinth*?"

"I've heard of it, but haven't read it."

"You might enjoy it. It's set in modern day Carcassonne where Alice, a young woman volunteer on an archeological expedition, discovers evidence of the Crusade against the Cathars."

"I'll look for it." Judy looked at her watch. "I suppose we should think about wandering over to Austerlitz to catch our train. Any other major historical events that have occurred in Carcassonne since the thirteenth century that I should read about in your book?"

Laurent took out his pocket watch. "Yes, perhaps in fifteen minutes we should head over to the station. In my book, you'll read about how England's Black Prince tried and failed in 1355 to conquer Carcassonne during the Hundred Year's War. In 1659, the *Treaty of Pyrenees* transferred the entire region around Carcassonne to France. Since then, its military significance has become less important than its economic significance as the economic center concentrated on the woolen textile industry... until in more modern times..."

"Yes?"

"After the Nazis conquered France in 1940, they set up a French puppet regime in Southern France known as 'Vichy France', which included Carcassonne, and headed by the Nazi collaborator Marshall Petain. Soon thereafter, the Nazis created the *Service for Mandatory Work*. This organization sent soldiers into the Carcassonne region to seize all young able-bodied Frenchmen and send them to Germany as slave labor to augment the Nazi labor force there. Many of these young men never returned to France as they were either worked to death or executed."

"I never knew anything about this history either," Judy said.

"That's not surprising as very little has been written about it, especially since many prominent French citizens were involved with the Petain regime. Much of what I learned about this period I heard first hand from my great uncle who served with a French Resistance group known as the Maquis. In addition to resisting the Nazis, the Maquis also took advantage of Carcassonne's geographic position along the main rail lines to create underground coordinating points for Jews and allied soldiers who had escaped capture and sought to escape via Spain to British controlled Gibraltar. Of course, many of the Maquis were captured by the Nazis and sent to a concentration camp located about forty kilometers from Carcassonne."

"Terrible. So your Uncle survived?"

"Yes, although he had many narrow escapes. He passed away back in 1998."

Laurent again looked at his watch. "And now, Ms. Alexander, we probably should begin our short walk to the station. Having made this particular trip many times, I can tell that it is best we arrive at the station an hour ahead of time. That would allow us to board the train at least half an hour before departure and to enjoy a glass of wine in the Club Car before retiring to our cabins. I take it you have booked a private cabin in the sleeping car?"

"Yes. I'm hoping to get a good night's sleep before arriving in Carcassonne tomorrow morning, but your stories of Carcassonne have so fascinated me that I fear I may stay up too late to read all the details in your book."

"As an academic, I am always very flattered that anyone would read any of my books and papers. If you would care to accompany me, I will show you the shortest way to our train and sleeping car."

Judy rose and picked up her roller bag and briefcase. "Thank you. I'll follow you."

After leading Judy through the byways of Paris Austerlitz station to the Night Train to Carcassonne on track 27, Laurent helped Judy find her compartment.

"If you'd care to join me in the Club Car after you settle in, I'd be please to tell you anything more you'd like to know about Carcassonne," he offered solicitously.

Judy opened the door to her compartment. "Thank you, Professor. I'll join you in a few minutes after I freshen up."

CHAPTER THIRTY-EIGHT

Soon after the train had left Austerlitz Station, Judy found Professor Laurent in the Club Car nursing a glass of Cabernet Sauvignon.

Laurent rose as she entered. "I wasn't sure if you would come, but now that you have, may I interest you in a Cabernet, or perhaps you would prefer a Merlot."

"What do you recommend?" Judy asked.

"I prefer the Cabernet, but the Merlot served here is also excellent."

"The Cabernet will be fine, though I hope it will not put me to sleep before I have a chance to read your book this evening."

"I fear the combination of both the wine and the book may do both, Ms. Alexander, but on the chance that it may not, please make yourself comfortable."

He motioned to the large chair across from his table. "May I also interest you in a Baked Brie. Francois over there makes an excellent Brie?"

Judy sighed. "We didn't really eat much at Starbucks, did we… and I am a little hungry. So perhaps a Brie would be nice."

"Of course." Laurent motioned to the white-coated Francois who came out from behind the bar.

"A Cabernet for the lady, and two of your excellent Brie, Francois."

"Yes, Professor," said Francois as he bowed and retreated to the kitchen behind the bar.

"So you really are a professor," said Judy, actually relieved to hear that a third party recognized him as such.

"Did you doubt it...but I understand. A Lady traveling alone must always be wary. I'm sure you have heard many tales from men who approach an attractive young woman such as yourself in your travels."

"I'm sorry, but yes. Thank you for understanding."

"Well, now that I seemed to have gained your confidence, perhaps you would permit me to ask a question. You said that you were traveling to Carcassonne on a case. I must confess that I can think of only one case that recently arose in Carcassonne, and that was in the Old City."

Judy paused for a long moment before tentatively answering. "Yes, Professor. I am representing a friend of a friend, Muriel Wright, who has been accused of a very serious crime that occurred recently at the Hotel Ville Fortifiée. I am coming to Carcassonne to see what I can learn about the circumstances of that crime."

Laurent took a deep breath. "I thought as much as soon as you told me that you were coming to Carcassonne on a legal matter ...the terrible murder of an Englishman, the son of an English Lord. Such a crime has not been committed in the Old City for many years...indeed, as long as I can remember...and I have lived in the Ancient City all my life."

"Can you tell me what the feeling is among your neighbors in the City?"

"There are only fifty-one of us who live permanently within the walls."

"Really? That few?"

"Yes, there are very few private homes within the ancient wall. The main City of Carcassonne below has a population of about 50,000. Most of the people who work within the wall come up from the modern city below."

"And you are legal counsel to the young woman accused of that crime?"

"No, not exactly. A London solicitor represents her, but I have agreed to assist both my friend's friend and her counsel by conducting my own independent investigation to find who really killed Arthur Edgeware. At that point, I may assist whoever is ultimately assigned to represent Ms. Wright in court should charges be lodged against her in England."

CHAPTER THIRTY-NINE

*B*ien. As Judy disembarked, she found Professor Laurent waiting for her in the station hall.

"Sleep well?" he asked as he took Judy's roller bag. "If you'll wait here, I'll get my car and meet you out front."

"Thank you."

The drive up the hill to the Walled City took only minutes. Laurent parked in his reserved space outside the Narbousisse Gate.

"If you give me your hotel reservation, I'll show it to the gate master. It's only a short walk to the Hotel Ville de Fortifiée."

He led Judy down a narrow winding street to the Hotel, through its medieval entrance to the reception desk, and rang the bell. In moments the desk clerk appeared.

"Good morning, Professor," said the clerk.

"Good morning, Pierre. I believe this young lady has a reservation for...for room..."

"Room 213," said Judy, examining her reservation.

After getting the key, Laurent led Judy up one flight of stairs and down the hall to her room.

"After you freshen up, perhaps you'd like to join me in the dining room for breakfast. I will try to track down my cousin."

"Can you give me an hour?"

"Shall we say...?" Laurent checked his watch. "Shall we say 8:30? Breakfast is buffet."

An hour later Judy found Laurent in the dining room speaking with a middle-aged man who seemed to be in charge.

"Ah, Judy," said Laurent "I'd like you to meet my cousin, Martin. Martin this is Judy Alexander."

Martin bowed. "My pleasure, Madame. Welcome to Hotel Ville de Fortifiée. I hope you enjoy your stay in Carcassonne." Martin excused himself, and Laurent and Judy settled down for a breakfast of cappuccino, croissants, and fruit.

"So did your husband not wish to accompany you on this trip, if I may ask?" Laurent asked.

Judy hesitated to answer, as she had anticipated that the question of her attachment would soon arise. She hoped her answer would not compromise his offer to assist her.

"I am not married, but I am…engaged. That is there is a significant other."

She looked closely at his expression to judge whether her concerns were justified.

"I would be very surprised if there was not. But since you are not married, perhaps you would not…"

Judy quickly changed the subject. "Professor, I wonder if it might be possible to arrange an interview with your cousin this morning."

He smiled, and rose. "Of course. If you will excuse me, I shall talk to him now, and see what I can do."

Laurent took a seat in his cousin's office. Martin sat behind his desk and looked at his cousin with skepticism.

"She's quite a beauty, Bernard. Wherever did you find her?"

"We met in a Paris Starbucks if you can believe it."

"Bien, cousin. You've always been outstanding in your profession, but you've been most unlucky in love."

"You'd do me a great favor if you would speak to Ms. Alexander. She's a British barrister and representing the young woman who spent the night with this Arthur Edgeware on the night of the murder."

"Oh no, Bernard…must I? I've been going over all this with the police for weeks now, and I don't know how I can help her. We've already lost business over this whole terrible affair."

"But you'll do it as a favor to me? I would owe you for a very long time."

Martin sighed. "Very well, but …"

"Could you spare her a moment now?"

Martin shrugged. "Sure. Send her in."

"Come in Ms. Alexander, and please have a seat," said Martin when Judy appeared at his office door. He spoke in passable English but with a thick French accent.

Judy nodded and sat. 'Merci, Monsieur."

"Well, Ms. Alexander, you appear to have made a conquest. My good cousin has asked me to see you. Please understand that this is quite irregular, as I am not sure our local constabulary would approve of my speaking with a British barrister representing their prime suspect in the murder of this British citizen."

"I understand, and I am most grateful. I only have a few questions."

"Procédez, Madame."

Judy withdrew the file of pictures Jake had taken at Arthur Edgeware's funeral and handed them to Martin.

"Do you recognize the faces of any of these people who were guests here on the night of the murder?"

Martin took the file and began to look at the photos, but said, "I doubt if I would recognize any of them. Please understand that I do not normally have direct contact with our guests, although I am familiar with a number of regular visitors."

"So you don't recognize any of them?"

"I'm sorry, no. Perhaps Pierre, my head desk clerk might be able to."

"He was on duty the night of the murder?"

"Yes, and he has already given a statement to the police."

"Would you mind if I showed him the pictures."

"No, but please be discreet. Please don't ask him or show him any of these pictures while he is serving any of our guests."

"Of course. Now…sir may I ask if you might have a list of the guests who were checked in on the night of the murder."

At this, Martin seemed to balk. "I'm afraid that information is confidential, Madame."

"But you do have such a list, which you perhaps gave to the police."

Martin shook his head, but finally said, "I cannot give you a list, but…"

He rose from his chair, walked over to an adjacent file cabinet, pulled out a file, and handed it to Judy.

"Madame, you may look at this list which I provided to the police, but you may not take it with you."

Judy nodded. "Thank you."

He watched while Judy surveyed the names.

One name caught her eye. "Sir, how difficult would it be in France to give a false name when checking into your hotel? I mean you require any visitor to produce a passport when checking in, do you not?"

"Yes, it would be quite difficult. We are required to download on to a national database the names and numbers of all passports that our guests provide when checking in. The DGSE would immediately notify us if any passport we download does not match with passports provided by all foreigners when entering the country."

"The DGSE?"

"Directorate General for External Security."

Judy stood, leaned over Martin's desk and pointed out the name that had drawn her attention. "You received no feedback from them regarding this name?"

Martin looked at the name. "No, nothing. I would remember if I had, and no doubt be contacted by a representative of the Directorate."

"But you would know if you had?"

"Of course."

"The list indicates that the passport provided for this person was by a British national."

Martin looked at the list. "It appears so, yes. It is a name you recognize?"

"I will have to confirm, but possibly. Now, could I possibly ask if you have a list of your employees who were on duty on both the evening of March 28 and the morning of March 29? I assume you provided such a list to the police."

"Of course...but again..."

"I assume that such a list is not confidential. I would be most grateful if you could let me see that list."

Anxious to conclude the interview which he had promised his cousin to give, Martin took the list of guests and returned it to his file cabinet. He then took out another file and handed it to Judy.

"This is the list of employees on both the evening of March 28, and the morning of March 29.

Judy surveyed the list. After a few moments she said, "I see there were only seven employees on duty on the evening of March 28...and three of them remained on duty until 10 AM on the morning of March 29."

"Yes, on the evening before Ms. Wright checked out, there were only three employees on duty—Pierre at the desk, and two cleaning attendants."

"Cleaning attendants...during the night?"

"Yes. Of course they do not use vacuums during the night but they do polish the floors, dust and so on."

"And I take it that the police interviewed the cleaning attendants?"

"Yes, they interviewed both the two night shift cleaning attendants, as well as the maids who came in early on the morning of the March 29."

"Including the maid who found the victim in room 213?"

"They were all interviewed," Martin paused.

"Yes?"

"Well, except one…Musa Sani, one of the two on the cleaning night shift."

"Why didn't they interview him?"

Martin grunted. "They couldn't. He doesn't speak English. He's an undocumented immigrant from Nigeria, presently under our supervision while he awaits his asylum hearing."

"The police couldn't provide an interpreter?"

"No. Apparently he speaks only a language called Hausa, I think, or something like that. Anyway there was no indication he knew anything. No one around here or in this region speaks that language."

"So he was not actually interviewed?"

"Not to my knowledge."

"How do you give him instructions on his duties here at the hotel?"

"Our head attendant just shows him…not hard to show someone how to dust and polish floors."

"And he still works for you?"

"Yes, he'll be with us for another month or so until his asylum hearing."

"Would you mind if I talked to him as well?"

"Be my guest, but good luck on finding a Hausa interpreter anywhere around here."

Judy rose and held out her hand. "Thank you, sir. You've been a great help."

Judy found Bernard waiting for her in the hotel lounge.

"Was my cousin of any help, Judy?"

"Yes I think so."

"Bien, if you have some time, perhaps I could show you some interesting sights here in Carcassonne."

"I'd like that very much. What sights did you have in mind?"

"Perhaps you would permit me to show you the Inquisition Tower, the Basilica of Nazarius and Celcus, the Porte

Narbonnaise, all the places that inspired Walt Disney's production of *Sleeping Beauty*."

Judy gently clasped Bernard's wrist. "I would love to, Professor, but could we make it this evening? Your cousin gave me permission to interview several of his employees, and I'd like to get those interviews completed before the day is out."

"Of course, Judy. The restaurants open late in the evening here in Carcassonne. Shall I come by at 9 this evening?"

"I'll look forward to it. Now, I must go."

Judy immediately retired to room 213 and called Jake.

"Hi Judy, I have news..."

"As do I!" Judy interrupted. "Listen!"

"All right, you first."

"Jake, I think I know who killed Arthur Edgeware."

"I'm listening, "Jake said calmly, waiting to hear what she had to say before giving her his own alarming news.

"Jake, first, I need you to find an interpreter for me."

"Interpreter? What kind?"

"Someone who speaks Hausa."

"Hausa? Never heard of it."

"It's one of several different languages they speak in Nigeria."

"Okay, and what do I do once I find such a person."

"Do whatever you have to do to get such an interpreter down here to Carcassonne. Pay whatever it takes, but I need this right away."

"Whew! I'll see what I can do, but I can't imagine I can pull that off and get someone there before tomorrow sometime."

"Just do what you can."

"All right...now, are you going to tell me who killed Arthur?"

"I can't tell you now. First, I need to interview the desk clerk who was on duty here on the evening of March 28-29, and then..."

"Yes, then..."

"Then…to be sure…I need to talk to a cleaning attendant, a Nigerian who works here. I don't think he knows anything, but he's apparently the only potential witness the police didn't interrogate. Once I'm satisfied that I haven't missed anything…"

"I take it one of those pictures I gave you panned out?"

"I think so."

"Is it my turn to tell you my news?"

"Sorry, of course. Tell me."

"Are you sitting down?"

"No, stop it, Jake!"

"It's not good, Judy."

"Just tell me."

"They've charged Muriel."

Judy was stunned. "What? Who? The French? The UK's going to extradite her?"

"They've charged her right here. Crown Court London, and she's been arrested and taken to Broozefield Jail in Ashford."

CHAPTER FORTY

*I*gnoring the Queen's Counsel marquee posted on Michael Hodges' office door, Braxton Thomas did not bother to knock. Instead he threw open the door, slapped a file on Hodge's uncluttered desk, and confronted his former mentor.

"Good heavens, my boy," said the startled Hodges as he looked up from his copy of the *London Times*, "what on earth are you about today?"

"I think you know Michael, and I think it's insufferable and utterly transparent," sputtered Braxton as he tried to control his anger.

"Braxton," Michael replied indignantly, "for the first time since I tutored you in the art of trial advocacy, I must confess that I have absolutely no idea what you are talking about."

Braxton took a deep breath and sat without being invited to do so. In a voice as calm as he could muster, he said, "Archie's list of Crown appointments came out today."

"Yes, I know," said Hodges as he nonchalantly picked up the file containing the Crown appointments. "I see you went to the effort of making a file of it, though I can't imagine why you would bother to do that. The list is public knowledge and posted in chambers. I think Archie is pleased that we are finally picking up more Crown appointments. So what is your problem here, Braxton?"

"The CPS has appointed you to prosecute Muriel Wright in the Crown Court."

Michael picked up the file and perused the list. "Yes, I see that. So?"

"Don't be coy, Michael, and don't think I don't know exactly what you're up to. I'm sure you called up every outstanding marker you have with your past contacts at CPS to engineer this appointment."

"Now why on earth would I do that?"

"Why on earth would you want to take on a case that you know will be high profile, that you think will be a slam dunk, that will re-establish your waning Queen's Counsel credentials, that…that…"

"That what, my boy?" Michael's tone changed from one of sincere puzzlement to one of irritation at being unfairly insulted—by a former pupil, no less.

"…that will let you engage with Judy Alexander, the woman you've been lusting after ever since you invited her… us…to your country compound, whom you can't stand stealing the media limelight from you on your lofty QC perch."

Hodges stood in indignation. "How dare you!" he shouted. "I take you under my wing, teach you everything you know, and how do you know Alexander is even going to represent this Muriel Wright? Hmmm? Tell me that! The last you told me, she would never consider representing this woman, Muriel Wright, which is understandable since she has neither the experience nor the skill to take on such a case."

Braxton rose in reaction, and for several moments the two barristers stood in defiant confrontation.

At that moment there was a knock at the door, which Braxton had inadvertently left ajar. Kitty, the chambers librarian peeked in. "Is everything all right in here? I could hear you two all the way down in the library."

"Yes Kitty," said Hodges with annoyance. "Mr. Thomas and I were just having a spirited discussion about a case—nothing to concern you. Everything is fine. Now off you go. Shut the door if you will."

Braxton turned and smiled at Kitty.

"Yes. Mr. Hodges." Kitty looked dubiously at the two men, and scuttled away.

After the two sat, Braxton was the first to back down.

"I'm sorry, sir. I was out of line."

"Perfectly understandable, my boy, but I'm afraid Judy has got you all muddled up, and I must say that if this continues she'll have the whole chambers muddled up. Perhaps you should consider either fishing or cutting bait with her."

Braxton began to respond to this, but then decided he had no desire to engage with Hodges over his love life, such that it was. In any case, it was none of his business. Instead, he said matter-of-factly:

"I think you are right that Judy would never take the Wright case."

"She's told you that?"

"Not in so many words…"

"I'm glad to hear it. I have no desire to go up against a novice with such little felony defense experience. No glory in that, my boy, I assure you."

"Why is this matter not being handled in the manner of an extradition? The killing occurred in France, not the UK."

"I'm not sure why I'm telling you this, but since you seem to have this interest through Judy…"

"Don't tell me anything you don't feel comfortable telling me."

"Then you didn't hear it from me, but the fact is that the PM has no interest in getting sideways with the EU, or France for that matter. They already have their hands full negotiating the details—always the devil to pay in the details—of Brexit. On the other hand, the Foreign Service does not want to set a precedent of complying with every extradition demand from an EU country—it still wants to use that as a bargaining chip."

"A bargaining chip?"

"Absolutely. Her Majesty's government has much more important fish to fry than this Muriel Wright matter. Fortunately, the facts in this case have given the government an easy out."

"How so?"

"Apparently the Thames Valley Police have evidence that elements of the crime—the alleged crime occurred in the UK in that town near Brookwood Cemetery…"

"Woking, I believe…"

"Yes, I believe that's it…Woking…apparently this Muriel Wright bought a fair number of Ambien capsules in Woking before accompanying Arthur Edgeware to France and to Carcassonne. According to the autopsy report provided to Thames Valley by the Gendarmes, there was evidence that the pills were administered to Edgeware at least twenty-four hours before the pair arrived in Carcassonne."

"And the CPS thinks that's enough to give the UK jurisdiction to try the case? That seems a bit thin. Wright may have consumed all the Ambien she bought herself long before leaving the UK, and someone else could have administered the Ambien to Edgeware."

"Entirely possible, and I'm sure that whoever ends up representing Wright in Crown Court will make that very point in moving to dismiss the case for lack of jurisdiction, but you miss the point."

"Which is…"

"Which is that it lets the government off the hook. I'm sure the PM could care less if Wright is acquitted or convicted. Either way, the government can show France that it is taking the crime seriously, and prosecuting it vigorously even as it declines to consider extradition. The Crown will, of course, invite the French to send any witnesses and evidence to the Court as it deems appropriate."

"And which you will duly introduce on their behalf during the presentation of the prosecution's case in Crown Court."

"Of course. I would be bound to do so."

Braxton did not want to renew with his former mentor the contentious altercation that had gotten both of their blood up, but he could not disguise his skepticism over Hodge's true motivation in engineering his appointment. He sat back, folded his arms, and said:

"I'm still curious as to why you would even want to lead the prosecution of this case. From what I understand, this will not be an easy case to get a conviction. The evidence is almost completely circumstantial, and Muriel Wright will be the most fair-faced and innocent-looking young school teacher ever to find herself in the dock at Crown Court. It will be hard for any jury to envision her as a vicious knife-slashing murderess, not to mention the lack of any real motive."

"Au contraire, my young friend, establishing motive will be the least of my concerns. If we can show that she had even an inkling that the untimely death of her poor schoolteacher husband might make her the richest woman in the UK…"

"Good luck on that, Michael. Right now, there seems to be little doubt that it was Arthur's brother Chester who was the first-born, and if there were such a doubt, no one would have a greater motive than Chester Edgeware, who stood to inherit upon Arthur's death regardless of who was proven to be first born."

Hodges shrugged. "Perhaps you should take on this woman's defense yourself, then…and talking of media-hyped match-ups, what would be more dramatically compelling than the former pupil going up against…"

"His Queen's Counsel mentor? How about going up against the barrister beauty from America who has become the hero of the women's movement against domestic violence. Aren't you in the least concerned about losing to her? I don't see how that would enhance your reputation as one of the UK's greatest advocates. Or have you taken up the modern celebrity mantra that any publicity is good publicity?"

Hodges smiled impishly, but said nothing in reply.

"On my God, that's it isn't it? You don't care whether you win or lose! You'll be happy just basking in the media limelight, talking to reporters, reveling in *Daily Mirror* headlines like 'Beauty versus the Beast: Will the American Barrister Charm the Jury into an Acquittal?'—or any other such sensationalistic nonsense. Of course, you'll be chivalrous in defeat, gallantly heaping praise on your beauteous protagonist for her valiant defense of an injured woman, pontificating about the jury system, how you respect the jury's judgment even though you might disagree with it. The leaders of the women's movement will praise you for your graciousness and magnanimity in defeat. I get it, Michael. I really do! "

Hodges broadened his smile and shrugged his shoulders. "I'm afraid you've got it all wrong. I suppose it could turn out as you surmise, though I assure you I wouldn't welcome it, but aren't you forgetting something? You yourself just said that Judy would never defend Muriel Wright. You know what I think? I think you are worried that she will take this case after all, and that she'll get so wrapped up in it that you'll be left out in the cold. Maybe permanently."

"Touché."

Braxton rose and picked up the file. "You're wrong," he said defensively, "and I regret that you've taken this appointment on false assumptions about Judy, about me, about both of us."

"We shall see. I still think you should take the case and see if you can use the things I taught you to make your own reputation on a high profile case. However, I would understand if you wouldn't feel confident going up against your old mentor."

Braxton walked toward the door, but then turned around. "As it happens, I'm now on my way to St. Pancras to pick up Judy. I can assure you that if Judy is even considering defending Muriel Wright, I will use all my powers of persuasion to convince her that it would be the wrong thing to do."

"Why is that? Because you think Muriel Wright is actually guilty or because you think Judy might lose even if Muriel is innocent?"

Braxton considered replying, but thought better of it and turned back toward the door.

"Braxton!"

The pupil turned again to face his graying mentor.

"You know," Hodges, continued, "who would have known back in those early days when as my pupil you hung on my every word, that it would ever come to this. I can only hope that, whatever happens with all this, that we can remain friends.

"Sure, Michael, sure. That's what we barristers do. I owe you a lot. We'll always be friends."

"Give my best to Judy."

CHAPTER FORTY-ONE

"*T*hanks for picking me up," Judy said breathlessly as she scrambled into the Spitfire outside St. Pancras, threw her bag into the back, and gave Braxton a peck on the cheek.

"Happy to do it, Meow. With you so busy these days with this Muriel Wright case, I guess I need to take advantage of every opportunity to see you."

Judy sat back and sighed. "I know, and I'm sorry. You can imagine how stunned I was to hear that the CPS has decided to prosecute here in the UK. I thought it best to return to London right away. Jake called me yesterday morning, and of course I called you right away."

"I got the news from Archie just a short time before you called. You were right to return right away. I'm sure you'll want to start looking for the top flight barrister to represent Muriel."

As the Spitfire stopped behind a double-decker London bus and Braxton waited while a long line of passengers embarked, Braxton turned and looked at Judy to see if she had a reaction to his suggestion. Whatever her expression might have been, he did not see it as she had turned to gaze out the left window.

When she did not reply, he said, "So, did you find what you were looking for…down there in Carcassonne?"

Judy turned back and said, "I wasn't really looking for anything specific. I mainly just wanted to get the lay of the crime scene, and hope I might find some evidence that the Gendarmes had missed."

"And did you?"

Judy turned back and nodded pensively. "I think so. I did find a witness whom the police had not been bothered—or were too lazy—to interview."

"Really! An important witness…who saw something?"

"Yes, someone who could be a very strong witness as a matter of fact."

"I see. And where is this witness now?"

"I called Jake, and he made arrangements for him in Paris."

"Paris? Why so far away from Carcassonne?"

"Jake was concerned that the Gendarmes might get wind of the fact that I was interested in him and had talked to him. There were people in the Hotel Ville Fortifée who saw me with him. It turns out that he is undocumented, or at least in the early stages of obtaining a residency permit. Jake didn't think I should risk the chance that he might be deported before being able to give evidence."

"I would think the Gendarmes would welcome any evidence relevant to the case."

Judy turned and gave Braxton a skeptical look. "Not if his evidence was contrary to their narrative that Muriel Wright killed Arthur Edgeware."

"So this mystery witness's statement might be contrary to the police narrative, as you put it?"

"Yes, I think so."

"Then wouldn't it make sense to make this witness available to the police so that he can tell them what he told you, whatever that was. I mean, if this person really is as important a witness as you say he is."

Judy shook her head. "He doesn't speak any English, his French residency status is shaky, and even if the police believe him, which is doubtful, his statement wouldn't be sufficient beyond a reasonable doubt to convict the person I have now come to believe committed this crime."

"And that would be?"

"Brax, I really don't feel comfortable telling you who I believe murdered Arthur Edgeware. I know I would need more than just this one witness to convince a jury, and in the meantime, I have to keep an open mind should additional evidence come to my attention."

"So you're not absolutely sure of who killed Edgeware?"

"No, Brax. I'm not absolutely sure, but whoever does represent Muriel doesn't need to convince a jury absolutely that another person committed it. He or she would only have to raise a reasonable doubt about whether Muriel committed the crime."

"So all you're really saying is that the testimony of this mystery witness of yours might be sufficient to raise a reasonable doubt as to Muriel's guilt, but not enough to convince a jury to convict this other person, should he or she ever be charged, and who you believe actually committed the crime."

Judy took a deep breath, and paused before replying, "Brax, could we talk about something else right now? I'm really tired, and I'd just like to get back to my flat, take a hot bath, and get a good night's sleep."

"Sure, I'll be happy to drop you off. I'm just feeling a little bummed, to be honest, that you don't feel you can confide in me. I told you before that I want to help you with this case, but I don't know how I can help you if you don't let me in on your thinking at this point. I assume you've confided with your Jake friend about who the killer is."

"Jake is the one who gave me the set of pictures he took at Arthur's funeral, and my witness in Carcassonne identified one of the persons in that set of pictures as the one he saw enter Arthur's hotel room in the early morning of the murder."

"Early in the morning…you mean after Muriel left the room to catch her train?"

"Yes. So, of course, Jake and I have discussed the importance that photo identification might have in a court of law."

"But you don't want to tell me what person this witness picked out."

"I told you, not now! Who knows whether this witness' testimony will even stand up in court under cross-examination, and I can't even be sure I'll be able to produce him in court."

"So you have this witness stashed away somewhere in Paris until such time as you might summon him."

"I asked Jake to try to arrange for him to come to London while we wait for the trial, but Jake says that would be a lot trickier."

"I'm sure it would be. The UK still checks the passports of those who cross the channel, but aren't you still sticking your neck out harboring a fugitive like that?"

"Stop it, Brax! I'm not harboring a fugitive and I resent the implication. My witness has not been charged with any crime, and all I've done is have Jake provide him with a place to hang out in Paris. If this case gets to the point where the CPS and the Thames Valley Police would be willing to listen to what my witness has to say with a view toward possibly dropping the murder case against Muriel, I will definitely make him available."

"So the witness is a man."

"Let me finish. Yes, he's a man—so what—as if that makes any difference, but if the CPS is bound and determined to prosecute this case against Muriel in Crown Court, I will definitely call him to the stand."

"You will call him to the stand? You're not seriously considering representing Muriel yourself! You told me you only agreed to help Muriel find out who killed her husband!"

"I know that, and I have no wish to represent her in a legal capacity, and you're right, I've made no such commitment to Muriel, and yes, I know I'm far too inexperienced to represent Muriel in a murder case, but yes, if she asked me to—if that's what Muriel really wants, I'd consider it. Why is that such a problem for you! You obviously think very little of my abilities!"

Braxton did not reply, but tightened his grip on the wheel as he maneuvered the Spitfire around another bus.

Judy bristled. "Brax, I'm tired of talking about all this now. Listen, just let me out on the corner. Thanks for picking me up. My flat's only two blocks away, and I can walk."

Braxton too flinched, found an open alleyway, swung the car into it, and switched off the ignition.

The two sat in stony silence for several minutes, before Braxton finally said, "I'm sorry, sweetie."

Another several minutes passed before Judy quietly said, "It's okay. I know I'm not qualified to represent Muriel in Crown Court—at least not without serious backup, and without the full support of Mayfield, and Muriel of course, but I've tried cases in Crown Court before, and won two of them. I think I could do it if it came down to it—and if it did, that you would support me."

"It's not that. I know you could do it."

"Then what?"

Brax took a long breath and very slowly blew it out. "Before I came to pick you up, I had a talk with Hodges."

"Oh, God. What did he have to say?"

"The CPS has appointed him to represent the Crown against Wright."

"You're kidding!"

"I wish I were."

"How did that even happen…I mean…"

"He masterminded the appointment—no doubt about that. He's still has lots of friends in higher places, and several of his former pupils are at CPS."

"But why? He isn't even interested in criminal cases."

"No, he's fine with criminal cases as long as we represent the Crown or parties in lucrative civil cases. It's the criminal defense cases he disdains."

"But why is he interested in this case in particular? What's his interest in Muriel Wright?"

"I doubt if he cares two hoots about Muriel Wright."

"Then what?"

Braxton looked at Judy and fixed his gaze. "It's you he wants."

"What do you mean, he wants me? That doesn't make any sense. I know he's a letch, but we put up with it because… you know, you were his pupil and all. He can't exactly make moves on me in the courtroom."

"No, he gave up on that the first time we visited him in Newbury."

"What a bastard too! He knows you and I are…"

"You and I are what, Judy?"

Judy fell silent for a moment. She finally said, "We've talked about this. You know you're the only one in my life."

"I know that."

"I told you, when this case is over, we'll go away together. I told you I'm ready to think about having another child…"

"Sweetie, you're missing my point here. He knows he's in the twilight of his career. He knows he can never have you sexually."

"Oh God…"

"…even though he's been obsessed with you since the first day you stepped into chambers."

CHAPTER FORTY-TWO

"**I**s there no pretrial detention facility closer to Woke or Newbury?" Judy asked.

Muriel Wright's solicitor, Peter Mayfield, had kindly offered to drive Judy to Broozefield Prison in Ashford, county of Middlesex. There, they would both see Muriel and discuss her legal representation.

"No, I'm afraid not," replied Mayfield in his thick brogue accent. "Broozefield is a lot closer anyway—only about eighteen miles from London. We're on the M-3 now, and I'll be turning off in a minute to the A-4. We'll be there shortly."

"I seem to have heard about a jail in Reading. If the trial is to be in held in Reading Crown Court, wouldn't it make more sense to hold Muriel there?"

"Judy, love, you wouldn't want young Muriel to be held in the Reading Jail, I'll tell you that. It was one of the UK's most notorious jails before it was finally shut down in…2013 I think it was."

"Why was that?"

"Well first, let me ask you…where did you ever hear of Reading Jail?

"I'm not sure. None of my clients so far have been held or sent there."

"Have you ever read Oscar Wilde's poem "The Ballad of Reading Gaol?"

Judy thought for a moment. "Now that you mention it, it does ring a bell. I think I have…in English Class in College.

I guess that's where I've heard it. Wasn't it a poem that Oscar Wilde wrote about an execution he witnessed while in prison?"

"Yes, you have it right, love. Wilde was charged with engaging in homosexual conduct with the son of the Marquess of Queensbury, John Sholto Douglas, a notorious Scottish nobleman best noted for writing the "Queensbury Rules" for boxing. Regina v. Wilde the case was called. "

"And Oscar Wilde was convicted?"

"Oh, yes and punished severely. Back in 1895, they called it 'gross indecency" and it was a serious crime, just below the crime of murder. Wilde was sentenced to two years at hard labor, and at the Reading Gaol a sentence of hard labor meant exactly that. At the time of his conviction, Wilde had become one of England's most renowned playwrights and poets, second only to Shakespeare, and famous for *The Importance of Being Earnest* and *The Picture of Dorian Gray*. In the Reading Jail he was condemned to 'Walking the Wheel" for twelve hours a day to the point of exhaustion. It broke his health utterly, and he was required to declare bankruptcy, resulting in the loss of all his possessions, including his home and all his books and manuscripts."

"But he survived?"

"Barely. Penniless, homeless, his health broken, and the victim on the streets of what we would now call relentless bullying and hate crimes, he borrowed money from his few remaining friends to flee to France, where he died alone in a Paris Flophouse at the age of forty-six."

"Unimaginable."

"One thing they couldn't take away from him was the historical court record of his valiant defense at his trial."

"Yes, I remember now. I was a student in my late partner's evidence class at Oliver Wendell Holmes School of Law—his name was Professor Robin Hammond—and he assigned us to read the transcript of the cross-examination of Oscar Wilde by the Crown Prosecutor."

"Ah yes, the great Sir Edward Carson."

"It's coming back to me now, Peter. Robin had us watch a video tape of Professor Irving Younger's Ten Commandments of Cross-Examination. One of his commandments was that a cross-examination should be short, brief, and succinct. It should be a 'commando raid, not the invasion of Europe... and I still remember Professor Younger's reservation that his commandments were primarily for the use of the inexperienced cross-examiner—not to be good, but to avoid being bad!"

"I saw you cross-examine the husband in the..."

...the Tomlinson case."

"Yes, you definitely followed his commandment to keep your questions short and succinct, and you were most effective."

"Thank you, but I now remember Younger referring to the cross-examination of Oscar Wilde, and saying that the virtuoso was free to ignore his commandments at any time. He used as an example Carson's cross-examination, which Younger noted, 'ran to some three hundred pages and every word vibrant with interest. Can you imagine cross-examining Oscar Wilde at the height of his powers? But none of you is yet Sir Edward Carson, so until you are, remember, never, never violate these commandments!'"

"An interesting trivia detail regarding that historic courtroom confrontation between England's greatest barrister and its foremost literary icon. Did you know that Wilde and Carson were classmates at Trinity College and knew each other quite well?"

"I didn't know that."

"Hold on, love," said Mayfield as he changed lanes sharply. "Got to make this turn-off to the A-4."

Now safely settled in the left lane of the A-4, Judy asked, "Tell me about this Broozefield Prison. I trust it doesn't put its inmates on the treadmill twelve hours a day."

"No, no treadmills, but it's earned its own brand of notoriety."

"How so?"

"Just a few years ago, a young woman named Natasha Chin died there under circumstances of what a Board of Inquest later found to be a case of extreme neglect and systematic failure."

"How did she die?"

"She had been violently vomiting for nine hours straight while incapacitated in her cell. Medical personnel were finally called but never appeared because the bell that would have alerted them supposedly malfunctioned. By the time medical personnel finally arrived, she had suffocated to death in her own vomit."

"Oh…poor Muriel."

"There have been other similar deaths, but since then the Board of Prisons has implemented some reforms."

"Peter, how do we get her out of there? Is bail even a possibility?"

"Possible, but not very likely. Whoever we find to represent her will of course request bail for her, but for murder—a definite long shot."

"Bail is never granted in such cases?"

"No, that's a misconception. There have been cases where bail is granted, but only with special circumstances."

"Like what?"

"Ties to the community for one thing, no criminal history…"

"Muriel fits both of those grounds. She lives with a close friend near Newbury, and has no prior convictions."

"It would help if she hadn't been fired from her job as a teacher."

"That was because she was charged, not because she was convicted of anything."

"Although there is no death penalty in the UK, life imprisonment is not uncommon in cases such as this."

"Such as what?"

"Such as in cases of murder for money, which are considered particularly heinous, that plus she'd definitely be considered a risk for fleeing the country, and now with all this Brexit mess…"

"Peter, the weight of evidence thus far gathered points toward Lord Edgeware's estate passing to Chester as the first-born."

Peter shook his head. "That is to be determined at trial. You and I both know that the Crown will be able to come up with at least some evidence showing that Arthur may well have been the first-born. Most important will be if the Crown can come up with any evidence that Muriel knew that there was at least a possibility that Arthur, and thus herself as his spouse, might inherit several billion pounds."

"In that regard, I wonder if there is some way to establish before the criminal trial whether Arthur was in fact first-born or not."

"In probate court you mean?"

"Yes, in probate. If the Probate Court finds that Chester was first-born, it would mean Muriel had no motive."

"Not necessarily. What's more important than who was in fact first-born is whether Muriel had reason to believe that Arthur might inherit. That would be enough."

Judy sighed.

"In any case," Peter continued, "I've looked into the possibility that the Probate Court might act before the criminal case against Muriel takes place."

"And…"

"All my sources tell me that the Probate Court will not convene until after the Crown Court reaches its decision in the murder case against Muriel, which is understandable. If Muriel is convicted of murdering Arthur, British law would not permit her to inherit in any case—even if Arthur was found to be first-born."

"So, there is…"

"Hold up, Judy. We're in Ashford, and just coming up on the prison. Bear with me, there's a turn I have to make. I haven't actually been here in a while. Most of my criminal clients in the past several years have been males, and Broozefield is a woman's prison."

"Is this it?" asked Judy as Peter parked in a spacious lot surrounded by well-kept gardens and manicured lawns. The buildings were of brick and looked like manor houses. "This looks more like a luxury resort than a prison."

"Yes, the exterior fools a lot of people, but looks can be deceiving. The community here would never have tolerated a prison in their town if the exterior were not esthetically pleasing."

"Wow. I'm impressed, though. So far."

"Listen, Judy, before we go in to talk to Muriel, perhaps we should talk about what recommendations we are going to make to her about her representation in court."

He pulled a packet of seventeen pages from his brief case and handed it to Judy. "I've taken the liberty of making a copy of the Legal 500. It's a list compiled by the *Times* and updated every year, of the top five hundred lawyers and barristers in England. It ranks them, and also sets forth their fees."

Judy perused the list and flicked through the pages. "I don't know, Peter. I'm inclined to think that Muriel is going to need the very best barrister that she can retain."

He said, "That's all well and good, but the top barristers come with the highest fees." Anticipating Judy's question, he pulled out a separate list that he had compiled of the UK's top barristers—none of whom were in residence at the Quadrangle.

"The very best barrister in the country," he continued, "is Michael Godfrey. He gets a retainer of 1.5 million pounds."

"Whew!"

"Yeah. Also up there is labor Peer David Goldberg. I've never heard of him ever losing a criminal case. His retainer is about the same."

Judy continued shaking her head in amazement.

"Then there's Thomas Gerald-Martin. His fee pushes two million. He's the one whom the celebrities and high-ranking cabinet members go to when they're in trouble. I give you these names, only because I wanted you to know who is the best—for a price—but I know Muriel is not in any position to retain such counsel, at least not from her own resources."

Mayfield, who was aware that Judy had her own resources, but had no idea of their magnitude, waited for Judy's reaction.

"Peter...I could...I could handle these fees."

"You mean you would consider using your own resources to retain such counsel for Muriel?"

"I could...yes, I could."

"I don't know, Judy. I'm also not sure that would be wise."

"Why not? If I have the resources, and can afford it?"

"Even aside from whether you would be willing to pay out that kind of fee for someone you really hardly know..."

"I think I've come to know her."

"Yes, but aside from that. There may be other complications you should consider as well."

"Like what, Peter?"

"Well, the ethics in such a case are quite explicit. You realize that if you pay such a fee on behalf of another...and I'm not saying it isn't done, friends, family, often hire counsel for their loved ones or friends...but if you do that, the rules of ethics would require you to almost completely give up any control of the case. Any barrister so retained would have only one client—Muriel. In other words, not you. Any barrister so retained would not and could not, ethically allow you to take part in any of the decision making and trial strategy. That would be a matter solely between this retained barrister and his client, and any communication between the barrister and Muriel would be privileged."

Judy nodded. "I understand that."

"And you'd be willing to pay the fee, and then step aside?"

Judy thought a moment. "Yes, I would."

"I think I hear a 'but' coming."

"Peter, I haven't given you the details of all the information I am privy to which I have obtained from my… investigator."

"Jake."

"Yes, Jake. I also haven't told you what I found out when I went to Carcassonne, including, more importantly, a witness."

"Judy, if you wish me to continue as Muriel's solicitor, you will need to provide me with all the information, as well as details about this witness you have found."

"I know that, and I will, regardless of who Muriel ultimately retains to act as her trial counsel."

"Then I'm not sure what your concern would be about retaining the best counsel…assuming you can afford it."

"I can."

"And stepping back to serve as…I don't know, just an investigator."

Judy shrugged. "I don't know. Look, let's talk to Muriel and see what she says, and what she wants, and go from there."

"Okay then," said Mayfield as he clapped his hands. "Let's go in and see Muriel!"

CHAPTER FORTY-THREE

After registering with the deputy clerk at Broozefield, Judy and Peter retired to the reception area to wait for a prison deputy to escort them to an interview room. They were surprised to see Samantha already sitting and waiting.

"Samantha," said Judy with surprise, "I didn't know you would be coming today."

Samantha rose, approached Judy, gave her a hug and said, "When I called here to ask if I could see Muriel, they told me that her lawyer had already booked an interview session with her today at this time. I decided to come meet you here so we could see her together. Do you think that would be all right?"

Judy turned to Peter. "Samantha, I think you know Mr. Mayfield, Muriel's solicitor."

"Yes, good morning Mr. Mayfield," said Samantha, offering her hand.

"Peter," Judy asked, "would it be all right if Samantha joined us?"

"Have you already checked in at reception?" Mayfield asked Samantha.

"Yes, sir. They said I'd have to check with you, though."

Mayfield paused as he considered his answer. "Ms.... Sterling is it?"

"Yes, sir."

"I have no problem with the three of us seeing Muriel together for the first half hour I have reserved. Judy and I need to discuss her options for retaining trial counsel, as well as ascertain if she wishes me to continue as her solicitor. As you are her friend…"

"Muriel's closest friend…" Judy added.

"Yes, as Muriel's close friend, I have no problem with you participating in that discussion."

"Thank you."

The three sat back down. Samantha said, "I hope they are treating her all right. I've been googling about this prison. It's the biggest woman's prison in the UK, but it doesn't have the best reputation. I still don't know why they're keeping her here rather than in London."

"I must confess I don't know," answered Mayfield. "That's something I will have to look into, though I suspect it may have something to do with the fact that the CPS may anticipate the possibility of this case becoming something of a media sensation, perhaps even a circus. Controlling media access in this location would be easier here in Ashford than in London. I also understand that any trial, if it comes to that, would be held in Reading Crown Court, which is close by."

"Dear God, Mr. Mayfield, do you really think it will come to that?"

"At this stage it's hard to say, Ms. Sterling. To be honest, from what I know of this case, I don't believe there is a strong case against Muriel. The prosecution's case is entirely circumstantial, no real forensic evidence to speak of—at least none that I've seen. I have further reason to believe that this prosecution has more to do with political considerations relating to the government's ongoing Brexit discussions with France than the merits of the case itself."

Samantha covered her face with her hands and stifled a sob. "Oh poor Muriel! I can't believe it. She's done nothing to deserve this! She's done nothing wrong!"

"If the prosecution is determined to pursue this case as one of murder in the first degree, and Muriel persists in proclaiming her complete innocence, I don't see the prosecution accepting any plea less than one of guilty of murder in the first degree. The prosecution position is likely to be one of 'either she did it or she didn't. Either she slit the victim's throat in the most callous manner imaginable, or she didn't. I'm afraid that's the way they will see it. So yes, I think a plea agreement is unlikely, and a trial is a very real possibility."

Judy put her arm around Samantha who sobbed, "Muriel would never plead guilty to something she didn't do. I know her!"

At that moment an officious female prison deputy appeared. "Mr. Peter Mayfield, counsel for Muriel Wright?"

Mayfield rose. "Yes, I am Ms. Wright's solicitor."

"Follow me to the pre-trial detention wing. Are these two women your assistants?"

"No, this is Judy Alexander, who has been representing Ms. Wright in a semi-official capacity."

"Semi-official?" asked the deputy.

"Ms. Alexander is a barrister, and has been advising Ms. Wright since she became a suspect in this matter. Ms. Sterling is a close friend of the prisoner."

"Very well, but keep in mind that this interview has been approved by the warden and Crown Services as a consultation with legal counsel. Any other persons can accompany you only under your responsibility, and you must remain with them for the entire duration of your interview."

"Understood."

The three followed the deputy down a long corridor to a heavy locked door with a window. The door buzzed open to a crowded processing room in which a number of correction officers and clerks milled busily about. After all three signed the interview log, after which they were led to a holding room.

"Do you wish the prisoner to be cuffed, counsel?" the deputy asked.

"Not at all. She is not a risk."

"Very well." The deputy opened the door. "Have a seat. The prisoner will be brought in shortly."

The three sat around a small table. There being only three chairs, Mayfield decided to stand.

Moments later, the door re-opened and Muriel appeared looking gaunt and frightened.

"I will be back in an hour," said the deputy. "Tap on the door if you wish to leave before then, or wish additional time. If you do request additional time, we may or may not be able to accommodate you."

Mayfield nodded, and the deputy shut the door and departed.

Samantha rushed over to hug Muriel, followed by Judy and Mayfield, both of whom took her hand.

Muriel sat and looked blankly at all three.

Mayfield said, "Ms. Wright. I'm Peter Mayfield. We've talked on the phone, but I've never met you."

"Yes, thank you all for coming."

"How are they treating you?" asked Samantha.

"Okay, I guess. I have my own cell, which is nice, I guess. I'd be afraid if I didn't. Most of the girls don't have their own cell."

"I'm glad to hear that," said Mayfield, "but we don't have much time, Muriel. I'm preparing paperwork now in preparation for petitioning for bail. Right now, I think it's important that you decide who you want to represent you in court. I'm your solicitor, and can prepare documents and motions, interview witnesses, but in court you will need a barrister."

Muriel looked confused and looked around the table. "I thought Judy was representing me in court."

"Muriel, "Judy interjected, "we talked about this. I agreed to advise you and help you find who murdered Arthur, but as for representing you in court, I told you that if you were ever formally charged you would need a barrister—one much more experienced than I. Your solicitor, Mr. Mayfield here, has a list of very experienced and most eminent barristers from which you may choose."

Muriel shook her head. "No. I have no money. I can't…"

Mayfield turned to Judy as he said, "Ms. Alexander has agreed to retain on your behalf any barrister you might choose to plead your case in Crown Court."

"No, no, "Muriel protested. "She's already helped me with your fee, Mr. Mayfield. I couldn't let her do that."

"Muriel, you are most fortunate to have someone like Ms. Alexander to support you and who believes in you. I strongly advise you to at least consider my recommendations. I've prepared a list…"

"No thank you, sir, but I want Judy. She knows I'm innocent." Muriel turned to her best friend. "Don't you agree, Samantha?"

Samantha nodded and turned to Mayfield. "I did see Judy in Court. She was so good—the way she cross-examined that husband—she was amazing, had the jury in the palm of her hand. How would that work, anyway? I mean, if Muriel did hire one of these other barristers? Would Judy still be able to, you know, assist that barrister in court, maybe as what they call…"

"Second chair?"

Mayfield knew that none of the barristers on his list—all of them QC's—would ever agree to have the young and inexperienced Judy Alexander, an American and a female, sit second chair beside them. They all had a reputation to protect, and each of those barristers would have a whole team of experienced barristers and solicitors in support.

"I don't think that would be likely," Mayfield continued. "Judy could still help them, compile evidence, that sort of thing."

"You mean run errands for them," said Samantha. "Besides, Judy already has her own investigator. Would Judy have any input with regard to courtroom strategy and tactics?"

Mayfield knew that if Muriel retained any of the barristers on his list, they would have little use for Judy, other than perhaps for decoration.

Mayfield shrugged. "Probably not."

"You know what I think," said Samantha. "I think if Judy takes this case, and manages to get her share of women on the jury, they will identify with Muriel's plight and see it for the political charade it really is—a charade masterminded by men, politicians, bureaucrats, who have their own political agenda."

"I'm not sure the political angle is something we can educate the jury about as a matter of admissible evidence."

"If the media is good for anything, I think you can count on them to ferret all that out."

"And the men on the jury?" Mayfield interrupted.

"She'll have them eating out of her hand. Just look at her, Mayfield. I saw it in the Tomlinson case. They were ready to give her anything she asked for."

Judy shook her head in embarrassment. "Samantha! Please! Peter, don't pay any attention to any of that. It's not true."

There was a long silence as everyone waited for Muriel to say something.

Finally, Muriel said, "I want Judy."

The other three now looked at Judy to hear her reply.

"Muriel, you don't have to decide now…think about it."

Muriel shook her head. "I want you, Judy. No one else."

CHAPTER FORTY-FOUR

*B*raxton gave a light and tentative tap to Judy's office door.

"Come in!"

Braxton stood in the doorway for a moment as Judy looked up.

Judy held out her hand to the chair in front of her desk.

"So you're taking the Wright case," he said.

Judy nodded. "I didn't really want to, Brax. All your arguments for me declining the case made sense. It wasn't that. But Muriel was quite firm that she wanted me, and only me, to represent her in Crown Court."

"You could still have said no…for her sake."

"She's terrified, Brax, as I'm sure any of us would be being charged with a crime we did not commit. In the end, she's going to be her own star witness, and to be credible she's got to be comfortable with herself on the witness stand. That's what this case will all come down to. Either the jurors will believe her, or they won't. I feel she can be comfortable with me representing her."

"That's all very fine, Judy, but do you really think you can be comfortable dealing with all the complex legal issues in this case?"

"I take it you're referring to the issue of territorial jurisdiction, the tricky question of bail, the admissibility of evidence regarding alleged alternative perpetrators…"

"Let me stop you there. You know that Hodges is going to object to any evidence you try to introduce to show that someone else might have murdered Edgeware…and I emphasize might."

"I know that—he'll object on grounds of relevance."

"Hodges and company will argue that it is Muriel who is on trial and that any attempt by you to turn the trial into one against other possible hypothetical perpetrators will only distract the jury and create the risk of confusion that will outweigh any possible probative value."

"Except that with regard to at least one of the alternative perpetrators, I have an eyewitness who is willing to testify under oath as to what he saw."

"Eyewitness? You mean the witness you've stowed away in Paris? He will testify that he saw a person killing Edgeware?"

Judy hesitated. "No, not exactly. He didn't see the actual murder being committed, no. However, he did see a person who entered Arthur Edgeware's room after Muriel had already left the Hotel Ville Fortifée. And I also have a witness—the hotel clerk—who will testify that Muriel signed out and left the hotel at 4:00 AM on the morning of March 29…"

"And your secret witness will testify that he saw a particular person enter Arthur's hotel room at…"

"About 4:45 AM—45 minutes after Muriel checked out and left to catch her early morning train to Paris. The police have their own evidence that Arthur was murdered sometime between 3 AM and 5 AM on the morning of March 29—which leaves both Muriel and this other person as the only two people who could have murdered Arthur."

"Not quite…someone else could have entered Arthur's room after Muriel left at 4:00 AM and either before or after this other person entered and left Arthur's room at 4:45 AM. Did your witness say whether he saw this other person leave Arthur's room?"

"No…just when he entered it. So regarding the legal issue of relevance, and whether such evidence would confuse the jury with very slight evidence pointing to other possible killers, I can certainly make the point that this particular other person had at least as equal an opportunity to kill Edgeware as Muriel."

"Opportunity, perhaps. However, I think you're forgetting that Muriel had a slighter bigger motive if she was aware that Lord Edgeware passed away just two days before in England on March 27, and that she might inherit several billion pounds. Have you been able to come up with a motive for this 'other person' you say your witness saw entering Arthur's room at 4:45 AM?"

"Not yet…unfortunately."

"Without showing a motive, Hodges will make a good case for the court to exclude your witness's testimony on grounds of relevance. Besides, it doesn't sound like this witness of yours is going to carry a lot of credibility."

"Why? Because he's a candidate for deportation and speaks Hausa.?"

"I didn't say that. I'm just saying that he sounds like a thin reed upon which to hang your defense."

"Perhaps it wouldn't be enough to convict this other person, but just like in our American system of justice, I only have to raise a reasonable doubt."

"Well, good luck with that. By the way, have you notified Thames Valley about this witness?"

"As a matter of fact I have. Mayfield has already given them his sworn statement and offered to let anyone from their office go to Paris and interview him if they could line up and pay for an interpreter who peaks Hausa;"

"Did they take him up on that offer?"

"No, they weren't interested in sparing the manpower for that purpose or in trying to track down an interpreter who could speak Hausa; nor were the willing to have the French police do it either."

"Why not?"

"I think both the Thames Valley and the CPS want to have as little to do with the French as they can get away with and still show that they are pursuing the case."

"Interesting…so what credence did they give to the affidavit itself?

"The CDI at Thames Valley acknowledged that a man named Musa Sani signed a statement to the effect that he saw a person enter Arthur's hotel room at 4:45 AM on March 29."

"I take it that they were not impressed."

"Nope. They were skeptical and said fire away—that they already had enough evidence to convict Muriel even if this Musa Sani character so testified."

"Interesting, but why did you even feel you needed to alert the police to Musa Sani's statement? The ethics rules only require you to list the witnesses you expect to call at trial; you don't have to tell the prosecution what they will say if called—at least not in criminal cases."

"I couldn't afford to pass up the chance that they might decide to dismiss the case once they became aware that I had such a witness."

"No such luck, I take it."

"Of course not. The Crown is bound and determined to follow through with this case using what they believe is overwhelming circumstantial evidence—for the political reasons you and I have discussed."

"All right. What about the jurisdictional issue? Do you feel equipped to argue that?"

"No, which is why Peter will move to dismiss the case for lack of territorial jurisdiction in Magistrate's Court as soon as possible."

"Mayfield? He's hardly experienced in that area of law either."

"Which is why I've given him carte blanche to consult with the best legal talent available."

"And you are covering that cost as well I take it?"

Judy ignored the question, as she knew Braxton already knew very well that she was covering all costs in Muriel's case. Braxton knew better by now than to initiate a quarrel on that subject.

"We don't expect to win on the jurisdiction at issue, "Judy said, "but it could be a basis for appeal if Muriel is convicted at trial."

"I could help on that as well. In fact, why not let me sit second chair with you at trial?"

Judy thought for a moment before saying, "Actually I've already talked with Peter about that. He doesn't think it would be a good idea."

"Really? Why not?"

"He doesn't think you'd be comfortable sitting second chair with me. You are far senior to me. He doesn't think it would work out. "

"Hmmm. Do you agree with him?"

"I think so, dear, "said Judy sympathetically. "I really do. Think about it. With your greater experience you might feel you need to...there'd be a temptation...even subconsciously..."

"To take over the case, start calling the shots..."

"Yes, something like that."

"And would that be so terrible if I did?"

"In this case, I think it would."

Braxton sat back, filled his cheeks with air and slowly exhaled before saying, "You really want to take on this case alone?"

Judy shook her head. "Not at all. I'll need all the support I can get—especially from you. Every day during the trial, I'll need someone to talk to besides my solicitor and investigator, someone I can lean on for moral support...and advice, who cares about me and my client, of course. Can you understand that?"

"Sure. I do. If that's what you want. Of course, I'll be there for you, but in the great hall of Crown Court, with QC Hodges and his minions facing you across the bar, you want to stand alone."

"With Muriel, yes."

"All right. If that's what you want. Of course. May I ask a question, though?"

"You know you can."

"The person whom this Musa witness identified going into Arthur's hotel room. You said it was someone whose photograph you showed him?"

"Yes. He identified a picture from the set of photographs Jake took at Arthur's funeral."

"So the person whom you believe to be the killer was at Arthur's funeral, then."

"Might be the killer. As I said, Musa's testimony wouldn't constitute absolute proof of this person's guilt, but could raise a reasonable doubt in the minds of the jurors about Muriel's guilt."

"So my question is…"

"Brax, honey, I'll tell you who Musa identified when and if I actually get him here to testify. Until then, I don't want to jinx it."

"All right, I'll be patient. However, can you at least tell me the names of those in the set of photographs that you showed Musa? When you go about raising reasonable doubt by suggesting alternative suspects who could have murdered Arthur, I trust you're not going to put all your eggs in one basket with this Musa witness. Who else will you suggest or imply might have murdered Arthur?"

"I think there are at least seven people—all of whom were at the funeral—who could have done it."

"Seven! Wow. Chester Edgeware, of course."

"Yes. He certainly had the strongest motive, especially if he was worried that Arthur might in fact have been first born."

"So his wife Madeleine, as well, then. She had a lot to lose if her husband turned up a cropper. That's two."

"James Holliston. He not only had a professional reputation to protect, but very possibly a substantial monetary motive as well if Chester had bribed him to forge the paperwork and documents that might have shown Arthur to be first born."

"That's three."

"Then there's Muriel's' ex-husband, Norman Yates, who had the classic motive of all jilted boyfriends and husbands."

"To kill Arthur?"

"To frame Muriel and put her away for life in revenge."

"Okay, that's four."

"And then there's Jeremiah Jones, the doctor who delivered the Edgeware twins. He would have had a motive not only to preserve his professional reputation, but also to protect his ill-gotten gains if it was discovered that he forged the medical records to show that Chester was first born."

"But he's dead now."

"Yes, but that doesn't mean he couldn't have killed Arthur."

"And he was at the funeral?"

"Yep, he sure was."

"So that's five...and...?"

"Heidi Wentworth. She had a similar motive as Jeremiah Jones, though perhaps not as strong."

"She was at the funeral, and among the photographs?"

"Yes."

"I didn't know that."

"Heidi is the third female in the set, the other two being Madeleine and Muriel."

"So that's six then."

"A picture of Samantha' husband, Eddie Sterling, was also one of the photographs in the set. Of course I already knew he was at the funeral."

"The husband of Muriel's friend, Samantha? What motive could he possibly have?"

"As to motive, I can't yet say, but he is one person about whom Muriel has not been forthcoming, and I am concerned that she may be holding something back. Every time I have brought up his name to Muriel, she has pretty much clammed up. Something may have gone on there. Jake has also learned that for some time Eddie worked for a financial outfit in London at which Arthur's brother Chester was a partner."

"So seven, then. And you think any one of those seven may be the murderer?"

"Either in person or by murder for hire. With the exception of Norman Yates, they would all probably have had the financial wherewithal to hire a contract killer."

"But you still have a primary suspect, which you're not ready to divulge to me."

"I don't want to say until I'm sure. At this point, in preparing for trial, I want to concentrate on how to best raise reasonable doubt and win an acquittal for Muriel. Finding the real killer and discovering proof that would convict that person is, for the time being, only a secondary priority."

"How sure are you that the real killer is one of the seven you listed?"

"Oh, of that, dear Braxton, I'm absolutely sure."

"One final question, Meow, and then I will desist. Is your strategy at this point to be one of delaying the trial as long as possible in order to give you more time to find the killer?"

"Ordinarily, I suppose I would try to delay. But in this case, Muriel is now in a very nasty place and most unlikely to win bail, though Peter will try his best. I fear for her health if she stays in that Broozefield much longer. Assuming Peter fails in winning bail, I plan to do everything in my power to get this case through Magistrate's Court and to trial in Crown Court Reading as fast as possible.

CHAPTER FORTY-FIVE

"*H*ey Girl, where have you been?"

Amber's face lit up on FaceTime with the skyline of Houston in the background.

"Oh Amber," said Judy, holding out her mobile as she sat up in bed. "I'm so sorry. I know I've missed several of your calls. This case I've been working on has taken so much of my time."

"Never mind excuses. I didn't mean to wake you, but you deserve it for being so naughty. What time is it there?"

"Let's see, its 6 AM here, so it must be…what, about midnight in Houston? I deserve it, but actually, you did me a favor by waking me. I really need to get going today."

"Working on that same case, I assume?"

"Yes, Muriel Wright. She's now been charged with murder, and she wants me to represent her in Crown Court."

"Wow. Your first murder case, I take it."

"Yes, and that's what worries me. Muriel has a good solicitor, though. His name is Peter Mayfield and he has a lot of experience. Of course, I also have Jake and his whole investigatory team at my disposal, so I feel I have plenty of back-up. Peter is also taking care of all the preliminary motions in Magistrate's Court."

"Like what?"

"Last week, he petitioned for bail. It was denied, but we expected that. His motion to dismiss on jurisdictional grounds was also denied."

"Jurisdictional grounds?"

"The CPS claims that when Muriel bought Ambien pills in the UK, she initiated the first step in her murder plot, and therefore the UK has territorial jurisdiction. I think it's bullock, but it may give us grounds for appeal if she's convicted."

Amber smiled at Judy's familiar use of British slang. "Bullock?"

Judy laughed. "Sorry. It's just a word I hear every day."

"And the CPS is…what again? I know you told me, but…"

"Crown Prosecution Service. They make all the decisions to prosecute major crimes."

"Oh yes…and the solicitor handles all the…"

"Pretty much everything except for actual representation in Crown Court."

"I wish we had a system like that here. I get so tired spending most of my time on motions, paperwork, and wheeling and dealing cases in smoke-filled back rooms. Well, not so much actual smoke these days, but you know what I mean."

"I certainly do. Well, hop the pond and join me as a barrister."

"Right. Now tell me. Any major strategic decisions coming up in this Muriel case? We promised to continue brainstorming with each other on our cases, and I was hoping to get your thoughts on a case I just got."

"Tell me!"

"No, your case sounds much more interesting. You first. We can talk about my case later."

"Well, I was going to call you about a major decision I thought I was going to have to make; but now it appears that that decision is out of my hands."

"Tell me anyway."

"Remember I told you that a major issue in this murder case was going to be whether Muriel had a motive to kill the victim, Arthur Edgeware?"

"Yes, you said that the prosecution would probably need to prove that Muriel knew that she might inherit billions of pounds if the victim…"

"Arthur…"

"Yes, if Arthur died, and he died exactly two days after his father died. And since Arthur and Muriel were married, Muriel would stand to inherit Edgeware's billions."

"And they still haven't figured out who inherits from the father's estate? I thought you said it would go to the first-born, or something."

"That's still the problem. As twins, Arthur and his brother were born only fifty-seven seconds apart, and a determination of who was born first depends on the medical records which may or may not have been forged, or the object of all manner of nefarious chicanery."

"I remember you telling me about all that. Sounds messy. But you also told me there might be evidence that the delivering doctor made some kind of a mark on the body of the first-born at the time of delivery."

"Yes, and I can think of only one person who would be able to provide evidence in support of a petition for exhumation—a certain Nurse, Heidi Wentworth, who was present at their delivery. The doctor who delivered the twins was killed in a suspicious hit and run accident."

"I remember you telling me that you couldn't decide whether it would be better to seek an exhumation, which might confirm that Arthur was first-born and thereby make Muriel a billionaire if he was, or to forego seeking exhumation because exhumation might confirm Muriel as the sole heiress."

"And thereby provide the prosecution with a motive for Muriel to kill Arthur."

"Yes, I was struggling with that decision, especially since Muriel said she'd support exhumation, despite such exhumation possibly providing the prosecution with a motive for her to murder Arthur."

"And you're still struggling with that decision."

"Actually, no, because that decision is now out of my hands."

"How so?"

"Last Tuesday, the prosecution filed a petition in Magistrate's Court for Arthur's exhumation, and neither Muriel, nor I as her advocate, are in any position to oppose it since doing so would make it look like we have something to hide."

"Shit! So the prosecution thinks exhumation will help them prove motive! How do you think they even found out about the body marking on the first born?"

"I was wondering about that myself, and there's only one answer, because the only way I knew about the possibility of body marking on the first-born is that Muriel herself told me that Arthur had mentioned it to her before he died."

"And the answer is…"

"The only person who could have told Valley Police— who would have in turn told CPS—is…"

"Don't tell me. Heidi Wentworth."

"Yep. It's the only way they would know. I expect to see her name on the prosecution's list of endorsed witnesses."

"When will you get such a list?"

"As early as next week."

"Next week? Has a trial date already been set, then?"

"Oh yes. Didn't I mention that?"

"No, when is it?"

"September 27, in Crown Court Reading."

"Oh my God, Judy, that's just six weeks away. No wonder you feel under the gun. You couldn't delay the trial, file a few more motions, or just ask the court for more time to prepare?"

"I could, but both Peter and I have Muriel's instructions. She's rotting in a terrible women's prison with no chance of bail, and she doesn't want to stay there for months waiting for trial. She just wants this nightmare to end…quickly…one way or another."

CHAPTER FORTY-SIX

"K_ISS!"

For the past six weeks during which Judy had been preparing Muriel Wright's defense in the upcoming case of Regina v. Wright, she had been guided by the advice of the great trial lawyer, Irving Younger: "Keep it Simple, Stupid!"

Three days before the beginning of the trial, she had set up shop in a two-bedroom suite at the St. Martin's Arms in Reading. This would relieve her from having to commute every day from London. Peter Mayfield had also taken a suite down the hall so that he would be available for consultation as the need arose. Jake remained back in London, on 24/7 call to communicate any additional evidence he might discover during the course of the trial.

She now sat back, perused the transcript of the previous days empaneling of the jury, consisting of seven men and five women, and prepared her opening statement for the next morning. She was determined to make her opening both short and to the point. The first draft read:

Ladies and Gentlemen of the Jury,
This is a case about love and broken dreams. Muriel Wright, the accused in this case, is a young woman, born into a family of modest means, who dreamed of becoming a schoolteacher. She loved children, working with them, teaching them, and preparing them for life. In pursuit of that dream, she had little time for romance...until she meet a young man, Arthur Edgeware. He was also a schoolteacher, and he had the same

values and dreams as she. They fell in love, and both hoped to find a co-educational public school at which they both could live and teach young children—a school that might provide them with a modest cottage where they could live together and raise their own family someday. Such dreams, which to many of us might seem so modest, gave these two young people the hope for a loving and happy future. It was with such hopes that they married.

Then on March 29 of this past year, those dreams were shattered when the pair took a holiday together, staying at the Hotel Ville Fortifée in the medieval town of Carcassonne in France. After several ecstatic days of sightseeing and enjoying each other's company, Muriel had to leave the hotel room at about 4:00 AM to catch a train back to England. Arthur had not planned to leave until later that afternoon to travel to a symposium in Budapest, and so at Muriel's insistence, he slept in. Several hours later, long after Muriel was on her way back to London, Arthur Edgeware was found brutally murdered in his bed in the hotel room.

The investigating French Gendarmes were quick to conclude, after a perfunctory investigation that revealed no forensic evidence whatsoever, that it surely must have been Muriel who committed the murder—for no other reason, apparently, than that Muriel had left the hotel prior to the discovery of the victim's body. Certainly, no motive was ever ascertained by the French investigators.

What political ramifications might be in play to explain why this case is being tried here in England rather than in France is a matter you will not be asked to consider. However, the prosecution will doubtless try to imply that Muriel may have had a motive to kill Arthur Edgeware. Their so-called proof of motive? That Muriel might have known—and I underscore might have known—that there was a chance she could inherit from Arthur's father if it was determined that Arthur was the first-born and thereby sole heir to his father's estate.

In fact, we shall show that a number of other persons, and one in particular, had a clear and powerful motive to remove Arthur Edgeware from this earth. The prosecution will also ask you to completely disregard the fact that Arthur and Muriel were soulmates with a common dream of teaching children, or that any such inheritance, no matter how unlikely to ever materialize, would have been relevant to them only to the extent it might further their dream of teaching young children.

Muriel is most eager to tell her story, and for you to hear it.

It will be up to you to judge her demeanor, her sincerity, and most of all her honesty.

If you believe that this young idealistic and loving young woman, against whom the prosecution can muster not a shred of forensic evidence, was capable of committing such a detestable and frightful crime purely on the basis of very shaky circumstantial evidence...then you must complete the nightmare she has endured thus far, and send her to prison for the rest of her life.

I submit to you, however, that when you hear her story, you will go into the jury room after hearing all the evidence, and render a unanimous verdict of NOT GUILTY.

After reading and re-reading the draft of her opening, Judy began to rehearse delivering it without notes, when Mayfield knocked on her door.

"It's me, Judy," he called out breathlessly.

"Come in, Peter. What is it?"

Peter entered, waving a document.

"Hodges just gave me the results of the exhumation!"

CHAPTER FORTY-SEVEN

Judy woke at 4 AM, and went to the mirror to practice her opening statement without notes. After making a few revisions, and practicing her revised versions several times until she was satisfied, she turned to Hodges' list of endorsed prosecution witnesses. Although she had anticipated a longer list, it appeared that he too had opted for the minimum number of witnesses necessary to make the prosecution's very circumstantial case.

She perused the list of witnesses—only six in all:

1) French Police Inspector Hugo Marceau, who presumably would describe the evidence he found at the murder scene at the Hotel Ville Fortifée in Carcassonne;

2) Dr. Herbert Fournier, the French pathologist, who would give his opinion as to the manner and time of Arthur Edgeware's death;

3) Dr. James Carter, who prescribed Muriel the Ambien pills prior to Muriel's trip to Carcassonne;

4) Martin Aubert, the hotel manager, who would testify to the exact time on the morning of March 29 that he unlocked the front door of the Hotel Ville Fortifée to let Muriel leave for the train station

5) Dr. Phillip Landry, the London pathologist who examined Arthur Edgeware's body, which was exhumed, and determined that there was indeed a half-moon tattoo on Arthur's left buttock which was visible only under ultra-violet light.

6) Ms. Heidi Wentworth, who would testify that she was present at the birth of the Edgeware twins, and that she observed the delivery doctor, Jeremiah Jones, apply a tattoo or

other marking upon the buttock of one of the Edgeware twins. However, she admitted that she did not notice which twin was given the tattoo and she had no idea why a tattoo was applied.

An hour later, there was a tap at Judy's door. Surmising that it could only be her erstwhile solicitor, she quietly opened it. It was indeed Peter, who was looking uncharacteristically disheveled.

"Peter!" she said in a loud whisper, "what are you doing at this hour of the morning? You look terrible! Have you been up all night? Court doesn't convene until nine o'clock."

Holding a document folder, Peter dashed over to the desk chair, sat, and handed Judy copies of the written statements that each of the prosecution witnesses had previously given to the police and prosecution. Attached on the top of this packet of statements was a separate document, which Peter had drafted.

"What is this?" she asked.

"A proposed stipulation of facts. I've been working on it all night, and researching the law of procedure which gives us good grounds to submit it to the Court in the form of a proposal."

Judy was mystified. "A stipulation of facts? For what purpose?"

"After the court recessed last night, a thought occurred to me. We have the written statements of all the prosecution witnesses. The Crown was obliged to provide us with those statements."

"I know, and I've read them many times. I've also prepared my cross-examination for each one of those witnesses, based on those statements. So what?"

"It occurred to me, Judy, that we don't disagree with any of those statements. In fact we agree with everything each one of them has said in those statements, and to which they are certain to testify in court today."

"What are you talking about, Peter?"

"Don't you see? There's not a single fact to which Hodges' witnesses will testify that we don't accept as true. That being the case, there's absolutely no reason why his witnesses should have to testify at all."

Judy, still puzzled, shook her head.

"I have a recent case in which the procedure of using a stipulation has been officially upheld—Rex v. Holdren, High Court, 2019. All we have to do is offer to accept as true all the facts to which Hodges' witnesses would testify if called."

"That wouldn't hurt our case?"

"Not at all! We're simply agreeing to what each witness claims they saw. Look, Inspector Marceau will testify as to what he saw at the crime scene. Do we have any grounds to say he's lying about what he saw?"

"No, I suppose not..."

"And do we have any basis to dispute the pathologist's estimate of time of death—between 3 AM and 5 or 6 AM on March 29?"

"No..."

"Muriel does not contest that Dr. Carter prescribed her Ambien. Muriel agrees with Martin Aubert about the time she left the hotel on March 29. The London pathologist, Dr. Landry, confirms that there's a half-moon tattoo on the left buttock of Arthur's body. No basis to dispute that."

"I see what you mean."

Heidi says she saw Dr. Jones apply a tattoo to one of the twins, but admits she didn't notice to which twin he applied it. I don't see how her testimony hurts us. In any case, it just confirms what Muriel said that Arthur once told her."

"What about my cross-examination?"

"What's to cross-examine? The only reason to cross-examine any of those witnesses is to undermine their credibility, but you concede that you can't deny that they're telling the truth. Every time you cross-examine a witness, you're sending a message to the jurors that witness' testimony has hurt you. In our case, they don't hurt us in the least. You can then argue in summation that none of the sworn statements of the prosecution's witnesses are inconsistent with what Muriel's live testimony will be—namely that when she left the Hotel Ville Fortifée at 4:00 AM on March 29, Arthur Edgeware was alive and sleeping soundly. Either the jury believes her or they don't. If they believe her, the jury must acquit. If they don't they convict. It's as simple as that."

"So you're saying we just offer to stipulate to the facts set forth in the prosecution witnesses' statements, and ask the judge to read those statements to the jury and instruct them to accept them as true."

"Exactly."

"But what if Hodges doesn't agree?"

"Why wouldn't he agree?"

"Maybe he'll insist that he's entitled to the moral weight of his witnesses' testimony. After all, he's already subpoenaed them at considerable expense, and they are now standing ready to be called to the stand. Hodges will want his day in the sun, calling all those witnesses."

"The law is on our side if you propose this stipulation. The whole purpose of stipulations is to spare the jury from having to consider evidence on matters which are not in dispute."

"You don't think the judge will scold us for not offering this stipulation prior to the Crown going to all the trouble of subpoenaing all these witnesses?"

"No because, even if we had offered the stipulation earlier, the Crown would still have needed to subpoena these witnesses in order to be prepared for rebuttal. I know this judge, Sir Anthony Sweeney, and I've sat in his courtroom on numerous cases. He hates inefficiency and wasting the court's time. My guess is that he will require the Crown to accept our offer of stipulation."

"I get it. I think."

"If Sweeney orders Hodges to accept the stipulation proposal, he'll probably give Hodges an hour or two before lunch to review the statements. After lunch, he'll then have the Recorder read the sworn statements to the jury."

"How will that work, exactly?"

"The Recorder will simply stand before the jury, and announce: 'The Crown and the Defense have agreed that if the following prosecution witnesses were to testify under oath, they would testify as follows...' The recorder would then read each prosecution witness's statement to the jury. This would probably take less than an hour, rather than the two days it would take if these witnesses were called to the stand."

"So when should I be ready to put on our defense?"

"Assuming that Sweeney accepts our stipulation, and the Recorder finishes reading the statements to the jury by this afternoon, probably no later than tomorrow morning. We have just three witnesses: Jake, who will authenticate the photographs he gave you of those who attended Arthur's funeral; Musa Sani, who will identify the photograph of the person he saw enter Arthur's hotel room shortly after Muriel left the Hotel Ville Fortifée; and of course, our star defense witness..."

"Muriel."

"Yep. It will all come down to her testimony—what she says on the witness stand and how she says it—particularly during Hodge's cross-examination. I tried to horseshed her—that is go over her testimony again and again to make sure she doesn't say anything that would be irrelevant or inadmissible under the rules of evidence—but I finally decided she doesn't need any coaching, just a caution to always tell the truth. I've told her that she just needs to stay calm, answer the questions slowly and deliberately, and look the jurors in the eye. I think she'll be fine. I also sent her a change of clothes—a knee length black skirt and white blouse with a black bow tie, and black flats. When I met with her last Friday for my final interview with her, I told her that you suggested that she cut off her waist-length hair."

"Oh, you put it all on me. Thanks. She loves her long hair. Does she hate us for asking her to do that?"

"She resisted the suggestion at first, of course, but after I told her that I had made arrangements—after rather extensive negotiations with the warden I might add—for a top London hair stylist to come to her cell, Muriel relented. She understood that such long hair wouldn't necessarily go down well with the jurors."

"Did Muriel say what hairstyle she wanted?"

"I think she said a bob, or something like that."

"I think that would like nice on her."

"I'll leave that to you girls. Listen, I checked in with Jake last night. As you know, he's hunkered down with Musa Sani at the Comfort Inn down the road. He'll be ready to go whenever we call. "

"And our interpreter?"

"Yep, she's on call too. She preferred to make her own accommodations here in Reading, but says she can be here within ten minutes when we're ready for her."

"I know it took Jake a long time to find a certified Hausa interpreter. They're pretty hard to find." Judy looked at her watch. "It's almost eight. Should we start walking over?"

Peter walked over to Judy's window where he had a good view of the Courthouse down the street.

"As I anticipated, the line is already forming to get seats in the gallery. This will be the biggest court spectacle Reading has had in recent memory. I heard that several French correspondents are in town as well. I guess you saw the Mirror in yesterday's edition."

"Actually, I've been assiduously avoiding the press. I don't want to be distracted."

"Just as well," Peter said as he pulled out the previous day's edition of the Mirror and waved it.

Judy grabbed the edition. "Oh, all right! I'll take a look."

He smiled as he saw her reaction.

"Oh no!" she exclaimed.

It was a blow-up of the original cheesecake picture of her jogging in the park under the headline: "American Barrister Takes on the Edgeware Murder Case in Reading: Will She Use her Beauty to Charm the Jury?"

She shook her head as she read the inside story. "Where do they even get this stuff? There are five women on the jury."

"It's a big case, love…it has all the elements the tabloids love. You can't blame the press for playing it up."

Judy folded up the paper, threw it in the rubbish, and said, "Let's go, Peter."

"Wait up. I need to get my roller bag. Be right back."

While she waited, she called Braxton on her mobile.

"Braxton, are you coming?"

"Of course babe, I'm coming into Reading station now. This is your big day, huh?"

"Probably not today. They empaneled the jury late yesterday, and the prosecution is set to begin today. However, Peter prepared a stipulation proposal in which we accept the truth of the statements of all Hodge's witnesses. What do you think?"

"Come to think of it, I think it's brilliant. I wish I'd thought of it. It will make your client the center of attention, and take Hodges down a peg or two by taking him off the stage for most of the trial. Does Peter think the judge will buy it? Hodges may put up a stink."

"Peter thinks Judge Sweeney will order it. Why spend a whole day presenting facts that both sides agree with. In final instructions, the judge will instruct the jurors to take the stipulated facts as a given in reaching their verdict."

"That will make this case a pretty short murder trial— just two days, it sounds like. I've actually seen several murder cases take less than two days—not like in America where inexperienced counsel tend to drag out such cases and bore the jurors to tears."

"Three if you count yesterday when they seated the jury. It was too late yesterday to take testimony after the judge gave them opening instructions. But yes, Muriel's testimony shouldn't take more than an hour."

"Unless Hodges tries to grandstand with an unnecessarily long and boring cross-examination…"

"I hope he does. I think Muriel can handle it. Oh, wait. Peter just came back with his roller bag. See you in the Court. I reserved a seat for you—two benches behind me."

"I'll be there. Let me know if there's anything I can do. Bye, sweetie."

"All right," said Peter. We're off. I know a back entrance to the courthouse if you want to avoid the obstacle course of journalists on the way."

"Lead the way!"

CHAPTER
FORTY-EIGHT

"**A**ll rise!" thundered the Usher as High Court Judge Anthony Sweeney, suitably arrayed in peruke, black gown, and red tippet, entered the Crown Court.

The Reading Crown Court, built in 1861 had been the main venue for the assizes ever since after Abington County Hall ceded that jurisdiction to Reading in 1867. Modeled after the Old Bailey in London, its design consisted of a symmetrical main frontage with seven bays facing onto the Forbury. The august central section consisted of five bays with Doric columns.

The largest courtroom in the courthouse was known as Old Shire Hall, and could accommodate forty-three spectators on the ground floor, and another eighty-seven in the gallery. The admission of spectators was on a first-come first-serve basis, with no reservations allowed except for a handful of certified journalists, court personnel, and five selected persons designated by both Crown and Defense Counsel, including solicitors. The remainder of the railbirds and the curious could secure admission only if they were among the first in line. Many of these had been waiting since the early hours of the morning. All those admitted were required to deposit their mobiles, purses, and all other personal items at the front desk before entering the courtroom.

"Be seated!" intoned the Usher after the judge had taken his seat on the high bench. After a minute of shuffling and whispering among the spectators, the Usher admonished, "Silence in court!"

"Are counsel ready for the Usher to bring in the jury?" asked Judge Sweeney.

Michael Hodges, Q.C., rose and replied, "The Crown is ready, My Lord."

"Ms. Alexander?" the judge asked.

"My Lord," replied Judy, "before the jury is brought in, the Defense has an offer to stipulate, which if accepted by Learned Counsel and the Court, we believe would be in the interest of justice, and expedite these proceedings considerably. I believe your office was provided with a copy of our proposal earlier this morning?"

Judge Sweeney leaned over the bench and whispered to the Court Clerk who handed him a copy of Judy's proposed stipulation.

After taking several minutes to read the stipulation, he said, "Ms. Alexander, do I understand you to say that you are prepared to accept the truth contained in the sworn statements of all the Crown's endorsed witnesses?"

"Yes, My Lord. That is correct."

"Ms. Alexander…this is the first time I have seen you in the court. I hope you know what you are doing. You understand that by accepting the truth of these sworn statements you are waiving all right to cross-examine each of the witnesses who provided these statements. "

"Yes, My Lord. The Defense finds nothing in these statements that is inconsistent with our defense."

"Mr. Hodges," asked Judge Sweeney, "I take it you have provided the defense with the sworn pre-trial statements of all your witnesses."

"Yes, My Lord." replied Hodges, looking a bit flustered by Judy's last minute offer to stipulate. It was something he had not anticipated.

"Nevertheless," Hodges continued, "we do not wish to accept Ms. Alexander's most generous offer to stipulate to the truth of these statements. Several of our witnesses have come from France to participate and testify in these proceedings."

"Mr. Hodges, I am not sure why you would want to…let us say…look a gift horse in the mouth here. Ms. Alexander has offered to accept the truth of all your witness's statements.She is in effect accepting that all your witnesses, if called to the stand, would testify to matters which are now not in dispute. That would certainly be a waste of this court's time, not to mention in violation of the rules of evidence which permit only evidence that goes to disputed facts."

Hodges now sputtered, "My Lord…we have witnesses… they are here…the jury has a right to observe their demeanor on the witness stand…"

"For what purpose Mr. Hodges?"

"To enable each juror to evaluate the credibility of my witnesses…"

"What credibility is at issue if the defense accepts their written testimony as both truthful and credible? Mr. Hodges, need I remind you that there is currently a backlog of 58,000 cases awaiting trial in Crown Court. I have no doubt that if you call all the witnesses you have endorsed, it will take at least a full day, if not several days to elicit their testimony. However, if we have the Clerk read these written statements, I anticipate that you might be able to wrap up the case for the Crown in less than an hour. I have to take that into consideration. Is there anything else, Mr. Hodges?"

"I do take exception, My Lord. It would have been considerate if My Learned Friend had given a bit more notice that she would make such an offer…"

"I agree, "said Judge Sweeny. "However, I am inclined to give Ms. Alexander the benefit of the doubt here, and assume that she only made this offer to stipulate after careful consideration, and did so only in light of recent events beyond her capacity to predict. Is that correct, Ms. Alexander?"

"It is, My Lord, with apologies to My Learned Friend, and to the Court, My Lord."

Before sitting, Judy turned around briefly to catch a glimpse of Braxton who was seated two benches behind her. He smiled and nodded.

Beside Braxton was a *Times* journalist, who was busily writing in his notes: "When Michael Hodges was in his prime at a time before the UK abolished the death penalty in 1998, he gained renown as the Crown's favorite prosecutor—the 'Beast'— who had sent many a criminal defendant to the gallows. Now, in his dotage, but still hanging on to his Q.C. status, it appears that the American female barrister, Judy Alexander, has won the first round against him. In this battle between the Beauty and the Beast, it now seems Ms. Alexander has set the stage for the defense to take center stage, while reducing the prosecution to presenting its case in the form of what looks to be a dry monotone reading of statements to the jury by the Court clerk."

"Is there anything else before we bring in the jury?"

Hodges managed to recover momentarily his poise by asking, "My Lord, would it be possible to grant an hour's recess so that I may provide to each of my witnesses a copy of their pre-trial statements? I would like to give them an opportunity correct or amend their statements before they are read to the jury."

Judge Sweeney looked up at the Court' clock. "Very well, it being ten o'clock now, we will reconvene at 12:30 to allow everyone to take an early lunch. I anticipate that the reading to the jury will take about an hour. If Mr. Hodges has no other evidence, might we expect for the Crown to rest at around 2 PM? If that is the case, the defense will have the rest of the afternoon to present their case. How many witnesses will you call for the defense, Ms. Alexander? "

"Three, My Lord, including the defendant Muriel Wright."

At this moment, one of Hodges' investigators approached Hodges and left a note for him to read. Hodges read it, and said, "My Lord, if I might have a moment."

Judge Sweeney looked annoyed, but said, "A moment, counsel. No more."

Hodges looked up and said, "My Lord, I have been advised that a Defense witness, a Mr. Musa Sani is present in Reading."

"Is that a problem, Mr. Hodges? The defense has indorsed a witness by that name."

"It's not a problem, My Lord, but we did not anticipate that this witness might actually appear. Our latest information was that this witness was in France and in a deportation status. Given that it is now likely that he will testify for the defense, we believe that the testimony of the investigating office in this case, DI Raymond Stone, may now also be necessary."

"You did not previously indorse this witness?"

"No, your honor. We did not think we would need him."

"Ms. Alexander?" the judge asked.

In fact, Judy was delighted that Hodges would call DI Stone to the stand. She had considered indorsing Stone as her own witness, but for strategic reasons had decided not to. Now that Hodges would call him, she would be able to cross-examine him, which she could not have done had she indorsed him.

"I have no objection, despite the late indorsement, My Lord."

"Very well, Court is adjourned until 12;30.

"All rise!" intoned the Usher.

Braxton met Judy as she left the courtroom. "Here, let me help you," he said as he took her roller bag.

"Thanks!"

"You were great, by the way. "Want to grab a Cappuccino at Starbucks? Just down the street."

"Sure, but I've got to make some calls."

At 12:30 sharp, court reconvened. The jury was led into the courtroom, and moments later the Usher announced, "Bring in the Defendant, Muriel Wright."

There was a hush in the courtroom as a court deputy led Muriel to the dock. All heads craned to see the young woman who would either be convicted and sent to prison for life, or set free and very possibly become the richest woman in England. She was dressed neatly in the modest ensemble Jake had sent her, and sat demurely with neither a smile nor a frown. Her hair was fashionably styled, cut short in a light brown bob, and any make-up she wore was barely discernible, giving the impression of youthful freshness, understated beauty, and innocence. Peter had done a good job preparing her for this first appearance before the jury.

Judy looked carefully at the jurors' faces to see if she could discern any indication of their impression of the defendant in the dock. Although she could not, she was satisfied that it was favorable.

At Judge Sweeney's direction, Hodges rose to give his opening statement, a dry and predictable summary of the brutality of the crime of the crime charged, and the overwhelming evidence of the defendant's guilt. He also explained how and why the testimony would be in the form of a reading by the clerk of the witnesses' uncontested sworn statements by the clerk. He concluded by stating his confidence that, after hearing all the evidence, the jurors would have no choice but to find Muriel Wright guilty of murder in the first degree.

With the conclusion of his opening, the Court Clerk began the tedious reading of the prosecution witness's sworn statements to the jury.

For the spectators in the gallery who had expected to see a parade of interesting prosecution witnesses followed by dramatic cross-examination, it was a disappointment. The clerk's monotone delivery put almost everyone to sleep. Many in the gallery would have left, had the Usher not made it clear that anyone leaving before the court adjourned would not be permitted to return.

It was only when Hodges called his last witness, DI Raymond Stone that interest perked up.

"Please state your name and occupation," Hodges asked after Stone was duly sworn.

"Raymond Stone, Detective Inspector, Thames Valley Police."

"What is your involvement in this case, Inspector?"

"Our department was asked by the French Gendarme to investigate and interrogate the defendant, Muriel Wright. She had been seen leaving the scene of a crime committed at the Hotel Ville Fortifée in Carcassonne, France."

"And did you so?"

'Yes, sir. She admitted that she left the hotel room that she shared with the victim, Arthur Edgeware, at 4:00 AM in the early morning of March 29, but claimed that Arthur was asleep when she left. We later received an autopsy report that the victim was murdered between 3:00 AM and 5:00 AM on that same morning. Further investigation revealed that the defendant purchased Ambien shortly before she traveled to Carcassonne with the victim, and the autopsy later confirmed that the victim had been drugged with an overdose of Ambien shortly before he was murdered."

"Did you later receive information from a Mr. Jake Everett that he had located and spoken to a Mr. Musa Sani who claimed that he had seen a certain male person enter Arthur Edgeware's room after the defendant Muriel Wright left the Hotel Ville Fortifée on the morning of March 29?"

"Yes, we did follow up on that lead, and determined that it was unreliable. We were not able to confirm Mr. Sani's statement. "

"You talked to other staff and guests who were at the Hotel Ville Fortifée on March 29?"

"I did not, but the French police did, and so advised us."

"Did Mr. Everett also show you a picture of the man whom Mr. Sani claimed he saw enter the victim's room?"

"Yes."

"Did Mr. Everett tell you who the person was in the picture?"

"He did, and we made every attempt to track that person down. With no luck. We do not believe that person is currently in England. We have reason to believe that he may currently be in Gibraltar."

"Gibraltar?"

"Yes, sir. However, without further confirmation of Mr. Sani's claim, we did not, and do not now, believe that this person was a viable suspect. We did consider him a person of interest, of course, and would like to have spoken to him."

"So without being able to confirm Mr. Sani's claim, you did not believe it was worth pursuing."

"My Lord," said Judy as she rose, "perhaps My Learned Friend might refrain from leading his witness so assiduously."

"Point taken," said Judge Sweeney. "I think you know better."

"My apologies, My Lord, and I shall rephrase. So, Detective Stone, did you or did you not believe that it was worth pursuing the person in the picture which Mr. Everett provided you."

"We did not believe it was worth pursuing."

"One final question, detective. Who was the person in the picture that Mr. Everett showed you?"

At this, Judy rose. "My Lord, I have made no objection to this witness's testimony thus far, despite his reference to a number of hearsay statements purportedly made by Mr. Everett to this detective. While we could argue the hearsay issue at this time, I would like to inform the court that within the next hour I intend to call both Mr. Jake Everett and Mura Sani to the stand as defense witnesses. Perhaps it would be best to let my Learned Friend ask Mr. Sani directly what he saw on morning of March 29, rather than asking for this witness to repeat double hearsay."

"Mr. Hodges?" Judge Sweeney asked.

"I withdraw the question, My Lord. However, if My Learned Friend does call this Mr. Sani, he should not be permitted to testify. Any such testimony by Mr. Sani would have no relevant bearing on the case against Muriel Wright, and the probative value of his testimony would be substantially outweighed by the danger of confusing and misleading the jury."

"Very well, Mr. Hodges. You can make that argument when Ms. Alexander calls Mr. Sani as a witness. Do you have anything further, Mr. Hodges?"

"No, My Lord. The Crown rests."

Judge Sweeney again looked at the clock. "I see that the time is now 2:00. We shall take a short recess, and return at 2:30, at which time the defense may call its first witness. Will you be ready to proceed at that time, Ms. Alexander?"

"Yes, My Lord."

"Very well. We are adjourned until 2:30."

CHAPTER FORTY-NINE

*P*eter waited outside the courtroom door in hopes of catching Judy as she left.

"Judy, over here!"

"Oh, Peter!" exclaimed Judy as she spotted him. "So glad you're here. We've only got thirty minutes before court reconvenes and I have to go back in and begin our defense. Sweeney seems bent on getting this case to the jury today. Where's Sani? Is he here?

"Just down the hall…Jake is with him. "He pointed to where Sani was sitting and looking blankly into space, obviously disoriented."

Judy waved to Jake, who waved back with a thumbs up.

"So he's ready to go?"

"I hope so. I have to say he's a little…shaky. I think he's afraid some immigration officials are going to suddenly appear and take him away."

"That's not going to happen is it?"

"Not at all. Jake and I worked together to get him a temporary judicial visa based on your subpoena."

"How long?"

"Just three days, and then he's back to France. If he's not, then yes, immigration will be on top of him…and me as well, since I've guaranteed he'll be on the Chunnel back to France by then. French immigration officials will take it from there.

"But he's ready? He knows why he's here?'

"I've gone over his testimony several times, so fingers crossed, yes."

"And the interpreter?"

"Yes, she's here as well, sitting on the other side of Jake. Ms. Idara Gado."

"I thought we'd have more time to discuss this, but I'm thinking of calling Jake first, then Sani, and then finish our defense with Muriel."

"In most cases, I'd agree with that order. Finish strong with our star witness—in this case, Muriel. But I've been thinking…perhaps we should put Muriel on first."

"Why? Tell me your thinking quickly."

"You realize that we haven't yet told Muriel who Sani is going to identify as the one who entered Arthur's room after Muriel left."

"Is that a problem?"

"I think it could be. I've horseshedded Muriel in preparation for her testimony, but if, right before she testifies, she hears who it was who entered Arthur's room….it might…"

"Might what…"

"Discombobulate her. I think we should let Muriel testify first. Depending on how that goes, maybe we won't have to risk calling Sani at all. His testimony is going to be shaky at best."

"Hmmm…I don't know, Peter. "

"Look, Hodges is going to ask Sweeney to exclude Sani from the witness stand on grounds of unreliability and relevance. Judges have been pretty tough on allowing alternative perpetrator testimony unless the defense has clear and convincing of evidence of the guilt of an alleged alternative perpetrator, and Sani hardly fits that bill."

"So you think I shouldn't call Sani at all…after all the trouble I went to in tracking Sani down in Carcassonne, stashing him in Paris, getting the judicial visa, and brining him here? Really?"

"The way things stand now, yes I do to be perfectly honest. First I think Sweeney will probably exclude Sami's testimony, and even if he allows Sani to take the witness stand, I think Hodges will tear him to pieces on cross. Hodges may be over the hill, but he's still a Q.C., and shredding a vulnerable witness like Sani on the witness stand would be a slam dunk— even for him."

Judy shook her head. "I hadn't thought of that. You know I think the person Sani saw is the one who killed Arthur."

"I know that, and you could be right, but if Muriel is acquitted, you'll have plenty of time to gather such evidence, submit it to the authorities, and salvage Muriel's reputation which would be ruined even if she is acquitted. But if you put that terrified kid on the witness stand now and let Hodges tear him to pieces, it will allow Hodges to finish on a strong note. In fact, I wouldn't be surprised if Hodges doesn't even follow through with asking Sweeney to exclude Sani from the witness stand. I think Hodges would like nothing better than to have you put Sani on the stand. I can guarantee you that on closing, Hodges will characterize your calling Sani to the witness stand as a desperate attempt to salvage an unwinnable case."

"Peter, I know you have far more experience than I, but…"

"Look, you've already put Hodges on the back foot by persuading Sweeny to permit the reading of his witnesses' testimony to the jury. That really took the wind out of his sails."

"So you think we should just call Muriel as our only witness…put all our eggs into that one basket?"

"Yes, as long as Muriel holds up under Hodges' cross. I've rehearsed Muriel with what to expect on cross by taking the role of Hodges and throwing at her every cross question I can think of that he might ask. She was good, and I think she's up to it."

"And if she isn't?"

"If she folds, then, okay…we'll have no choice but to call Jake and Sani and hope for the best. In any case, on closing you can still direct the jury's attention to what other persons had a motive to kill Arthur, not the least Chester Edgeware. You can be sure that Hodges will use the still ambiguous evidence of who was first-born to suggest that Muriel had a motive."

"Five minutes!" bellowed the Usher. "All those with tickets must be seated now!"

"Okay, Peter. Let's do it. After Muriel steps down, give me a frown if you think we should call Jake and Sani."

"Right. By the way, Samantha is in the upper gallery, and asked me to give you her best. She got one of the last seats."

"She's a good friend. I know her presence is a great comfort to Muriel."

Judy turned and entered the courtroom just moments before the Usher closed the door.

The cry of "All rise" reverberated through the courtroom as Judge Sweeney entered, followed by "silence in court!"

Surveying that counsel and all courtroom personnel were present, Sweeney intoned:

"Ms. Alexander, you may call your first witness."

Judy rose and took a deep breath.

"My Lord, the defense calls Muriel Wright to the witness stand."

CHAPTER FIFTY

Accompanied by two court deputies, and under the gaze of a packed gallery, the jury, court personnel, and a high judge in full judicial regalia, Muriel took her seat in the dock. Although she appeared poised, with neither a smile nor frown upon her face, she looked frightened. Surely, everyone in the courtroom would understand and sympathize with the young woman in the dock.

After the court clerk administered the oath, Judy rose, but paused to give Muriel time to gather herself until the gallery became completely silent. Knowing that the case would turn on the cross-examination, Judy had decided to keep her direct examination skeletal—the better to minimize details and better highlight Muriel's passionate protestation of innocence. It would also give Hodges less detail to work with on cross.

"Please state your full name."

Muriel answered crisply. "Muriel Bonham Wright."

"That is your birth name?"

"Yes ma'am."

"You were previously married, and during that marriage took the last name of your husband?"

"Yes, ma'am."

"And you reverted to your maiden name after you were divorced from your first husband?"

"Yes, ma'am."

"Did you subsequently remarry?"

"Yes, Ma'am."

"And whom did you marry?"

"Arthur Edgeware."

"At the time of your marriage to Mr. Edgeware, did you announce that marriage to family and friends?"

"No."

"And why was that, Muriel?"

"After graduation from university, I planned to become a school teacher. That was what I always wanted to do ever since I was a child. After the divorce from my first husband, the only such position I could find was teaching French at a girl's school...it was called Brianhurst...which required me to be in residence, and which could not provide accommodations for a spouse. I did not understand that this requirement forbade me from marrying—only that if I did marry I must be in residence and could not cohabit with my husband at the school during the school term. The school provided me only with a small room. In light of this policy, Arthur and I thought it would better not to announce our marriage until we could find a coeducational school which could provide marital accommodations."

"Did you subsequently meet with Arthur Edgeware during holidays when you were not required to be in residence?"

"Yes ma'am. I had one weekend a month when I had no residential duties."

"Were you aware that Arthur Edgeware was the son of a very wealthy man, Lord Chester Edgeware?"

"Arthur did mention that to me, though neither of us thought it was important. All we both wanted was to find a school where we could both teach and be provided with marital accommodations...a little cottage, perhaps, where we could raise a family together. Arthur was not interested in his father's wealth, and neither was I."

"Muriel, some people might find it difficult to believe that neither Arthur nor you cared about a possible inheritance. Some might even think it un-natural, or even un-human. Did Arthur ever intimate to you that he might inherit a substantial fortune from his father?"

"No ma'am. Not at all. We had our own dream to be together, and we needed no grand inheritance to make that dream come true. In fact, it would hinder us. Arthur told me that his father had always told him that he was leaving his estate to his first-born child—so as not to split the company assets."

"Did Arthur ever acknowledge to you that his brother Chester was first born?"

"Oh yes ma'am. Even though Arthur and Chester were identical twins, Chester was born fifty-seven seconds before Arthur."

"Arthur told you that?"

"Yes ma'am."

"Did Arthur tell you how he knew that?"

"He said he never disputed it…that it was documented in medical records."

"Arthur never expressed any resentment that his brother would inherit his father's entire estate?"

"Not at all. He said such an inheritance would only bring us trouble. Arthur wanted nothing to do with his father's company. To be honest, I think he hated the whole idea of being involved in that company in any way. He knew if he inherited it, he would have to run it. He didn't want to have anything to do with it."

"Muriel, tell us about a trip you and your husband took to France last March."

"It was during my school's spring break, during which I had four…or maybe it was five days, I don't recall, without any residential duties. It was the first time Arthur and I had real chance to be together for any period of time."

"Where did you go?"

We went to Carcassonne in France. It is a medieval city, near the border with Spain. I had read about it, and thought it would be a great place to take some of my French students for a holiday field trip during which they could practice their French."

"Directing your attention to the evening of March 28 of this year, and the morning of March 29, did you and Arthur share a hotel room?"

"Yes ma'am…at the Hotel Ville Fortifée. I had to leave early that morning…about 4:00 AM…to catch a train back to England. I had to resume residential duties at Brianhurst at 5 PM on March 31."

"Did Arthur accompany you at that time?"

"No, he had to stay and catch a train later that day to Budapest for a language symposium. I told Arthur there was no reason for him to take me to the station…that I could take a cab, and he could sleep in."

"What was Arthur's state at the time that you left your room?"

"He was sleeping, but I must have wakened him when I was taking my shower, because he asked me to come over and kiss him goodbye."

"And did you?"

"Kiss him goodbye? Of course."

"And then what did you do?"

"I went to the front desk and asked the manager to unlock the hotel's front door so I could leave and get my cab. I had called for a cab the night before, and it was waiting for me outside the front gate to the fortified city."

"Did you then catch the train back to England?"

"Yes ma'am."

"And when did you hear about Arthur's murder?"

"Not until two days later in the early afternoon."

"The afternoon of April 1?"

"Yes, ma'am. A friend picked me up at Reading station and took me back to Brianhurst.

Judy now paused, and waited a long moment before asking her final question:

"Muriel, did you kill your husband?"

Without hesitation, Muriel answered firmly and deliberately, "No ma'am, I most certainly did not kill my husband. I loved my husband deeply and would never, ever harm him in any way!"

"Thank you, Muriel"

Judy turned to Hodges and said:
"Your witness."

CHAPTER FIFTY-ONE

With a portentous air, Hodges rose to conduct his cross-examination.

"Ms. Wright...let's talk about the circumstances of your marriage to the now unfortunately deceased Arthur Edgeware. I would like to show you what has been marked as Crown Exhibit #3 and ask if you recognize it."

The clerk took the exhibit from Hodges and handed it to Muriel.

"Do you recognize that document?"

Muriel perused the exhibit. "Yes, sir."

"What is it?"

"It is the form I filled out when I applied for the position at Brianhurst School."

"That is your signature at the bottom of the form?"

"Yes sir."

"Please read the question on line 4."

"The question asks whether I was married."

"How did you answer?"

"I wrote 'no' as my answer, but...."

"So you lied on the application form, did you not? Please answer yes or no."

"Yes, sir."

"So would it be fair to say that you obtained your position at Brianhurst under false pretenses?"

"Arthur and I saw no harm in it, sir, since Arthur never came upon the school grounds, and thereafter we only saw each other on holidays."

"I'll repeat the question, Ms. Wright. Did you obtain your position under false pretenses?"

"Arthur could not support us on his rather meager salary."

"Answer yes or no, please."

"Yes. We saw no harm. I am a Catholic, sir, and was brought up not to have sexual relations before marriage. I think Arthur and I supposed that there was no greater harm in doing so than when a young man who wants to join the military understates his age."

At this, Hodges turned to Judge Sweeney. "My Lord, could the witness be instructed to answer my questions without additional commentary."

Judge Sweeney sighed, rolling his eyes slightly, but said to Muriel, "Ms. Wright, you must confine your answers to the question asked. If your counsel wishes you to explain your answers in further detail, she will give you an opportunity to do so on redirect."

"Yes, your Honor. I'm sorry, your Honor."

"Now Ms. Wright," Hodges continued, "having obtained your position at a girls' school under false pretenses, you decided to carry on with your plan of deception by deceiving your employer, your coworkers, friends, and family."

Muriel started to explain why Arthur and she had decided to keep their marriage secret from friends and family, and also explain that she had never actually lied to friends and family, but rather had just not volunteered the information—an important distinction, she thought. Nevertheless, she realized such an answer would appear argumentative—something Mayfield had advised her to avoid on cross-examination.

"Yes, sir."

"Thank you, Ms. Wright," said Hodges with condescension and an air of minor triumph.

Sitting up in the gallery, Braxton wondered if Hodges planned to come up with any question more consequential than that which established Muriel's benign motive of not wanting to engage in premarital sex until after marriage. So far he was racking up very few points.

"In fact, Ms. Wright, I put it to you that the real reason you deceived Arthur's family about your marriage was that you knew they would see you as a seducer whose primary interest was becoming very rich someday by Arthur's inheritance."

"No sir!" Muriel answered indignantly. "Arthur and I loved each other. Arthur always made it clear to his family that he wanted none of their money, and wanted nothing to do with Edgeware Industries, which he thought was a corrupt and unethical organization!"

"My Lord!" Hodges protested.

Braxton smiled again. So far, Judy's erstwhile client was holding her own on the witness stand.

"I'm sorry, your honor," said Muriel before Judge Sweeney could reply to Hodge's objection.

"Continue, Mr. Hodges," said the judge without ruling.

"Ms. Wright, having so far provided us with your sad tale of poverty and privation as a simple schoolteacher, perhaps you could tell this jury how you were able to afford a stay at the Savoy Hotel in London," Hodges reviewed his notes, "on the evening of March 24 of this year."

"Arthur and I both saved the money for our trip to Carcassonne. I had been working for several months by then, and I saved every penny, and so did Arthur. It was our chance to be together as husband and wife on a delayed honeymoon."

Hodges was about to protest that Muriel's answer was not responsive, but saw that Judge Sweeney did not appear in a mood for another objection. In fact, Muriel's answer had been responsive, as Hodges had asked how she could afford a night at the Savoy and she had answered quite succinctly.

"Six hundred pounds a night at the Savoy. It appears that you really saved your pennies, Ms. Wright."

At this, Judy rose. "My Lord, is my Learned Friend asking a question, or prematurely making a comment?"

"I withdraw the question," said Hodges before Judge Sweeney could respond. Turning back to his witness, he said, "Ms. Wright, I take it that you have a severe sleeping problem. Is that correct?"

"No sir. I sleep quite soundly, thank you, though perhaps you might understand that a person unjustly accused of murder without any evidence whatsoever might have trouble sleeping from time to time."

A wave of giggles rippled through the gallery.

"Silence!" the Usher intoned.

"My Lord!" Hodges protested.

"Continue with your examination, Mr. Hodges," intoned Sweeney with an expression of 'just get on with it'. "Perhaps if you asked your question more directly."

From the rafters, Braxton smiled and shook his head. Did his old mentor realize he was getting a beating?

Looking increasingly flustered, Hodges asked, "Ms. Wright, did you not, on February 14 of this year purchase two packets of Ambien sleeping medicine at a pharmacy in Woking?"

"Yes, by doctor's prescription."

"So you were having trouble sleeping at that time."

"Yes, my ex-husband had been stalking me around that time, and there were several times when I felt unsafe."

"And prior to your trip with Arthur did you not ply him with a number of those pills?"

"No sir. Prior to our trip, I had discarded most of the pills. I woke in the middle of the night after taking one of them, got up, and passed out on the floor. I felt like those pills could be dangerous, so I kept only a few of them, planning to maybe take one of two of them during my travels to relieve jet lag or such."

"You heard the statement of the French Pathologist which stated that an overdose of Ambien was found in Mr. Edgeware's body."

'Yes, sir."

"I put it to you that before you even began your trip to Carcassonne, while you were in London, that you gave Arthur

Edgeware a number of those pills—pills which later made him unable to defend himself when you later decided to cut his throat!"

"My Lord!" Judy protested. "My Learned Friend has overstepped his bounds with such an improper question, which in fact is not a question in the proper sense, assumes a fact not yet proven and which is, in any case, a matter for this jury to decide."

"Mr. Hodges," Sweeney said sharply, "I ask you again to ask your questions directly, without reference or inference based on matters not yet proven in this court."

"Yes, My Lord, I shall rephrase."

After shuffling his notes, Hodges continued:

"Ms. Wright, did you ever give any Ambien pills to Arthur, and if so, when did you give him those pills?"

"I did give him a couple of pills because shortly before we left on our trip, Arthur came down with a severe cold, hacking and coughing. It was severe enough that I suggested to him that we cancel our trip and that he consult his doctor."

"What did he say to that suggestion?"

"He would have none of it. He said we had planned this trip for many weeks, saved our money, made our reservations. He said he would be fine. However, during our first night, at the Savoy, he woke several times in the night with coughing spasms and seemed unable to get back to sleep. I gave him several Ambien pills, but how many he took over what period of time, I have no idea. I didn't monitor him."

"How many is 'several'?"

'I think maybe three or four. He didn't take them all at once, of course. He never asked me for more during our trip, and I had already given him all the ones I had anyway."

"You are also aware from the French investigation that your fingerprints were found on a bottle of cough medicine in your hotel room at the Hotel Ville Fortifée."

"I was not surprised to hear that. On the night before I had to leave Carcassonne, Arthur told me that he had already used all the cough medicine in the bottle he brought with him on the trip, and asked me to go out and buy him another. I guess he didn't want our last night to be one in which he would be up coughing all night. "

"And of course you did so."

"Did what sir?"

"Go out and buy him a bottle of cough medicine."

"Yes, sir, but when I gave it to him, he told me it was the non-drowsy kind. Rather than ask me to go out and get the nighttime cough medicine, I suppose he might have put the contents of his Ambien capsules into his cough medicine, so he could both sleep and suppress his cough."

From his perch in the gallery, Braxton suppressed his smile as he realized that his old mentor was losing it—a far cry from Hodges' earlier days when he rarely, if ever, let an opposing witness get the better of him. He might be having his day in the sun, but the sun was not out for him today. At least not yet.

Hodges continued: "You have said that on the morning of March 29, when you were dressing to leave the hotel to catch your train that you woke Arthur up. Is that correct?"

"Yes sir."

"And he kissed you goodbye."

"Yes sir."

"And when you left, you say he was sleeping?"

"Yes sir."

Hodges paused and shuffled through his notes. Braxton noted that his last several questions had been one of the worst cross-examinations he had ever heard, accomplishing nothing more than allowing the witness to repeat on cross-examination what she had already testified to on direct. It violated one of the honored commandments of cross-examination: never allow a witness to repeat on cross what they have already testified to on direct—because, as the premise of the commandment goes, if the jury hears a witness's story once, they may believe it; if they hear it twice, they will probably believe it; and if they see evidence in writing, nothing on this earth will convince them it isn't true. In light of this travesty of a cross examination—it verged on the pathetic—Braxton wondered if the CPS had not purposely appointed Hodges as Crown Counsel just to get the French off their backs, and put a not-so-merciful end to Hodge's career, or at least get him off the QC role.

Hodges now seemed to grope for the next question. After several moments, Judge Sweeney asked, "Mr. Hodges do you have any further questions?"

"Ugh, no My Lord."

"Ms. Alexander, do you have any re-direct?

"No, My Lord," Judy answered promptly.

"Very well, does the defense have any more witnesses?"

"My Lord, might I have a few moments to consult?"

"I will give you two minutes."

Wow, thought Judy, this judge really wants to finish this case today. Should I let that happen? Except for the few hits Hodges managed to score with his questions about Muriel's failure to answer truthfully the marriage question on her job application, Muriel had held up well. Even those hits may have been softened by Muriel's explanation of not wanting to engage in pre-marital sex. In this day and age, might the jury find that notion refreshing? Perhaps it would be better to let the trial case end now, especially since the judge seemed so determined to end it. Did the judge think the whole prosecution was a farce to begin with, not worthy of wasting more precious court time? Was he perhaps aware that with so little real forensic evidence, this case against Muriel would never have been brought to trial in the first place but for the political ramifications of the UK's Brexit negotiations with the EC? In light of this, should she risk letting Hodges redeem himself by giving him an opportunity to tear Sani to pieces? Although she thought not, she nevertheless thought it prudent to consult with Peter and Braxton.

"Might I have five minutes, My Lord?"

"One and a half minutes and counting, Ms. Alexander."

"Yes, My Lord."

Judy turned back toward the gallery to get a signal from both Peter and Braxton. Both shook his head—with only a slight motion so as not to be conspicuous.

Judy turned back to address Judge Sweeney.

"My Lord, the defense rests."

"Very well." Sweeney fixed his gaze on the courtroom clock. "I see it is now 4:00. We shall recess until 4:30, at which time we shall hear closing arguments and I shall make my comments on the evidence to the jury. After that, the jury may retire for deliberations.

CHAPTER FIFTY-TWO

At 4:30 sharp court was reconvened in Reading Crown Court, and the doors shut.

Crown Court Judge Sweeney gave a perfunctory commentary on the evidence to the jury, highlighting that while there was little if any forensic evidence connecting Muriel Wright to the crime charged, circumstantial evidence, if sufficiently cogent, could sustain a finding of guilt beyond a reasonable doubt. If the jury could not decide on whether the circumstantial evidence was sufficiently cogent to sustain a finding of guilt beyond a reasonable doubt, they must turn to the testimony of the defendant and judge her credibility.

Hodges' closing, while anything but perfunctory, suffered more from theatrical emotion—it urged the jury to consider the probabilities that could be drawn from the undisputed facts in the case. These undisputed facts included that Muriel Wright left her hotel room in Carcassonne only an hour or so before the body of her husband was found. What were the probabilities that some unknown person, unidentified by any of the guests and staff at the hotel, had somehow miraculously gained entrance to the Hotel Ville Fortifée that had been locked down for the night, proceeded in a bee line to Arthur Edgeware's room only moments after Muriel had left the hotel, committed the hideous murder, and then miraculously escaped from the hotel unseen?

Hodges conceded that Muriel's motive could not be definitively established, given that Heidi Wentworth could only testify that Jerimiah Jones had indeed marked one of the Edgeware twins with a half-moon tattoo—a fact confirmed by a pathologist's autopsy of Edgeware after disinterment—but could not testify from personal knowledge as to whether the half-moon tattoo indicated who was the first-born, or whether, like the mark of Cain, it indicated who was second-born. Why disfigure the first-born? Although the issue of which son would inherit Lord Edgeware's estate was admittedly unresolved, how could the jury discount the motive created by even the possibility of Muriel inheriting several billion British Pounds?

While Judy's closing was fervent and impassioned, it was also understated, which gave it more credibility than Hodges' closing. Arthur Edgeware's tragic death was simply too convenient for too many people who stood to gain from that death—not least Arthur's brother Chester who also stood to inherit billions, the professionals both legal and medical who had much to lose if implicated in creating the conflicting documents relating to which Edgeware twin was first-born, and not least Muriel's ex-husband who had stalked and terrorized Muriel in the months before Arthur's murder.

In place of raw emotion, Judy concluded her closing with a measured appeal for justice for a wronged and innocent woman whose only crime was to be in the wrong place at the wrong time.

"Is it safe to convict this young woman against whom there is no forensic evidence? No bloody shirt, or clothes, no murder weapon belonging to the defendant, no eyewitness… nothing! Not only is there no evidence in this case, there is evidence that there is no evidence—which is impossible. In our justice system, the prosecution must prove that the defendant is guilty beyond a reasonable doubt. It is your sacred duty to apply that principle to the facts in this case. Go back to the jury room, apply that principle, and come back with the only just verdict of not guilty."

There was a hush in the gallery as Judy sat.

After the judge gave final instructions to the jury, the trial was adjourned, and the jurors retired to consider their verdict.

Braxton and Peter met Judy at the door.

"You were great, Judy," said Braxton.

Peter agreed.

"I thought we might retire to the Brewdog across the street while we wait for the jury's decision. Best pub in Reading, and very convenient."

"Sure boys, why not? The clerk will ring my mobile when the jury returns."

"Allow me," said Braxton as he took Judy's roller bag.

"Thanks, I'll follow you."

Moments later the three settled into a quiet corner table at the Brewdog. As they passed several other tables, Judy could not help but overhear some of the conversation.

"Do you think they'll believe her?" came one loud comment from a woman at a table for five near the bar.

"Well, what do you think?" Judy asked when they were seated.

"I think you did everything you could," said Braxton as he waved for a server.

"One thing I've learned, is that you can never guess what a jury will do," said Peter. "I've stopped making predictions, because half the time I've been wrong when I do."

"Three pints?" Braxton asked when the served arrived.

"That's fine," said Judy.

"Me too," said Peter.

"Peter and I both agree you did a wonderful job, Judy. But the question is, how do you feel about the case...win or lose, I mean."

"Win or lose? Hmmm."

"You look..."

"Conflicted? I guess you could say that. To be honest, there are things about this case I still don't understand. I could never put together all the pieces of the puzzle, and yes, that bothers me."

"If you win, which I certainly hope you will, it won't make any difference, will it?"

"For me it will. Winning is one thing…or losing, for that matter…but what bothers me is that in either case I haven't done what I promised to do."

"Like what?" Braxton asked.

Judy toyed pensively with her fork. "When I first took on this case, I did not do so as a barrister. I only promised Muriel that I would help her find whoever killed her husband. I haven't done that."

"To be honest, Meow, you couldn't really expect to do that. It's not like in some of those old Perry Mason re-runs we used to watch, where good old Perry would cross-examine a prosecution witness, who would then break down weeping, and confess. It doesn't work that way in real life—or in real courtrooms or real cases."

"I know that, Brax. Besides, I waived my chance to cross-examine Hodges' witnesses when I proposed to have the clerk just read their sworn statements to the jury. I didn't think any of their evidence was inconsistent with our theory of defense which was simply that Muriel didn't do it."

"Which I thought was a master-stroke," Peter piped in. "It put old Hodges on the back foot, and I don't think he ever really recovered."

"I have to admit, though, I would not have stipulated to any statements by James Holliston if Hodges had indorsed him."

"Why, do you think Holliston was crooked?"

"Let's just say I would like to have probed that possibility on cross."

"You could have called him as your own witness."

"No, I couldn't cross-examine my own witness."

"You could have asked the judge to declare him a hostile witness."

"I decided against it."

"I agree you would have been up against a stone wall," said Peter. "So what else bothers you?"

"After talking to Sani, I think you know my best guess was that Muriel's ex, Norman Yates, killed Arthur out of rage and jealousy."

"Yes. We certainly went to a lot of trouble to bring Sani to the UK to testify."

"I also knew it would be flimsy testimony. Hodges would have crucified him. I'm just glad I didn't have to call him to the stand. Thank God that Muriel's testimony was credible enough that we didn't need to."

"I think you made the right decision. So what's your problem?"

"While I did have Sani's identification of Yates, the only motive I could think that might incite Yates to commit murder— just to frame Muriel—never rang true for me. I mean, why not just kill both Arthur and Muriel?"

"Being accused of murder brings its own kind of hell…"

"Yates couldn't count on Muriel even being charged. No, that motive just doesn't work for me, and I don't think it would have worked for the jury."

"I assume Jake tried to track Yates down so you could at least call him as a witness."

"Oh yes, Jake tried, believe me. He got as far as tracking Yates down to Gibraltar…then lost the trail."

"Sounds like a dead end. So are Holliston and Yates the only loose ends that bother you?"

Judy shook her head. "I still don't understand who killed Jeremiah Jones out there in Wales."

"He could have confirmed who was first born."

"Exactly."

"That puts Chester back in the crosshairs if he thought Jones could confirm that Arthur was the true first-born."

I know, but as you know, Peter, Jake could not find a shred of evidence to link Chester to that killing…and to be honest, I don't' see Chester doing something like that. Bribing Jones, oh yeah I can see that. I can even see Chester hiring those thugs to dig his brother up to avoid the risk that a court ordered exhumation might show that Arthur was first born, but killing him—I just don't see it. But now that I mention it, the botched grave-robbing attempt has also found its way into my basket of loose ends to which I have no answer."

Braxton decided to break back in to the conversation. "Can I ask a question?"

"Of course, Brax. Fire away."

"Where does all this leave you with regard to whether Muriel or Chester will inherit Lord Edgeware's estate?"

"Peter, you want to take that one?"

"I think we had all been hoping that Arthur's autopsy would finally resolve the question of which Edgeware twin was first-born. Unfortunately, it did not. As Hodges had to concede in his closing, Nurse Wentworth could only testify that Doctor Jones had marked one of the twins with a half-moon tattoo. She didn't see which twin was in fact first-born or whether the tattoo marked the child that was first born, or the one who was not first-born."

"So who will decide it?"

"I understand that the Probate Court had postponed proceedings until this criminal trial against Muriel Wright is resolved—apparently in hopes that the question might be decided, and the Probate Court wouldn't have to resolve it. Now that's not going to happen regardless of whether Muriel is acquitted. That's a question the Probate Court will have to decide. Good luck to them!"

Judy's mobile vibrated. She read the text.

"Ok, boys. The verdict is in."

CHAPTER FIFTY-THREE

*B*raxton stopped short in the hallway of the Quadrangle when he noticed that Judy's office door was ajar. It had been over a week since Muriel's acquittal, and Judy had not come into chambers since then.

Braxton tapped on the door jam. "Are you receiving visitors?"

"Come in Brax," said Judy softly.

Braxton sat. "I got your texts, but I was worried. Are you okay? I would have thought you'd be basking in the limelight of your great victory in the Reading Crown Court. I brought you this morning's *Mirror*."

"No thanks. I've read one or two of them but I've told them all I'm not giving any interviews."

"Why not? They're all most complimentary on your performance in court. I don't understand after such a triumph in Reading Crown Court. The whole chambers is talking you up as the next female Q.C. Archie says the phones are ringing off the hook from solicitors wanting you to represent their female clients in divorce court."

"No Brax…"

'Instead, you seem to have spent the last week hunkered down in your condo as if you needed to recover from some kind of devastating defeat."

I don't deserve the credit for winning Muriel's case. For one thing I was lucky to get a judge who seemed to be more interested in concluding in record time—for what reason I can't imagine, but it certainly didn't help the Crown's case."

"How can you say that your skills were not decisive in winning an acquittal in a very difficult case rife with political underpinnings? You took a case that most of us wouldn't have touched with a ten foot pole, made great tactical and strategic decisions...."

"On Peter's advice. I owe him a lot too."

"...gave a superlative opening statement, and your closing was brilliant. You had the jury eating out of your hand. Your star witness held up under the withering cross-examination of our favorite Q.C."

"Hardly withering. Hodges was terrible and you know it."

"Well, it was his last hurrah, I suppose. I just heard he's announcing his retirement, though I'm not too sorry for him. He needed something like this to make him realize he would be far happier as a country squire."

"Having Jake at my beck and call—at great expense of the kind that most defendants could not afford—gave me a great advantage. Without his investigatory help, Muriel would probably have been convicted."

"I'm sure Jake did give you an upper hand, but Muriel certainly did her part holding up as she did under cross-examination. I must say she was good."

"Maybe too good."

"Really? What do you mean?"

Judy shook her head. "Brax I came into the office today at 4 A.M...to think. For the last week Jake has been feeding me some very disturbing information gleaned from his small army of investigators, and digital sources which may not have been obtained through... strictly legal channels—information that had Jake been able to provide to me before the trial, would have made a huge difference. In fact, if I had had this information in timely fashion, I would never have agreed to represent Muriel in court."

"Wouldn't all that be rather moot now? Muriel has been acquitted, and depending on the outcome of probate she may soon be one of the richest woman in the U.K.—not a bad person to have as a client in the future."

"No, it's not all moot for me, Brax…and do you think I give a whit about having rich clients? I know I haven't been completely forthright with you about my financial resources which have freed me from the mundane task of earning a living and fostering a successful professional career. You know my reasons for choosing the life of a barrister."

"I know."

Judy held up a thick file. "I have here documents, photographs, video clips from CCTV…I had no idea the UK has no many of them…CCTV is on every street corner, in every business, even in hotels…that tell a very different picture from what the jury heard last week."

"Judy, I have no idea what Jake has belatedly provided to you, but please consider the ramifications if you…"

"That's precisely what I have been doing…considering… and I made a decision. Yesterday afternoon I called Peter, and asked him to arrange that five people meet me at Chester Edgeware's estate this evening at 8 o'clock."

"What five people, may I ask?"

"Chester and his wife Madeleine, of course…since I have reasons for wanting to meet at their house…and Muriel…"

"Why should Muriel come? She's a free woman now. Its not like you can subpoena her."

"I had Peter tell her, and it's true, that I have very important evidence about which of the Edgeware twins was first-born. She'll be there, believe me. She has several billion reasons to show up to hear what I have to say, as do Chester and Madeleine."

"And the others?"

"James Holliston…"

"Holliston? Why him?"

"Let's just say that he will want to address matters that relate to his professional reputation and livelihood…and Samantha."

"Samantha? Why would you want her there?"

"That is more personal, but as Muriel's closest friend I believe she will be there."

"Would you like me to be there?'

Judy smiled. "No Brax, I think this is something I need to do myself."

"Okay, Meow. As you wish. You've done great so far without me. I take it that if all goes well you will resolve all those loose strings you talked about last week while we were waiting for the verdict."

"I hope so, yes."

"Including, who really killed Arthur Edgeware?"

Judy did not answer.

"I see you're determined to do this, then."

"Oh yes, Braxton, I'm determined to do this."

CHAPTER FIFTY-FOUR

*J*udy's Uber arrived at the front gate of Chester Edgeware's estate at precisely five minutes after 8 o'clock. Around her shoulder she carried an arm bag containing a number of organized files.

Madeleine Edgeware opened the door.

"Why, Ms. Alexander. Please come in," said Madeleine with exaggerated politeness. We are all waiting with bated breath to hear what you have to say."

"Yes, hello Ms. Edgeware, and thank you."

"Please follow me to the drawing room."

Judy followed her host to see all five of her interested parties seated in a semicircle. Whatever Peter had told each of them, it had been enough to induce them all to appear.

"Hello, Judy" said Muriel, who was seated demurely on a Georgian chair at the far left of the semicircle. "I didn't get a chance to thank you after the trial. I had to return to the prison for several hours as they processed me for release."

"Hello, Muriel. Yes, I knew that would be the case, so I did not linger in Reading after the verdict was read."

Judy nodded in acknowledgement at Holliston and Samantha.

After a very pregnant pause, Chester rose from his center chair to say, "I must say you have aroused our curiosity, Ms. Alexander, bringing us all together like this, though I for one cannot imagine what interests all of us here have in common. I must say that many of us were surprised by the verdict, though I confess to some chagrin at the ineptness of the Crown prosecution."

Chester looked over at Muriel with a look of obvious disdain, as did Madeleine. "I trust this will not take long, as I think we all have other matters best attended to on this lovely evening."

"I will try to be as brief as possible," said Judy, "but I think the information I have in my possession will be of some interest to all of you."

"Then get on with it!" Holliston grumbled impatiently.

Judy withdrew a file containing Xeroxed copies of what appeared to be a hand-written letter, and handed out copies to each of the five.

As each of the five perused the copies, Judy said to Chester, "You may recall that soon after the death of your father on March 27 of last year, you visited Parkington Abbey where your father had been in residence ever since being diagnosed with Alzheimer's."

"Yes, what of it?"

"You went there to retrieve your father's personal items. However, you decided not to take from your father's room a large cabinet, which you doubtless thought would be too heavy to conveniently cart away. Do you know what became of that cabinet?"

"I can hardly remember. I probably told the staff to discard it—after I had retrieved all my father's papers from its drawers."

"In fact, Mr. Edgeware, the staff at Parkington Abbey gave it to a man who offered to cart the old cabinet away for a nominal fee. That man was my investigator, Jake Everett."

Chester looked up from the letter with an expression of apprehension.

"Mr. Everett has spent the last six weeks tearing that cabinet apart and going through it with a fine tooth comb," Judy continued. "He spent weeks slicing the thinnest slivers of wood to look for a cavity that might contain a document. It wasn't until three days ago, however, that he just discovered the hidden cavity that he was looking for."

"Why would this Mr. Everett do such a thing?"

"Perhaps the more interesting question is why your father would have hidden away this letter in the first place. At my instruction, Mr. Everett was looking for something that Lord Edgeware might have wanted to preserve after he was consigned to Parkington. I had reason to believe your father was afraid that if his memory deteriorated further while in residence at Parkington, his hopes for insuring his legacy would not survive his death."

Judy paused several more minutes to allow everyone to finish reading the first page of the letter. The handwriting was difficult to read, but legible. As one after another turned to read the second page, Judy continued:

"It was Lord Edgeware's wish that only one son inherit his company. He feared that if he left the company to both sons, it would be broken up, or tied up in litigation. That was why his will specifically referenced the age-old canon of primogeniture—the same principle which Parliament had codified into law to preserve the most efficient food-producing estates of the empire. But he also wanted the son who most capable of running his company to inherit, even if that son might be the second-born."

Judy paused and then resumed:

"And so Edgeware came up with a scheme which would enable him to both adhere to the ancient canon, while also retaining the option of choosing the son most worthy and capable. I guess you could say he wanted to 'have his cake and eat it too'."

"How do you know this letter was even written by my father?" Chester protested.

"I'll be coming to that, and I assure you that your father's handwriting has been thoroughly authenticated, although I'm sure you yourself could authenticate the handwriting as your father's. As the letter makes clear: your father bribed both Dr. Jones and Mr. Holliston to prepare two sets of documents—one confirming that Chester was first-born, and the other set confirming that Arthur was first-born. At a later time of his choosing, Lord Edgeware planned to tell both Jones and Holliston which set of documents to release prior to his death."

"My father always told me I was the most worthy and qualified to inherit!" Chester exclaimed.

"That may be true, Mr. Edgeware. But in his later years, he began to have doubts—about your ethics, your honesty, and proclivity to risk the company's reputation by engaging in… shall we say…your extracurricular activities."

Chester rose from chair. "I don't have to listen to this. You are in my home as a guest. I'm going to ask you to leave!"

Madeleine said soothingly, "Chester, dear, I think we should listen to what else this woman has to say. We know its rubbish, but perhaps we should hear it all."

Chester snorted, but sat.

"To save time, perhaps we might flip to the last paragraph of the third page. Despite Lord Edgeware's plan to wait as long as possible before having to decide which set of documents should be produced in any court, he also wanted to establish beyond any doubt or dispute, which son was in fact first-born."

As everyone read this final paragraph, one after another looked up in astonishment. Muriel was the last to finish reading it.

Muriel's face lit up with obvious delight. "My God, Judy, Arthur really was the first born!"

Judy nodded. "Yes, Muriel. Lord Edgeware writes quite clearly that he ordered Dr. Jones to mark the first born, not the second-born, with the half-moon tattoo. With this letter in evidence, I would expect the probate court to find that you are the sole heir to Lord Edgeware's estate."

Muriel stood up. "I can't believe it! I always knew Arthur Edgeware was first born!"

"Did you really, Muriel?" Judy asked. "No one knew for sure until this letter came to light."

Muriel looked at the other four, all of whom sat in stunned silence. Madeleine in particular looked horrified. Chester sat stone-faced, revealing no emotion, while Muriel sat with her face still glowing with excitement.

Samantha too was silent, but said nothing, not sure what emotion to reveal.

Judy now turned to Holliston. "Mr. Holliston, does any of this come as a surprise to you?"

"I will wait until this letter is authenticated before I make any comment."

"I can believe that Lord Edgeware withheld from you who, in fact, was first-born. But do you deny that Lord Edgeware gave you two sets of documents with instructions not to produce either set until Edgeware gave you further instructions? I know that you provided the set showing that Chester was first-born to the Court that appointed you as Conservator of the estate pending probate. Since you did that sometime after Lord Edgeware was adjudged incompetent to manage his affairs, I take it that you made the decision on your own."

"I'm not saying anything, Ms. Alexander. This is not the time and place."

"I'm sure it's not, especially if you not only made that election without Lord Edgeware's instruction, but also did so without informing the court that you were in possession of two separate sets of documents. I think you know you could be disbarred and ruined for perpetrating such a fraud on the court—a fraud which would only be made more serious if you did so as a result of a bribe."

Holliston shifted uncomfortably, but did not respond.

"I put it to you, Mr. Holliston that if what I suggest is true, it would provide you with an ample motive to murder Arthur Edgeware."

Holliston now exploded, his face distorted in anger. "How dare you! This is outrageous! I will not sit here and listen to such rubbish from a publicity-seeking American floozy who somehow managed to insert herself into a British chamber! Just because you got a miraculous acquittal for Muriel, doesn't give you the right to…"

"James," Chester said, "we know its rubbish, but like Madeleine says, we'd better hear her out...the better to know what slander we can expect to hear from this woman in the future, and the better to advise counsel we retain to sue her for libel."

Holliston sat sullenly.

Samantha, who had not yet said anything, now asked, "Judy, can I ask why I am here? I mean, other than to hear that Muriel is to inherit, though I'm most pleased to hear that my good friend will finally get her due in life."

"Samantha, I asked you to come as Muriel's friend and confidante. I also wanted to ask if you had any explanation for the animosity between Muriel and your husband."

"Eddie?"

"Yes. Did you have any suspicions about Eddie and Muriel?"

"No, not at all...other than Eddie hates it when I have any house guest at all, and of course, he doesn't like it when I go out."

Judy turned to Muriel. "I got the feeling from one of our first conversations that Eddie was..."

"Yes, Judy, that's true. Eddie was always coming on to me." Muriel turned to Samantha. "I didn't want to tell you. But he was."

"Oh my God, Muriel, I had no idea! I'm so sorry."

"Why would Eddie take chances like that in his own house?" Judy asked Muriel. "Was he hanging something over your head, perhaps, in return for giving him what he wanted?"

"Like what?"

"Like Eddie telling you that he saw you, several times, visit Chester's office?"

"Why no, not at all. Where did you get that idea?"

"Bullocks! Another outrageous insinuation!" Chester blustered. "I never saw Muriel in my life until I heard that she had seduced my brother into marrying her."

"Is that all, Ms. Alexander?" Madeleine asked, obviously anxious for what she considered a needless session to end. "If so…"

"I won't be much longer, Ms. Edgeware. Please indulge me a little longer."

"I have a question," Holliston now piped. "I see that you obviously have a number of unsubstantiated suspicions about all of us. May I ask why you have not called Nurse Heidi Wentworth here this evening so that you might give her the third degree as well? After all, she too was present during the delivery of the Edgeware twins."

"A fair question, Mr. Holliston. The answer is that I don't think Lord Edgeware would have wanted anyone beyond you and Dr. Jones to be aware of the his double-set scheme. That would have involved an unnecessary extra risk of disclosure, not to mention having to offer an additional bribe. No, I believed Nurse Wentworth's sworn statement that she saw one of the twins being tattooed but was not in any way privy to Edgeware's double-set scheme—as you were, Mr. Holliston."

Holliston shook his head in exasperation.

"If that's all, Ms. Alexander," said Chester.

Before Judy could respond, Madeleine, who had been looking all this time at Muriel with hatred in her eyes, said, "You mentioned something about my husband's extracurricular activities. I have no doubt that it is all another lie. Nevertheless, I'd like to hear it now, if you please."

Judy nodded, and withdrew another set of files from her briefcase. As she did so, Madeleine said:

"Ms. Alexander, if you think you will get away with depriving my husband of his rightful inheritance, I can tell you that he—all of us, except Muriel of course—will spare no expense, leave no stone unturned, to expose your lies and insinuations. This little gold-digger you managed to get off—how, I have no idea and don't want to know—will never, ever steal what is rightfully ours!"

Judy did not respond directly to Madeleine, but instead asked Muriel a question:

"Muriel, what can you tell us about Oliver's Gentleman's Club in London?"

Muriel turned ashen. "What? What do you mean? I've never heard of…"

Judy held up several documents. "I know Muriel. You didn't tell me yourself, and I think I understand, but now it's best that you tell us."

Muriel, now obviously in distress, looked around the room. "It was after my divorce from Norman. He abused me terribly, but he never paid me a dime in alimony. I was desperate. I was going to be out on the streets…homeless. I looked everywhere for work…but nothing."

"This was before you finally got your job at Brianhurst…"

"Of course! I would never have worked for Oliver's if I had gotten a teaching job. It wasn't what you think. I didn't have to dance or anything like that. I just had to…chat up wealthy men, have them order drinks…"

"Get them drunk, run up an exorbitant tab…"

"I only had to talk to them. I wasn't a prostitute, if that's what you mean. Why are you even asking me this, Judy? You're my lawyer."

Yes, and that job is completed. You were acquitted, and I have now found evidence that will probably make you a very wealthy woman, but I need your honest answer."

"Okay, yes, I worked at Oliver's…just for a few weeks, before I found the job I wanted at Brianhurst."

"Later, did you ever tell Arthur about your work there?"

"No I couldn't…"

"Of course she couldn't," Chester shouted. "She couldn't tell my brother she was a slut! But better leave the bitch alone, now. It's humiliating enough for the family to know Arthur was even tied up with the likes of her."

Judy now looked directly into Chester's obviously very concerned eyes. Then she took a yellow document, which looked like a summons, and turned back to Muriel.

"Muriel, do you recognize this paper?"

With obvious mortification, Muriel looked at the paper and put it aside.

"Muriel?"

"Judy, why are you doing this?"

"Please answer, Muriel."

"It's a summons."

"For what?"

"Fraud, confidence, disorderly conduct..."

"In fact, you were accused of taking advantage of an elderly man, plying him with five hundred pounds a glass watered-down alcohol, and running up a tab of over five thousand pounds. What was your commission on that, Muriel?"

"The charges were dropped."

"Only after Oliver paid off the victim."

"Why are you doing this, Judy?"

"I always knew Muriel was a whore," said Madeleine, spewing out Muriel's name with undisguised venom.

Judy turned to Chester. "Sir, I have one more file I would like to bring to your attention, but perhaps it would be better if your wife was not here when I reveal it to you."

"I shall certainly not remove myself from this room while this travesty continues," Madeleine protested.

Chester, looking nervous, said, "Dear, perhaps it would be better it I listened to her calumnies first. We can talk about it later."

Madeleine stood up and left in a huff.

"Now, what is this mysterious file you want me to look at?" Chester asked, resigned that he must now listen to whatever lies Judy had in store for him.

Judy handed him several pages of documents and digital downloads.

"Sir, "Judy began as she handed him the papers, "we have eye-witness testimony that you visited Oliver's Gentleman's Club on numerous occasions last fall, and that your exclusive host on those evenings was Muriel Wright."

Chester was silent.

"We also have evidence that Muriel did indeed visit you numerous times at your office, and that you and she were often together behind locked doors for long periods of time."

"Even if that is true, which it certainly is not, what does that have to do with who murdered my brother?"

Judy produced eleven eight by ten digital photographs of Chester, over a period of several weeks, visiting such hotels as the Savoy and the Ritz. In each case the CCTV security cameras caught clear images of Muriel following Chester into the hotel, and on each occasion entering his room—for the night.

"Cameras don't lie, sir," said Judy.

"All right, so I had an affair with Muriel. So what?"

"I suggest that you had more than an affair, sir. In fact, you were obsessed with her, and promised her that once you had inherited your father's estate, you would divorce your wife, and marry her. You should never have confided to Eddie Sterling your intentions to marry Muriel, Sir. If necessary he will testify."

"So you think I had my brother killed, just because I wanted to marry Muriel?"

"Actually, I don't think you murdered Arthur, though you would certainly have had a motive to do so if you thought Arthur might somehow inherit and take Muriel away from you. After all, you knew by now that Muriel would only marry the brother who inherited, regardless of whether it turned out to be you or Arthur. Now that Arthur is gone, you'll still be free to marry Muriel. If Muriel now inherits your father's fortune—and I assure you this letter has now been thoroughly authenticated by the best handwriting experts in the UK—you can still enjoy your father's fortune as Muriel's husband."

At this, Muriel stood up and laughed. "Chester, you old tiresome fool. You're pathetic. Do you really believe any woman would marry someone as ancient as you without your money? I'm sure Madeleine only married you because you convinced her you would inherit, and I'm sure she'll be taking off once she finds out you won't."

There were gasps in the room at this revelation.

Chester was speechless. "Muriel, I thought…I thought you wanted me…like I wanted you. You told me…"

"Muriel," Judy interrupted, "I know all about you and Norman. You see the file I'm holding now? It documents that on numerous occasions you slept with Norman even after your divorce. Your divorce from him was a fraud…though legal, of course. It had to be if you were to inherit from either Arthur or Chester. But like everyone else—except Lord Edgeware himself before he was declared incompetent, you couldn't be sure which brother would inherit, so you and Norman, in conspiracy together, decided to play both ends against the middle. After the divorce, you had plenty of time to make whoopee together whenever you weren't having to sleep with Chester. First you seduced Chester, and then just to be sure, you tracked down poor penniless Arthur."

"A nice story, Judy, but you have no proof."

"Don't I? If you care to look at it, I have a transcript of the police interview conducted two days ago with Norman, who has been hunkered down in Gibraltar, waiting for you. Once he realized that you did not intend to ever go off in the sunset with him, he tried to leave for South America. The Gibraltar police caught him boarding a plane to Belize."

"You…" Muriel hissed.

"In exchange for a promise of leniency, Norman sang like a bird—told the police everything—how, at your instigation, he ran over Dr. Jones in Wales, hired two thugs to try to rob Arthur's grave—all to increase your odds of winning a fortune from fifty percent to one hundred percent. Norman even told the police how, after he alerted you on an untraceable burn phone that Lord Edgeware had died, you phoned him back on your own burn phone and told him to get down to Carcassonne as fast as he could. You told him that he should enter the hotel during the daylight hours, hide in a broom closet until you left at 4:00 AM so he wouldn't have to register before the hotel closed down for the night, and then slit Arthur's throat after you left. Shall I go on?"

"You might as well finish your fairy tale."

"After he murdered Arthur in cold blood, he then exited the hotel after the hotel's front door was re-opened in the morning, but before the staff found Arthur's body."

"No one will believe a total loser like my ex-husband. He has a long record, and except for those silly charges for disorderly conduct, which were dropped, I have a clean record—thanks to you, Judy. Even if what you say is true, and I deny every word of it, I've been acquitted of having anything to do with the murder of Arthur. I can't be tried again…and since I've been totally exonerated, I also can't be denied my inheritance on grounds that I killed the victim from whom I inherit. I checked that out myself Judy."

"I'm sure you did."

Just at that moment, Madeleine, who had been listening from the balcony, entered the room.

In her right hand, she held a SIG Sauer P328 handgun. As everyone watched in horror, she first approached her faithless husband. Then, before anyone could speak, she turned toward Muriel.

"Don't'" cried Muriel.

"Bitch!" Madeleine fired two shots into Muriel's chest, and finally a third before Judy managed to wrest the gun from her hand.

CHAPTER FIFTY-FIVE

*B*raxton scanned the available tables at the Brass Monkey and looked for Peter Mayfield. He found him guarding a corner table that would offer them some privacy before the early evening crowds.

"Is Judy coming?" Peter asked.

Braxton looked at his watch and said, "she'll be here."

"What'll you have?"

"A pint of anything is fine."

"Coming up." Peter waved for a server and ordered three pints of the house ale.

"So," said Peter, "how is she holding up?"

"She's been pretty devastated by last week's turn of events, as you can imagine."

"I think we all were. I should have been there, but she insisted on going alone to meet all those characters at Chester Edgeware's estate."

"That's Judy. I should have been there too."

"The tabloids don't seem to know what to make of the whole thing. This morning's story in the *Times* talked about Norman Yates' arrest in Gibraltar, and his 'wild accusations' about Muriel Wright, but apparently chalked them up to the little weasel trying to save his skin. What does Judy think?"

"You can ask her. I asked her, but she hasn't really said whether she thinks Muriel actually did what Yates claims she did, but she has no doubt that Muriel lied to her about a lot of things—not least that she carried on with Yates after their divorce, and, almost worse, had an affair with Arthur's brother,

Chester. For Judy, that's enough to question her entire decision to represent Muriel. She regrets it, and blames herself for not seeing through Muriel from the beginning. I'm afraid its shaken her confidence."

"A lot of Yates' accusations against Muriel seem to jibe with the facts. They certainly explain how Yates knew where and when to go Carcassonne. I suppose, if Muriel were still alive, she could always, if pressed, admit that she did carry on with Norman after her divorce, and might even confess that she let Yates know that she might come into a fortune if Arthur died, but still deny she asked him to kill Arthur. You know, like Henry II saying to his henchmen, 'will no one rid me of this troublesome priest.' I suppose it's all moot now."

"Not necessarily for Judy. I think Judy just wanted to get to the truth."

"Well, she definitely got her baptism by fire with this case, but if she wants to continue in her career as a barrister, she'll have to learn what we had to learn the hard way. It is not the defense lawyer's job to believe or not believe a client—that's a job for the jury—but only to provide the most zealous defense possible within the bounds of ethics. It is all part of the adversary system of justice. The defense counsel is just one cog in the system, and the system depends on the defense performing that function zealously. Judy certainly did that. "

"I know all that Peter. You're preaching to the choir. I'm just not sure Judy sees it that way. If she sees herself as having used her skills—not to mention her ample resources, not available to most defendants—to acquit a murderer, she's not likely to forgive herself."

"She didn't acquit Muriel, the jury did. You've probably heard that the Quadrangle's phones are already ringing off the hook asking for Judy to represent them."

"I can tell you Judy doesn't care about that. She doesn't need to."

Peter took a long swig of ale. "Braxton, you and I have known each other for some time. Let me ask you a question. If

Muriel were still alive, do you think she would have become the richest woman in the UK?"

"I think so, yes. The letter Judy's investigator uncovered established without a doubt that Arthur was in fact the first-born. Since Muriel was acquitted, the probate could not have denied her Arthur's inheritance on grounds that she was implicated in the murder of the one from whom she inherited."

"You don't think the CPS could have tried Muriel again after hearing what Yates had to say?"

"Theoretically, the Crown might have been able to re-try her, yes. As you know, since the passage of the Criminal Justice Act of 2003, defendants acquitted of murder in the UK can be retried if the prosecution later finds evidence that was not available at trial. Remember the case of Michael Weir in 2019? After he was acquitted of murder, the police found DNA evidence that conclusively proved his guilt. He was re-tried for murder, and convicted. It's not like in the United States, where the double jeopardy clause of their constitution forbids such re-trials."

"I wonder if Muriel knew that."

"Probably not, or she wouldn't have made some damaging admissions just prior to being shot by Madeleine."

"More to the point, I wonder if Madeleine knew that Muriel, at least in theory, could have been re-tried, though I doubt if the CPS would have wanted to re-try the case based on the evidence of a known criminal such as Yates. But yes, if Muriel were re-tried and convicted, she would have been ineligible to inherit. Chester would then have inherited."

"I'm sure Madeleine didn't stop to think it through. She was so maddened by Chester's admitted infidelity, for which she rightfully blamed Muriel, that I'm sure she pulled that trigger out of pure jealous fury. 'Hell hath no fury', etc. After all, as Madeleine saw it, when Muriel stole Chester, she also stole Chester's inheritance."

"Where is Madeleine now?"

"Broozefield, last I heard."

"Well, it sounds like she'll need a good woman's lawyer, and she'd find no one better than…"

"Peter, don't you dare mention that possibility to Judy, even in jest."

Peter held up his hands in submission. "Sorry."

"Sorry about what?" came the voice behind the table.

"Darling!" gushed Braxton. "You've come! Welcome back to the world of the living. We were worried about you."

"Never mind that. I've come, boys, but only on one condition."

"And that is…?"

"I don't want to hear a single word about this case, about Muriel Wright, or Madeleine Edgeware, or…"

"Not a chance, dear," said Braxton. "Not a chance. Now sit and tell us what you'd like to talk about."

Judy turned to Peter and said, "Peter, would you mind giving Brax and me a moment?"

"Of course," said Peter, who stood and bowed. "I'll leave you two lovebirds to yourselves. If you need me, I'll be up at the bar."

Judy smiled. "Thanks, Peter."

"So, Meow, what should we talk about?"

Judy withdrew two envelopes from her purse.

"Remember how you promised to take me on nice long trip after this case was over?"

"I certainly do."

"I think the last time we talked about it, we narrowed the choices down to either the Galapagos or Easter Island."

"I do remember something like that, yes."

"We couldn't decide, though."

"Whatever you choose, darling, is fine with me."

"Oh no, that's not the way we're going to do things from now on."

"Then what…"

Judy held out the two envelopes. "Pick one. Fair is fair."

"Really? Okay." Braxton took a deep breath and picked the one on the right.

"Open it."

"Well?" Judy asked.

Braxton sat back and smiled as he read the brochure.

"Well, "he said with a dispassionate air, "it looks like we're going to Easter Island."

Judy matched his smile and leaned over. They kissed, oblivious to all around them.

THE END

COMING:
MURDER ON EASTER ISLAND
(SIXTH IN THE JUDY ALEXANDER
MYSTERY SERIES)